Decoy Zero

BOOKS BY JACK MARS

LUKE STONE THRILLER SERIES

ANY MEANS NECESSARY (Book #1)
OATH OF OFFICE (Book #2)
SITUATION ROOM (Book #3)
OPPOSE ANY FOE (Book #4)
PRESIDENT ELECT (Book #5)
OUR SACRED HONOR (Book #6)
HOUSE DIVIDED (Book #7)

FORGING OF LUKE STONE PREQUEL SERIES

PRIMARY TARGET (Book #1)
PRIMARY COMMAND (Book #2)
PRIMARY THREAT (Book #3)
PRIMARY GLORY (Book #4)

AN AGENT ZERO SPY THRILLER SERIES

AGENT ZERO (Book #1)
TARGET ZERO (Book #2)
HUNTING ZERO (Book #3)
TRAPPING ZERO (Book #4)
FILE ZERO (Book #5)
RECALL ZERO (Book #6)
ASSASSIN ZERO (Book #7)
DECOY ZERO (Book #8)
CHASING ZERO (Book #9)
VENGEANCE ZERO (Book #10)
ZERO ZERO (Book #11)

DECOY ZERO

(An Agent Zero Spy Thriller—Book #8)

JACK MARS

JACK MARS

Jack Mars is the USA Today bestselling author of the LUKE STONE thriller series, which includes seven books. He is also the author of the new FORGING OF LUKE STONE prequel series, comprising three books (and counting); and of the AGENT ZERO spy thriller series, comprising ten books (and counting).

ANY MEANS NECESSARY (book #1), which has over 800 five star reviews, is available as a free download on Amazon!

Jack loves to hear from you, so please feel free to visit www.Jackmarsauthor.com to join the email list, receive a free book, receive free giveaways, connect on Facebook and Twitter, and stay in touch!

Agent Zero – Book 7 Summary (recap)

Having been forced back into the agency's service, CIA Agent Kent Steele is put on the trail of a mysterious ultrasonic weapon, pursuing a radical group with an unknown agenda and in possession of a silent but deadly machine nearly impossible to track. Yet new memories plague his mind with old secrets. Though tormented by his shadowy past, Agent Zero must put the safety of millions above all else—though it may be too late for him to save himself.

Agent Zero: While pursuing the insurgent group responsible for ultrasonic attacks around the United States, old memories from Zero's haunted past resurfaced in the form of assassinations he carried out early in his CIA career. Uncertain if they were real or fantasy, Zero sought help from the Swiss neurologist Dr. Guyer, who gave a grim diagnosis: deterioration was evident in Zero's brain, and though the speed at which it would proceed is unclear, Guyer believes it will eventually kill him. Zero kept the news to himself, deciding to instead live whatever life he has left to the fullest with his daughters and a rekindled relationship with Maria.

Maria Johansson: Having defied orders from both the CIA and the president, Maria stepped down from her position as deputy director and returned to the post of special agent. Through Zero's own admission, she is aware of recent memory issues he's been having, as well as his perceived past as an assassin.

Maya Lawson: After an attempted assault by three boys in a West Point locker room, Maya left the military academy—though not before learning that her younger sister Sara had gone missing from the rehab facility she'd been sent to. Maya rescued her from beneath a boardwalk mere moments before an attempted trafficking and brought her back home. Maya battles to reconcile the obvious darkness in herself, and whether or not the path she's chosen is the best one for her.

Sara Lawson: Still struggling with her drug dependency, Sara was checked into a Virginia Beach rehab facility by her father. She escaped on her first night there and, her addiction getting the better of her, threw caution to the wind in search of a fix. After a harrowing near-trafficking incident under a boardwalk, Sara was rescued by Maya and Alan Reidigger and brought home.

Mischa: The only survivor of the insurgent group behind the ultrasonic attacks, Mischa is a twelve-year-old Russian girl who was indoctrinated from a very young age and trained as a spy and killer. Zero and Maria apprehended her and turned her over to the CIA for holding.

President Jonathan Rutledge: The former Speaker of the House ascended to the Oval Office after the impeachment of his predecessors. Though he considered stepping down, Rutledge was bolstered by Zero's perseverance and decided to remain in office and do whatever good he can.

Table of Contents

PROLOGUE

The ship itself was a modern work of art.

Sixteen meters from bow to stern, she was capable of comfortably accommodating up to fourteen souls while only requiring three to crew her efficiently. Twin dual-calibration inboard engines combined for fourteen hundred horsepower and a top speed of two hundred forty kilometers per hour. Low-observable technology made her virtually invisible to radar, sonar, infrared, and nearly all forms of electromagnetic detection. Her hull was wrapped in a reflective coating that, to look upon her up close, cast a silvery aspect that almost appeared fluid, mimicking the ebb of the water in which she sat low-slung when at rest. But from any distance approximately three hundred meters or greater, she would appear as no more than a nebulous blur; a ripple of heat perhaps, a reflection from the ocean, or a trick of the naked eye.

It was for this reason she was dubbed *Banjjag-Im*, or in the transliteration from her native Korean to the diverse crew's shared language of English, she was simply called *Glimmer*.

Yet for all of *Glimmer*'s tools and fittings, she was still merely a vessel—not only in the maritime sense, but also in the literal definition of being a container, a method of conveyance for a far greater treasure. Like a gilded chest or an ornamental jewelry box, what *Glimmer* held in her belly, hidden within the curved ribs of her hull, beneath an automated aluminum hatch and mounted upon a hydraulic lift, that was the genuine masterpiece, the magnum opus of those who kept her secret.

Park Eun-ho considered himself staggeringly fortunate to be considered among them. At age twenty-nine, he was the youngest of the crew by nearly a decade, but his work in theoretical plasma ballistics had been indispensable to the project—and as of today, would no longer be theoretical. The thought made him outright giddy, though he tried his best to hide it and maintain the solemnity of his colleagues. He had to admit, even if only to himself, that his interest in the field had initially been spurred by video games. Outwardly, he could wax rhapsodic for hours about the influence of science fiction on real-world applications—cell phones, touch screens, virtual reality, artificial intelligence, even energy drinks—all of those impossible dreams that had persisted to become scientific fact.

He had been recommended by his mentor, Dr. Lee from the University of Seoul, and for the first several months Eun-ho had hardly any idea what he was actually working on, outside of the desired payload and, quite obviously due to the nature of his research, that it was a weapon. Eventually the research needed to come together, and the various engineers that comprised the top-secret efforts were convened.

Eun-ho would later discover that only two men had been fully privy to the details from the start: a general with the Ministry of National Defense, and a high-ranking politician close to the president, both from the government of what he would call *Hanguk* (Romanized from his native language to *Korea*, if they were speaking in English), the country that the western world referred to as South Korea. Eun-ho hadn't met either of these men, nor were they aboard *Glimmer* as she made her maiden voyage, with Park Eun-ho one of the twelve currently aboard her.

It was a privilege that just a tiny part of him was regretting.

Nearly three hours prior they had departed from the southwestern shore, in those strange hours that, depending on perspective, could be considered very late at night or very early in the morning. *Glimmer*'s home while in port was a rural culvert on a stretch of rocky beach surrounded by hazard signs warning travelers that the area was littered with unexploded land mines from the Korean War (which, of course, was not true). Under the cover of night, the twelve of them boarded the miracle ship and piloted her out into the North Pacific Ocean, maintaining an unimpressive speed for the first eighty kilometers. *Glimmer* was veritably undetectable, but they were not taking any chances when it came to US satellite surveillance or their spying neighbors to the north, the country that still called themselves *Choson*.

The part that Eun-ho had mild regrets over was not the hour or the circumstances, but rather the time of year; early February was cold enough, and out on the ocean it was outright bitter. Wind slipped easily over the vessel's streamlined hull and bit into Eun-ho savagely. The occasional spray of frigid ocean spittle stung his cheeks. The inboard engines were stunningly silent, more of a thrum beneath his feet than an audible sound, though it could have been partially attributed to the hood of his downy parka, pulled up over his head and drawn tight around his face.

And though the engines were mostly quiet, the crew remained somber and silent, as if the excursion required some sort of reverence. Among them were researchers, experts, doctors of various sciences that Eun-ho could not begin to guess and was disallowed from asking. Even their full identities were not known to each other; Eun-ho was known to his eleven comrades only as "Park," the anglicized pronunciation of which from his non-Korean cohorts rankled him slightly. In his native tongue, the name was pronounced more like "Bahk."

Still, he did not bother to correct them.

To his left on the cushioned bench seat near *Glimmer*'s stern was a man known to him as Sun, a fellow Korean researcher whom Eun-ho might have believed was a carpenter or some other sort of tradesman based on the calloused state of his fingers and knuckles. To his right was a European with a square, clean-shaven jaw and sandy hair impeccably parted and so slicked with pomade that even the freezing wind did not ruffle it. The European's age was difficult to discern; he could have been a hardened thirty, a healthy forty, or anywhere in between. He spoke seldom, and softly when he did. By Eun-ho's best guess he was Dutch.

But most notable about the European's appearance was the angular pistol holstered at his hip, matte black and clasped snugly in a matching nylon holster. Despite the fact that he was sitting almost quite literally upon one of the most powerful and revolutionary weapons in the world, the sight of the pistol on the man's hip was somehow more unsettling.

"Pardon," Eun-ho asked over the gently roaring wind. His English was excellent; he'd been studying it since he was seven. "What is that for?"

The European regarded him evenly. "Security."

Ah. He was not Dutch after all. The raised voice required to speak audibly over the wind was consonant-heavy and, to Eun-ho's ear, sounded German.

Still, the answer was not entirely satisfactory. What need did they have for security out here, almost five hundred kilometers southeast of Japan? No one knew they were here. No one was looking for them. *Glimmer* was nigh invisible.

Perhaps, Eun-ho thought, *in the event that any change their minds about what we have done here.* He glanced around as casually as he could muster at the red, chapped faces of his colleagues. Would any among them have a change of heart after seeing the weapon's destructive power?

As if in answer, the whine of the inboard engines wound down and the ship slowed. Eun-ho felt a chill run through him that was not from the freezing water or biting wind. The sun was rising, turning the dark water blue and gracing the sky with streaks of pink.

"Gentlemen." The man called Kim—only Kim—stood near the bow and addressed them all with his gloved palms out, and then repeated the phrase in English for the sake of their non-Korean friends. His owlish glasses and receding hairline made him a veritable stereotype of the weapon-building scientists that Eun-ho might have found in a science-fiction novel. "Today is momentous. It is a culmination of two years of our collective hard work. It is unfortunate that this event can be witnessed by so few. But rest assured, my friends, the world will remember your names."

"Only if the damn thing works," Sun grunted under his breath.

Eun-ho held back a chuckle.

"Let us begin," said Kim. He nodded to another, who stood at a complicated three-person control panel just behind *Glimmer*'s steering column and wheel, separated from the rest of the boat by a thick windshield that Eun-ho knew to be bulletproof. The man pushed a key into a slot, twisted it, and punched a four-digit combination into the keypad.

The aluminum doors in the ship's center rose with a heavy whir, opening outward like a pair of Bilco doors. A deeper, more resonant hum began as the hydraulic lift was activated. In moments, the weapon rose from *Glimmer*'s bowels like an angelic presence making itself known. It was a beautiful sight to behold.

Even the most educated on the matter would argue that a plasma railgun was the stuff of theory at best, fantasy at most—and yet, they had built one. Two years of round-the-clock commitment, fractured relationships, personal lives fallen by the wayside, some of the brightest minds of both the eastern and western worlds, and a frankly obscene amount of money later, a weapon thought never possible to exist existed.

At full height upon the hydraulic lift, the weapon stood about three meters taller than *Glimmer*'s hull. The two parallel rails—essentially, the "barrel" of the weapon—were six meters long, a pair of ultra-sturdy electrodes along which an armature of ionized gas-like particles would slide at a velocity more than seven times the speed of sound. The railgun's effective firing range, as far as their predictive models could tell, was two hundred forty to three hundred and twenty kilometers—or one hundred fifty to two hundred miles.

Sun's words echoed in Eun-ho's head. *Only if the damn thing works.* Of course, all of the railgun's systems were integral, but he liked to think that his own work on the weapon was arguably the most important; after all, if the weapon could not fire its plasma projectile, it would be utterly useless.

He was not superstitious, but still he crossed the fingers of one hand.

"Here," Sun grunted as he held out a pair of thick black binoculars.

Eun-ho took them with a nod. "Where?"

Sun pointed, and Eun-ho looked. He could just see it out there, visible as a vague shape in the still-rising sun. The garbage barge was seventy meters long and piled high with refuse from Seoul. It was unmanned, and a few dim lights around its perimeter were the only warnings anyone would get to keep ships from colliding with it. The barge had been anchored here three weeks prior, specifically here in this spot, specifically for this purpose.

It was only eighteen kilometers away. Today's test was a maiden voyage, so to speak, not to test full range but efficacy, targeting, power—and, as Sun had so astutely pointed out, that the damn thing worked.

"Ready," said Kim.

The railgun crackled to life. Eun-ho knew that it took eight seconds to ready its charge, during which the operator would deftly enter the coordinates and, in just a few seconds, the weapon would autocorrect its trajectory to match.

"Ready," the man at the console parroted.

Kim glanced around at his expectant colleagues. Then with a curt nod of his head he said, "Fire."

It happened so quickly that Eun-ho did not even have time to register it. In an instant, or even less than an instant, a blue spark of plasma danced down the length of the railgun's electrodes. It was gone just as quickly. There was no earsplitting crack to accompany it, no sonic boom, no high-pitched whine ringing in his ears. There was simply an odd sound—like a *thoom!*—and a microsecond of blue plasma. Barely more than a flash, a glimpse.

And in the second instant, eighteen kilometers away, the garbage barge exploded. Even from this distance the force of it made him shudder. One moment the barge was barely on the horizon, even with binoculars; the next, it was a fiery burst arcing into the sky, pieces of it sailing in various directions for hundreds of meters, lighting up the early hours of the morning.

And, seconds later, those flaming pieces sizzled and sank in the freezing waters of the North Pacific Ocean.

In moments like this, many great men had the aptitude of foresight to prepare a statement, knowing or at least suspecting that their quote might appear later in a history text, or regurgitated on the internet, or at the very least noted by another who was present. But Eun-ho had prepared no statement, and in that moment only one syllable escaped his throat.

"Huh."

The test had gone spectacularly well. The damn thing worked perfectly. Where there once was a barge, there was now nothing at all but frothing waters. The destructive force of the railgun was immense—not nearly that of a warhead, but it was not an explosive weapon. It was a tactical weapon, a precise weapon; its goals were small, more strategic, and could even be mobile. The railgun would be most adept at sinking ships, shooting down planes, or even defending against missiles. Its ability to course-correct almost instantly and the plasma projectile speed of Mach 7 made it virtually impossible to defend against. Its only disadvantage was the eight seconds it took to charge before firing, and even that paled in comparison to long-range missiles, torpedoes, or battleship cannons. Its relatively small size lent to mobility, and stealth capabilities meant that it could go virtually unseen by any enemy, even at close proximity.

The plasma railgun could change the face of modern warfare. But that was not its intention, at least not as far as Eun-ho and his colleagues had been told. Despite the many billions it had cost to create the weapon (South Korea had the tenth-highest military budget in the world) they would produce five more, and together the half-dozen railguns would protect not only the border between them and those to the north, but any would-be enemy or invader. They did not seek to become a stronger military power or to destroy anyone who was not an aggressor; it was about protection, safeguarding their people, and nothing more.

And he, Eun-ho Park, was among those responsible for the welfare of his people. He had helped make such a thing possible. Even the biting wind of February on the ocean could not detract from the immense feeling of pride swelling beneath his parka—

"Dr. Kim!" the man behind the console shouted suddenly. "A boat!"

Eun-ho's head swiveled quickly at the distressing call, and his eyes widened when he saw that the man was not looking at the radar display of his console—but pointing over the bow. A boat was indeed approaching, no more than fifteen hundred meters out and bouncing on the white-tipped crests as it closed the distance.

The weapon's test had distracted them all from keeping their eyes open. They had assumed they were safe out here.

"What the hell?" Dr. Kim grunted. "Who...?"

Eun-ho realized then that he still had Sun's binoculars in his hands. He lifted them to his face and focused in. He did not know much about boats, but enough that he could tell the approaching ship was not military, nor was it nearly as new as *Glimmer.* The chipped and faded hull told him that this boat had been through some wear and tear...and were those bullet holes in its sides?

He looked to the deck and nearly gasped aloud. The men gathered there were dressed for cold weather, but the exposed areas of their dark skin told him that they were African. And the guns cradled in their hands told him that they were not friendly.

Eun-ho did not know much about boats, but he knew loads about weapons, and he recognized an AK-47 when he saw one.

"Sir," he said meekly to Kim. "I don't know how to explain this, but I believe they are…pirates."

"Give me those!" Kim all but snatched the binoculars from Eun-ho's hands. The balding doctor's jaw went mildly slack even while the lenses were still against his eyes.

Of course they had all heard tales of modern pirates, particularly those that hailed from Somalia. But they were a territorial lot, their victims being those that sailed the Gulf of Aden, the Arabian Sea. Certainly not the North Pacific. They were thousands of miles from their hunting grounds.

The German was on his feet then, staring off the bow with an eagle-eyed squint. He unclasped the nylon holster at his waist and drew the matte black gun in such a fluid motion that it seemed like the weapon simply appeared there in his hand.

But it was Sun who spoke next.

"Turn the weapon on them."

Dr. Kim wheeled on him with a look of utter incredulity. "Are you mad? You would have us simply kill them?"

"They have guns," the German murmured. "Assault rifles."

"They've seen," Sun insisted. "They saw us fire the weapon, and they are coming for it. There is no doubt. Turn it on them."

A lump of panic congealed in Eun-ho's gut. It was strange to think that after all of this time and research, he had never once considered that this masterpiece of a weapon might be used to end lives. He would be a part of that. His own hand had crafted the projectiles. Yet here they were, faced with a genuine threat and little other recourse.

"You have about fifteen seconds to decide," the German announced in his harsh accent, louder than any words Eun-ho had heard him speak before.

"No," Kim said firmly. "We can outrun them easily. Get the engines going!"

"We need to lower the weapon first…" stammered the man at the console.

"Then do so!" Kim screeched. "Now, quickly!"

"But they have *seen!*" Sun insisted again.

"Ten seconds," the German interjected.

A burst of automatic gunfire tore at the air, so loud and crisp over the water that Eun-ho instinctively threw his hands over his head. He felt the thrum of the hydraulic lift lowering the plasma railgun back into the confines of *Glimmer*'s hull. He heard the shouts—the panicked, argumentative ones of his colleagues, but now others, guttural and angry and unintelligible to his ear, speaking a language that was not Korean or English or Mandarin, which Eun-ho was also fluent in, but sounded angry and demanding and deadly all at once.

When he dared to look again the pirate skiff—for he had made the mental assumption by now that they were indeed pirates—had drawn nearer and slowed, pulling perpendicular to *Glimmer*'s bow so that moving forward would be impossible.

"Full reverse, now!" Kim snapped as the hatch doors closed over the railgun.

The man at the console wrapped his hand over the throttle as a single, sharp report made Eun-ho's shoulders jump. The pilot's head jerked to the right as a cloud of red mist settled over the sea behind him.

The German lowered his pistol. The silence and incredulity of the ensuing moment was crushing; the man at the console slid to the deck. The pirates watched. Eun-ho's colleagues fell absolutely still. His legs felt as if they were made of stone, rooting him to the ship's deck.

And in that vacuous moment, the German turned and dispassionately fired a second shot into Dr. Kim's forehead.

That jarred them into action. Several shouted. Two rushed forward, Sun and another man—Bong, if Eun-ho recalled correctly. They reached for the German but he simply twisted his body and, instead of bothering with the pistol, he threw out an elbow. It connected with Sun's nose with a sickening crunch, blood arcing backward with the toss of his head and spattering the front of Eun-ho's parka. With the same smoothness that he had drawn his weapon, the German spun the pistol in his palm, bringing it around at the same time, and caught Bong just behind the jaw with its grip.

Eun-ho's legs turned to jelly and his knees buckled, sending jolts of pain through his legs as they struck the deck. Two more shots rang out, *pop-pop* in quick succession, and even though he had closed his eyes by then the telltale sound of two bodies falling followed.

There was a splash, and then another—colleagues that had chosen "flight" as their fight, flight, or freeze option. But even as terror coursed through Eun-ho, he knew that ultimately they had chosen the latter—freeze. In the frigid North Pacific in February, they would be dead in less than a minute.

Pop.

Pop-pop.

These were not the tearing bursts of automatic weapons; these were the single shots of the matte black pistol. The pirates were not firing, he realized; they were *waiting*. Waiting for him to finish so that they could claim the railgun. The German had betrayed them. The man who had been responsible for their safety had been their undoing.

When at last Eun-ho mustered the courage to open his eyes again, *Glimmer*'s deck was awash in blood but still spotless white in others. Four of the African pirates had boarded, pairing off and tossing the bodies of his colleagues over the side.

The German stood beside him, the pistol loosely and casually gripped in his left hand as if it was a mere accessory.

"Why?" Eun-ho asked, or tried to. But all that escaped his throat was a breathy hiss.

"Just a young man," the German murmured, his voice soft again, sounding much the way it had when Eun-ho had erroneously guessed he was Dutch. "But it is often young men that suffer most in these sorts of matters."

Eun-ho could not help but flinch slightly as the barrel of the gun pressed against his temple. He closed his eyes again. The breeze was cold, but the morning sun felt pleasant on his face.

CHAPTER ONE

Zero lay on his stomach in the snowdrift, hoping that he was low enough to the ground and far enough from the cabin to be obscured as the sun set across the prairie. He cursed the lack of foresight to wear white; the fleece-lined synthetic jacket was beige, close enough in theory but undoubtedly standing stark against the pure-white snow. The balaclava over his face was black because—well, because it was difficult to find one that wasn't black, especially on as short notice as he had.

He held the monocular to his eye again and scoped the cabin in the distance. Still no movement. But he was certain this was the place; the question was whether or not his target was inside at that moment.

Zero wished he had better gear. He was only vaguely aware of what he might be walking into, and none of it was good. He had the cold-weather clothes on his back. He had the monocular. He had a gun, a small silver Walther PPK with a three-point-three-inch barrel and a six-round capacity. Many believed that the PP series stood for "pocket pistol," since they were so easily concealed, but it actually stood for *Polizeipistole*—quite literally, "police pistol"—which was made all the more amusing by the fact that it was currently concealed in his right jacket pocket.

Zero had no radio, no motion detectors, no listening devices, not even a phone. The CIA could track him by phone ... or perhaps more dangerously, his daughter Maya could track him by phone. She hadn't believed for a second that he was seeing a nerve specialist in California for the traumatic injury to his hand from a couple years earlier. As usual, she was right.

Zero was not in California. He wasn't even in the United States. Instead, he was lying half-buried in a snowbank in the northeastern corner of Canada's Saskatchewan province. Thanks to having to resort to paper maps and pens, he had only a nebulous idea of where he actually was in relation to anything else. The landscape was little more than a wide swath of prairie as far as the eye could see, marred only by snow that had been arranged by wind into small ridges of drifts here and there, and the occasional leafless tree.

And, of course, the cabin.

It sat about five hundred yards away from his current location, just a single-story modular affair that looked neither old nor modern. It was roughly the size and shape of an eighteen-wheeler's trailer (which Zero surmised was how it had arrived here) and had been unceremoniously propped upon a foundation of cinder blocks, some of which seemed to have settled since the cabin's weight had set upon them, causing the building to sit at an angle of about three degrees.

To the cabin's eastern side Zero could see a stainless steel cistern, which must have been collecting melted snow and groundwater. Even at his distance he could hear the faint rumble of a diesel-powered generator, though he couldn't see it from his vantage point. And there were clearly two small solar panels on the roof. The cabin was small, self-sustaining, and almost completely off the grid.

Almost, or else he might never have found it.

After what felt like hours the sun finally vanished behind the horizon, darkening the plain enough that Zero felt comfortable moving. He was thankful for that, because the night brought with it a plummeting temperature that bit into him even with his cold-weather precautions. Northern Saskatchewan in February was anything but forgiving.

Before carefully setting off toward the cabin, he did a quick mental check. It was an exercise that he'd started doing daily, and then almost hourly, and now just second-naturedly to ensure that his memory was not slipping or failing. First he thought of his daughters, Maya and Sara, eighteen and sixteen respectively. In his mind's eye he brought up their names, their faces, their ages, the sound of their laughter. Then he thought of Maria Johansson, her cascading blonde hair and slate-gray eyes that some-how managed to look flat and bright at the same time. And finally, he thought of Kate, his late wife.

"Kate." He actually murmured her name aloud, more out of ceremony than anything else, like an "Amen" punctuating a brief prayer; her name was the first thing he'd for-gotten when his latent memory lapses began to crop up. He remembered her name. He remembered her face. Her scent, her laugh, and the tiny hiss of fuming breath when she was irritated. He remembered that she was murdered by a former CIA agent named John Watson, a man Zero had once called a friend. A man who had fled and gone dark after Zero had decided not to kill him.

And then he moved, slowly and carefully making his way toward the cabin, stepping heel-toe and shifting his weight with each footfall. He couldn't do much about leaving tracks in the snow, but at least he could keep his steps from crunching.

The exercise, the "mental check" as he was calling it, was about more than just ensuring he hadn't temporarily lost anything. A little over eight weeks ago, he had visited the Swiss neurologist Dr. Guyer, the same man who had implanted the memory suppressor in his head in the first place, as well as the man who had told Zero, in no uncertain terms, that his brain would continue to deteriorate at an unknown rate, that his memories would fade and potentially vanish forever, and that the damage to his limbic system would, in all likelihood, eventually kill him.

All of which lent greatly to his reason for stalking a remote cabin in Saskatchewan at night in the dead of winter. He needed to go back to the beginning, to seek out someone who could give him more answers. At least he hoped.

He paused about fifty yards from the cabin and lowered himself to one knee, staying like that for several minutes, completely silent and watching. Zero saw no lights on from within. Conserving energy, perhaps? Or maybe the windows were boarded. Maybe there was no one home. But he could hear the chugging of the diesel generator even clearer now; if there was no one inside, why would it be running?

Zero rose to his feet and stalked forward again. Though it was night, he could still see the exterior façade of the cabin and did not notice anything like cameras or detectors or perhaps automated gun turrets that would tear him to shreds the moment he stepped into their sensor range. As ridiculous as it sounded, it was a legitimate concern, considering his target.

He realized then that his hand had slipped into his pocket and was gripping the PPK. He released it. He wouldn't need the gun, not here. He'd only brought it as a precaution.

But as Zero reached the front door of the cabin, he was keenly aware that this was as far as his careful planning would take him. He'd imagined the scenario a hundred times, especially with the hours he'd spent lying in the snow drift, but had no way of telling what was waiting on the other side of the door. If this was an assault, it might have been easier; ordinarily he would burst in, gun drawn and ready for anything. Shoot first and ask questions later.

This time, however, he simply twisted the knob. It turned easily, unlocked. He pushed the door open and took a small, cautious step over the threshold. As he'd suspected from the outside, the cabin was entirely dark. But still the generator hummed from somewhere behind it.

This is a trap.

No sooner did his brain remit the message than he took another small step forward. The tile under his foot gave way just slightly, no more than a quarter of an inch.

A pressure plate.

Zero froze.

"I wouldn't lift that foot if I were you." The voice was familiar, yet seemed to come from everywhere, as if it was cast through an omni-directional microphone. "Put your hands up, please."

Zero did as the voice told him. "I'm not armed," he said, but hours of being silent and out in the cold had made his throat tight and his voice hoarse.

"You are," the engineer contradicted simply. "You've been lying in a snowbank for about four hours. There were hidden cameras on you from two of the trees. A large rock you passed about a hundred yards out was actually a full-body scanner. You have a pistol in your right jacket pocket. Just keep your hands up and your foot down."

A light clicked on, a bright white LED that made Zero squint. Beyond it, a silhouette appeared from a small rear room.

"Bixby," Zero said.

The silhouette paused.

Slowly Zero reached up and did what he should have done before he'd even entered the cabin; he grabbed the fabric of the balaclava and tugged it off his head. His hair was matted and stray wisps were plastered to his forehead with sweat.

"Oh," said Bixby. The disappointment in his voice was palpable. "I didn't think they would send you. But I guess I should have figured."

"They didn't," Zero insisted calmly, both hands still hovering near his ears. "I swear they didn't. No one sent me. I'm here on my own and alone."

Bixby took one step forward, being sure to stay out of arm's reach but close enough that Zero could see him better, just in the edge of the LED's corona. Last time he had seen the eccentric CIA engineer and inventor, Bixby had been wearing a soft purple silk shirt under a black three-button waistcoat. He still had his signature horn-rimmed glasses, but now he wore a simple flannel shirt and blue jeans. He hadn't shaved in several days, the early growth of a gray beard matching the salt-and-pepper of his hair, which appeared to have been hastily combed out of habit and hygiene but not care.

There were bags beneath his eyes, and his skin had something of a sallow quality. Zero imagined that Bixby hadn't gotten much sleep in the two months he'd been on the run from the CIA.

"How do I know you're telling the truth?" Bixby asked carefully.

"You said you scanned me, right? I brought a gun as a precaution." He realized how lame the excuse sounded when he said it aloud and to a man who believed Zero was there to kill him. "I have no phone. No radio. No tracking devices. You would have seen that."

Bixby shrugged slightly with one shoulder. "Do better."

"We're friends."

"We were—"

"We *are*," Zero said adamantly. He could see in the older man's eyes that he wanted very much to believe it. How many times had Bixby prepped him for an op? How many bad jokes had they exchanged? To think that Zero was there for an assassination was laughable—at least to him. But Bixby couldn't be too cautious. Not after what he'd done.

Two months earlier, Zero and his team had stopped a band of Chinese mercenaries and their Russian leader from melting down a nuclear reactor at a facility in Calvert Cliffs. Bixby had helped by making modifications to a machine called OMNI, a CIA supercomputer capable of spying on any cell phone, tablet, computer, radio, or smart device in the continental United States. Its very existence was intended only for the highest clearances; it was extremely immoral, highly illegal, and insanely expensive.

Bixby's modifications to OMNI also caused irreparable damage to the supercomputer. As not only the one who had done the damage but the only man who could fix it, Bixby fled and went dark. There were no doubts between the two men in that tiny cabin that if the CIA ever found him, there would be no arrests, no trial, no prison sentence. There would be only a bullet and a shallow grave, which was why Zero had taken every precaution to get here.

"How did you find me?" Bixby asked.

"Do you think maybe you can disarm whatever I'm standing on first?" Zero asked, gesturing to the depressed pressure plate beneath his foot. "What is it, anyway? A mine?"

"Of course not," Bixby replied. "Bombs are messy. You know me better than that."

"Ah." A sonic weapon, most likely. If Zero had to guess, taking his foot off the plate would activate a carefully directed sonic blast that would cause instant dizziness and nausea, and give him one hell of a headache, if not actually rupture his internal organs.

"Take off your jacket," Bixby ordered. "Slowly. And toss it to me."

Zero did as he was told, first tugging off each thick glove, slowly, and then unzipping the fleece-lined coat and shrugging out of it. He tossed it away and Bixby caught it by the collar. Only then did the engineer reach into his own back pocket and produce a small black remote. He flicked a single button and nodded once.

Even so, Zero held his breath as he lifted his foot, only breathing again when nothing happened. "Thanks."

"Sit over there," Bixby said flatly. Zero had been so concerned about whatever he was standing on that he hadn't really gotten his bearings; they were in a single room that operated as living room, dining room, and kitchen. The room in the rear must be a tiny bedroom, and he assumed there was a bathroom somewhere and not much else.

Zero did as he was told and took a seat in a small wooden chair.

"How did you find me?" Bixby asked again.

"Wasn't easy," Zero admitted. And that was certainly true; the eight weeks it had taken to locate the remote cabin was far longer than any mission Agent Zero had ever been on. "I went to your apartment after you vanished, and after the CIA did a sweep. Noticed what you took, what you didn't take. You did a pretty good job covering your tracks, but I saw that all of your cold-weather gear was gone. Not sure the agency even knew you owned it. I also knew you wouldn't stay in the US, so we narrowed it down to the most likely countries you might run to—"

"We?" Bixby interrupted curtly.

"Reidigger helped," Zero admitted. When it came to finding people, Alan was nearly as adept as he was at making them disappear. "I also remembered that one really rough winter when you complained about the arthritis in your hands," he continued. "You said that Trexall was the only medication that helped when it was that cold. So putting that together, and with the help of a certain Danish hacker that we both know, we tracked all new prescriptions of Trexall from our list of countries you might have fled to and then cross-referenced them against identities until we found one that wasn't actually anyone. Thousands of names. Took several weeks. But then we got a hit on a man in Saskatchewan named Jack Burton, who happened to share the same name as the main character in your favorite movie."

The corner of Bixby's mouth curled slightly into something that was almost a smile. "You remember that?"

"I do. So I came here, visited the pharmacy that gave you the pills. Tried to bribe the pharmacist with a thousand dollars to tell me where I could find you. He told me no. I thought it was a dead end—until I thought of something else. I asked the pharmacist if he'd ever heard the one about Orion's Belt."

At this Bixby did actually grin. "It's a 'waist' of space."

Zero knew there were few things that Bixby loved more than an awful pun or a down-right cringe-worthy joke, and as one of the only other humans he interacted with in eight weeks, the pharmacist must have heard them all.

"That convinced him that I knew you, and that I needed to find you," Zero concluded.

"Why?" Bixby asked.

"Because we're friends."

The engineer nodded, though his gaze was far away. "Yeah. I guess we are. But I'm not going back, Zero. I can't, and we both know it."

"Let Alan help you," Zero pleaded. "He's very good at making people disappear—and I mean really disappear, not the CIA way. He can get you a new identity, a new life. Not..." Zero gestured at the tiny modular cabin around them. "Not this."

Bixby pulled out the second wooden chair, opposite the small table between them, and took a seat with a heavy sigh. "Are you still working for them?"

"I have to. You know that." The only reason Zero wasn't in prison or worse, like the Moroccan black site H-6, was because he'd agreed to return to Special Operations.

"Friends or not," Bixby said, "if you're still with them, then you being here is trouble for me. I can't let you help me. Or Alan. I made my choices and I'm going to live with them. Besides." He grinned again. "This isn't so bad. It's only the first stop on a long journey. Trust me."

Zero blew a long sigh through his nose, knowing that he wasn't going to win this. But convincing Bixby to accept his help was only half the reason he was here; in fact, it was intended as a bargaining chip for the far more personal part of his visit.

"There's more. I need... help."

Bixby raised an eyebrow. "Oh?"

Zero sighed, unsure of how much or how little to explain. "The memory suppressor," he began. "You co-invented it. And lately I've been experiencing some... let's call them 'side effects.' Bad ones."

"Zero..."

He ignored Bixby and pressed on. "There must be something in the design that could help me. Or, I don't know, a way to undo it. There must be something you know that I don't—"

"Zero—"

"I need help, dammit!" He pounded the table with a fist.

"*Zero*," Bixby said again, forcefully. "Listen to me, please. What happened to you was unprecedented. I mean, they tore the damn thing out of your head with a pair of pliers. No one expected that. No one planned for that. To be honest, I'm surprised you recovered anything at all. Even if I could help..." Bixby gestured to the tiny cabin around them. "I'm sorely lacking in anything I'd call resources."

"Yeah," Zero said quietly. He stared down at the surface of the wooden table. He'd come all this way for nothing. He'd spent weeks seeking out a man who didn't want to be found for nothing. There were no answers to be had here or anywhere else. His own brain would eventually kill him, and he had to live with that until he wasn't anymore.

A full minute of silence passed between them before Bixby gently cleared his throat. When Zero looked up again, the engineer was holding out the jacket.

7

"I'm sorry," he said. "I'd invite you to stay the night, but you know I can't take any chances."

Zero understood. Even with all his careful planning, the agency had ways to find him if they thought there was a reason. Satellites, subcutaneous tracking chips, good old-fashioned spy networks... every minute he lingered was another minute he was putting Bixby in danger.

He took the jacket, stood, and slowly pulled it on. "I'm assuming that if anyone were to return to this place, there'd be nothing here."

Bixby smiled sadly. "Assume that." And then he said again, "I'm sorry."

Zero nodded once and headed for the door. "Take care of yourself, Bixby."

"... Wait."

Zero froze in mid-step, one hand reaching for the knob, his brain immediately assuming there was another forgotten booby trap.

"Just wait a second." Bixby took off his glasses, rubbed his eyes, and pushed them back on. "I ... I lied to you. Before. When I told you that you were the first person to ever have the suppressor installed."

Zero whirled around. "What? You lied?"

"Under threat of death? Yes. But all things considered, that ship seems to have sailed." He chuckled slightly in spite of himself. "The suppressor that was installed in you wasn't our first. Before that, there was another prototype. And there was a *single* human trial. About a year before your suppressor disappeared from my lab. A male, early to mid-thirties. Affiliated with the agency."

Another person who had a suppressor installed? Suddenly this trip was entirely worth it.

"An agent?" Zero asked.

"I don't know."

"Where is he?"

"I don't know."

"Who was he?"

"I don't know that either."

"What *do* you know?" Zero asked in exasperation.

"Look, he was just 'Subject A' to me," Bixby said defensively. "But there is one thing. After it was installed, as he was coming out of anesthesia, the neurosurgeon called him Connor. I remember that clearly. He said, 'Do you know who you are, Connor?'"

"Is Connor a first name or a last name?" Zero asked quickly.

"I don't know. That's all I have," Bixby told him. "You and I both know how the agency operates; he's probably long dead. Any record of him is probably wiped. But... maybe it's worth something. If you tug at that thread hard enough."

Zero nodded. It *was* worth something, he just wasn't sure what yet. "Thank you." He held out his hand, and Bixby shook it, possibly for the last time ever. The engineer wasn't easy to find the first time around, and he wouldn't make the same mistakes twice. "Please, be safe. Disappear. Go lay on a beach somewhere for the next twenty years."

Bixby grinned. "I'm Irish. I burn easy." The grin faltered. "Godspeed, Zero. I hope you find what you're looking for."

"Thanks."

But as Zero headed back out into the cold, impossibly dark night of Saskatchewan, he couldn't help the thought that ran through his head.

I hope I remember what I'm looking for.

CHAPTER TWO

The Saudi king's funeral was, as expected, quite opulent. At least this one was; the one that the world would see on news networks, the publicly held funeral, after the traditional Islamic rites were honored and the more intimate occasion with immediate family. This was the funeral attended by heads of state, Saudi nobility, and leaders of industry, held in the gilded and marble-columned courtyard of the royal palace in Riyadh. Rather, *one* of the royal palaces, Joanna reminded herself as she stood solemnly among those mourners present, heads bowed reverently and foreheads sprinkled with sweat beneath the bright Saudi sun.

She was the representative from the United States, though she could not help but feel slightly out of place in a black blazer, black silk shirt with its collar crisply folded, and black pencil skirt. Combined with the fact that it was seventy-eight degrees outside, the affair was stifling even in the shade. She tried her best not to let it show.

Joanna Barkley was a woman as pragmatic in mind as in her wardrobe. She had no misconceptions about that aspect of herself, though others often seemed to. As a teen, her notion to become a senator in the state of California was seen as a pipe dream by her teachers and peers and even her prosecutor father. But Joanna saw the clear path, the logical trajectory that would get her there. It was simply going to be. And at age thirty-two, she fulfilled the dream—or notion, to her—and was elected to the United States Congress as the youngest female senator in history.

Four years later, and barely more than two months ago, she made history yet again when President Jonathan Rutledge named her as his vice president. At thirty-six years of age, Joanna Barkley became not only the first female vice president in American politics, but tied John C. Breckinridge as the youngest.

Though inwardly sober and practical, somehow Joanna could not avoid being characterized as a starry-eyed daydreamer. Her policies were met with a similar derision as her childhood aspirations—all of which she had accomplished and more. To her, overhauling the healthcare system was not at all an impossibility, but simply something that needed a thorough and incremental plan to bring to fruition. Pulling out of conflicts in the Middle East, achieving peace, fair trade, even eventually sitting behind the desk in the Oval Office herself…none of it was unfeasible or impractical.

At least not in her eyes. Her detractors and rivals, of whom there were many, would say differently.

At long last the procession came to a close, ending with a tall man with a gray beard and a leftward hook to his nose murmuring a prayer, first in Arabic and then in English. He was dressed entirely in white from throat to ankles; a priest, Joanna assumed, or whatever they called themselves. She was not as well-versed in Islamic culture as she knew she should be, especially now that these sorts of visits and diplomatic missions were on her shoulders. But two months had hardly been enough time to prepare, and her term thus far had been a whirlwind of events, not the least of which was unified peace between the United States and Middle Eastern countries.

King Ghazi of Saudi Arabia had lost his lengthy battle with an undisclosed illness, the nature of which the royal family had not been inclined to share with the world. Joanna assumed it was something that may have been perceived to bring shame or ignominy to his name and she would not begin to guess. As the prayer came to a close, the procession of leaders, diplomats, and tycoons silently retreated into the sanctity (and air-conditioning) of the royal palace, away from the press and lenses of cameras. A curious thing, Joanna thought, considering how private the royal family seemed to be.

But before she could step inside, a voice called to her.

"Madame Vice President."

She paused. The speaker was none other than Prince Basheer—rather, King Basheer now, the late king's eldest son of seven. He was tall and broad-shouldered, perhaps even puffing his chest out slightly, if she didn't know better. He wore entirely white, much like the priest, save for his head covering—*what was it called?* she scolded herself—which was a red-and-white checkered pattern that, admittedly, reminded her of a picnic tablecloth. He kept his beard cut short, the end of it pointing downward like an arrow, black but flecked with gray despite his relatively young thirty-nine years.

"King Basheer." She nodded to him while congratulating herself on remembering the correct title. "My condolences, your highness."

He smiled with his eyes, though his mouth remained a tight line. "I must admit that getting used to the title may prove difficult." Basheer's English was excellent but Joanna noticed that he smacked his lips with each hard consonant. "I understand your visit will be short-lived. I hoped that we may have a word in private."

It was true; the flight plan was already registered. She'd wanted to be back on the jet within the hour. But diplomacy dictated that she not reject the offer from a grieving son, a newly minted king, and possible ally—especially since the US government had little idea where now-King Basheer's loyalties may lie.

Joanna nodded graciously. "Of course."

King Basheer gestured for her to follow. "Right this way."

She hesitated, catching herself just before blurting out, "*Now?*" Her gaze flitted back to the still-filing procession. Basheer had just put his father in the ground; surely there were more important matters to attend to than speaking with her.

A tight knot of apprehension formed as she followed a few strides behind Basheer, into the palace and through a receiving room for dignitaries the size of a modest gymnasium. As servants couriered refreshments to other visitors, Joanna skirted the edge of them and into a small antechamber. She noticed movement in her periphery; the tall priest in white was following her silently.

More than a priest, she thought. *An advisor, perhaps? Though in their culture they may be one and the same.* She fought to recall the term for this sort of person—Imam, was it?

Whoever he was, the tall priest (as she was now accustomed to thinking of him) closed the thick double doors to the antechamber behind him. It was only the three of them in this room; surprisingly, not a single servant or guard present. Divans and thick cushions in dizzying colors were arranged in some sort of feng-shui-meets-Middle-Eastern sensibility, and even the windows were dressed in heavy velvets.

This was a room where secrets were discussed, a room without ears. And though she did not know what was about to be discussed, Joanna Barkley knew it was precisely the reason she had hoped to return to Washington quickly.

"Please," said Basheer, gesturing wide to any of the seats in the chamber. "Sit."

She did so, on a cream-colored divan, but did not recline or make any effort to be comfortable. Joanna sat on the edge of the cushion with her back straight and her hands in her lap. "To what do I owe such an audience?" she dared to ask, skipping any formalities that may have been in store.

Basheer allowed himself a rare smile.

It was no secret that relations between the United States and Saudi Arabia had deteriorated somewhat ever since King Ghazi had fallen ill. Ghazi had been an ally, but when the disease took over and he fell out of the public spotlight, those who should have been speaking for him were oddly silent. The monarchy in Saudi Arabia was the absolute power and held sway over all branches of government, so the US found it prudent to begin furtively following the movements of Crown Prince Basheer.

They did not much like what they had found.

To make matters worse, Joanna was well aware that the former prince adhered strongly to Sharia law and had an obvious disdain for women in power. In his mind they were not and would never be equals or peers. She was beneath him, plain and simple.

"I would like to speak briefly about the future of relations between our great countries," the king began.

Joanna smiled in kind. "Before you speak your mind, your highness, you should know that I lack the authority to authorize any sanctions on behalf of my country."

"Yes," the king agreed. "But anything discussed in this meeting can be relayed to the president in turn."

Joanna held back a scowl at the suggestion that she was a messenger, but said nothing.

"I understand that America is hosting the Ayatollah of Iran this week," Basheer continued.

"Indeed we are." Joanna had organized the visit herself; a key part of President Rutledge's efforts to bring peace between the US and Middle East was a strategic alliance with Iran. They were aiming high, but as most things in her life, Joanna approached the problem diplomatically and without bias and found that a solution was very possible. "Our countries are reconciling. A treaty is currently being drafted by the United Nations."

The priest in white flared his nostrils; it would have been nearly an imperceptible movement had he not been standing like a statue beside the double doors. As stock-still as he was, the facial twitch might as well have been a vocal snarl.

"I understand you may not be completely, uh, how would you say—up to speed," Basheer said haughtily. "As you are new to office—"

"I'm new to *the* office," Joanna interrupted. "I assure you, I am not new to office."

What am I doing? she scolded herself. It was not at all like her to clap back to condescension or even outright derision. Yet something about this young king and his statuesque advisor riled her in a way she'd never felt before. It was more than a disdain for her personally; it was a disdain for her gender, a general outlook that the entirety of womanhood was beneath them. Yet she knew she had to keep herself in check. This was her first major diplomatic mission since taking the office of vice president and she would not let it go awry.

Basheer nodded. "Of course. What I meant to say was, you may not be aware of the history between our countries. That is, Saudi Arabia and Iran. We are sworn enemies, and as such we cannot condone such a treaty. There is a saying: 'The enemy of my enemy is my friend.' By the same logic, the friend of my enemy is my enemy."

Joanna chewed the tip of her tongue, biting back what she would have very much liked to say to the headstrong king. Instead of poking holes in faulty logic she said, "Then might I ask what you suggest, in your wisdom, sir?"

"A choice, Madame Vice President," Basheer said simply. "An alliance with Iran is an affront to my country, my people, and my family."

"A choice," Joanna repeated. The notion that Basheer expected the United States to choose peace with only one of the two was ludicrous—unless, she reasoned, he was testing her. "I hope you understand that our goal is peace with all Middle Eastern nations. Not just Iran, and not just Saudi Arabia. This is not personal; this is diplomacy."

"I cannot help but take it personally," the king replied instantly. "As the new monarch I will be expected to show strength—"

"And you still can," Joanna interjected, "by joining us. Peace is not a weakness."

"Peace is not an option," Basheer corrected. "The history of tensions between our nations transcends what you may have learned in books or reports—"

Anger flared inside her. "With all due respect—"

"And yet you insist on interrupting!" the king snapped.

Joanna winced. Clearly Basheer was not accustomed to anyone speaking over him, let alone a woman. "Your highness," she said, keeping her voice measured, "I don't think this is a terribly appropriate time to speak about this. Not to mention that I am in no position to simply grant what you're asking."

"What I am *owed*," Basheer told her.

"Nor would I," Joanna raised her volume, "even if I was." There was fire in her now that she could not ignore or extinguish. "We are well aware of your…ties, King Basheer. Your personal alliances with some rather unsavory factions."

She immediately regretted it as Basheer narrowed his eyes at her. Not only had she let slip, in a roundabout way, that the US had been monitoring him, but also that they were aware of growing connections between the Saudi royalty and aggressive insurgent groups both within and outside their borders.

"Leave," Basheer grunted.

That's been the plan all along, Joanna thought wryly as she stood. In lieu of anything else to say she simply offered a curt, "Thank you for your hospitality," and turned on a heel toward the door.

"I don't think you understand," said Basheer loudly. "I am not only asking *you* to leave. I am telling you that the United States is to vacate my country. The embassies are closed, effective immediately. Any and all American troops, American citizens, American diplomats are hereby deported. Until your government comes to their senses and is willing to speak seriously about this, we are severing ties."

Joanna Barkley's mouth fell open slightly as she attempted to gauge if Basheer was being genuine or calling a bluff. All indications pointed to him being deadly serious. "You would make us an enemy out of spite for Iran?"

"You have made me your enemy first." Basheer motioned toward the door without rising. "Go and tell your president that."

There was nothing more to be said. Vice President Joanna Barkley pulled open the door to the antechamber without a single glance at the stoic priest that still stood alongside it. She was met right away with the din of a hundred chattering voices; she had almost forgotten that the funeral procession was ongoing. But she paid them no mind as she crossed to the far side of the wide auditorium, where her two Secret Service members waited.

"Let's go," she told them curtly. "And get President Rutledge on the phone before wheels are up."

She feared that she had failed in her first diplomatic task as vice president, one that should have been simple and routine. But moreover, she feared that peace with one Middle Eastern country would only mean war with another.

"The insolence!" Basheer growled in Arabic as he paced the antechamber. "The audacity! This is why America is failing. This is why they will fall. Rutledge is weak. That woman is insufferable. Was she Saudi, I'd have her publicly executed!"

The sheikh had not moved from his position for several minutes, despite how much he had desired to draw the thin blade hidden in his sleeve and rake it across the American politician's throat. He took two long strides into the room, his lanky legs carrying him several meters toward his king. "Patience, highness. This is not a moment to lose composure. This is the time for discipline and tact."

Basheer nodded, though his lips were still curled in a snarl. "Yes," he agreed. "Yes, you are right. Of course."

Under normal circumstances, a tribal sheikh like Salman would never be at the right hand of the king. But while others had ingratiated themselves to Ghazi, Salman had looked to the future and turned his attentions to the eldest son, Basheer, who would one day be king. Since the prince was sixteen years of age Salman had used every opportunity to whisper in the boy's ear. To remind him of his greatness. To encourage that he would be a stronger king than his father ever was. To ingrain the necessity of the fall of the West and the expansion of the Saudi kingdom in equal measure. Salman would never, could never be king—but he could stand at the king's side, and his name could be known the world over in the same breath.

"I'm afraid I've acted rashly," Basheer muttered. "This will not bode well for us."

"On the contrary," Salman assured him. "You've shown that your will is strong. Next we must prove that you have an equally strong hand."

"How? Tell me how," Basheer implored him. "If they are successful in a treaty with Iran, we will have no allies. We will look foolish before the world. We cannot stand against the US army. We cannot afford a war with them."

"No," Salman agreed, placing a spindly hand on the young king's shoulder. "We cannot. But we may not need to. There is a plan, highness, one already in motion. And if we see it through, the western world will learn a painful lesson—and the world will watch our rise."

CHAPTER THREE

*D*on't worry
        About a thing,
    'Cause every little thing...
    'Cause every little thing...

"Dammit," Zero murmured. "You know this." He'd been whistling the tune while reciting the lyrics in his head—the girls had asked him multiple times to stop singing—but he'd never gotten caught on that line before. "What was it?"

"Are you talking to yourself?" Sara asked as she entered the small kitchen of his apartment in Bethesda, Maryland. She wore sweats, her blonde hair was a disheveled mess on her head, and judging by the dark circles under her eyes she'd forgotten (or neglected) to wash the mascara off her face the night before.

"Sure am." Zero kissed the top of her head as she pulled open the refrigerator. "Morning, sweetheart."

"Mm," Sara said in response as she retrieved the jug of orange juice. She'd been staying with Zero ever since Thanksgiving—ever since she had escaped from the rehab clinic he'd sent her to and ended up under a pier and nearly kidnapped. She was sixteen, almost seventeen now, he reminded himself, though her features were mature enough to pass for at least a couple of years older. It was painful enough that his girls were growing up, even more so that the trauma she had been through had aged her prematurely, but most of all that she looked more like her late mother with every passing day.

"What are you making?" she asked, craning her neck over his shoulder to peer into the pan.

"Oh, this? This, my dear, is a frittata." Zero plucked up the frying pan, shook it twice, and then expertly flipped the frittata in the air once.

Sara wrinkled her nose. "Looks like an omelet."

"It is omelet-esque. Omelet-adjacent, you might say. Like if an omelet and a pizza had a baby. A frittata."

"Please stop saying—"

"Frittata."

Sara rolled her eyes as she took a long gulp from the orange juice. "You're weird."

"Hey, Squeak," Maya announced as she entered the kitchen. "Let me get some of that." She was dressed in shorts and a hooded sweatshirt, sneakers on and a sweatband over her forehead. Her dark hair was cut short in something close to a bob—a "pixie cut," the kids called it—and while her younger sister's features were reminiscent of their mother, Maya's youthful face was much more the shadow of Zero's.

Maya was staying with him as well, making the two-bedroom apartment feel cozy yet a bit cramped at the same time. His girls, almost-seventeen and nineteen respectively, had been sharing a room but hadn't complained once. Zero chalked it up to the amount of time they'd spent apart while Sara was living in Florida and Maya had been enrolled at West Point. But his eldest had skipped the remainder of the fall semester, and now the spring semester as well, and though he hadn't broached the subject yet he was hopeful that she would eventually return and finish her education.

Sara passed the orange juice to Maya, who took an ample swig. "Maya, hasn't Dad been weird lately?"

"You mean weirder than usual? Yeah. Definitely."

"First of all," Zero said, "get a glass. I didn't raise a couple of heathens. Secondly, how am I weird?"

"You've been singing a lot," Maya said.

"I stopped doing that when you asked."

"Now you whistle a lot," Sara told him.

"What's wrong with whistling?"

"Are you cooking a frittata?" Maya asked.

"He's been cooking a lot," Sara said as if he wasn't even in the room.

"Yeah, it's weird," Maya agreed. "It's like he's ... happier."

"Why is that weird?" Zero protested.

"In this family?" Sara scoffed. "It's weird."

"Ouch." Zero held a hand over his heart and mimed a heart attack. "So sorry for trying to enrich the lives of those I love."

"I don't trust it," Sara side-mouthed to her sister.

"Where were you last week?"

The question came so suddenly that Zero almost got whiplash. His eldest stared him down with one eyebrow precipitously high on her forehead, waiting.

"I told you. I was in California..."

"Right," Maya said, "seeing a specialist for your hand."

"Right."

"Except that I checked with our health insurance provider and no paperwork was submitted," Maya said casually. "No deductible paid. So... where were you last week?"

I was tracking a blacklisted CIA engineer to see if he could tell me why my own brain was trying to kill me. That was the truth, but not only would he not tell them that—his apartment could be bugged, for all he knew—but they had no idea about his lost memories, his recent issues, or the dire warning that Guyer had given him.

So instead he forced a coy smile and said, "Maybe it's none of your business."

Maya mimicked the fake smile perfectly. "Maybe you shouldn't lie to your daughters."

"Maybe I'm trying to keep them safe."

"Maybe they don't need you to."

"Maybe—"

A brisk knock at the door interrupted him. To Zero's chagrin, it was still his first instinct to reach for the Glock that was hidden in the silverware drawer. Despite the number of times his own home had been raided, he had to remind himself that terrorists did not knock first, and forced his muscles to relax and shook it off as Maya called out, "It's open!"

The apartment door swung open and a woman entered. She was two years younger than Zero, not yet forty, though she could pass for a decade younger if needed. When they weren't on an op, she wore her thick blonde hair down, cascading around her shoulders in a way that perfectly framed her face and slate-gray eyes. She was dressed in slim-cut jeans, black boots, and a downy black coat. Zero had seen her at her best, in evening wear and gowns, and at her worst, with blood on her face and a gun in her hand, and yet the sight of her still always made his heart skip a beat.

Maria strode into the kitchen, gave Zero a kiss on the cheek, and dropped a white box on the counter. "Morning all! Brought croissants."

"Perfect." Maya plucked one up and took a bite. "I could use the carbs before my run."

"But frittata," Zero murmured.

"Maria, settle something for us," Sara piped up. "Has Dad been weird lately?"

Maria frowned. "Weird? I don't know about weird. Different though. Happier, maybe?"

"Told you." Sara grabbed a croissant.

"Are you sticking around?" Zero asked her as he transferred his unwanted, omelet-adjacent dish to a plate.

"Just dropped in on my way," Maria told him. "I have to go to Langley."

"On a Saturday?" Zero raised an eyebrow.

She shrugged one shoulder. "Paperwork."

"Paperwork," he repeated. He knew perfectly well there was no paperwork. "Paperwork" was the excuse they gave one another when they couldn't tell the truth but didn't want to outright lie—the irony, of course, being that "paperwork" was in fact an outright lie.

"And where were you last week?" Maria asked with faux innocence.

Zero smirked. "Paperwork."

"Touché."

Maria didn't know about Bixby, and Zero intended to keep it that way.

He quickly shifted gears. "Will I see you tonight?"

"Definitely." She smiled and grabbed a croissant from the box. "But I have to run. Taking one for the road. Call you later."

"Gotta run too," Maya added. "Literally."

"I'm gonna take a shower," Sara announced.

"Hey, wait!" Zero called out as they all tried to leave the kitchen at once. "Hang on a sec." Three expectant faces turned back to him. "Um, I was thinking... Valentine's Day is just a few days away. So maybe don't make any plans."

They glanced at one another. "Who?" Maya asked.

"All of you. Any of you. I want to spend it with all three of the women in my life."

"Uh... sure. Okay." Maya nodded.

"Sounds great," said Maria.

"Like I said," Sara muttered. "Weird."

And then they were gone, the front door and bathroom door closing behind them at almost the same time.

Zero sighed at his frittata. "Guess it's just you and me, pal." He grabbed the plate and took a seat at the small counter bar.

Outwardly, everything seemed great in his life. He and Maria were officially dating again, and the last couple of months had been like starting their relationship anew. He'd kept the apartment in Bethesda, and she'd kept the small bungalow they'd once co-inhabited, but who knew? Maybe soon they'd live together again. He had both his girls with him, which had been nice. He'd been actively trying to give them space and let them make their own decisions—after all, one was now an adult and the other was technically emancipated. And no matter how weird they claimed him to be, they'd certainly noticed the positive change in his demeanor.

And change he had. Zero had been making genuine efforts to better himself, starting with expanding his culinary skills, spending more time with the girls, coming up with fun things for them to do as a family, and including Maria in as much as possible. He wanted to live life to the fullest ... because he had no idea how much life he had left.

Guyer had no idea. Neither did Bixby. And if the two most brilliant minds he'd ever encountered couldn't give him answers, he doubted anyone on the planet could. He would keep losing memories. New ones would still occasionally resurface, like the remnants of assassinations carried out in his younger days as a dark agent with the CIA. But he had determined that he needed to look forward, not backward. His past was his past, and his future was in question.

He knew what he needed to do: he had to find the agent that Bixby had told him about, this man named Connor, the one who had undergone the memory suppressor. The chances of the guy still being alive were slim, and if he was, the chances of Zero finding him were far slimmer.

Still, he had to try. And at the same time he had to continue trying to make the most of the time he had left, to be a positive influence in the lives of those he loved. He had to know that after he was gone, these were the times they would remember. This was the version of him they would think fondly back on.

Because eventually his brain would kill him—if the pain of keeping so many secrets after promising honesty didn't kill him first.

CHAPTER FOUR

Maria Johansson swiped her keycard through a vertical slot in the wall of a white, cinder-blocked corridor in a sublevel of the CIA's Langley headquarters. There was a loud buzz, the sliding of a heavy electronic bolt, and the steel door unlatched with a heavy *chunk.*

This was just one of four sublevels beneath the George Bush Center for Intelligence—four that she knew of, and probably others that she didn't. Even as a former deputy director, she was not privy to all of the agency's secrets and was not nearly foolhardy enough to believe she ever would be.

Still, it was a small wonder that her keycard still worked. Back in November, after stopping the Chinese insurgent group and their ultrasonic cannon, she had stepped down from her post and resumed life as a special agent. Yet they had not yet revoked the clearances that came with the position.

And she was pretty sure she knew why.

Maria pushed the door closed behind her and nodded to the single gray-suited security guard who sat behind a beige desk, reading a copy of *Sports Illustrated.* "Morning, Ben."

"Ms. Johansson." The retired agent made no attempt to move, let alone check her ID and scan her keycard.

"Should I sign in...?" she asked after a moment of awkward silence.

Ben grinned. "I think I remember what you look like since Thursday." He bobbed his head down the corridor. "Just go on back."

"Thanks."

The heels of her boots clacked against the tiled floor and echoed from empty cells as she headed toward the final one on the left side of the hall. There were no other prisoners on this sublevel; this was intended as a temporary holding station, usually reserved for domestic terrorists, war criminals, rogue military, and the occasional traitorous agent. It was a way station en route to far worse places, like Hell Six in Morocco—or a simple hole in the dirt.

She hated lying to Zero. That's how she was referring to him these days, as Zero. He'd asked her to stop calling him Kent last month. No one referred to him by his former CIA alias anyway; he wasn't really Kent Steele anymore. And barely anyone he associated with regularly called him by his real name, Reid Lawson. He was simply Agent Zero. Hell, even the president called him Zero. So Maria did too.

Though "paperwork" isn't technically a lie, she reminded herself. That was their code for "it's a secret and I'd rather you not ask about it." In fact, just last week, when he told the girls that he was going to California, he'd told her that he had to take care of some "paperwork."

So she didn't ask. Well, she did playfully mess with him that morning, but it wasn't in earnest. Besides, what was she supposed to tell him? *I've been visiting a CIA prisoner and murderer for the last couple of months and I'm embarrassed to admit it.*

Of course not. That sounded terrible.

The cell was twelve feet by twelve feet, with a floor and ceiling of concrete and walls made not of bars but two-inch reinforced glass. A grid of half-inch holes in the side facing the corridor made communication possible with the prisoner inside. There were no windows, but far worse was the fact that there was no discernible door. Maria was not even sure how the cell was accessible; a hidden panel in one of the glass facades, most likely, but not even slightly apparent. It was a psychological maneuver intended to demonstrate to the prisoner that there was absolutely no way out.

Maria's heart broke a little every time she saw that glass. Even though there was no one else here, possibly on this entire sublevel other than Ben the guard, it afforded no privacy. Inside was a small cot with blanket and pillow, a tiny bathroom area that consisted of a sink, toilet, and shower head—all open, all exposed—and a single steel chair, bolted to the floor.

But today the denizen of the cell was seated cross-legged on the cool cement floor squarely in the center of the cell, the most open part of their tiny habitat. Likely, Maria assumed, to give themselves the illusion of having some space.

"Good morning," Maria said. She had to speak a bit louder than she normally would so that the girl could hear her, even through the drilled holes in the glass.

"Hello." Mischa did not turn to look at her, not at first. But that was the way she was, the way she had been since Maria had started to visit her. She would play aloof for at least a short while—perhaps not playing, but acclimating.

The girl was twelve, blonde-haired, green-eyed. Maria would even call her pretty, though the expressionless façade she usually had on flattened her features. She wore simple blue polyester/cotton scrubs, like a nurse in an ER, which lacked pockets or zippers or anything metal. Her feet were bare. She was typically sullen, spoke little, and could kill a man three times her size with little effort. The last time Maria had seen her without two inches of glass between them she had indeed tried to kill her and Zero.

"I brought you something," Maria said in Russian. She was unsure exactly what nationality the girl was, but her English was perfect and unaccented. Over many visits Maria had discovered she was equally gifted in Russian, Ukrainian, and Chinese.

At Maria's elbow was a small rectangular hatch in the glass with a looped handle. She tugged it open and deposited the croissant she'd grabbed earlier from Zero's apartment. The door on the other side, on Mischa's side, was rigged so that it could not be opened at the same time—not that it mattered. The girl never took any of the food she brought until after Maria was gone.

"Should still be warm," she added.

"*Spasiba*," Mischa said, almost too quietly to hear. Thank you.

"Are they feeding you enough?"

The girl merely rolled one shoulder in a shrug.

Maria closed her eyes for a moment to stymie the threat of tears that suddenly came over her. She didn't know why she got so emotional when she came to visit, but at least once per visit a wave of sorrow hit her powerfully to see such a young girl alone in an underground cell.

Mischa had been among the Chinese group with the ultrasonic weapon. Her handler was a redheaded Russian, a former sparrow and spy named Samara who had defected and joined the Chinese in a terrorist plot on US soil designed to look like an attack by Russians. Samara and her cohorts were now dead. Mischa alone survived. Yet no country spoke for her or claimed her; she was disavowed the world over.

The primary reason she remained here in the Langley sublevel was certainly not because the CIA was above sending her to the Moroccan black site. No, it was because the agency could not actually prove that she had committed any crimes. No one on the team—not Zero, not Strickland, and certainly not Maria—had made any statement against her or detailing her actions.

They simply didn't know what to do with a possibly dangerous, possibly brainwashed, highly trained, definitely lethal child. And so she remained.

But Maria didn't see any of that. She simply saw a girl who, over the course of a couple of months, had shown her glimpses of vulnerability that proved she was still human.

"What is it?" Mischa asked.

Maria realized her eyes were still closed. She opened them and smiled when she saw the girl looking at her quizzically. "Um... to be honest, I'm sad."

"Why." She asked it like a flat statement rather than a lilting question.

"I'm sad for you," Maria explained. "That you have to be here."

"I've been in worse places," the girl said simply.

"That's no excuse," Maria told her firmly. "You deserve better. You're not an animal. Maybe..." She stopped herself. *Maybe I could negotiate to get you a cell with a window*, was what she had planned to say.

But it would still be a cell.

Maria had first visited the girl only a few days after her initial incarceration, and had been coming twice a week since then. For the first several visits Mischa did not even look at her, let alone say a single word. The next several visits after that were spent convincing the girl that she was not there to hurt or torture her. Maria did not want information. In fact, she didn't want the girl to say anything at all about her past life, and that was the absolute truth; the cell was being monitored by both video and audio, and any discussion of Mischa's past might uncover indiscretions that could get her a one-way ticket to a far worse place.

It had taken seven weeks for Maria to learn that the girl's favorite color was purple and that she liked Tootsie Rolls—though there was a strong indication that Mischa had never had any other type of candy. So Maria brought her some. After that it became a ritual for her to bring some morsel of food and, with the permission of Ben the guard, slip them through the small rectangular door in the cell.

Maria knew she was being watched, but she didn't care. In fact, she was pretty certain the reason she still had her deputy director clearances was *because* she was visiting the girl. As long as she was doing it on her own time, no one else had to do anything but watch, listen, and hope that some information came of it.

Maria lowered herself to the floor and sat cross-legged just beyond the glass, her knees almost touching the surface. "Would you like to play a game?"

Mischa looked at her from the corner of her eye for a long moment. "What sort of a game?"

"It's called 'Never Have I Ever.' Have you heard of it?"

The girl shook her head slightly.

"It's very easy. Hold up three fingers, like this." Maria knew that the girl was not going to talk openly, but she hoped that disguising some questions as a game might get her to open up more. "I'll start by saying something I've never done, but I'd like to do. If you've done that, you put one finger down. Then you say something that you've never done. If all of your fingers are down, you lose."

Mischa stared at the floor for several seconds, long enough for Maria to think that her ploy was not as clever as she'd originally thought.

Then the girl slowly lifted one arm and held up three fingers.

"Good. I'll start. Um ... never have I ever been to the Bahamas."

The girl's three fingers stayed up.

"Okay," Maria said, "now you pick something."

"I have never ..." the girl murmured. "Played soccer."

Maria slowly folded one finger down. "But you'd like to?"

Mischa nodded once.

"Did you see other kids playing it? Or on TV?"

"On a television. It looked ..." She trailed off for a moment, as if searching her memory for the right word. "Fun."

Maria held back her smile. That was the biggest admission she'd gotten out of Mischa yet. "That's good. My turn. Never have I ever eaten candy until I was sick."

The girl's brow furrowed. "Why would you want to do that?"

"Well, you wouldn't *want* to, I guess. But sometimes people tend to overdo it."

Mischa's three fingers stayed in the air. "I have never had a friend."

Maria quickly bit her lip to stifle the sharp gasp that nearly escaped. She hadn't expected that sort of candor and it took her off guard, gripping her heart suddenly like a vise.

"I'm sorry," she said softly as she lowered her second finger. "Maybe we should stop."

"But I am winning."

An involuntary smile broke on Maria's lips at that. "You're right. You are. Okay. Uh ... never have I ever raised a garden."

Her three small fingers remained up, and Maria held her breath at whatever she might say next.

"I have never met my mother."

Maria let her breath out slowly. It was an awful statement, but not one that was all that surprising. She imagined that Mischa was likely abandoned, or orphaned, or possibly even taken by the Chinese or Samara or whatever group had trained her. She lowered her last finger and put her hands in her lap.

"You win," she said. The game had backfired on her completely. Outside of wanting to play soccer, the only thing Maria learned was that the girl's life had been just as terrible as she'd previously assumed. If only ...

"Mischa," she said suddenly. "I can't promise that you ever will. Meet your mother, that is. But I *can* promise other things. I can promise that you won't be in here forever." She spoke quickly, as if she was afraid the words might stop flowing if she paused. "You'll get to play soccer, and you'll have friends, and … and you can eat candy until you're sick if you want to. You can have all those things." Maria blinked back tears, surprised at the flood of promises and instantly regretting them. She could try, but she couldn't actually promise anything. "You *should* have all those things."

"How can I believe you?" the girl asked.

Maria shook her head, knowing she was only digging a deeper hole for herself if she failed. "We start small, I guess. Let me bring you something. Not just food. Tell me something you would like. Something to do? A … a toy, or a ball, or …?" She had no idea what the girl might be interested in.

Mischa thought for a moment. "A book."

"A book?"

"Dostoyevsky."

Maria laughed a little in surprise. "You want me to bring you Dostoyevsky—?"

"*Notes from the Underground.*"

"Wow. Um … okay. Yes. I will. I promise." Maria rose to her feet. "I'll come back in a couple of days, and I will bring you the book."

"Thank you, Maria." It was the first time the girl had ever referred to her by name. It felt nice, hearing her say it, but somehow foreign at the same time.

"And Mischa? You were wrong about one thing. You do have a friend."

Maria started back down the hall, boots clacking and echoing on the concrete. She did not turn back to see, but she heard the telltale click of the small steel hatch, where the croissant lay, and she smiled.

She didn't know how she was going to convince anyone to release Mischa, or to even allow her some measures of privacy and space, but she was going to try like hell. The girl had given her the first clear indication that she wasn't entirely indoctrinated, that she was still just a child after all, one who wanted friends and to play sports and to have a family.

Maria would make that happen for her. There was no taking back the promises she'd made so hastily, and there was no other choice but to keep them.

CHAPTER FIVE

Zero wore sunglasses and a black skull cap, his jacket collar riding high as he pulled open the door to the office of Third Street Garage in Alexandria, Virginia. His outfit was probably overkill, but ever since he'd successfully found Bixby he'd been trying to stay as incognito as possible when seeking information. The agency had tracked his whereabouts before when he hadn't been expecting it; it was entirely possible that they still were.

The small office was empty, except for a steel desk with an old computer and two guest chairs. He heard muffled music coming from the garage and headed that way, pulling open the second door to find himself auditorily assaulted by CCR's "Bad Moon Rising" blaring from a stereo that looked old enough to have been made the same year as the song.

He pressed the stop button—*is that a cassette tape?*—but Alan continued belting out the next few bars, very off-key, from beneath a cherry 1972 Buick Skylark.

"That's the best part of the song," he grumbled as he rolled out from beneath the Buick on a squeaky creeper. "Give me a lift, would you?"

Zero grabbed Alan's meaty hand and grunted as he hefted the larger man to his feet. Alan groaned too, though Zero knew it was an act. Alan was broad-shouldered and carried some extra weight around the midsection, but beneath it were layers of tuned muscle from a career spent as a CIA operative. His thick beard, now flecked with gray, and trucker's cap obscured his features and further perpetuated the identity of a simple mechanic, but Alan Reidigger was much, much more than that—not the least of which was Zero's best friend for as long as he could remember.

"You're a little early," Alan noted.

"Are you suggesting it's not ready?" Zero asked, gesturing toward the car.

"Oh, it's ready. Just thought I'd have a little more time for chorus practice. Come on, hop in." Zero slid into the passenger seat as Alan got behind the wheel. He twisted the key in the ignition and the engine roared to life, chugging powerfully beneath the hood.

Alan was a lot of things, and possibly a bit paranoid was among them. He was convinced that his garage had been bugged by the CIA no matter how many times he swept it. Zero had no idea who the Skylark belonged to, but behind its tinted windows and with the engine rumbling, no cameras or audio equipment would see or hear them.

"So what'd you find?" Zero asked.

"Me? Nothing." Alan pulled an already-stained handkerchief from his flannel pocket and wiped his greasy hands. "But maybe Santa left you something in the glove box."

Zero reached for it and pulled out the thick three-ring binder that was inside. Between the plastic covers were at least a hundred and fifty pages. "Jesus, Alan. Did you hack the CIA database?"

"Of course not," Reidigger said indignantly. "I paid someone to do it." He grinned, the corners of his beard curling. "That right there is the known identity and current where-abouts of every person affiliated with the CIA with the first or last name of Connor in the last six years."

"Impressive." Zero did a quick flip of the pages, seeing just a glimpse each of dozens of faces, ID photos most likely, with paragraphs of personal information beneath each one. "I'm waiting for the 'but.'"

"But," Alan said, "I've already been through it all, and…"

"And not a single mention of memory suppression." Zero shook his head. "I didn't expect there to be. I'm looking for someone who disappeared without a trace. Where what they claim in the files doesn't match the kind of person he was, or his job description."

"Maybe if you'd let me finish." Alan sniffed. "I've already been through it all for that, too. Look, Zero, I'm very good at making people disappear if they want to, and I learned most of that from the agency. Your guy is either dead or isn't in that binder, and there's a good chance he doesn't exist anywhere. Not on any paper or in any computer."

"He's gotta be somewhere," Zero muttered. "Even just one needle in the haystack that they forgot to scrub. A secret bank account, or a gym membership, or an expired warranty…"

"And how do you presume we go about finding that?"

"I don't know." He opened the binder to a random page and scanned it. "I mean, how do we know it's not this guy? He was an agent alleged KIA in Lebanon on an op. That could be a lie."

"It could," Alan agreed, "but that would mean he's dead. You don't want that either."

"No. I don't." *Think, Zero. There must be something you missed.* "Let's at least agree that he must have been an agent. We're the easiest to make vanish. They could have said that he was sent off somewhere, never came back…"

"You're speculating." Alan warned. "And if anyone's watching, this is going to start looking weird."

"Yeah," he murmured. Their little in-car meetings couldn't be too long just in case there actually were prying eyes watching. "You're right."

Alan reached for the ignition, but Zero didn't move just yet.

What am I missing?

Bixby's words, from the week prior in Saskatchewan, ran through his head.

"After it was installed, as he was coming out of anesthesia, the neurosurgeon called him Connor. I remember that clearly. He said, 'Do you know who you are, Connor?'"

"Wait!" Zero reached over quickly and stopped Alan from turning off the car. "That's it! I can't believe I missed it. The neurosurgeon called him Connor!"

"Huh?"

"That's what Bixby told me," he explained quickly. "I've been so fixated on finding this Connor that I didn't even think about trying to find the neurosurgeon! How many of them could be in CIA records from the last five years? A hell of a lot fewer than this, I bet!" He shook the binder excitedly. Instead of a hundred or more possibilities, they could narrow it down to—well, Zero wasn't even sure. A few dozen, maybe less?

Alan sighed. "Okay. So you want me to run another…"

"I want you to run another search, yeah."

"You know that binder cost me five grand."

"I'll buy you a drink." Zero grinned, but it faded quickly. "Please."

"You know I'd do anything for you, pal." Alan cut the engine; there was no "but" to his statement this time. It was a simple fact, and Zero knew it. Alan had saved not only his life more than once but also the lives of his daughters. He had bent over backwards to help Zero out of a jam more times than he could count. Alan had even faked his own death, given up his life for a few years and went on the lam, all for Zero's sake.

Even worse was that the opposite was true. He would do anything for Alan… yet Alan had never asked him for anything. At least not anything as significant as what he'd already done and would still do for Zero. The engine ceased, but the silence that ensued in the cab of the Skylark was just as roaring.

"Thank you," Zero said quietly. "You know I wouldn't get very far if it wasn't for you."

"You'd be dead if it wasn't for me." Alan grinned, even though it was the truth. "So we find the neurosurgeon..."

"Get whatever intel he knows..."

"Find the agent..."

"And hope he's not dead," Zero finished.

"Piece of cake," Alan chuckled, but it faded quickly. "We're going to find this guy. But you're going to owe me *two* drinks."

The community center smelled like cedar chips for some reason. Every room, even the halls, smelled like a hamster's cage. Sara figured it was probably from the playground outside, but it was February, for Christ's sake; the windows were closed and the ground was frozen. Why did it still smell like cedar chips?

She tried not to think about it as she maneuvered the brush in gentle strokes. There were fourteen in the class, people ranging from her age up to a hunched, balding man that she presumed was in his sixties. They were stationed at easels and stools in a circle, at the center of which was a bowl of wax fruit on a pedestal. Still-life, they were calling it.

Sara almost chuckled to herself. Still-life. Up until just a couple of weeks ago, that would have been a pretty apt metaphor for how she'd been feeling.

The art teacher was a frail-looking bohemian-styled woman named Ms. Guest, who wore kaftans and owlish glasses and head scarves over her frizzy mane of blondish hair. She made slow laps around the circle of students, pausing now and then to murmur words of encouragement like "yes, good" and "excellent perspective, Mark."

Sara felt her spine stiffening instinctively—defensively—as the teacher paused behind her easel.

"My," Ms. Guest breathed in her ear. "Such vision, Sara. There are no wrong answers, but please share with me: what inspired you to paint the banana pink?"

Her first instinct was to mess with this woman, to look up at her in wide-eyed earnestness and say, *What do you mean? Is that not the right color? That's how it looks to me.* Instead she bit her tongue and considered an answer that a community center art teacher might find deep.

"Because," Sara said with a dramatic flick of her brush, "everyone else's is yellow."

Ms. Guest put a hand over her heart. "My dear, you are going to do great things in this world."

Sara held back a snort as the teacher moved on. Maybe the art class was a mistake. But she hadn't drawn or painted anything in quite a while, and even though she loathed the therapist at that ridiculous excuse for a rehab center, there might have been just the tiniest iota of merit to her words when she suggested that Sara should find a passion, something she loved, something she could cling to in her dark times. So painting it was.

There were still dark times. The worst of her addiction felt behind her; even the cravings were less severe now. She hadn't touched as much as an aspirin since Thanksgiving. But still she feared the darkness in her, the too-real possibility that her demons might come clawing back at any moment. That they might take her completely by surprise one day and overwhelm her, drag her into a black mental chasm from which she wouldn't be able to escape.

Again she almost laughed at herself. *Such a tortured soul you are.* If Maya was here she might suggest that Sara used self-deprecating sarcasm as a coping mechanism.

But Maya wasn't here, so instead Sara painted pink wax fruit. In the evenings she studied for her GED. Ordinarily she wouldn't have felt quite as inspired as she should, but—and she would never admit this openly—seeing her dad's change in attitude of late was actually a bit inspiring. Despite how much she made fun of him, it was a welcome change.

Still super weird though. People didn't just change like that. There was always a reason, a catalyst. Hers was clearly recovering from drug addiction. Her dad was keeping his motivation from them, she knew that much. But she had her own problems, and so did Maya, so neither of them pried any further.

"I'm afraid that's our time for today," Ms. Guest announced. "I have to get over to my ceramics class. You can leave your paintings here to dry, but please clean your brushes before you leave. Thank you!"

Sara sighed. She'd been painting her apple orange and was considering just turning it into a pumpkin, but that would have to wait. She dutifully cleaned up her station, hefted her backpack on one shoulder, and headed down the cedar-smelling corridor.

She took her time, shuffling her feet, not at all in a rush for the cold bike ride back home. Maya had offered to pick her up when she was done, but Sara didn't want to put her out or have to rely on anyone. Besides, the chilly air whipping her face kept her alert.

She peeked into various rooms of the community center as she shuffled down the long corridor toward the exit. There was some kind of a kids' gymnastics class going on, just a bunch of tykes rolling around on mats and trying to do handstands. She passed by a pottery class, an ESL course, a computer lab...

The door on her left was mostly closed, just ajar a few inches, not enough for her to see inside. But as she passed it, a snippet of conversation floated to her from inside.

"I promised myself I would never go back to heroin."

Sara froze, quite literally mid-step with one foot in the air, and craned her neck toward the door.

"But as you can guess," a woman said somberly from inside, "my addiction had other plans. One really bad afternoon, it got to me. I knew a guy, just down the street. I called him up."

There was a sign on the door, just a sheet of white paper with some words printed in black ink, held by its corners with scotch tape.

Common Bonds
Sharing Trauma, Sharing Hope

"It was just a few minutes." The woman inside lowered her voice, almost to the point that Sara couldn't hear. She pushed the door gently, a couple inches wider. "I left my two-year-old son in the apartment alone, but it was just for a few minutes." Inside the room, Sara could see women seated in a semicircle, facing one another, their expressions subdued, almost funereal.

"But in those few minutes, my ex-boyfriend—the father of my baby—decided to stop by." The woman speaking stared at the floor. Her skin was pale and she wore no makeup, her brown hair pulled into a simple and hasty ponytail. "I got back with a baggie in my hand to find my son in his arms. That was the day I lost him..."

A face suddenly filled the partially open doorway, startling Sara into a gasp and a small jump backwards. A woman smiled out at her, looking somehow youthful and matronly at the same time, like the sort of suburban soccer mom who would invite her kids' friends to stay for dinner and not take no for an answer.

"Hi," the woman said quietly, as not to interrupt the meeting behind her. "Are you here for Common Bonds?"

"I, uh..." Sara cleared her throat and shook her head quickly. "No. I'm not. I was just peeking. Sorry."

"That's okay." The woman took a small step into the hall and gently closed the door behind her. "We're a support group for women who have experienced different sorts of trauma. Drug addiction, domestic abuse, PTSD, depression ... We share our experiences, and through each other we find—"

"Common bonds," Sara muttered. "Yeah, I get it."

The woman smiled. "Right." Then she did something strange—she looked Sara right in the eye, and she furrowed her brow as if frowning, though the smile never left her lips.

Sara did not like the look at all. It was like the woman was ... reading her.

"Are you sure you don't want to come in? You can just sit and listen. You don't have to say anything."

"No. Thank you. I'm ... good." Sara took another step backwards. "In fact, I was just leaving." She'd done fine on her own without rehab; she certainly didn't need a "support group."

She turned, but the woman kept talking. "I'm Maddie, by the way."

"Sara," she called over a shoulder.

"It was nice to meet you. I'll see you around, Sara."

No, you won't. Sara hurried on her way down the corridor. Suddenly the February chill in Maryland felt a lot more welcoming.

CHAPTER SIX

Maya stared at the cell phone in her hand. The call log was open, the number was right there. She just had to tap it.

Maybe tomorrow.

She sat cross-legged on her twin-sized bed, tucked into a corner of the bedroom opposite Sara's with about three feet of space between them. The quarters were, at times, a bit cramped—but not all that unlike the barracks she'd grown accustomed to at West Point. And Sara had had four roommates when she lived in Jacksonville, so the accommodations were fine with both of them. They had, on more than a few occasions, had to turn their dad down from offering them the bigger of the apartment's two bedrooms.

Maya tossed the phone onto the bedspread next to a largely ignored copy of *Ulysses* (a "triumph in masochism," as her dad called it) and a half-eaten protein bar. She wanted to make the call. And she would. Just not today.

The number, if she had the gall to call it, would connect to the office of the dean of West Point, Brigadier General Joanne Hunt. Dean Hunt's office had called Maya no fewer than four times in the past two weeks, though they had not left voicemails or any other indication of why they were trying to reach her.

They didn't need to; she knew why. After a harrowing experience in a girls' locker room and an altercation with three boys in which Maya had badly beaten two of them and nearly killed the third, Dean Hunt had graciously offered her the rest of the fall semester off, pending her return in January after winter break.

But Maya had not returned, and it was too late to do so now. She'd missed too much. She had unnecessarily prolonged her education by at least six months—a huge blow to her goal of becoming the youngest CIA agent in the history of the organization.

She just needed some more time. That's what she had told her dad and her sister. Just a bit more time with them, and to herself, and she would return. But she knew damn well that every day that went by without her making the call and promising to return next semester was one more day to consider never going back at all.

The apartment's front door opened and Maya stiffened for a brief moment, a natural reaction to the number of times someone intending to kill or kidnap her family had broken into their home. But she'd grown to recognize her father's footfalls, his frustrated sigh when the door stuck a little having expanded with the cold, and she breathed easy.

"Honey, I'm home!" he called out.

"Who's 'honey'?" Maya called back with a smile.

"Whoever answers to 'honey,' I guess."

"It's only me here."

He appeared in the doorway, smirking. "In that case, hi, honey. Where's your sister?"

"Art class at the rec center."

"Right. Forgot she was doing that. But I'm glad she is. Does she need a lift?"

"Rode her bike."

Her dad blinked. "In February?"

"She said she likes the cold. Keeps her alert."

"Huh. And she calls me weird."

Maya slid off the bed and followed him out to the kitchen, where he dug around in the fridge and came out with a light beer. After popping the cap, he ran one hand through his hair and sighed before taking a sip.

"You're frustrated," Maya observed.

"Nah, I'm fine. Happy as a clam." He tried to play it off with a grin, but she could tell. "Actually, that should be 'happy as a clam at high tide.' You know that saying dates back to 1841? Some even attribute it to Robert E. Lee ..."

He trailed off as she folded her arms and lifted an eyebrow. "You're frustrated. Or upset about something. Maybe both. You didn't take your shoes off when you came in, went straight for a beer, did the hair-and-sigh thing—"

"That's not a real thing," he argued.

"And now you're deflecting," she finished. "I'd bet money you were less than a minute away from suggesting we order pizza tonight." Pizza was his go-to dinner option for nights in which he had too much on his mind.

"Fine, busted." He added in a mutter, "Sometimes I wish I'd raised dumber kids. Or maybe just less observant ones."

"You want to tell me how those 'errands' went?" Maya asked.

He thought about it for a moment, and then said, "Put on a jacket."

She retrieved her coat and followed him out onto their small balcony, barely large enough for two chairs and a small glass table between them. But they didn't sit; her dad shut the glass door behind them and leaned against the railing.

Maya buttoned up her jacket against the chilly winter air and folded her arms. "Spill it."

"I've been looking for someone," he told her, keeping his voice just low enough for her to hear. "An agent, or someone that used to be one about five years ago or so. Named Connor."

"First name or last name?" Maya asked.

He shrugged. "No idea. He might be dead. And if he's not, he's been hidden very well."

She frowned, wondering why her dad would be looking for a presumably dead agent. "What do you need from him?"

Her dad took an annoyingly long pull from the bottle and then murmured something under his breath. Maya couldn't quite make it out, but it almost sounded like he said "paperwork."

"What?"

"Nothing," he told her. "I can't really tell you. It's a ... work thing."

"I get it." But from his demeanor, and the fact that he wasn't currently out there with CIA resources conducting a full-scale manhunt for this guy, she surmised that it was not at all a work thing. "And you're telling me this out here on the balcony in the frigid cold because ...?"

He didn't say anything in response, but instead shot her a flat look. It took her a moment to interpret it, but when she did her stomach turned.

"Oh my god, you don't actually think ...?" She stopped herself from actually saying it aloud. He thought their apartment might be bugged in some way.

"I don't know for sure. Alan did a couple of sweeps, but they tend to get creative."

Maya shook her head in disgust at the thought that everything she said, possibly everything she did—not to mention that of her little sister—was being recorded to some CIA database somewhere. She'd once had a tracking chip implanted just under her skin, and the thought that her whereabouts were always known was creepy enough.

But to actually be watched ... it brought back the memory of those three teenage boys at West Point, hiding in a locker room, waiting for her to come out of the shower so they could attack her. Who knew how long they'd been there, what they'd seen ...?

She pushed the thought out of her head forcefully. Her dad knew the bare minimum about what had happened and she was not about to rehash it now. It was her problem to deal with, just like he had his.

"What do you plan to do next?" she asked.

He waved a hand dismissively. "There's a doctor, or there might be, who knows him. Or knew him. Don't know yet. I'm waiting on some info from Reidigger." He smiled over his shoulder at her. "Come on, let's go back in."

"Hold up. If you're not supposed to talk about it, why are you telling me all this?"

He stared at her for a moment, long enough for her to think that he wasn't sure of the answer either.

"Because," he said at last, "when I'm frustrated, talking to you makes me less frustrated."

He gave her shoulder a squeeze and they headed back inside, just in time to find Sara closing the front door behind her. She pulled off her wool cap, her nose and cheeks reddened and chapped from the wintry air.

Sara took one look at their dad and nodded once. "So pizza for dinner, then?"

He threw both hands up. "Am I really that predictable?"

Maya grinned—but then she noticed that there was something about Sara that didn't feel quite right. She moved stiffly, and it seemed like it was from more than just the cold. Even after pulling off her parka, her younger sister kept her elbows tucked close, almost defensively.

"You okay?" Maya asked.

Sara sniffed. "Yeah. Just, you know, my usual bullshit."

"Language," her dad called from the kitchen. And then, "Yes, I'd like two large pies..."

"I'm good," Sara assured her as she headed toward their shared bedroom.

Maya didn't believe it, but she knew it wasn't her place to ask. They all had their problems, and they all dealt with them in their own ways. For a family that had promised each other honesty, they seemed to keep a lot of secrets. But it wasn't a matter of dishonesty; it was a matter of independence, of being responsible for themselves.

It also, admittedly, got pretty lonely sometimes.

But maybe it doesn't have to be. She thought about this missing Connor person. There had to be a way to find the guy...maybe even a way that someone as smart as her could figure out. Maybe something that she could do for her dad to show him, instead of just telling him, that he didn't always have to be alone with his problems.

If only she could learn to take her own advice.

CHAPTER SEVEN

President Jonathan Rutledge eased back on a striped sofa in the Oval Office, slipped his feet from his loafers, and propped both heels up on the polished coffee table before him. He was fairly certain that the sofa, one of two that were perpendicular to the executive desk, had not been there yesterday, but he couldn't be sure. Usually the room was so abuzz with activity, advisors and joint chiefs and administrators scurrying here and there, that the furniture became more of a backdrop than décor. Compounded by that was his wife, Deidre, who had tasked herself with "helping" the White House design team to redecorate every room once a week, or so it felt to him.

It was a nice sofa. He hoped it stuck around the office for a while.

Rutledge had nearly gone the way of the furniture last November. Just a few short months ago he'd been seriously considering resigning from the office of the presidency, deeming himself unfit for the job. He'd been promoted from Speaker of the House straight up to the top of the ladder by virtue of his predecessors' immense scandal with Russia, and it had taken some time for him to become accustomed to the position, the powers it granted, and the responsibility it required.

But that was behind him. He'd made the decision to remain in office, and then he'd named California Senator Joanna Barkley as his vice president. She was doing a stellar job so far. Their approval rating was sky-high; Rutledge was even polling well among conservatives. There had been a very minor setback for a couple of days in mid-December when he'd made the grievous error of dyeing his hair to its original chestnut brown. He'd only done it because the gray streaks had been bothering him, not for vanity or to look youthful but to preserve his own self-confidence. Yet for a solid two and a half days the media pundits couldn't help but gabble over what Rutledge was trying to prove. Apparently dyeing one's hair had not found its way into the big book of unwritten presidential laws. Like those before him, he was expected to age either in a distinguished way or terribly.

This was one of those very rare moments in which he was alone, and he was enjoying it with his jacket hanging and his black-socked feet up on the table. Of course he was never *truly* alone; there were cameras on him and at least two Secret Service members posted just outside the office doors. But it was enough, and he'd take the little moments when he could—because they were so few and far between, barely filling the cracks between the much bigger moments like mortar between bricks.

The US's relationship with Russia had been on a tightrope for a couple of years now, even before Rutledge's time as POTUS. And now China too was on the wrong side of things. The trade war had ended and the Chinese government was playing nice, but only because Rutledge himself had threatened to leak the entire ordeal of the ultrasonic weapon and the identities of the commandos sent with it. There was a truce currently, but one that was fragile as glass and could shatter the moment the Chinese saw an opportunity.

Yet something had to give. Rutledge knew it, and even had an idea, but it was Barkley who made him believe it could be done. She had a way about her of taking immense, seemingly impossible problems and turning them into several-step solutions. She would have been a great mathematician, he mused; to her every problem broke down into the simplest components.

The goal, simply put, was peace in the Middle East. And not just between the United States and each member country, but between all countries as well. It was farfetched, to be sure, but any step that could be taken would be one in the right direction.

And after two months of meetings, of planning, of hoping and of hearing out naysayers, of strategizing and ingratiating, of speech-writing and nightmare-having, it was happening.

"Tomorrow, the Ayatollah of Iran is coming to Washington."

He said it aloud, just to himself in the otherwise empty Oval Office, as if daring someone to burst in and contradict him. But it was true; the supreme leader of Iran, a man who once publicly vowed that he would never capitulate to the United States, a man who had demonized the entire country, was due to arrive the following day—first to visit the UN building in New York, where a treaty was currently undergoing a last-minute review. And then the Ayatollah would travel to Washington, DC, to meet with Rutledge to sign the mutually beneficial treaty that would ensure not only peace between them but promised aid to the Ayatollah's people, and (in a perfect world) help to alleviate Islamic xenophobia stateside.

Rutledge was nervous, but cautiously optimistic. If the Ayatollah agreed to the terms of the treaty, it not only would make history but would also become the pace car for other Islamic nations to follow suit.

Or most of them, he thought bitterly. Barkley had spared no detail briefing him on her recent trip to Saudi Arabia for the late king's funeral and the ensuing demands of the prince—or rather, new king. Already US troops were leaving command posts and pulling back to neighboring nations. The embassies were being emptied. Rutledge had boots on the ground over there that were trying to keep it under wraps from the American public as much as possible, but that was an insurmountable task; rumors swirled and reports came out of Saudi Arabia through other outlets.

Eventually they would fully address the currently fragile state of things between Iran, Saudi Arabia, and the US. Sooner than later there would be action plans and press conferences.

Eventually. But it would have to wait until after the Iranian leader's visit. He'd spent too long making this single visit possible.

A brisk knock on the door not only shook him from his thoughts but startled him enough that he yanked his feet from the coffee table and sat up straight, as if his own mother was about to catch him with his feet on the furniture.

"Mr. President?"

He cleared his throat. "Yes, come in, Tabby."

The left door of the cream-colored pair opened just enough for Tabitha Halpern to stick her bob-length head of auburn hair in. "I'm sorry sir, but you're needed right away in—"

"Let me guess." Rutledge rubbed his forehead. "The Situation Room."

The White House Chief of Staff frowned. "Did someone call?"

"No, Tabby. Just an educated guess." He reached for his shoes. "One week. Just one week I'd like to go without a crisis. Wouldn't that be something?"

The John F. Kennedy Conference Room was located in the basement of the West Wing, a five-thousand-square-foot center most commonly called the Situation Room—and fittingly, since the only reason President Rutledge ever had to step foot in it was when there was a situation.

And there's always a situation, it seems.

Two Secret Service agents led the way with another pair behind him, while Tabby Halpern strode double-time on her five-foot-four frame to keep pace while reading from a single-sheet briefing she'd received just moments ago. It was something about South Korea and a stolen ship; Rutledge was still fairly lost in his own thoughts.

Please don't be a catastrophe. Not on the eve of such a historic visit.

Already present around the polished conference table were the usual suspects and familiar faces—most of them, anyway. Secretary of Defense Colin Kressley stood before his chair beside the Director of National Intelligence, David Barren. Across from them was CIA Director Edward Shaw, a man who moved as if his spine was made of steel and his mouth existed only to grimace. The two men on either side of Shaw were unknowns.

Vice President Barkley was not in attendance, he noted, though protocol generally dictated that her presence was optional for meetings such as this one, depending on the nature of the situation and whatever she had her hands in at the time.

"Gentlemen," Rutledge greeted as he and Tabby swept into the room. "Please, have a seat. I don't think I need to remind any of you what tomorrow is or how important this visit could be. Someone please tell me this is either a security briefing or a surprise party."

No one so much as cracked a smile; if anything, Director Shaw's frown deepened. Rutledge reminded himself to stifle his generally cavalier demeanor while in a room designed to deal with disasters.

"Mr. President," said General Kressley's gruff baritone. "Two days ago, at approximately seventeen hundred hours Eastern Standard Time, a satellite over the North Pacific Ocean detected a very brief, very powerful energy spike a little more than three hundred miles southeast of Japan."

The president furrowed his brow. He had only been half-listening to Tabby en route to the Situation Room, but she had mentioned a missing ship.

"At the time, the energy spike was written off as a powerful surge of lightning or potentially an explosion from a geothermal pocket," Kressley continued. "But we now have reason to believe that it was something else entirely…"

"Excuse me, General," Rutledge interrupted with a raised hand. "The briefing said that South Korea was missing a boat. If there's a point to this energy spike thing, can we get to it faster?"

Kressley stiffened a moment, but nodded to Director Shaw.

"Sir." Shaw folded his hands upon the table, a strange habit that Rutledge noticed whenever the former NSA director spoke. "Less than thirty minutes ago, the South Korean government shared a classified internal dossier with the Central Intelligence Agency. If what they are saying is true, they have developed a very powerful weapon and mounted it upon a small stealth ship. During the weapon's initial test on the Pacific Ocean—the energy surge that the Secretary of Defense was just describing—the ship was attacked. The crew was entirely killed. The ship and the weapon were stolen."

A hiss of breath escaped Rutledge's throat, matching the feeling of deflation he was suddenly feeling. There was a lot of information to digest in a very short amount of time.

"This weapon." Rutledge's voice was low but still carried in the otherwise silent room. "This weapon was developed in secrecy?"

"Yes sir."

"And tested in secrecy."

"That is correct, sir."

"And the South Koreans waited two full days to tell us that it was stolen." Rutledge just needed to confirm that all he had heard about his so-called allies on the Korean peninsula was accurate.

"Affirmative, Mr. President." Shaw paused for a moment before adding, "It seems they were initially optimistic about their chances of recovering it. But now they're asking for our aid in the matter."

Rutledge gritted his teeth. This was worse than he could have imagined. Not only did someone out there have their hands on whatever this weapon was, but it was not a good look for alliances to break down while trying to create a new one.

"What's the weapon?" he asked.

"For that," Shaw said, "I will defer to Dr. Michael Rodrigo." He gestured to the man on his left, easily the youngest in the room at not a day over forty. "Our top advanced weapons technology expert, and head of R&D for the US Navy."

"Thank you, Mr. President," Dr. Rodrigo said hastily. "It is an honor to be here and to consult on this matter for you—"

"What's the weapon?" Rutledge asked again.

The doctor adjusted his tie. "Well, sir, if the dossier from South Korea is legitimate, then they have created a plasma railgun."

Rutledge blinked. He'd heard the term "railgun" before, and knew that the Navy had some working model of one somewhere, but still it sounded like something out of a science fiction movie. "A what?"

"A plasma railgun," the doctor repeated. "To be frank, up until now this type of weapon has been purely theoretical. In fact, it would be difficult to fully believe its existence until the missing ship is found—"

"Or until the weapon is used," Kressley grunted.

"Well... yes," the doctor agreed. "Suffice it to say that the railgun is a projectile weapon with the capacity to destroy any single target from a few hundred miles away."

"A projectile? Like a missile?" Rutledge asked.

"No, sir. Missiles can be scrambled, shot down. Missiles can be seen coming. I've already examined the Korean schematic; this weapon would fire a plasma projectile at several times the speed of sound. There is no defense for this, other than something getting in its way."

President Rutledge squeezed his eyes shut, feeling a headache coming on. "You say that South Korea has been searching for two days. Do they have any leads on the ship's whereabouts?"

Shaw shook his head. "None, sir."

"None. Perfect." Rutledge scoffed. "With all of our satellites, how difficult could it be to find one boat in the ocean?"

"With all due respect," said Dr. Rodrigo, "very difficult. This ship has some of the most advanced stealth capabilities I've ever seen. We can't forget that our own military shares information and resources with the South Koreans, and that they have the tenth-largest military budget in the world—"

Rutledge abruptly held up a hand and the doctor fell silent. "Do they at *least* know who took it?"

No one spoke. Director Shaw stared at his folded hands. DNI Barren adjusted a cufflink. At last it was Tabby Halpern who said it, hesitant as she was.

"They do, sir. A Navy vessel in the South China Sea spotted a boat passing by several hours before the energy surge. No one thought anything of it at the time, but they snapped a few photos. Imaging has traced the boat's origin to a home port in Mogadishu."

"Mogadishu?" Rutledge repeated, bewildered. What the hell was a boat from Mogadishu doing in the South China Sea?

"Sir," Tabby elaborated, "the South Koreans have strong reason to suspect the railgun was stolen by Somali pirates."

Under the conference table, Rutledge pinched his own leg. No, he wasn't dreaming this, though he wished he was.

"Just to recap what we're talking about here," the president said slowly. "You're telling me that *pirates*... have stolen an invisible ship... with an impossible weapon... from one of our closest allies... who were developing it in secret. And now those pirates have a two-day lead on us. Does that about sum up the situation?"

"Yes, Mr. President." Tabby nodded. "That is what we're dealing with."

"I can't handle this right now." Rutledge rubbed his face with both hands. "And I don't mean I'm incapable of doing so; I mean I literally do not have the time, energy, or mental capacity considering what's on the line. You're all in this room for a reason, and that reason is to handle situations like this one. So handle it." He pointed toward his left, at Kressley. "Consider this full authorization to do whatever you have to do—drone flyovers, full satellite surveillance on every square foot of water between the attack site and Mogadishu. I want ships dispatched from Diego Garcia immediately and ready at a moment's notice."

Kressley nodded, but Dr. Rodrigo spoke up again. "Sir, I'm not sure I truly stressed just how untraceable this ship will be—"

Again Rutledge silenced him with a hand. "Doctor, your concern has been heard and noted." Yet he knew he had little choice but to defer to the doctor's expertise. They needed something more than just technology; he needed actual eyes out there. Someone looking for this boat. Someone he could trust to get the job done.

"Shaw," said the president. "I want *him* on this."

Director Shaw chewed his lip pensively for a moment, an expression that suggested he knew this was coming. "Sir, I'm not sure this sort of operation would be relevant to his expertise."

Rutledge bristled. "I apologize if that sounded like a request, Shaw. It wasn't."

"If I may, Mr. President." At last the man on the other side of Shaw, furthest from the president, spoke up. He was short in stature, five-seven at best, and looked like he could have been Shaw's accountant. His nose and chin were angular, almost pointed, in a way that was reminiscent of a rodent. A rat, perhaps? No—a weasel was more like it, Rutledge thought.

"And you are?"

"Deputy Director Walsh," the man said with a deep nod of his head. "I've been the head of the CIA's Special Operations Group of Special Activities Division since early December."

Ah, thought Rutledge. *Another carryover from the NSA, I'm betting.* Shaw was hiring from his former agency; this Walsh person couldn't have looked less CIA if he was wearing Bermuda shorts and Groucho Marx glasses.

"We have a number of extremely qualified, highly trained agents who are ready to take this right away. In the next thirty minutes, we could have an entire team of former SEALs and Black Ops personnel en route to the attack site—"

"Walsh, was it?" Rutledge interrupted.

"That's right, sir."

"You're Zero's new boss?"

Walsh sat a little straighter in his chair. "I am, sir."

President Rutledge stood from his chair and rounded the table until he stood beside—or more accurately, stood over—the much smaller man. Then he stuck out a hand.

Walsh glanced nervously at Shaw before taking the president's hand and shaking it gingerly.

"A pleasure to meet you," said Rutledge. "I'm your boss's boss's boss. And I wasn't asking. Call him. Or I will, and at the next meeting, someone else will be sitting in your seat."

CHAPTER EIGHT

Zero pulled his SUV into the sprawling parking of the George Bush Center for Intelligence, the headquarters colloquially known simply as Langley for the unincorporated Virginia community in which it sat. Being a Sunday, the lot was at maybe a quarter capacity, which meant the perimeter of the parking lot was visible, surrounded by tall trees that shrouded even the blacktop from the outside world. In the springtime those trees were lush and vibrant green, but now they were leafless and skeletal, giving Zero the impression he was surrounded by a grim forest.

He'd gotten the text message only a half hour prior—from an unknown number, of course, and with the simple message of *Langley. 30 min.* He didn't need to know the number to know who it came from: his new boss, Walsh, a former deputy director at the NSA who was now heading Spec Ops Group. Or, he thought wryly, more likely from one of Walsh's lackeys. The deputy director was a thorough delegator.

Zero and his team had been used sparingly in the past few months, ever since the ultrasonic weapon and the near-meltdown of the Calvert Cliffs reactor. *No,* he corrected himself, *not Zero's team. Not anymore.* Once upon a time he'd headed the team, but then he'd quit the agency, gone into retirement for more than a year. Circumstances and the threat of a lengthy prison sentence had forced him to return, and with Maria stepping down from deputy director last November, it was now her team to lead.

Lately the most exciting op they'd been on was two days of surveillance on a suspected terror cell in Argentina that had turned out to be a camp of political refugees. They'd been doing grunt work, plain and simple, rookie stuff. Deputy Director Walsh and his old pal Director Shaw had a clear and undisguised disdain for Zero and his colleagues since the events of last November, and Zero had no reason to believe that today's briefing would be any different.

The deep rumble of a truck engine disturbed his thoughts, and a moment later a familiar ruddy pickup pulled in opposite him. The truck looked like it was old enough to have seen the Civil Rights Movement; its color could only be described as "rust," and the noises that came from beneath the hood suggested it might collapse on its axles at any moment. But Zero knew that the truck was as much a ruse as its driver. That old bucket of spare parts could outmaneuver and outrun an Interceptor if it had to.

Zero folded his arms and did his best to suppress the grin on his face as Alan Reidigger ambled out of the cab, his sour expression notable even behind the bushy beard and trucker's cap. "Morning. They called you in on this one?"

"Mm," Alan grunted, clearly not happy about it. He'd been given the same ultimatum as Zero: come back to the CIA, or spend the rest of his life in prison. Not only did Alan despise the agency, but he made it his personal mission to use whatever opportunity he could to make lives more difficult. Case in point, he'd still refused to return as a full-fledged agent; on paper he was labeled an agency asset, which was something of a catch-all euphemism for an errand boy whenever they needed him.

"Where's Todd?" Zero asked.

"You didn't hear? Broke his arm two days ago, rock climbing."

"Huh. Some guys get all the luck." Zero hadn't spoken in a while to Todd Strickland, the youngest of their team. Strickland was only thirty, a former Army Ranger still boyish in facial features but chiseled from marble from the neck down. Had he not been recruited by the CIA he might have been cast as Captain America. "That's too bad," Zero quipped. "I like seeing the two of you stand next to each other. It's like the before and after of a Special Forces vet."

"Ha-ha," Alan said flatly as a sporty white coupe joined them. Maria slid out, her nostrils flared and blonde hair unusually flat on her head, still slightly damp.

"Thirty minutes?" she said with a huff. "Got the message while I was in the shower. Didn't even have time to blow-dry my hair." She slammed the door shut. "We all know this is going to be a bullshit call anyway."

"You're cute when you're angry." Zero took a step toward her, with the intention of a kiss, but stopped himself short. There were cameras, even here in the parking lot, and the less Langley knew about their personal lives the better.

Maria flashed him an understanding smile before turning and leading the way toward the main building of the Langley campus, Zero and Alan flanking either side.

"You guys talk to Todd?" she asked as they walked.

"Not lately," Zero told her, "but I heard. Broke his arm rock climbing?"

She let out a snort. "Please. Don't believe that for a second. Our boy tripped on his cat going down the stairs."

Maria and Zero shared a laugh, and even Reidigger chuckled a little. Zero could hardly imagine the tough, ass-kicking combat veteran tripping down some stairs. They entered the building and strode across the marble floor, shoes echoing across the expansive atrium as they trod over the huge circular emblem embossed beneath their feet, a shield and eagle in gray and white, surrounded by the words "Central Intelligence Agency, United States of America."

"Walsh said to meet at his office," Maria said over her shoulder.

Zero frowned. That was atypical for a briefing environment; typically those were held in one of the conference rooms, an innocuous enough term for a room that had been swept thoroughly, debugged, and was wired with transmitters to scramble any unwanted cellular and radio signals.

Something about all of this, from Reidigger's inclusion to meeting in Walsh's office, felt to Zero like it was not going to be a run-of-the-mill grunt-work operation.

"Say, Alan," Zero said quietly as Maria handed her badge to a security guard at the entrance to the corridor and stepped through the metal detector. "Did you happen to get that part I ordered?" He knew that Alan would pick up on the meaning; he wanted to know if his hacker contact had compiled the information on CIA-affiliated neurosurgeons.

"Not yet," Alan said gruffly. "Couple of days."

Zero nodded as he stepped through the metal detector's frame, and then Alan, each scooping up their personal belongings again before heading to Walsh's third-floor office.

But when they arrived at his door, Zero was surprised to see their boss of the last few months emerging, locking the door behind him with a briefcase in one hand and a manila folder under an elbow.

"Ah," he said flatly. "Agents." His spine stiffened and the chest beneath his suit and tie puffed slightly. It was a reflexive move that Zero had noticed almost every time he interacted with Walsh; the deputy director was almost a half-foot shorter than him, and seemed to draw himself up whenever standing beside Zero.

"Sir," said Maria. "Are we going elsewhere for this?"

Walsh frowned. "For what, Agent Johansson?"

"The briefing, sir."

"No, no need to go elsewhere." Walsh set down the briefcase and held out the manila folder to her. "Here."

"What's this?" she asked without taking it.

"That is a sealed envelope, Agent."

"I see that, sir," Maria replied just as tartly. "But why are you handing it to me?"

"Because I'd like you to take it," Walsh said, his tone clipped.

This was a game and Zero knew it. There was no love lost between them and Director Shaw. The man had clear disdain for the way that they defied orders and still got results—or perhaps more appropriately, defied orders in order to get results. Shaw was as much about authority as he was about being recognized as one. And since Walsh and he were cronies, their new boss did not much care for their tactics either. The two of them had attempted to inundate them with subpar assignments, trying to break them like wild horses, and it seemed that failing that, they'd resorted to passive-aggressive pettiness.

"This *is* your briefing," Walsh said at last, still holding the envelope. "You will take it. You will go downstairs to R&D, where the necessary gear for this operation has been apportioned. You will then—"

"But Bixby's gone," Zero blurted out. He hadn't been down to the subterranean lab since November and Bixby's disappearance, and had no idea that it was still in use.

Walsh bristled at the interruption. "Yes, Agent Zero. We are well aware that our former head engineer has turned traitor and gone AWOL. But that does not mean we simply shut down the department that he used to run."

Zero clenched his jaw to keep his tongue behind his teeth. Walsh was trying to push his buttons; Bixby was no traitor, and it was no secret that he and Bixby had been friends. If they knew, or even suspected, that Zero had seen him as recently as he had, he'd find himself in a pit in Hell Six before lunchtime.

"As I was saying," Walsh continued, "you will take this. Retrieve your gear. There is a jet waiting on the government runway at Dulles. Once you are wheels-up, only then should you open the briefing package, and follow its instructions to the letter. Am I clear?"

"Sorry," Reidigger grunted, digging a pinky into his ear. "Didn't catch that middle part."

"You're clear," Maria said. She snatched the envelope from him. "*Sir.*"

"To the letter, Agents." Walsh plucked up his briefcase and nodded to them. "Happy hunting." He strode past them toward the elevators.

"Ass," Maria muttered.

"Hunting?" Zero said. He eyed the envelope in Maria's hand. This wasn't how briefings were handled. This wasn't how information was shared. Something was amiss here, and it was in that envelope.

"Come on." Maria led the way back to the bank of elevators and pressed the down arrow. Once inside the car, she swiped a keycard and punched in a sequence of floor buttons on the panel. The elevator rumbled in the shaft, taking them down to one of several underground levels beneath Langley.

The elevator ride was entirely silent; all of them knew that there were cameras and mics sensitive enough to pick up even whispers. It felt like it took forever, but at last the doors opened onto a hall with cinderblock walls painted gray. There were no windows, and only bare fluorescent bulbs lit their way. The facades to the left and right were interrupted occasionally by heavy steel doors.

They weren't even three steps out of the elevator when Maria said, "Hang back a sec." She stuck a thumb into the corner of the flap and tore the envelope open. "I'm not waiting around to see what we're walking into. Never have before, not starting now."

Zero grinned. The same devil-may-care, anti-authority traits that made her a great agent had also made her come to loathe the position she'd briefly held as deputy director. It helped that those same traits had an extra benefit of making her twice as attractive.

Maria tugged a sheaf of white paper from the envelope, twelve to fifteen pages tops, three-hole punched and tidily fastened with brass brads. To Zero it looked like a book report, or a paper he might have gotten from one of his students when he was a professor of European history, in what felt like a lifetime ago.

She thumbed through the first few pages, scanning quickly. "Huh."

"Huh?" Zero mimed.

"Looks like South Korea made a weapon. Put the weapon on a boat. A couple days ago they lost the boat and the weapon." Then she laughed in a half-chuckle, half-scoff. "To Somali pirates?"

"Pirates?" It was the first time Reidigger had sounded even slightly interested since they'd arrived. "Sounds fun."

But Zero had other questions on his mind. "What weapon?"

"A railgun," she said thoughtfully. "A plasma railgun."

Zero frowned. He wasn't exactly familiar with railgun tech, but by way of a rudimentary fling with physics he was fairly certain that such a thing wasn't supposed to be possible. "Are you sure? That doesn't sound legitimate."

Maria's gaze lifted from the paper to him. "We stopped an anarchist group with weaponized smallpox they'd mined out of a millennia-old glacier, and you're going to question this?"

"Fair point," he conceded. "What's the rest?"

She flipped the next few pages, her frown increasing with each one until finally she murmured, "Son of a bitch."

"Hmm?" Reidigger asked. He and Zero both leaned over her shoulder to see what she was seeing. It was a list—a lengthy bulleted list, in bold typeface.

"Instructions," Maria said. She snapped the sheaf shut. "Actual step-by-step instructions of how they want this operation handled. They want us to go to South Korea. Charter a boat. Take it out to the coordinates of the weapon's testing site, where it was last seen, which is in the middle of the damn Pacific Ocean..."

"There won't be anything to find," Zero interjected. They'd lose precious time, entire days, going out there for nothing and they were already behind on this.

"I know," Maria agreed. "Because they don't *want* us to find anything."

"I'm not sure I follow," Alan admitted.

But Zero did. "This wasn't their idea." Judging by Walsh's demeanor and the instructions in the envelope, he could assume that the decision to send them must have come from someone else—and if he had to guess, he'd bet it was his new pal President Jonathan Rutledge. The president had personally lauded him for his efforts in stopping the ultrasonic attacks, and had even invited him back to the White House twice (though on both occasions, Shaw suddenly had some urgent matter for Zero to handle).

"Rutledge," he told them. "Rutledge forced their hand on this."

"This is exactly why I didn't want to come back to the agency." Alan tugged off his trucker's cap and ran a hand over his matted hair. "So our bosses would risk national security to make us look bad?"

"Not necessarily." Maria was studying the report again. "This weapon was stolen thousands of miles from here. A boat of that size would never make it to US shores. And since we're talking Somalis, they'd likely bring it back to their home port and organize a buyer. This weapon doesn't seem like a threat to the United States. They've also got drones, Navy ships, satellites, the works looking for this thing. So... yeah, they can afford to make us look bad."

"Then screw it," Alan said. "Let's go to South Korea, charter a boat, and do some fishing. Consider it a mini-vacation. Let the Navy find it. If they're so intent to make us look inept, let's be inept."

"No," Maria cut him off. "No, we're going to find it. Just not the way they want us to." She pointed at something on the page. "We're going here."

Zero peered over her shoulder and saw what she was pointing out. A Somali boat was identified in the South China Sea as one that made its home port in...

"Mogadishu." He nodded. "Feels like the right play."

"Not even out of the gate and already disobeying orders." Reidigger put his oil-stained cap back on. "Sounds about status quo."

"We'll have to convince the pilot," Zero warned. Walsh had made it clear that the waiting jet already knew where they were supposed to be heading.

"Don't need him," Alan said with a shrug. "I can fly."

"We'll figure that out later." Maria dropped the envelope to the floor, rolled up the report, and stuck it in her back pocket. Then she gestured to the steel door that would grant them entry into what used to be Bixby's lab. "First, let's see who's behind door number one."

CHAPTER NINE

Most who worked for the Central Intelligence Agency were unaware of the multiple subterranean levels beneath their feet. Of those who were, most knew the lab as Research & Development—which was, in a way, partially true. Research did occur down there, as did development, though what was being researched or developed was kept highly classified.

Even Zero, for as often as he had been down there over the course of his career, knew only a fraction of what actually went on in the bowels of Langley. He knew that the super-computer OMNI had dwelled down there before Bixby had decommissioned it. He knew the lab was where Bixby had invented new weaponry and new defense systems, and sometimes even reverse-engineered stolen tech from other countries and militaries, improving it and finding ways to use it against them in the same capacity.

The first thing he noticed upon entering was the scent. The lab smelled like fresh solder, a sort of burning odor that wasn't unpleasant or harsh but still foreign enough to register as something possibly being on fire. As Maria pushed into the cavernous lab, Zero found himself hesitating, feeling strange to be back in the place that had been a second home to a man he had most recently seen living in fear in a remote region of Saskatchewan.

With that thought came the reminder of why he went there in the first place—his own brain, trying to kill him. Losing memories. The other agent, the man called ...

Shit. What was the name again? He panicked briefly. That wasn't the kind of information he could afford to forget. He took a calming breath and reminded himself that Alan knew it too. It would come back to him, he was sure.

Just stay focused, he told himself.

The underground lab was large as a hangar, the ceiling overhead high as a gymnasium and lined white wall to white wall with powerful halogen bulbs that burned as bright as day. Shelving units, computers, and arrays of machinery the function of which Zero could barely begin to guess were arranged lengthwise in the shape of a huge H. As they made their way further into the lab, Zero saw blue sparks popping from the tail of what appeared to be a miniature Predator drone as two white-coated technicians in goggles worked on it.

"Excuse me," Maria called out to them. "Who's in charge here?"

They looked up sharply as if they hadn't noticed that they weren't alone. "That would be Dr. León," one of them called back.

"And where would we find...?"

Before Maria could even finish her statement, a young woman rounded the corner from an antechamber of the lab not ten yards from them. To say "young woman" was almost an overstatement; to Zero, she looked like she might have been Maya's age. Her skin tone, dark eyes, and curly, shoulder-length brown hair suggested she was Latina, and she wore denim jeans, brown clogs, and a pink and white striped T-shirt.

Upon seeing them, the woman's eyes went wide and she stopped dead in her tracks, fumbling the clipboard in her hands. It clattered noisily to the floor.

"Oh! Oh my god, sorry!" She ignored the clipboard and hurried over to them. "Hi! Hello. Wow. It is so good to meet you! Wait, wait, don't tell me, please. You must be Agent Johansson."

The young woman grabbed Maria's hand and pumped it enthusiastically. Zero blinked several times. This was who was running Bixby's lab now?

"Um, yes, hi," Maria said, equally stunned.

"And that would mean..." The woman glanced between him and Reidigger, her gaze finally landing on him. "You're Agent Zero? Wow! He was right. You really don't look the part. I bet that comes in handy though, huh?" She grabbed Zero's hand and shook it vigorously, while he decided to ignore the backhanded compliment. For the most part, he really did still look more like a professor than a CIA agent. But then again, this young woman before him sounded more like a Valley girl than a doctor.

She glanced over at Alan. "I'm sorry, I don't know who you are, but I'm sure you're great." She sighed. "Wow. It is *so* good to meet you guys. I've heard so much!" Then she let out a nervous laugh. "Look at me, fan-girling all over the place here."

"Uh, sorry," Maria said carefully, "but who are you exactly?"

"Oh! Right. Of course. I'm Penelope. I mean, Dr. León." She cleared her throat. "I am Dr. Penelope León." She laughed nervously again. "You know what? Just call me Penny."

Zero smirked at Alan, who just shook his head slightly. "And you're running the lab now?" he asked.

"Yes I am," she said proudly. "It's a lot of work, but I'm managing." She looked from one of them to the next, and as she did, the smile faded from her lips. "You guys don't know who I am, do you? He never... mentioned me?"

Zero assumed that the "he" was Bixby, but wasn't sure the connection. "No," he said gently, "he didn't. I'm sorry... uh, Penny."

"Oh. That's okay." She laughed nervously again and waved a hand dismissively in the air. "He had a lot of secrets. Not like I had to be one of them, but... you know."

"So you were Bixby's student?" Zero asked.

"Student? I guess you could say that. More like a protégé. An understudy. I interned with him through my entire doctorate in applied sciences, and worked here in the lab ever since. But you guys know this is a big place, right? I was never, you know, out here. Front and center. He taught me everything I know." She gestured to her T-shirt and jeans before adding, "Except how to dress, am I right? He was always a snappy dresser."

Her gaze fell to the floor of the lab for a moment. Zero couldn't help but wonder why this young woman, who the CIA deemed qualified to take Bixby's place, had never been mentioned. Another of Bixby's secrets, maybe? She certainly didn't seem like it—though he had to admit that everything about her demeanor fit the bill of someone Bixby would keep around.

And there was something about her demeanor, subtle and just beneath the surface. It felt to Zero like she was trying to be intentionally disarming, yet guarded. *She's hiding something,* he realized. *But from us? Or from cameras?*

"Hey, do you guys want something to drink?" Penny asked suddenly. "I set up a little break room in the back, there's a fridge, we've got water, soda, juices... there's a coffee machine, though I don't know if you have that kind of time—"

"Dr. León," Maria said with just enough force in her voice.

"Penny, please," she corrected.

"Penny. Sure. We're here to gear up, and then we have to get going."

"Right." She laughed at herself again. "Of course you are. Of course you do. Right this way! Let me show you what I've got for you." She led them with a wave of her hand as she turned on a heel and strode quickly across the lab.

Maria exchanged a quick glance with Zero and Reidigger. "You trust this?" she asked quietly in Arabic.

"Not sure yet," Zero told her.

They followed her to a long, stainless-steel table upon which three black neoprene backpacks were waiting. "So, this is it," Penny said with a sweep of her arm. "Ta-da, I guess."

Zero frowned. A bag each for a major globetrotting operation? He grabbed the nearest one and unzipped it. Inside he saw a pair of binoculars, a first-aid kit, a bundle of nylon rope, a few flares...

He tossed the bag aside. These looked like emergency provisions for a camping trip. "Penny, what is this stuff?"

"Not even a gun in here," Alan grumbled as he sifted through another bag.

She smiled apologetically. "That was the approved list from Deputy Director Walsh. Sorry, guys, that's what I was given, so that's what we're working with." She let out another nervous laugh.

It didn't make sense to Zero. The envelope, the lack of proper equipment; what was Walsh playing at? It was one thing to want them to fail. It was another matter entirely to want them to ...

A-ha.

"I know what this is," he told his teammates in Arabic. "He doesn't just want us to fail. He doesn't even want us to go." Walsh was hoping they would lodge a complaint, or refuse to commit to the op under these circumstances, so that he could say they were uncooperative.

"Well, that's not going to happen." Maria took a step toward the doctor. "Penny. We need more than this, and you know that."

Penny's gaze drifted from one of them to the next as her smile evaporated. "I'm sorry, guys. Really, I am. But you gotta understand, I'm twenty-seven years old and never had another job. This is the opportunity of a lifetime for me. I can't do anything to jeopardize that." She took two steps backward. "I'm sorry," she said again, and then curtly spun and strode around the corner, vanishing into another part of the lab.

Alan scoffed. "I say we scrub it. Let Walsh send someone else."

Zero shook his head. "No." It wasn't just a sense of duty speaking. It wasn't just the thought of letting Walsh have his way. This young woman knew something, more than she was letting on, and Zero wanted to find out what that was. "Stay here a minute." He grabbed one of the backpacks and followed Penny around the corner.

The antechambers of the lab were like a maze, corridors that split off and emptied into rooms that led into other rooms. Luckily Penny hadn't gone far; he saw her through a small window in a white clean room, tinkering with something that looked like a transmitter.

He pushed into the room and set the backpack on the table before them, opening it up as if he was showing her something. There was one way to know if she was a plant, or truly a friend of Bixby's—the same tactic he had used on the Canadian pharmacy to find the elusive engineer.

As quietly as he could he asked, "Did you hear the one about the dyslexic insomniac atheist?"

Penny stared into the bag, but a sad smile touched her lips. "Yes." She set the transmitter down gently. "He stayed up all night wondering if there was a dog."

"He's alive." Zero's voice was barely a whisper, little more than a breath. "I've seen him." He reached into the bag for a pair of binoculars, as if he was showing them to her, for the sake of anyone watching. "But you knew that already, didn't you? So how about you drop the ditzy-girl act and help us?"

Penny smiled then and took a step back. "He was right. You really are quite good, Agent Zero." Suddenly her California demeanor was gone, replaced with squared shoulders and a stark British accent. "And you don't have to whisper in here. I've swept and debugged this room myself."

He was right—and she was sly. She'd led him back here on purpose so they could speak openly. The lab was being watched, or at least parts of it. Somehow she was in communication with Bixby, and he wasn't going to ask about that. But she hadn't been sure that she could trust him, same as he'd thought about her.

"What else do you know, Dr. León?"

"I know that Shaw and Walsh want you gone," she told him simply. "I know that they're afraid to try to have you killed because so many others have failed. Besides, they're bureaucrats; that's not their way. They won't fire you because Rutledge likes you. So they're trying to find a more elegant solution."

"Like have me quit?"

"Have you quit, prove you insubordinate—I don't believe they're that picky at this point, as long as you're gone. You're a wild card to them. They fear that eventually your luck will run out and you'll cause a catastrophe."

"Someday, probably," he allowed, "but not today. We're going to get this done. Do we have you on our side, Penny?"

"What do you need?"

"First, a private and secure line directly to you. We need someone helpful on the inside who can get us intel."

"Done," she said immediately. "And?"

"And we're going to need real gear. Some things that go bang. A few things that go boom."

Penny's gaze drifted toward the corner of the clean room. Zero hadn't noticed it before, but beneath a stainless-steel table was a large, rectangular black footlocker. "I may have foreseen things going this way," she admitted. "But I will warn you that I was deadly serious that I will not jeopardize my position here. This lab gives me access to information and resources that I have need for. If I notice anyone sniffing around, I will disavow having helped you in any way."

"Understood," Zero agreed. He sorely wanted to ask what "need" she had for the lab's resources, but held his tongue. She'd shared enough with him for one day.

"Take the bags and go," she instructed. "A van will meet you on the runway. And Agent Zero? Do try to look disappointed on the way out."

CHAPTER TEN

"That sneaky little bitch," Maria remarked on the way to the airstrip. Zero had waited until they were in the truck, en route to the airport, before recounting what had shaken out in the lab. And it wasn't lost on him that despite her words, there was admiration in Maria's tone.

"She'd make a good agent," Alan added.

"Point is, we've got an ally on the inside," Zero said. He was squeezed in the center of the bench seat of Alan's truck as they rumbled toward Dulles International Airport. There was no way they were going to take a CIA vehicle, and out of their three, Alan's was the only one they could say with certainty was bug-free.

He had to acknowledge that it was utterly ridiculous to live like this. But at the same time he was even more convinced that his own home was likely bugged, armed as he was with the knowledge that Walsh and Shaw would stop at nothing to get rid of the liability that he represented to them.

"Now we just have to convince a pilot who has direct orders and a registered flight plan to South Korea to take us to Somalia instead," Maria noted.

"Told you before," Alan grunted. "I can fly. Let's just leave him behind."

"Can't do that," Maria told him. "The less Walsh knows, the better. He's going to find out sooner or later what we're up to, but if we're overseas before that happens there's not much he can do about it."

Zero very much wanted to ask the glaring question on his mind—what exactly were they going to do when they got to Mogadishu? How were three very obvious Americans going to infiltrate and scope out a known pirate port? But he also knew that there were a few hurdles to leap between then and now, most prudent of which was getting there in the first place.

They arrived at Dulles and Alan slowed the truck to flash his CIA credentials to the guards at the gated entrance to the government runway. Beyond it, Zero could see the waiting jet, a Gulfstream G650 gleaming white even under a cloudy February sky. At least

Walsh hadn't stiffed them on transportation; but then again, he hadn't expected them to get this far.

But, Zero noted, there was no van as Penny had promised.

"She'll come through," he said aloud, as much to convince himself as his teammates.

Alan parked and the three of them climbed out of the cab. "I'll talk to the pilot," Maria announced. "Alan, keep an eye out for the van. I wouldn't be surprised if we've got eyes on us right now."

"You two go on," Zero called after them. "Gonna make a quick call." He pulled out his phone, realizing he'd have to leave it behind in Alan's truck. But first, he navigated his contacts and hit the green call button.

"Hey, Zero," Strickland answered on the first ring.

"Hi, Todd." Zero couldn't help himself. "How's your cat?"

"She told you?"

Zero snickered. "Don't sweat it. Listen, I'm getting called away, with Maria and Alan. Not sure for how long. Do me a favor and keep an ear to the ground, would you?"

"Of course," Strickland replied quickly. He didn't even need an elaboration on what Zero was asking; Todd had vowed that whether Zero was dead or alive, he'd keep an eye on the girls whenever possible. "But you and I both know it's hardly necessary anymore. They can handle themselves."

"I know they can." He couldn't tell Todd about his suspicions that his Bethesda apartment was bugged—not overtly, anyway. "I just want to make sure *someone* is watching."

There was a brief moment of silence before Todd said, "Yeah, man, you got it." Zero could only hope that in that moment Todd was coming to an understanding. "Be careful, yeah?"

"I will. Bye." As soon as he was off the phone with Strickland, he made another call. "Maya, it's Dad. Is your sister there? Put it on speaker."

"Hey, Dad," he heard Sara say in the background. It sounded like her mouth was full.

"I've got to do a thing," he told them. "Couple days minimum, maybe longer."

"Aww, does that mean we're going to miss out on our big Valentine's Day?" Sara asked, clearly sarcastic.

"Oh, don't you worry, sweetheart, I'll make it up to you," he quipped right back. "There's stuff in the freezer for dinners, and Todd is just a call away if you need anything."

"Dad, I think we'll be fine," Maya sighed.

"By the way, how is Boy Scout doing?" Sara asked behind her.

"Be nice. He saved your life. Love you both, don't do anything I wouldn't do."

"Love you too." Maya ended the call, and Zero stashed his cell phone in the glove box of the truck before jogging over to the plane. It was a beautiful jet—as well it should be for its price tag of sixty-five million dollars, which didn't even include the alterations the CIA had made to it. It could seat up to eight comfortably and twelve if necessary; its wingspan was narrow enough to land on a four-lane highway if it needed to (and in one precarious situation, Zero had needed it to), and thanks to a few modifications it could reach a top speed in excess of seven hundred fifty miles an hour.

The breeze blowing over the flat open tarmac was bone-chilling. Zero zipped up his black leather coat as he rounded the plane to the entry ramp side to find Maria, her arms folded and eyes narrowed, having what seemed to be a less-than-amiable chat with the pilot.

"I *know* what orders are," she was telling him, her tone tight. "I also know when to follow a lead. I'm telling you we have a lead, and this is where we need to go."

The pilot clucked his tongue. "Sorry, ma'am, but it was made very clear that my job would be on the line if I took y'all anywhere else."

Zero frowned. Something about the pilot's Texan drawl sparked something in his mind. He looked the man over; the pilot didn't look like the usual uniformed captain they had on these operations. He was around Zero's age, at or near forty, wearing an honest-to-goodness bomber jacket complete with fur-lined collar. His black hair was trimmed close, and he had a five o'clock shadow that he'd apparently groomed that way. He was, for all intents and purposes, trying to be walking stereotype of the maverick pilot.

And Zero ... knew him.

"Chip," he said suddenly, before he even knew why he was saying it. "Chip Foxworth, right?"

The pilot frowned. "Do I know you, Agent?"

"No. You wouldn't remember me. But I know you. You were a fighter pilot in the Navy. You flew Tomcats, I believe. You were going to go in for the Blue Angels, but the CIA scouted you first." Zero recited it all like there was a script in his head. This wasn't a new memory resurfacing; this was information, something he'd read or been told. It was a strange sensation, much like the first time he'd realized he knew Arabic and Russian. "You didn't make the cut. So you flew for them instead."

The pilot scoffed. "You tryin' to make friends here? Because you ain't doin' such a good job ..."

"No," Zero said, "I'm trying to bargain. You still want a shot at being CIA? You're talking to Agent Zero."

Chip looked him up and down. A wide smile broke out on his face, wide enough for Zero to see that he was missing a molar. "Get the hell outta here. If you're Agent Zero, I'm Madonna."

Zero folded his arms. "I know all this because I read your file." Back when he was head of the SOG team, even before the memory suppressor, he had reviewed each candidate for Spec Ops Group himself. "I liked what I saw. But it wasn't my call to make." That distinction would have gone to Shawn Cartwright, the then-deputy director who was now very much deceased. "You want another shot? We need you on our team."

The pilot scoffed and kicked at the tarmac. "Shit," he murmured.

"We got a van!" Alan bellowed from the other side of the plane. A moment later a white cargo van careened around the tail and screeched to a stop. A burly driver leapt out and yanked open the rear doors as Alan joined him. Together the two of them hefted the long black footlocker from Bixby's lab—Penny's lab now, Zero reminded himself—and carried it up the ramp and onto the plane, huffing and puffing the whole way.

The driver then jumped back into the van and sped away without a word. The entire exchange had taken all of forty-five seconds, and left Chip Foxworth seemingly bemused.

"Well?" Zero asked again, trying to pretend that he wasn't baffled by the expedience of the handoff. "Do we have a pilot or not?"

"All right," Chip relented. "Get on the plane, let's go." He led the way, vaulting up the ramp stairs in two bounds. The three of them followed, dropping into cream-colored leather seats and buckling up.

"Please keep your hands and feet inside the ride at all times," Chip called over his shoulder, leaving the cockpit door open. "We'll have to refuel in Europe, likely Zurich. But final destination: Mogadishu."

"Addis Ababa," Reidigger called back.

Zero frowned at that.

"Gesundheit?" Chip said.

"Addis Ababa in Ethiopia." To Zero and Maria he added, "Trust me. I know a guy who might be able to get us into the port."

"You know a guy," Maria repeated. "Of course you do."

The plane's engine whirred to life, and in moments they were taxiing down the runway. Zero leaned back against the headrest and closed his eyes. They would need to check gear, review the op, come up with a plan—but they had some time. He could relax for five minutes.

Or maybe not.

"You okay?" Maria asked quietly. She sat across from him, leaning over the aisle.

"Yeah, of course. Why?"

"You knew the pilot."

"I remembered reading his file once," Zero said honestly.

"Sure. But I saw the look on your face. You *just* remembered it. In the moment. Did it come back to you?"

"What are you trying to ask?" Zero said, perhaps a little too defensively.

"Are you still having memory problems?" Maria asked him point-blank.

"I ..." He knew he should be honest. But Maria knew about the memories that had resurfaced of his past, carrying out assassinations in the name of the CIA. She was there when they'd caused him to have a nervous breakdown. She was there when he'd put a gun to his own head. If he was honest now, she'd see him as little more than a liability to the operation.

"No," he said. "I'm straight. I'm good."

"Okay," she said, leaning back in his seat. "You promise?"

"I promise," he lied.

CHAPTER ELEVEN

"Let's see," Sara said as she leaned over the open freezer door. "Do you want frozen lasagna or frozen chicken tenders? Oh, and there's a frozen pizza in here too. Now I see why Dad wanted to learn to cook. I really should have been paying attention to that frittata."

There was no response behind her. Sara straightened, looking around, but her sister wasn't there. "Maya?" She closed the freezer and headed down the short hall to find her in their shared room, jamming clothes into an olive-green rucksack.

"Are you going somewhere?" Sara asked.

"For a little bit, yeah," Maya said without looking up. "There's something I need to do."

Sara shifted uncomfortably from one foot to the other. She didn't like the idea of being left alone here. "For how long?"

"Not sure. A day or two? Maybe longer." Maya opened her nightstand drawer and pulled out a lockback knife. She snapped the blade open, inspected it, and then folded it closed again. Into the rucksack it went. "If Dad comes back before then, tell him I went to visit friends on campus to reacclimate myself."

"So lie to him. Got it." Sara hadn't intended it as sarcastic as it came out; that was just her natural tone these days. Either way it had the desired effect. Maya set down the rucksack and turned her attention to her younger sister.

"Are you going to be okay?" she asked candidly.

"Me? Pssht. Yeah. Of course I will." Sara forced a grin. "It'll be great. I can stuff myself with frozen food, and I won't have to argue with either of you about what's on TV."

Maya smiled with half her mouth. "You call me if you need anything at all, and I'll come right home." She hefted the rucksack and brought it out to the kitchen, where she pulled open the silverware drawer and withdrew the black pistol that was hidden behind the cutlery tray. Sara watched as her older sister expertly ejected the magazine, cleared the chamber, and dropped both into her sack.

"There's a revolver in the closet," she told Sara. "I'm taking this one."

Sara felt a lump form in the pit of her stomach seeing her sister with the gun. The haste with which she was packing, the story about going back to school, and the need for a gun only amounted to one thing in Sara's mind.

Maya pulled on her winter coat and slung the rucksack over her shoulder. "I'm going to take an Uber to Langley and get Dad's car. I'll be able to charge my phone in there if I need to. Call if there's anything—"

"Maya, wait." Sara held her breath for a moment, mustering the courage to ask. "Are you going to kill those boys? The ones that attacked you?"

Maya's face fell slack in sheer disbelief. "Sara…no. No, of course not. God, no." She opened her arms and wrapped her in a hug. "No, I'm not going to kill anyone. This is just for protection. I don't know what I'm going to find."

"At least tell me what you're looking for," Sara said from Maya's shoulder.

Her older sister sighed. "Fine. But you have to keep this a secret. Dad's been looking for someone. Someone from his past. But he can't find them, so I'm going to try."

"Why? Why do you need to help him?"

Maya chewed her bottom lip for a moment. "Because," she said at last, "he won't ask for help. But I know he needs it."

Sara felt a pang of remorse at that. She was guilty of the same thing—they all were. "Can I come with you?"

Maya flashed her a thin smile. "I'm not sure that's a good idea. I know I can handle myself, but…" Her sister trailed off, but Sara didn't need her to finish. Maya wasn't responsible for her safety and couldn't guarantee it.

"It's okay," Sara said quickly. "I get it. Do what you have to do. Just, keep me updated."

"I will, I promise. Call me anytime. Be back soon. Stay safe!"

"You too."

And then Maya was out the door, into the chilly February air, and Sara was alone.

She stood in the foyer for a long time, not knowing what she should do, until she realized how stupid she felt just idling there. She made it to the kitchen and stood there instead for a while, elbows propped on the counter. She poked her head in the freezer again before deciding that she wasn't actually all that hungry, and resorted to turning on the TV.

After about fifteen minutes of lackadaisical channel-flipping, she settled on a nineties sitcom that she'd never really found all that funny before, but for some reason the background track of canned laughter turned up to a high volume made the apartment feel less empty. It even felt bigger now, somehow, without anyone else in it.

For the last two months, more than that now, Sara had been spending her time either here or at the community center. There were people there. There were people here. The main reason she'd never complained about sharing the close quarters with her father and sister was—and she'd never admit it to either of them—she was enjoying being close to them again, both literally and figuratively.

More than that, she needed it, because it helped her get outside her own head. Here and now, even with fake laughter filling the living room, her head was the only place to be.

She remembered reading somewhere that most of those canned laughter tracks used in sitcoms were recorded in the sixties, which meant that most of the people laughing were probably dead. And *that* thought didn't help anything.

At some point her stomach rumbled and she realized she was hungry after all. A glance at the clock shocked her—she'd been sitting there for more than two hours and hadn't actually registered a single plotline of the show that was on TV over her own swirling thoughts and gallows humor.

"You need to get out more," she told herself as she headed back to the kitchen. Her fingers were barely on the freezer door when someone knocked so briskly at the front door that she jumped nearly a foot in the air.

"Christ," she laughed at herself. "Chill out, Sara." She headed to the small foyer, pausing only briefly at the coat closet and remembering what Maya had said about the revolver hidden in there.

It's probably just a solicitor. Or maybe a Jehovah's Witness. Hmm, maybe I should *get the gun.* She snickered at her own internal joke as she took a look through the peephole.

She couldn't believe what she saw.

"Oh my god."

It couldn't be.

She unlocked the door and yanked it open, staring in disbelief.

Camilla flashed her an embarrassed smile. "Hey, girl," she said hesitantly.

Sara couldn't believe what she was seeing. Camilla, her roommate from Jacksonville, was standing at the door of her Maryland apartment. Her Florida life felt like a distant past, another life since she'd rented a ramshackle house with Camilla and three others. Since she'd been introduced to cocaine and Xanax. Since she'd been introduced to the drug dealer Ike, whom she'd stolen from, and almost killed herself on an OD.

But it was her, Camilla, in the flesh—or rather, in capri pants and a windbreaker in the dead of winter in the northeast.

Sara snapped out of it. "Jesus, you must be freezing! Get your ass in here, come on." She ushered Camilla in and shut the door, the older girl rubbing her hands together for warmth. "Come in the kitchen. I'll make some coffee." On the way down the foyer Sara turned the heat up several degrees, certain that wherever in the world her dad was, a shudder had just gone down his spine at her touching of the thermostat.

"Thanks." Camilla dropped a backpack onto a chair in the kitchen and glanced around. "Nice digs. This your place?"

"No. It's my dad's place." Sara's head was still spinning at the sudden intrusion as she filled the coffeepot with water. "Camilla, not to be rude, but what the hell are you doing here?"

Her former roommate smiled. "I know, I know. I'm so sorry to just drop in on you like this. I wanted to call when I got up here, but my phone died and I didn't know what else to do."

"How did you get this address?"

Camilla blinked. "You texted it to me. At Christmas? Remember I sent you a card?"

"Oh. Yeah." Sara barely remembered that because she'd thrown the card away. She had still been struggling and hadn't wanted the reminder of her former life. "Yeah, thanks for that."

Sara turned on the coffee machine and then faced her friend—her former friend, and enabler. The girl who had given her the first bar of Xanax. The girl who scored dimes for her so she wouldn't have to. She wanted to be mad that Camilla had just shown up so unceremoniously like this. She was ready to be mad... but then she noticed a few things that she hadn't at first.

Camilla was eighteen—no, nineteen now, Sara remembered, since her birthday was early December—but she'd always tried to look older with lots of makeup. There was no makeup now, not a trace of it, and her girlish features clashed terribly with the bags beneath her eyes and the creases around her mouth that heavy drug abuse had brought on early. Her hair was kinky and unwashed, pulled up in a sloppy ponytail. She had taught Sara how to pick clothes that flattered and accentuated her contours, but now Camilla wore a thin windbreaker and what looked like a man's tank top, loose on her skinny frame.

Frankly, she looked like hell, and Sara could guess why that might be.

"Why are you here?" she demanded.

"What, I can't drop in to see an old friend?"

"No," Sara said, "you can't. Not when..."

Not when I feel like I'm an inch away from relapsing at any moment. But she didn't say that. "Tell me the truth."

"Okay. Yeah." Camilla inspected the tiled floor. "There was this guy. He seemed nice at first, and it was fun for a while... until it wasn't anymore. I tried to break it off and he didn't like that. Started showing up at the house, and my job. I went to my parents' place. He even showed up there. Almost got in a fistfight with my dad but he ran off when the cops were called."

Sara took a deep breath. She didn't need this right now, but this wasn't the sort of thing there was ever a convenient time for. "Did he hurt you?"

Camilla shrugged one shoulder noncommittally. "I don't think he meant to," she murmured. "Just could use a place to lay low for a bit. Somewhere far away from that scumbag."

Sara leaned against the countertop and smoothed her hair. She doubted her dad would like this very much. She also knew he'd have trouble turning away someone in need. But he wasn't here. Neither was Maya. This was up to her.

"You clean?" she asked.

"Yeah. I am. Totally." To Sara's arched eyebrow she added, "I promise. Haven't touched anything in weeks."

"Let me see your bag."

"Seriously?" Camilla bristled.

"Seriously." Sara wasn't backing down from this. It was one thing to have her old partner in crime in the apartment; it would be another matter entirely if she was holding.

"Fine." Camilla waved a hand. "Go ahead."

Sara unzipped the backpack and rifled through it quickly. She found some clothes, some makeup, a few pieces of jewelry, a couple of hair products, and a tight roll of cash, thick as a Maglite and held with a rubber band.

"That's from the bar," Camilla said quickly. "It's everything I had."

Sara wanted to press her for the truth, but she also knew that Camilla was, or had been, an excellent bartender, popular locally and especially among older men. It wasn't uncommon for them to tip her as much as their drink cost. She dropped the money back into the bag and zipped it again.

"All right," she relented at last. "You can stay here for a few days. My sister and dad are both away, so you can sleep in my bed and I'll take Maya's. But if either of them get back and want you out, it's outta my hands, got it?"

Camilla nodded once. "Got it."

"And if you're lying and I catch you using, I'll throw you out in the snow myself."

Camilla's throat flexed. Sara had seen her friend's hotheaded *tica* roots show themselves on more than a couple occasions, standing up to guys twice her size, but at Sara's threat she merely nodded meekly.

"Got it. Um, bathroom?"

Sara pointed down the hall and Camilla scurried off, closing the door behind her.

She leaned against the counter and sighed. This was not at all how she'd imagined her evening going—but at least she wasn't alone. And if Camilla truly wasn't using anymore, this could be a real opportunity to help a friend. Something in the older girl seemed... different than it was before. As if something was broken. Whatever that guy had done to her seemed to have had a serious impact on her, enough to send her running from Florida to seek out a friend she hadn't seen in four months.

She thought of that support group in the community center. What was it called again? Oh, right—"Common Bonds." *Sharing trauma, sharing hope.*

She and Camilla shared trauma. Maybe they could share hope too.

But only if they could avoid sharing a relapse.

CHAPTER TWELVE

Maya used her dad's spare car key to unlock the SUV and slide behind the wheel. It wasn't hard to get past the gate that admitted entrance to Langley's parking lot; she'd simply flashed her West Point student ID and told them she was here to be interviewed for an internship. The guard had waved her through, him knowing that the security checkpoint inside the building would confirm her story and her knowing that she wasn't going that far.

She glanced up at the enormous compound, the white and teal contemporary structures, the dark blue windows.

Wonder which office will be mine.

She hadn't given up on her dream of becoming the youngest CIA agent in history, though if she ever made it back to West Point she would have serious catching up to do. One way or another it was going to happen. Maybe she would change her name so that no one accused her of nepotism; but then again, no one knew the great Agent Zero by his real name of Reid Lawson anyway.

That was for the best; she didn't want to have to explain to anyone that her goal had almost nothing to do with her father. In fact, she'd made the resolution at a point in her life when she was furious with him for the lies he'd kept from her and Sara. For the fiction he'd weaved around her mother's murder. No, Maya's motivation had come from her own experiences at the hands of Serbian human traffickers. It was those men she wanted to stop, to grind their industry to a halt, to see them imprisoned in dirt holes in the ground where the sun would never shine on their faces again.

Despite the dark thoughts, she smiled and waved to the kindly old guard at the gate house on her way out of the parking lot, him giving her a puzzled frown and her wondering if he'd even gotten a good enough look at her to place her face a second time. Unlikely, she decided.

As she navigated back to the main road, she reviewed what she knew in her head.

One: Dad is looking for a former CIA agent with the first or last name of Connor.

Two: There was a doctor involved. Was some kind of procedure done on this guy?
Three: Alan was helping him.

It wasn't much to go on, but she at least knew where to start. As she headed there, she thought about Sara and leaving her alone in the apartment. Sara was sixteen, almost an adult, certainly liked to act like one. But at the same time, she was more like her sister and her dad than she'd ever admit. She wouldn't ask for help when she needed it, and she'd definitely never admit that she didn't want to be alone.

Why? Sara's words in her head. *Why do you need to help him?*

It was a valid question, and not one she'd been entirely honest in answering.

Because I feel utterly useless. That was one answer. *Because if I'm ever going to go back to that school, I need to know that I'm capable. That I deserve what I want.*

If she was being honest, even only with herself, she needed to succeed where an actual CIA agent had not.

She parked the SUV two blocks from Third Street Garage and dialed Alan on her cell phone, but it went straight to voicemail. Maya wondered if he'd gone with her dad to wherever it was he'd gone. She left her rucksack in the car, opting for a smaller bag of necessities that anyone would think was a purse. Then she walked the short distance to the garage. She didn't actually think anyone was following her, but she couldn't shake her dad's suspicion that their apartment was bugged—and if the apartment was bugged, the SUV might be tagged too.

Third Street Garage was a simple place, a boxy building with three bays and a small attached office. Maya knew that behind this place, forming an L shape with the garage, was a small apartment where the burly mechanic "Mitch" lived. Mitch, who had once taken Maya and Sara to a WITSEC house in Nebraska for their safety. Mitch, who had taken a few bullets for them when members of a mercenary group came to seek them out. Mitch, who was the alias of former CIA agent and now CIA asset Alan Reidigger.

But the office door was locked. All three garage bays were shut tight. Maya cupped her hands around the small office window and peered in. It was dark inside. She unzipped the small purse; this was a perfect opportunity for her to exercise one of her "extracurricular" skills, the ones she had learned on her own time during West Point breaks when she wasn't going home or speaking to her dad.

Inside the purse was a pick set. She'd had plenty of time to practice when all the other kids and most of the faculty were gone home for holidays, picking the locks of other dormitories, of classrooms. One afternoon she'd gone down an entire corridor, unlocking every door, and then going back the way she came and locking them back up again.

She chewed her bottom lip as she worked the picks in both hands, feeling for the sliding pin tumblers as she kept an eye out for onlookers. After about two minutes she felt the final pin fall into place; the knob turned, and the door swung inward.

Hold up a second. One of the other skills she'd picked up had been profiling. She'd consumed about a dozen books on the subject, and while she wasn't particularly well-versed in practice, there wasn't much she didn't know about theory.

Alan is a paranoid ex–CIA agent. There's no way his defenses would be this thin if there was anything worth finding here.

She slipped into the office and closed the door gently behind her.

Unless he knew that others would think the same … which means anything worth finding would be cleverly hidden.

Maya quickly searched the small office, the drawers of its rickety steel desk, the undersides of the two ratty guest chairs, behind a wall calendar and under a loose corner of the carpet. She checked the decade-old desktop computer for hidden files. She stood on the desk and lifted a panel of the drop ceiling, finding nothing but dust.

Then she pushed through the door that led to the garage bays. Two of them were empty, but the center one was occupied by a red sports car, definitely older than she was but in absolutely pristine condition. It stood out like a sore thumb in this otherwise dark and gloomy place full of rusting tools and the smell of grease.

Maya circled it twice, slowly, thinking of Occam's razor as she did. The explanation that required the least amount of assumptions is usually the correct one. The car was mint; there were no smudges on the hood from greasy fingers lifting it for repairs. But, she noticed, there was the slightest of fingerprint oil on the driver's side door. A close inspection of the passenger side told her the same. Behind the exhaust pipe at the rear was a dark mark on the concrete where fumes had stained it.

Two men got in this car. Or one man got in on both sides. Car repairs don't require getting in the passenger seat. Someone turned it on and sat here with the engine idling for some time. None of those were assumptions; they were facts. The single assumption was that there was more to this car than met the eye.

Using the hem of her shirt, Maya carefully pulled up the door handle just once. Luckily the car was unlocked; a lot of car alarm systems were set to trigger on multiple pulls of a locked door. The door swung open smoothly, the interior smelling like leather and pine. She slid herself behind the wheel, wishing she'd had the foresight to bring latex gloves but also realizing she'd had no intention of breaking into Alan's garage to search for information.

The steering wheel was clean. As she'd suspected, this car had been detailed but not driven. But there was some dirt on the floor mats on each side. She had the increasing feeling that her intuition had been right, that two men had sat in this car, turned on the engine ...

So no one would hear them speaking if anyone was listening in.

"Yo, Mitch?"

Maya froze at the sound of a male voice drifting to her through the open door between the garage and office. She quickly leaned over, pulled the car's door closed—fingerprints be damned—and laid herself across the passenger seat.

"You here, man?" The voice sounded young. "Door was unlocked ... Mitch?"

If he heard me close the car door, I'm screwed.

Sure enough, a moment later there was a silhouette against the tinted window on the passenger side. The latch clicked, and the door swung open.

Maya, seated in the driver's seat with her legs folded against the door and her torso sprawled over the passenger side, found herself staring up at a young white guy, mid-twenties at best, with blond dreadlocks, a fuzzy patch on his chin, and an expression of utter bewilderment in his eye.

"Whoa!" The guy leapt back. "What the hell?!"

"Wait," Maya said lamely. "Just let me explain ..."

"Uh, no thanks. I don't want any part of whatever this is." Apparently this guy had the complete wrong impression about Mitch's garage. "I'm just gonna ... go." He spun on a heel to leave.

Maya couldn't just let him go. She planted one foot against the driver's side door and pushed off, propelling her body across the seats and headfirst through the open door. She tucked into a shoulder roll, came up on one knee, and threw out a hand. Her fingers just barely closed around the strap of the guy's messenger bag as he tried to scoot out the door that led to the office.

The strap went taut; the guy's legs flew out from beneath him, and he landed on his back on the concrete. "*Oomph!*"

Maya scrambled to her feet as the guy struggled to catch his breath. She kicked the door closed with one foot and put herself between it and him.

"Who are you?" she demanded.

"Me?" he wheezed. "Who are *you?*"

"I'm a friend of Mitch's. And I don't know you."

The guy rolled over with a groan and got to his knees. "Well, I'm a friend of Mitch's, and I don't know you either."

73

"That's ..." Maya frowned. "That's a fair point, actually. Fine. My name is Maya." She'd managed to stay honest so far, but now seemed like a good time for a slight pivot. "Mitch is ... away. He sent me here to retrieve information."

"Away where?" The guy staggered to his feet.

"None of your business. Who are you?"

The guy sighed resignedly. "Name's Jay. I work in ... IT."

Maya raised an eyebrow. "IT?" *A hacker. He's got the intel Alan was helping Dad get.* "I'm going to need that messenger bag."

Jay's left hand clutched the bag suddenly. Protectively. "Still don't know you. Where's Mitch gone?"

"He's gone ..." Maya bit her lip, wondering if she could play a trump card here—if this guy was snooping in CIA databases, he probably knew some things. Yet she scolded herself for even considering it, since she'd just been thinking about nepotism. "He's away with my dad. Maybe you've heard of him. Agent Zero?"

Jay's eyes narrowed at that, but Maya stared resolutely. Slowly a grin spread across his narrow face. "Agent Zero? You're telling me that *the* Agent Zero has teenage kids—"

"I'm nineteen—"

"Fine, that *the* Agent Zero has *adult* kids, and that Mitch works with him?" Jay laughed. "Prove it."

"Prove it?" Maya scoffed. "Prove that my dad is a secret agent? You think I carry a card around or something? I don't have time for this."

"Sorry. No proof, no bag, no info. I have no way of verifying that anything you say is—"

Maya kicked out suddenly, using her left leg to deliver a smack to the back of his right knee with the flat top of her foot—not to hurt him, but to buckle the leg. As his knee gave and his body pitched forward, she twisted her hips and kicked out again, this time with her right, the shin smacking solidly across his chest.

Neither blow was intended to harm him much, but the quick one-two sent him once again to his back on the garage's concrete, and elicited another "*Ooph!*" of deflated lungs.

"How's that for proof?" She knelt and scooped up the bag quickly. "Are you going to stay right there, Jay?"

He flashed her a weak thumbs-up.

"Good. Because that was me trying *not* to hurt you. I'm taking this." She slung the messenger bag over one shoulder. As she turned toward the door, she noticed a set of keys dangling there, and she bet she knew what they fit in. "These too. Now I want you to stay right there, just like that, until I'm gone." She slapped the black button for the middle garage bay and the door rumbled upward, bringing with it the biting February air. "Once I leave, count to one hundred. Then close this place up and lock it before you go. Mitch will be in touch."

Maya rounded to the driver's side of the Skylark and slid behind the wheel. The passenger side was still open; she leaned over to pull it closed, but not before issuing one last warning to the "IT" guy. "If you try to contact Mitch before he contacts you, I'm going to tell him *you* stole his car."

Jay muttered something that Maya was pretty sure was "bitch," but she let it slide and shut the door. A twist of the key brought the powerful engine to life, thrumming beneath her fingers on the wheel like a growling animal.

It wasn't the most inconspicuous ride she could have chosen. She was practically begging cops to pull her over. *But damn, it feels good.*

She backed out of the garage bay and drove the Skylark the few blocks back to her dad's SUV to retrieve her rucksack. After making sure no one was watching, she left the keys on the driver's side wheel well. She could call Sara later and have her retrieve it. The classic Buick was practically calling her name.

She got back into the Skylark and drove a couple of miles, eventually parking in the lot of a pharmacy to see what she'd taken from Jay. There was only one thing inside the messenger bag: a black binder, inside of which was about thirty neatly punched pages. It didn't take her long to discern that these were stolen CIA profiles on doctors—neurosurgeons, to be precise—all of whom had been contracted by the agency between four and five years ago.

That's a pretty specific timeline, she noted. There were nine of them in all. Two of them were marked as since deceased. But it was the final page of each surgeon's profile that caught her attention the most. They were bank statements, dated sometime during that year with a single transaction highlighted.

Every single one of the neurosurgeons listed had received a deposit in the tens of thousands from a company that was actually called General Consulting, Inc.

They really could have come up with something better than that.

Maya paged through the profiles. Two were dead. Another had retired and moved to California. She couldn't very well go hopping around the country after these doctors. A few were still active, it seemed, and even local.

There was a standout, however; one particular neurosurgeon, a Dr. Howard Bliss, had been the only one to receive a six-figure payment from General Consulting. He owned his own practice in the Flatiron District of New York, near Gramercy Park, and lived on the Upper East Side.

It was farther than she'd hoped to have to go. By the time she reached the city, it would likely be dark. His office would be closed.

Am I really going to drive to New York, go to this guy's house, and try to shake him down? A neurosurgeon with ties to the CIA, when I'm hardly aware of what I'm even looking for?

Maya started the car again, and for some reason the resonant rumbling of the Skylark's engine strengthened her resolve. She reminded herself why she was doing this in the first place. If she couldn't accomplish this one task, she didn't deserve the lofty goals she had set for herself.

Yeah. I guess I am.

CHAPTER THIRTEEN

Zero popped the latches on the large black footlocker at the rear of the plane and lifted the lid as the Gulfstream hurtled over the Atlantic at top speed. None of them doubted that Shaw and Walsh were tracking the jet and were well aware it was heading in the wrong direction, but there had been no attempt to contact them.

They want to see where we're going first, Zero reasoned. His superiors wanted to see just how many direct orders they would defy—the short answer, he knew, being "all of them."

At least Penny had ensured they were well supplied. Beneath the lid of the footlocker was a wide shallow tray laden with numerous gadgets and implements, not the least of which were flashlights, zip ties, sunglasses, radios with wireless earpieces, and a trio of satellite phones. He tugged on the tray and it lifted easily, unfolding into four tiers like an oversized toolbox. Beneath the first tray were weapons, including his favored Glock 19 and the compact LC9.

He couldn't help but smile; one of the black Glocks was clearly inscribed with a slashed zero on the barrel. He lifted it, the weight of the gun familiar enough to tell him it was fully loaded. His right thumb rested naturally on a soft oblong pad; a biometric trigger lock already encoded to his thumbprint.

Zero set the Glock down and let out a low whistle. In the lowest tray of the footlocker was a compact submachine gun, an Italian-made Beretta PMX. The weapon was sleek, deadly, and admittedly alluring.

"Wow," Maria said over his shoulder. "That's quite a collection. Is that a grappling hook?"

Zero chuckled. "I guess our new friend Dr. León thought of everything."

"What's this?" Maria reached into the center tray and lifted a square parcel encased in black nylon, about eighteen inches on each side and about four inches thick. Zero took it and turned it in his hands; whatever it was, it was dense but not heavy, and had two shoulder straps that connected with a third. The only identifying marks on it were three characters stenciled in white on the front of it. They said XI-B.

Zero frowned. Why did that sound familiar? Then it came to him—the XI-A had been a prototype, a design of Bixby's that comprised a sailcloth over an aluminum composite frame, compact enough to fit in a backpack when folded.

"It's a glider," he told her. This must have been a new design, perhaps something that Bixby had been working on before his disappearance. Zero had used its predecessor himself when he and then-President Pierson leapt off the Queensboro Bridge before it collapsed. "Sort of a personal hang glider."

Maria scoffed. "What exactly does Penny think we're going to be doing?"

"What exactly do *we* think we're going to be doing?" Zero shot a glance behind him at Reidigger, who was slumped in a leather seat, his trucker cap pulled low over his brow and his fingers laced over his protruding stomach. "You awake over there?"

"Nope," Alan grunted.

"What's in Addis Ababa?"

"I know a guy." Alan sat up in his seat and adjusted his cap. "We can't just walk into a Somali pirate port without some very convincing cover. I know a smuggler who operates out of Addis Merkato in the city. Trades with the Somalis, occasionally brokers a buyer for their, uh, 'acquisitions.' The railgun might be on his radar. If it's not, I think he could arrange to get us into the port undercover as part of his crew."

Maria nodded thoughtfully. "Okay then. That's ... a good idea, actually."

Reidigger eased back into his seat. "Saying 'actually' implies you expected the opposite."

"And this smuggler," Zero interjected. "You're on good terms with him?"

"Was," Alan muttered. "Once upon a time. Guess we'll see where the chips fell. For now, let's just say we're not going to call ahead."

Zero and Maria exchanged a concerned glance. She shrugged slightly, indicating that she didn't have anything better, when one of the satellite phones chirped.

Maria reached for it. "It's Penny. She's just confirmed that three US Navy battleships have been dispatched from Diego Garcia and are headed west, towards Somalia."

Zero nodded. That confirmed their suspicions; Walsh knew damn well there would be nothing for them to find in Korea or in the Pacific Ocean. It also meant he probably had a good idea of where the jet was heading.

He unzipped the black backpack and dumped the useless provisions onto the floor of the plane. "We can't take all this stuff, and we don't know what's going to be necessary. So let's split it up as best we can." He reached for the Beretta PMX. It was a little too large to fit in the bag, so he broke down the barrel and stock and stashed all three pieces in the bag.

He grabbed the XI-B, but then reconsidered and put it back in the footlocker. He wouldn't need it, and it would take up too much space in his bag. Although—the glider had saved his life once before.

Better to have it and not need it.

He stuffed the nylon parcel into the backpack with the broken-down Beretta machine gun. They had two other bags and needed to consider all options. After all, they had no idea what they might have to do.

A small part of him hoped the naval ships were successful and found the Somali thieves before they reached their port. Because if not, he and his team would have to walk into a literal pirates' den.

Including the time zone difference and travel, local time was a little after eight in the morning when the Gulfstream set down on a runway at Bole International Airport in Addis Ababa.

"Stay with the plane," Zero told Chip Foxworth. "No one gets in. Contact the US embassy here and let them know that the CIA is here on a brief stopover en route to another destination. Make it clear that there's no operation going on here and no reason for concern."

"Is that true?" the pilot asked.

"Probably not," Reidigger grunted as they disembarked.

They caught a taxi outside the central terminal and Alan sat up front, directing the driver to Addis Merkato. Zero marveled at the city outside the window; in a lot of ways it wasn't all that dissimilar to an East Coast city, the dense downtown in the distance packed with tall buildings and surrounded by waning urban sprawl. The major difference was that everything here seemed so colorful. Every corner was vivid and bright, not bland and concrete like he was accustomed to seeing in places like DC and New York. Even the citizens' clothing seemed more vibrant than he was used to, yellows and reds and greens in every shade.

Traffic felt as if it crawled along, a symphony of honking horns and shouting voices muted only by the taxi's closed windows, throngs of people weaving alongside and in front of cars.

I guess jaywalking's a popular thing here, he mused.

"You know," he said casually to Maria, "the Ethiopians use a different calendar than most of the world. They're technically about seven years behind us, in a way."

Maria smiled quizzically. "Is that so, professor?"

"Yeah. They use a calendar based on the Eritreans, rather than the Gregorian, but they disagree on the year that Jesus was killed—the year the rest of us started counting up from zero. Well, there's more to it than that. There's also the Coptic influence to consider, but in simplest terms—"

Maria pressed a finger against his lips. "Not that it isn't fascinating," she told him gently, "but I need you to put your game face on."

He nodded and kissed her finger lightly. She was right; it had been months since he'd done anything he would call legitimate fieldwork, and this was serious. They were going into this place blind, with no previous intel other than Alan's word.

Soon after, they arrived at their destination and Alan paid the driver. Addis Merkato was a considerable sight to behold; it was Africa's largest open-air market, if not the world's. A sea of people undulated before them like flocks of migrating starlings, heading this way or that among the seemingly endless rows of colorful stalls. Many of the stalls were shoddily fashioned from plywood, with discarded steel for ceilings when it rained. Others were little more than tables with an umbrella to supply some shade. Not that it was needed in February; the sun was out, but the weather was a cool fifty-five degrees.

Zero zipped his black jacket about halfway up. He'd pulled it from the footlocker, courtesy of Penny León, but he wasn't sure if it was reinforced with a layer of bullet-stopping graphene mesh or not.

It would generally be better if I didn't have to find out.

Alan led the way through the market. Despite his size, he navigated the crowd easily, slipping between and around people without pausing even a beat, his direction as purposeful as if there was a map in his head.

Zero couldn't help but wonder what exactly Alan had been doing in the two-year interim that he was missing. He'd vanished shortly after the memory suppressor was installed in Zero's head, and later resurfaced as the enigmatic mechanic Mitch, but he'd never opened up or spoken about the time in between. Clearly he'd been busy traveling and making connections, given the vast network of underground contacts he had. Gone was the round-faced jovial-yet-capable agent Zero had known years ago. Alan still joked, and he still cared deeply for his friends and went out of his way to prove it. But often it felt like genuine mirth had drained from him.

Reidigger turned left suddenly and entered a wide stall displaying a number of Oriental rugs in a dizzying array of colors, hanging from lines strewn like a spider web overhead. He weaved around them until they reached the rear plywood wall of the stall, hanging on which was the ugliest rug Zero had ever seen, an off-white thing with brown patterns swirling in a random way that made it appear as if it came already stained. Alan pushed it aside like a curtain to expose the narrow opening behind it and squeezed through.

Zero followed, Maria behind him, into a small courtyard of sorts, most hidden behind a box of stalls around it. "Courtyard" wasn't quite the right term; it was a square patch of dirt with a large white tent in its center that Zero quickly realized was made from a used parachute.

A bearded man stood at the tent's entrance. He had six inches and sixty pounds on Zero easily, and eyes so dark they were almost black. His zipped-up track jacket was tight enough against his torso to make out the unmistakable bulge of a machine pistol holstered under his left armpit.

"Is Hannibal in?" Alan asked gruffly.

The man said nothing in response.

"Tell him Mitch is here to see him."

The guard turned slowly and disappeared into the tent.

"He didn't look very happy to see you," Maria whispered.

"Yeah," Alan agreed. "He must be new."

A moment later the guard pulled back the flap of the tent and stepped aside to admit them entrance. Zero set his jaw as he followed Alan inside.

The tent was spacious, several degrees warmer than the open air, and dim, the only light provided by the glow of the sun outside. Directly in front of them a man sat at behind a simple wooden table, scribbling in what appeared to be a ledger of some sort. Beside his ledger, conspicuously, was a Desert Eagle.

Maria was right, Zero thought at the sight of the large gun. *I need to get my head in the game.*

The man behind the table wore a collared shirt that had likely been white once, now stained with sweat and streaks of dirt, the sleeves rolled up to the elbows to reveal thick forearms and several tattoos. He sported a thick beard on his chin, but no hair on his lip, giving him the aspect of some kind of menacing Mennonite.

But that wasn't what stood out about him the most. Zero noted the odd angle at which he clutched the pen, pinched between his thumb and forefinger—because the two center fingers of his right hand were missing.

The smuggler, Hannibal, set down his pen and rose from his seat, a grin slowly spreading wide as he did. "Mitchell! My friend. It has been too long. To what do I owe this surprise visit?"

He spoke with an accent that was difficult to place—not Australian, but something close. New Zealand, Zero assumed. But more concerning was the obviously false saccharine charm that he was laying on too thick.

"Hannibal." Reidigger nodded. "I need a favor. We need to get into Hamar Port."

"Hamar?" The smuggler stroked his chin. "You have business with pirates, Mitchell?" He grinned wide again. "You should know you could just come to me for all your extralegal needs."

"We're looking for something," Reidigger told him. "A boat was stolen from South Korea. Small. Fast."

Hannibal frowned as Zero studied his face carefully. Alan was careful not to mention the weapon, and Hannibal was either a stellar liar or had no idea what he was talking about. If the latter was true, it meant that the Somalis had not yet gone through the usual channels to offload it. And *that* meant that they still had time ... or that the railgun had been stolen for another purpose.

"You could get us in there as part of your crew," Alan continued. "Nothing's going down. We just want to scope it out."

"Hmm." Hannibal stroked his shaggy chin again thoughtfully. "I could do that, yeah. But, uh, what's in it for me?"

"You *owe* me," Alan said forcefully. "You're still alive, aren't you?"

"I am." Hannibal held up his right hand to show the two missing fingers, fleshy patches grown over the half-inch of stub left in each digit's place. "But they still took from me."

Zero wasn't sure what they were talking about and this wasn't the time to ask, but he could at least surmise that Alan had helped the smuggler out of a jam at some point, one that could have cost him his life—and it seemed that Hannibal thought the removal of two fingers was equivalent.

"I can get you to Hamar Port," Hannibal said. "I can get you to the docks. Hell, I can get you face to face with any crew that operates out of there. But again, I'll ask: what's in it for me?"

Zero knew they didn't have much to offer. It was unlikely he would accept a couple of submachine guns as payment when the guy likely traded weapons daily. They had the Gulfstream, but they weren't in a position to give that away in what would be the most one-sided transaction in the history of transactions. He had some money saved, but lacked access to it from Ethiopia ...

"You're hiding here," Maria said suddenly. Zero turned to her; she had her arms folded casually, non-defensively, staring Hannibal down coolly.

"Sorry?" the smuggler asked.

"You're hiding here," she repeated. "You're a wanted man. I'll tell you what I can give you. I can expunge your record from the CIA database."

Hannibal's eyes flickered wide. "You're CIA?" To Zero's left, the guard bristled, and the smuggler's gaze fell on the Desert Eagle on the table.

"Wait." Maria held up her hands to show she was unarmed and wasn't reaching for anything. "Yes. I'm Agent Johansson with the CIA. This is Agent Zero. We're working with Mitch as a specialist. We need to get into that port. If you can get us in there, I can wipe your record. You won't have to hide in a tent in a crammed marketplace anymore."

Hannibal seemed to be torn between grabbing his gun and taking the offer. At last his smile returned, and he waved the guard back with one hand. "Mitchell," he laughed. "What the hell have you gotten yourself into, working with the CIA?" To Maria he said, "I'll take that offer. Obviously a man like me operates on his word, and I expect my colleagues to do the same. What did you say that name was?"

"Agent Maria Johansson," she said clearly.

"Maria Johansson. Two s's, I assume?" Hannibal flipped open his ledger book and scribbled her name down. "Our verbal agreement dictates that if you screw me on this, I'm going to send men to hunt you down and kill you." He said it casually, almost jokingly, but in the moment Zero's most primal instinct was to leap over the table and strangle him for such a crass threat.

But he restrained himself. Instead he said a single word in Russian: "Wait."

Hannibal blinked at him. "Sorry, didn't catch that?"

Good. He doesn't speak Russian.

"You know you can't do that," Zero said quickly to Maria in Russian. "You don't have the authority, the access, or the skills. No offense."

"I don't," she countered in the foreign language. "But Penny does."

"Will she, though?" Maria was betting on her own life and putting everything down on a young woman they'd just met. "She took a risk on us. You think she'll do that for him?"

"Hey," Hannibal snapped, shaking a finger at them. "I don't like that. Makes me think you're having second thoughts."

"No second thoughts," Maria confirmed. "A deal's a deal."

Hannibal held out his hand over the table—his right hand, the one missing two fingers. Maria took it confidently and shook it.

The grin spread again across the smuggler's face, one that Zero was quickly recognizing as *shit-eating*. "All right, friends. Let's go to Hamar Port." He plucked up the Desert Eagle and slid it into a holster at his hip before rounding the table.

Before leaving the tent, Hannibal paused for a moment, looking Zero up and down as if seeing him for the first time. "Are you really Agent Zero?"

"Yeah. I am."

"Huh." The smuggler chuckled. "Thought you'd be taller."

Chapter Fourteen

Maya cursed herself for taking the Lincoln Tunnel into the city. Some event or concert had just finished at Madison Square Garden and traffic was brutal, even this late at night. She cursed and honked with the best of the New Yorkers, struggling to move the Skylark even a few feet at a time for more than an hour, all the while fully aware that she could have walked it faster than she was driving.

The fire-engine Buick got more than a few looks, stares, and wolf-whistles while she sat frustrated in traffic. At least she hoped it was the car.

It was after eleven p.m. by the time she reached the Upper East Side and her destination. She parked across the street from the address in the CIA file for Dr. Howard Bliss, a handsome three-story brownstone that Maya could only guess was valued north of three million. Out of all the street-facing windows there was only a single light on, and she couldn't tell if it was because the residents were home or because they'd left it on.

Now what? She supposed she could sleep in the car, wait for morning, or even follow the doctor when he left for his clinic. But she wasn't the least bit tired; quite the opposite, actually. She was wired, and she hadn't come all this way to just wait.

Before getting out of the Skylark she dug around in her rucksack for the Glock she'd taken from the kitchen back in Bethesda. It wasn't until it was in her hand that she realized how completely ridiculous she felt even holding it.

What am I going to do? Threaten a doctor at gunpoint? I won't need it.

Even so, she found herself ejecting the magazine and tucking both it and the gun into her purse. Then she got out, strode across the street, and before she could think twice about it, forced her thumb to press the doorbell.

She heard nothing. Was it working? Or was it inaudible from outside? Were the doctor and his family asleep in there? If they were, how might he react to such a rude awakening?

"Yes?" A curt male voice crackled to her right. She nearly jumped; she'd expected the door to open, but it seemed there was an intercom system worked into the brick that she hadn't noticed.

Get your head in the game, Lawson.

She pressed the white button on the panel. "Um... is this Dr. Bliss? Dr. Howard Bliss?"

"Who is asking?" the voice asked impatiently. "Are you a student?"

A student...? Oh. He can see me. She glanced upward—the small black dome of a security camera stared down on her. From inside, all the doctor saw was a young woman on his doorstep.

"No," she told the intercom. "Not a student. I'm..." She had to come up with something fast that would get him to the door. "My name is Mary. My father is a patient of yours. *Was* a patient of yours. I have a question, and I promise it will only take a moment of your time."

"Who? Which patient?"

"Please, sir." Maya put on her best pouting voice, though she realized it had been a while since she'd used it. "I'd rather not have this talk like this. It's something of an emergency. Just one minute." To lay it on thicker, she decided to try to appeal to his self-worth. "I was told you're the best neurosurgeon in the city. Maybe the whole state. Or am I mistaken?"

Bliss sighed audibly through the intercom. "Just... give me a moment."

Bingo. Maya quickly rubbed two knuckles in her eyes to make them appear tearful and red. For good measure she unzipped her purse as well, just in case she needed to reach into it quickly.

But you won't. You won't need to.

A moment later a deadbolt clicked and the door was pulled open hastily. Maya was a bit taken aback by the man on the other side; he was older than she imagined, easily into his sixties, thoroughly gray, wearing honest-to-goodness silk pajamas and a red robe with lapels, as if he had some sort of Hugh Hefner aspirations.

"Young lady," he said through his teeth, "this is very unusual and I was just about to go to bed. You have precisely one minute to tell me why you've bothered me at this hour."

"I need to know about a former patient of yours," she said quickly. "A man named Connor."

"Connor? Connor what?"

"I... I don't know," Maya admitted.

Dr. Bliss narrowed his eyes at her. "You said this was about your father, yet you don't know his last name? What's *your* last name?"

"He's not my father. But please, you must know something about what happened—"

"There is a thing known as physician-patient confidentiality," he spat. "Even if I knew who you were talking about, I wouldn't be able to tell you anything. And since you cannot even tell me who you are, I have absolutely no obligation to share anything with you. Please leave!"

With that, the doctor slammed the door in her face—or tried to. As he pushed it shut, Maya stepped forward quickly and wedged a shoe in the frame just in time for the door to close on her foot.

"Wait!" she demanded.

Dr. Bliss scoffed at her in shock. "That's it." He reached into a pocket of his red velvet robe and pulled out a cell phone. "I'm calling the police."

Maya wasn't sure what came over her. The sight of the phone, his dismissal of her, the hours she spent getting here and in frustratingly slow traffic, it all seemed to congeal into anger in her chest.

With the palm of one hand she shoved the door open roughly, sending the doctor stumbling back a step. She swung out her right hand, swatting at the phone. It clattered several feet away onto a carpet.

Her left hand plunged into the purse hanging from her shoulder, fingers wrapping around the grip of the Glock. As she kicked the door closed again behind her, the gun came out. It made her physically nauseous to point it at an innocent man, even if she knew it wasn't loaded.

You don't know that he's innocent, she reminded herself.

The doctor stared at her in horror. "What is this?" he said hoarsely. "A robbery?"

"No. I just want information. I don't want to shoot you."

"Then don't!" the doctor pleaded. "My wife... she's upstairs. Asleep. Please don't hurt her. Or me."

"I just want information," Maya reminded him. "And I think you're going to be honest with me, right?"

Bliss nodded fervently.

"Okay. For starters, are there cameras in here?"

He shook his head. "No. None here. Only on the stoop, and at the back door. None inside. We value our privacy."

"Good." Maya glanced around. They were in a high-ceilinged foyer, a chandelier over their heads and a set of stairs going up to the second level. To her right was an office; to her left was some kind of parlor or sitting room. "Let's go talk in there."

Dr. Bliss stepped backward, not taking his eyes off of Maya or the gun as he retreated into the parlor.

"Take a seat in that armchair," she instructed. He did so. "Thank you. Now I'm going to ask you some questions. Please be honest."

"Yes." Dr. Bliss nodded again. "I will."

"Okay." She took a deep breath. "Nearly five years ago—four years and ten months, to be exact—you were paid a sum of one hundred sixty thousand dollars from a consulting firm. You and I both know that the firm was a front for a government agency slush fund—"

"No," Bliss refuted. "No, no. That money was for my expertise! It was for textbooks. A series of medical textbooks that I helped compile and edit."

"Textbooks," Maya repeated flatly. She recalled how often during her childhood her own father, whose CIA cover had been a career as an adjunct history professor at the time, would go away for "conferences" and "research." He too had claimed to contribute to textbooks. It seemed a popular cover story for academic assets to the agency. "That's a lie and we both know it. What did I say about honesty, Doctor?"

Maya pressed the barrel of the Glock to his knee. Bliss sucked in a breath as his eyes clenched closed and every muscle in him stiffened. Of course the gun wasn't loaded—

But I never took the round out of the chamber.

She quickly pulled the pistol away, another wave of nausea pounding at her gut. She had control here, over the situation and over herself, but just the thought of putting a loaded gun against flesh without the intent to pull the trigger was too much for her.

She remembered something her dad once told her, when he had taught her to handle a gun. *You don't ever point it at someone if you don't mean to use it.*

"I'm sorry," she said quietly. "I don't want to hurt you. But I do want the truth. That money was not for textbooks or expertise or research. It was from the CIA, in exchange for something you did for them."

The doctor's chest was heaving now. He gulped. "Who sent you? How do you know all this?"

"No one sent me. No one else knows about this." Maya thought it best to try to ease the doctor's mind if she was going to get real answers out of him, even if it meant lying about the nature of her mission. "Beyond me, you have nothing to fear. It took me this long just to get to you, and I intend to see this through. You did something for them, and I believe it involved a man named Connor."

Dr. Bliss hung his head until his chin nearly touched his chest and he sighed resignedly, the way people often did when cornered in a lie. "Not Connor," he corrected her. "Connors. Agent Seth Connors."

"What did you do to him, Dr. Bliss?"

The doctor shook his head. "If you're on this crusade, then you already know, don't you?"

Nope, not a clue. But she couldn't very well tell him that. "I'd rather hear it from you than give you the opportunity to just agree with whatever I say. Walk me through it."

Bliss rubbed his forehead. "All right. But you must know, I never intended the outcome. If I'd known, I never would have agreed."

Maya bit back the quizzical frown and merely nodded once. "From the beginning."

"There was a chip." The doctor folded his hands in his lap, suddenly looking more like a vulnerable schoolchild than a respected medical professional. "A microchip, developed by the CIA. They contracted me because I was the best with some fairly new robotic surgery techniques at the time. I accepted it because...well, frankly, because I thought the very concept was a fiction and needed to see for myself."

"What was fiction about it?" Maya prodded.

"Memory control," Bliss said quietly. "Or, more accurately, memory suppression."

This time Maya couldn't help her expression of surprise. Of course she'd heard the urban myths that the US government had been experimenting with mind control and memory, but of every possibility that she might have imagined, that wasn't among them.

"The chip was supposed to only suppress certain memories," Bliss continued. "You see, Agent Connors was a volunteer. He'd lost a child, a daughter I believe, in a car accident."

"And he wanted to forget her?" Maya asked, appalled.

"I don't pretend to know that kind of pain," said Bliss, "and I can only assume you wouldn't either."

"So what happened?"

"I performed the procedure," Bliss told her simply. "I was aided by a nurse and a CIA engineer, one of the chip's inventors. It was relatively simple, actually. But when Connors awoke...well, you must understand that the chip was a prototype, the first of its kind. There were bound to be certain setbacks—"

"What sort of setbacks?" she demanded.

Bliss hung his head again. "Connors's entire memory was erased."

Maya could only stare. She had a thousand questions—chief among them being why her dad was after this former agent at all when he clearly seemed to have been a victim—but couldn't seem to form any of them.

"He still had perfect physical function," Bliss noted. "No loss in motor skills or even language. He knew how to load a gun flawlessly, how to cook a meal, how to drive a car. But he could not recall anything about who he was. Not even his own name. Everything that made him *him* was simply gone."

"That's monstrous," Maya said quietly. She was right; this man was not innocent at all, and suddenly the thought of holding a loaded gun to his knee was not as unappealing as it had been a minute earlier. "Was it permanent?"

"...In a way," Bliss said carefully. "After the failure, the agency wanted us to remove the chip to see if Connors would recover his memory. However, I argued that doing so could result in *more* damage, like physical impediments or further mental impairment. The engineer on the project agreed with me."

"So you left it in his head." Maya scoffed. She wasn't sure what was worse: putting it in there in the first place or the refusal to remove it. "What then? Did they kill him?"

Bliss shook his head. "Of course not. In order to improve the next prototype, they needed to monitor him for any changes, for better or for worse. Despite the chip not working in the intended way, its stability was still important to the endeavor."

Maya shook her head. "They kept him alive with no memory of who he is. No idea who his family and loved ones are. Everything he knew was gone, but they had to *monitor* him?"

"Young lady," Dr. Bliss said with some small force behind it. "Mary, was it? You're beginning to sound like he would have been better off with a bullet in his head instead of the chip."

Maybe she was. But that wasn't the goal right now. "So he's still alive. Where?"

"You're asking me? I have no idea where they put him."

Yet even as he said it, Maya noticed that his gaze faltered. His pupils dilated slightly, flickering to the left as they did.

"You're lying." The doctor knew where Agent Connors had been stowed away by the CIA, she was sure of it. "You accepted a six-figure payment to cripple a man's memory and take his entire life away from him. You'd have to be a sociopath to just walk away from that. You don't strike me as one."

"I can't," Bliss murmured. "I can't tell you. They'll kill me."

"And what, do you think this is a toy?" Maya threatened, waving the Glock in his face.

"You won't shoot me." Even as he said it he didn't sound entirely confident. "You need the information I have. And if you tried to wound me, my wife and neighbors would hear the shot and call the police."

Dammit. Of course Maya had no intention of shooting anyone, but now he'd gone and called her bluff. Her mind raced; all she needed was one more piece of the puzzle and she could get out of there. "This will all be far easier for everyone if you just tell me—"

"Howard?"

Maya and Bliss both turned their heads at the sound of a female voice calling down the stairs.

"Howard, are you down there? I heard voices. Is someone here?"

Maya nodded curtly to him and whispered, "Answer her. Make it good."

He cleared his throat. "Um... yes, Sharon. I'm down here. A student came by with a... an important question."

"At this hour?" Her footfalls were on the stairs.

Bliss's eyes widened in terror. "Please. Don't hurt her."

"Then tell me what I want to know." Maya lifted the Glock, aiming it through the open doorway of the parlor, at the empty space where Sharon Bliss would be any moment.

"Please!" Bliss whispered hoarsely.

"Tell me, or I put a bullet in her." Maya clenched her jaw. She had no intention of shooting the woman, but she had to make it look good.

"Fine! Fine. I'll write it down. Don't hurt her."

Maya shoved the gun back into her open purse. In almost the same instance, a woman stepped into her view from the parlor. Mrs. Bliss had high cheekbones and discerning narrow eyes.

"Oh, hello!" Maya said cheerfully. "So sorry to disturb you so late. I had an important question for Dr. Bliss, and I happened to be in the neighborhood." Before Sharon could ask anything further, Maya turned to the doctor. "Thanks again, I really appreciate the help. Can you write that prognosis down for me so I don't forget?" She reached into her purse for a pen and a scrap of paper, finding a stray pharmacy receipt.

"Uh... yes," he said breathlessly, seemingly still reeling. "Yes. Of course. Just one moment, Sharon, and then we can go back upstairs." He walked with Maya to the foyer. "What assurance do I have that you're being honest? That you're the only one that knows?" he whispered.

"None but my word," Maya told him honestly. She handed him the pen.

He scribbled down the address. "I don't ever want to see you again."

"The feeling is mutual." She took the pen and the receipt from him, and read the barely legible doctor scratch on the back.

John Graham. 501 Willow Street, Columbus OH

"He doesn't go by the same name anymore," Bliss pointed out. "Obviously. And I can't guarantee he's still there."

Ohio. The man was in Ohio, easily a nine-hour drive if she didn't stop at all. Suddenly she felt a lot more tired than she'd been when she arrived.

"For what it's worth," the doctor said quietly, "I do regret it. Deeply. Not a day goes by that I don't think about him."

Maya wanted to tell him that his sentiment was empty and meaningless to her, because Seth Connors, or John Graham, or whatever name he went by, didn't have the privilege of remembering anyone daily, for better or worse, thanks to Dr. Bliss. But she didn't say anything in reply. Instead she left wordlessly, heading back out into the frigid night and across the street to the Skylark. She let the engine warm up for a few minutes; the visit hadn't taken long, but it was still bitter cold out.

She felt exhausted. There was no way she was going to be able to drive to Columbus in one shot. *At least get out of the city*, she told herself. *Find a cheap motel, catch a few hours of sleep, and finish the drive tomorrow.*

She had to see this through. She had no idea what she would say to a man that wouldn't remember who he was—but he might be able to tell her what her dad might want with him.

CHAPTER FIFTEEN

Zero was uncomfortable.

The single engine of Hannibal's 1998 Cessna 206 was remarkably loud, so much so that even in the close quarters of the six-seat cabin they had to either shout to each other or remain silent, largely choosing the latter for the duration of the flight. Fortunately the distance from the airstrip in Addis Ababa to their seaside destination in Mogadishu was only about twelve hundred kilometers, or roughly seven hundred fifty miles, so takeoff to wheels-down would be just a little over two hours.

Assuming we get there in one piece. The plane dipped precipitously, causing Zero's stomach to lurch, and the wings wobbled a bit before evening out again. From the pilot's seat ahead of them, Hannibal flashed a thumbs-up to indicate no worries.

Zero would have preferred to have Alan flying; he'd even volunteered to do so, which Hannibal had swiftly denied with a curt reply of "My plane, I fly." He would have definitely preferred the Gulfstream and the practiced hands of Chip Foxworth, but they all understood without it needing to be said that landing in Mogadishu with a luxury jet that was usually reserved for royalty and high-tier celebrities was the absolute definition of "conspicuous."

And so he sat, strapped in with a seatbelt that he knew would do very little in the event of a crash, and hoped that the end of Agent Zero would not be at the hands of a smuggler who clearly did not have a pilot's license.

He reviewed their plan in his head to distract himself. It was simple enough; Hannibal would get them into the port under the guise of his crew, claiming that he needed a boat to pull off an important arms deal. Something small, light, and fast. With a little luck, that would get them close enough to the water to get a visual if the stolen boat and railgun were there. They had all studied the schematic en route to Addis Ababa and had a pretty good idea of what it looked like. Any visual confirmations would get discreetly tagged with a magnetic tracking device, supplied by Penny, and the information would then be supplied to the battle-ships from Diego Garcia to chase them down.

Meanwhile, Hannibal would fish for leads by mentioning hearsay about the South Korean heist and see if he got any bites. If at any point the Somalis caught on or their cover was blown, Reidigger would cause a distraction with a couple of flash-bangs.

Easy, Zero thought. Then he laughed at himself. *But you say that before every op right before things go sideways, don't you?*

The satellite phone vibrated against his thigh. Maria, seated alongside him, frowned as he pulled it out of his pocket. The number was, of course, blocked but he knew who it would be.

"Zero," he shouted into the phone, pushing it hard against his head and plugging his other ear with a finger.

The voice on the other end was still muffled.

"You have to speak up!" he told her. "I'm on a very loud and questionably stable plane!"

"...hear me now?" Penny's British-accented voice had to shout back.

"Yes! I can hear you. What do you have for us?"

"Nothing good, I'm afraid. I've just been alerted that a Gulfstream G650 was impounded at Bole Airport in Addis Ababa. I dug deeper... it seems your friend Foxworth is being detained at the US embassy there."

Dammit! Not only had they lost their pilot, but they'd lost their jet and the rest of the supplies in it that they hadn't been able to carry. They'd taken everything that seemed necessary and then some, but there were some toys in that black footlocker that Zero would rather have and not need than need and not have.

"Shaw?" he asked, wondering if the CIA director ordered the arrest of the pilot.

"Presumably, but not confirmed," Penny told him. "Will Foxworth talk?"

"I hope so." If Chip was at all savvy, he'd claim Zero and his team forced him to fly to Ethiopia, threatened him. Admitting that he flew them willingly and defied not only CIA orders but US government regulations would get him blacklisted at least, imprisoned at worst.

"I'm not sure it will matter," Penny admitted. "Shaw is certainly aware that you didn't go to Korea, yet there hasn't been a whisper of disavowing anyone. He's waiting for you to cock up."

"With my track record, I'm sure he won't be waiting too long," Zero mused. "Wouldn't want to disappoint him."

"This is serious, Zero. I know you have a reputation for breaking rules and getting away with it because you get results. But Shaw isn't like your other bosses. He's not going to send someone to try to put a bullet in you and write it off as KIA. He'll build a case, one that's meticulous and tight enough that even the president would look bad trying to revoke it. If he wants you gone he'll do it publicly, by ruining your reputation in whatever way he can. Don't give him any fuel for that fire."

"Says the girl who gave me big guns," he muttered.

"What was that? I didn't catch it."

"I said, we're going to be landing soon. I have to go. Don't worry about me, Penny. Just keep your eyes and ears open and let us know anything we can't find out for ourselves." He ended the call. It was kind of her to worry for him and he was growing more trusting of her with each phone call. But she was new to this. Shaw couldn't touch him and the director knew it. This was petty backlash from a frustrated bureaucrat because the system he'd helped build was now failing him. But Zero would not. With Maria and Alan at his side, he was going to find this weapon and the perpetrators.

For some reason, Maria's words from earlier rang through his head, back when they'd first read Walsh's operation report.

They've got drones, Navy ships, satellites, the works looking for this thing.

Then screw it, Alan had said. *Consider it a mini-vacation. Let the Navy find it.*

Zero couldn't do that. He had to find it now. From the moment they'd taken off from the runway at Dulles, he'd committed himself to it. Even before that, when they'd accepted Penny's furtive help. But why? Why did he feel so devoted, so bound to accomplish a mission that had seemingly been engineered for his failure and possible undoing?

To prove a point, he realized grimly. *To prove I can, and to prove that men like Shaw don't hold all the power.*

He didn't quite like that acknowledgment. It was easy to flip it, easier to call it something noble in the name of country and his fellow man. But the truth was that his own head-strong attitude, the same one he'd passed on to his daughters, had one hand on the wheel.

He didn't like admitting that, and he didn't like the roaring Cessna engine that forced him to stay quiet and stew in his own thoughts. He'd rather walk straight into a pirate port—which was convenient, since that was exactly what they were about to do.

Mercifully, Hannibal set the small Cessna down in one piece and without incident, though the wheels did bounce twice on the tarmac before settling. The four of them piled into a waiting orange Jeep with no roof or doors, supplied by some associate of the smuggler's, and set off for Hamar Port, four miles to the southeast.

"Remember the plan," Maria warned Hannibal from the passenger seat alongside him, her blonde hair whipping about in the open air. "You need a recap?"

"Not at all." The smuggler waved dismissively. "Easy as pie." He laughed. "I've always found that an amusing saying. My pies are terrible."

From the backseat, next to Alan, Zero watched Mogadishu go by. The city's downtown was in the distance to the west, with all the crime and violence that came with it. At least that might have felt familiar. Here, near the Indian Ocean, was a bizarre dichotomy that Zero was struggling to reconcile. On one hand, there were palm trees, white sand beaches, and crystal-blue water that could rival any tropical resort destination. There were also crumbling, dilapidated structures, rampant homelessness, trash littered nearly everywhere, and more than one shell of a burnt-out car that they passed in the short drive from the airstrip to the port.

Hannibal seemed completely unaffected by it, driving casually with one palm on the steering wheel while fishing a pair of aviator sunglasses from his shirt pocket. "Now listen up," he said loudly. "Couple of things going into this. First, no one is going to be happy to see you, even if you are with me. Hell, I don't exactly get warm greetings myself. This is business and that's it. I know you lot might find me charming and affable, but it doesn't get far with them.

"Second, don't do anything stupid or reckless. These guys love their guns. They love waving 'em around. They might even stick one in your face. But trust me on this: they don't shit where they eat. They're not going to shoot you in port, but they do like to look tough. With your training I'm betting instinct is to whip out your own, but try to resist so we don't all get dragged onto a boat and tossed to the sharks."

Zero frowned at Alan, not only because he didn't like the sound of that but also because Hannibal was right; his kneejerk reaction to staring down the barrel of a gun was to disarm and retaliate.

Maria glanced back at them over her shoulder as if reading his mind. "Guns in your bags," she ordered. "I don't like it much either, but we're not here to incite an incident. We're observing and reporting."

Zero unclipped the holster from his hip and slid it into the bag. The Ruger LC9 was strapped to his ankle; for a moment he considered leaving it there, but that would only be a chance to invite disaster. Into the black backpack it went too.

Hannibal slowed the Jeep and turned left, heading through a break in a chain-link fence that had so many sagging sections and holes cut in it that it was hardly worth standing at all. He eased the Jeep to a stop and parked right on the port.

Zero climbed out and took a quick look around. Hamar Port, at a glance, seemed fairly innocuous. The concrete ran right up to the edge of the ocean and spanned the coast for at least half a mile down its length, thick rusty eye bolts affixed into its surface to moor the boats that parked there. Small mountains of freight littered the dock, from enormous boxcar-sized cargo containers to stacks of wooden crates, to pallets piled high with miscellanea, wrapped and tied with coarse rope. Dark-skinned men worked to load or unload the boats that were docked there, parallel to the concrete abutment, some not even tied to anything but secured by a man with one foot in the boat and the other on land.

If it wasn't for the guns this might have even looked commercial. But they were glaring in their incongruity, tucked into pants, dangling from straps, or even cradled in arms.

"Hello!" Hannibal called out, waving his three-fingered right hand to two approaching Somalis. One was clearly older, perhaps around Zero's age (difficult to tell, considering the very different lives they'd each led), missing his left arm from the elbow down and carrying a machine pistol in the other.

The second Somali was stunningly young. He couldn't have been a day over sixteen. Sara's age. And he held an AK-47 tightly in his hands.

"I'll talk to them," Hannibal muttered as the two men approached. "Start looking for your missing boat. But don't wander too far from me, it'll look suspect."

The pair of pirates (Zero assumed they were pirates, since they were armed and in a pirate port) said something to Hannibal in their native Somali, something that sounded harsh and unwelcoming. Hannibal responded in kind, almost flawlessly, holding his hands palm out as a sign of no ill intent. Whatever they were saying, it seemed the two men did not like the look of Hannibal's crew.

"We need to do this quickly," Zero said. He hadn't been this nervous in a while. Something was telling him to get the hell out of there, fast. "See anything?"

"Nope," Alan conceded, his trucker's cap keeping the sun out of his eyes. "Small skiffs, a repurposed tugboat, couple of fishing boats ..."

"Same," Maria said flatly. "Would be great if we could use a pair of binoculars right now without sending these guys into high alert."

Zero scoffed. He didn't want to believe this had been a waste of time, but it was clear right before his eyes. This port was wide open and right on the water; there was nowhere to hide a stolen ship. There was nowhere for a boat to go but out to sea. There was no ...

Wait a second.

"Alan," he asked quietly. "Have you ever *been* to Hamar Port?"

Reidigger shook his head. "Can't say that I have...oh." Alan realized the same thing Zero had just been thinking. The CIA's intelligence had traced the pirate vessel back to Hamar Port, but the agency would have damn well known if this was what it looked like. A satellite image would have told them in mere moments that the stolen Korean ship wasn't here, and if that was the case, there would be no reason for the battleships dispatched from Diego Garcia to head here.

"This isn't Hamar Port," Zero told his teammates. They'd been duped.

"My friends!" Hannibal called out as he made his way over to them. "Bad news. My contacts haven't heard a peep about any South Korean ship, stolen or otherwise."

Zero was barely listening. In his periphery he saw the two Somalis edging closer, grips tight around their weapons. There were others approaching from the sides, a half dozen in all, maybe more behind them. Closing in.

"You speak Somali," Zero said to the smuggler.

Hannibal nodded. "Arabic too."

"And Russian?"

The smuggler flashed him a smile. "Afraid so, Agent."

He'd heard. Back in the Addis Merkato, Hannibal had known exactly what Zero had said to Maria in Russian. He'd heard and understood their exchange, Zero reminding her that she didn't have the authority to expunge Hannibal's record and Maria's noncommittal response to try to get Penny to do it.

"What now?" Alan adjusted the strap on his backpack. The smuggler flinched. None of them could go for their guns, secured in their bags. They'd be shredded by bullets in an instant. Hannibal had cleverly gotten them to stow their weapons, close as could be but woefully out of reach. "You going to kill us?"

"Kill you? Goodness no." Hannibal laughed. "No, these gentlemen are paying me for you. I've told them who you are and where you came from. Not sure if you know this, but Somali pirates make most of their money from ransoming hostages."

CHAPTER SIXTEEN

"Let's get those hands up," Hannibal instructed.

Zero did so, putting his hands at about shoulder height while slowly scanning in a semicircle. Eight Somalis in total were surrounding them, every one of them armed with at least a semiautomatic weapon if not one that would pump a dozen bullets into him in half a second.

"Hannibal," Zero said in Russian, "you know these men will never get their money. The CIA will disavow us. No one will pay a ransom." The unspoken part of that was their inevitable death and watery grave in the Indian Ocean when the Somalis grew tired of waiting.

"Huh." The smuggler stroked his bushy chin. "I suppose you're right. But see, Agent Zero, I get paid either way."

The nearest Somali to him, the young one that Zero had ascertained was little more than a teenager, punched the air with the barrel of his AK-47 and barked an order in his native language. "Go!" he shouted in English. "There!"

All three of them glanced over their shoulder as two of the pirates pulled open the doors to a steel cargo container, empty and black as night inside.

"If we go in there, we're never coming back out," Maria muttered. "Got any ideas?"

"One or two," Alan grunted. "But they probably won't end up well for us."

Zero glanced around desperately, his brain churning for an answer. There were too many guns on them ... but one notably missing. Hannibal had his sidearm, the Desert Eagle, strapped to his hip. But he hadn't drawn it. Did he think it wasn't necessary, with the Somalis closing in?

Or was part of what he told us actually true?

"Zero...?" Maria said nervously as they edged backward in small steps toward the container.

"Give me a sec!" If Hannibal was trying to avoid this from becoming a bigger incident than it needed to be, then maybe there was some truth to his statement. He racked his brain for what he knew about Somali piracy. In 2007, they'd killed a Chinese sailor when ransom was denied. It had made international news, because such events were rare. In fact, in most of the hijackings he'd heard of, the pirates had tried very hard *not* to kill anyone—because they were valuable. In 2009, a British couple, the Chandlers, was held by pirates for three hundred eighty-eight days, released when the seven-figure ransom was finally paid.

They don't want to kill us. It was still an enormous gamble, and he still had no idea if the jacket he'd taken from the footlocker was graphene-infused or not. Worse still was that while he and Maria had opted for one, Reidigger was without any potential additional protection.

"Their bags!" Hannibal shouted as they neared the dark maw of the cargo container. "Take their bags!"

A Somali edged closer, the barrel of his gun directed at Zero's center mass.

The bags…

Zero slung it down from his shoulders, holding it in both hands as if he was going to hand it over. "Graphene?" he hissed to Maria through clenched teeth.

"Not sure. Worth a try…"

"Alan, with me," he told them. "Split off."

"When?"

The Somali reached for the black bag.

"Now!" Zero surged to the right, toward the water, holding the backpack at face level and roughly shoving the Somali aside. Alan darted along with him, and Maria broke off in the opposite direction.

A chorus of angry voices rose, shouts filling the air, the backpack blocking his view of what he was sure was a small army of furious Somalis charging them.

But no gunshots rang out.

"Hey!" Hannibal roared. "Shoot them!"

Zero sprinted along the dock, Reidigger keeping a surprising equal pace despite his size, and scooted into a homerun-slide behind a stack of wooden crates. Alan collapsed beside him.

"They have guns!" the smuggler shouted, and then again in Somali. The warning seemed to give the pirates enough pause to not outright pursue them around their cover.

"That might have bought us ten seconds," Alan panted.

"Good. Give me some cover—" Zero winced as a thunderous gunshot split the air and half a crate exploded a few feet from his head.

He hazarded a quick glance through the hole it had made. Hannibal had his Desert Eagle out, aimed, ready to squeeze another shot, when three Somalis grabbed his arms roughly, spitting foreign curses that could only be sharp rebukes.

"Get off a me!" he hissed at them, but two more joined to take the large New Zealander to the ground. "Get off!"

"They don't want to shoot us," Zero said breathlessly, "because we're worth money." He tore open the backpack, intent to assemble the Beretta PMX, when a rip of automatic gunfire erupted, peppering the crates but not penetrating.

"They don't want to *kill* us," Alan corrected. "I'm not sure maiming is out of the question."

"Fair point." There wasn't time to assemble the machine gun. Instead his hand closed around something else in the bag—a smooth, thin canister. A flash-bang. Either of the pistols in his bag would be of no use against so many automatic guns, but the stun grenade would.

"Zero!" Alan pointed. About twenty yards away, near the edge of the concrete dock, was a large steel drum, painted blue and rusting at the lip. He understood immediately; if it was filled with oil, or fuel, it could be a useful distraction. But if it was empty...

Screw it. They'd already gambled with their lives, might as well go all-in. "Flash-bang out!" He yanked the pin and tossed the canister in a high arc over his shoulder, past their wooden crate barricade.

Then he covered his ears with his arms and squeezed his eyes shut.

Even with his head covered, the one-hundred-seventy-decibel blast rattled his bones. The stun grenade wasn't intended to kill or even grievously injure, but the enormity of the blast and the flash of brilliant light that accompanied it would blind and disable anyone within ten to fifteen yards for up to a full minute.

Zero dared to peer around the crates. The pursuing Somalis were scattered in the thin white fog of smoke, most on the concrete, a few attempting to stagger to their feet but falling onto hands and knees. The form of Hannibal was unmistakable among them, lying flat on his back and unmoving. Zero wondered—and even hoped, at least a little—that the flash-bang had landed right at the smuggler's feet.

"Let's go!" He and Alan tore off toward the large blue drum. But as they did, the high-pitched whine of a motor alerted them to a new pending threat as a narrow skiff roared toward the dock. The boat barely slowed as it pitched sideways, coming parallel to the dock so that the small crew, who had undoubtedly seen the flash-bang go off, leaped onto the concrete.

Alan wasted no time. He grabbed his pack in both hands by the shoulder straps and swung it upward, connecting right beneath the chin of the fastest pirate and sending the man off his feet, smacking into the dock with a force that sent all air from his lungs. As another pirate drew in, Reidigger feinted with the bag and threw a solid jab across the man's jaw.

With Alan indisposed, Zero got low into a tackling stance and put a shoulder into the drum. It didn't budge; it was definitely full of something, hopefully combustible, but at fifty-five gallons it weighed in at somewhere around four hundred and fifty pounds.

"Any time now!" Alan bellowed as he grappled with a Somali wielding a chipped machete. Some of the lot they'd disabled with the flash-bang were getting back to their feet, staggering but coming around. They had seconds.

Zero put both hands on the rusty lip of the barrel and pushed with all his might. His boots gripped the concrete, giving him traction as he gritted his teeth and leaned in with all his weight. The bottom edge of the drum slowly lifted, the contents inside tipping away from him, helping his efforts. With one final grunt, he pushed the barrel over onto its side. The rusting lid bounced away and the acrid scent of diesel fuel filled his nostrils as a wide pool spread rapidly over the dock.

Behind him, Reidigger caught the pirate's wrists as he chopped downward with the machete, twisting the blade out of the man's grip and eliciting a sharp scream of pain as bones snapped. He shoved the pirate away and dug into a pocket.

"Zero! Here!"

An object sailed in an arc toward him and he caught it deftly.

But when he looked down at it, he had no idea what he was looking at.

The object was palm-sized, rectangular, made of shining metal. But it had no buttons, no levers, no pins or triggers to pull. He was fairly certain he'd seen one before, but could not for the life of him determine what exactly it was or what he was supposed to do with it.

Oh no. The realization hit him worse than the pounding blast of a flash-bang. His memory was failing him. He'd forgotten whatever this thing was.

"Zero!" Alan was beside him then, Glock 19 in his hand. He dropped to one knee and emptied his entire magazine, fifteen rounds, in the general direction of oncoming Somalis that Zero had barely registered in his confusion. "Give it!"

Alan yanked the device back from him and flicked it open. The top half of it was on a hinge, Zero noted, cleverly hiding wheel and a fuse. Alan flicked the wheel, and a small flame leapt up; it was a wick, not a fuse.

A lighter, Zero suddenly recalled dully. The device was a Zippo lighter.

Alan flicked it, sending the Zippo and its flame tumbling toward the spilled fuel as he grabbed Zero by the scruff of the jacket and pulled him away. The heat was instant and intense as the fuel caught fire, spreading as quickly as the liquid itself had, flames dancing outward in every direction at once as they put as much distance as they could between them and the blazing fuel.

And then the wooden crates caught.

Zero had erroneously believed that the Somalis tackled Hannibal for firing at their would-be ransoms. But as the crates exploded, sending an enormous fireball skyward, and the shockwave of the blast sent Zero off his feet and down hard on the concrete, he realized that it wasn't about them. It was about the explosives inside the crates.

Zero gasped for air as he got to his knees, and then ducked again instinctively as another explosion blossomed behind him—a boat, the motor of which had caught and blew—and then a third, smaller blast from the skiff behind it.

Greasy black smoke poured into the air from several sources as cargo caught fire and burned. Zero was only vaguely aware of the shouting voices, no longer sounding angry and pursuing but desperate and entreating as Somalis rushed to try to extinguish the flames burning their boats and collected bounties.

"Come on," Alan grunted suddenly, grabbing Zero by the elbow and hefting him to his feet. Together they stayed low, dashing from cover to cover, using the smoke and littered dock as cover to reach the chain-link fence line. "You hurt?"

Zero didn't feel hurt, but adrenaline was still surging through him in the wake of the fireball. But his forehead felt wet; he touched it with two fingers that came back stained with blood. It was a superficial cut, no pain but bleeding copiously. "I'm fine. You?"

"Not hurt," Alan replied as he fished his Glock out of the bag. "But curious." He gave Zero a stern look that suggested they'd be talking about the Zippo incident once they didn't have more pressing matters at hand.

Together they stole along the fence, pistols out and ready, but unnecessary it seemed. The Somalis were busy trying to salvage what they could from the fire and explosions. Zero marveled at just how much damage it had done; it seemed like nearly half of this port had been destroyed, the fire still spreading, and he doubted that if there were any emergency services even available nearby that they'd be rushing to help the pirates.

After about two tense minutes that felt much longer, they reached the orange Jeep that had brought them to the port—as well as the man who had driven it. Hannibal's face was streaked with soot and he bled from both ears, as well as a cut over one eye as he slid into the driver's seat.

He didn't even hear them coming.

"Out," Alan grunted as he pressed the barrel of the Glock to the smuggler's temple.

"Now hang on…" Hannibal started, before Alan grabbed him by the arm and yanked him from the door-less Jeep. The smuggler sprawled to the ground hard, his left hand immediately reaching for the empty holster at his hip before he seemed to remember that he'd lost his Desert Eagle. He grinned sheepishly and held his hands palm out. "You wouldn't kill an old friend, now would you?"

Reidigger clenched his jaw as he glanced up at Zero, indicating the choice. The smuggler deserved it for what he tried to do to them—but Zero wasn't about to execute an unarmed man. He shook his head no.

So instead, Alan shot Hannibal once through the calf.

The smuggler yelped, both hands flying to the wound as blood ran between his fingers. "Son of a bitch!" he cried. "Oh, I think that hit bone."

Alan climbed into the driver's seat as Zero rounded to the other side. "Wait, what about Maria?"

"You really think she stuck around here?"

"I don't know, but we can't just leave her—"

"Look," Reidigger said harshly. "If we stick around here they're either going to come looking for us or others are going to show up. I doubt a place like this has any shortage of opportunists who would take advantage of the fire. In a situation like this, what would Maria do? What would you have done if you were her?"

"I would…" Zero sighed. "I would get clear. Shake anyone following. Find a safe place to lay low, and then make contact."

"Exactly. So that's what we're going to do right now." The Jeep's keys were already in the ignition. Alan gave them a twist and the engine rumbled to life. Behind the noise, Zero heard the shouts of Somalis; a quick glance down the dock showed that the fire was petering out somewhat, and the pirates had noticed their hostages' absence.

"You're not really going to just leave me here, are you?" Hannibal moaned, holding his shot leg. "They'll kill me!"

"Maybe not," Zero told him. "You know anyone that would pay your ransom?"

Alan slammed the gas and the Jeep lurched through the fence, away from the port and out into Mogadishu, to find some place to lie low until they could find out what had happened to Maria.

CHAPTER SEVENTEEN

"Graphene?" Zero hissed quietly to them as the Somalis attempted to corner the three of them into an empty cargo container.

Maria realized what he was asking; if the black backpacks that Penny had supplied them might be able to withstand a bullet if the shooting started. "Not sure," she replied. "Worth a try..." She let the strap of it fall slack off her shoulder as if she was going to relinquish it to the approaching pirate.

"Alan, with me. Split off," Zero whispered.

Maria did not like the idea of splitting up, especially not in a foreign city that none of them knew how to navigate, but she knew what he was trying to do—or at least she thought she did. He and Alan would make a break toward the water and in Agent Zero fashion, cause some sort of massive distraction while she slipped away to find somewhere safe for them to reconvene.

"When?"

"Now!" Zero and Alan split to the right, as she'd assumed they would. Maria darted the other way, slinging the backpack up in front of her face and bracing for a hail of bullets.

But none came. Instead she heard the furious shouts of pursuing pirates as she ducked around the side of the boxcar-sized container and sprinted its length. They were chasing, not shooting—and she supposed that if she'd had a moment to think about it, it made sense. No one paid ransom on a corpse.

No one pays ransom on disavowed CIA agents either, she mused as she ducked around the rear corner of the container and skidded to a stop. She slung the backpack over her shoulder and held her breath until the barrel of an AK-47 came into view. No one had taught pirates to clear corners; Maria ducked low, beneath the barrel, as she stepped out from behind her cover and sprang up again, right in the pirate's face. As she did she wrenched the rifle from his hands, inadvertently smacking the man under the chin with it as she did.

Holding the dazed pirate up in front of her like a shield, she propped the AK on his shoulder and aimed at his two compatriots who followed. They both froze in their tracks; they wouldn't shoot their own in the back any sooner than they would risk hitting her, their bounty.

Maria shoved her pirate captive backward and he fell limply into the other two in a tangle of limbs. She sprinted off again, still clutching the AK, and dove behind the relative safety of a pallet stacked higher than she was tall with what looked like aluminum ammo boxes. In any other situation, the irony of hiding from gunfire behind a supply of unspent bullets might have been laughable, but here it only served as a reminder. She popped the magazine from the AK—and then she laughed, though it was bitterly.

The rifle wasn't even loaded.

Suddenly a single booming shot rang out from elsewhere on the dock. Not an automatic weapon; if she had to guess, it was Hannibal's Desert Eagle.

Be careful, guys.

There were voices then, shouting to each other in a language she didn't understand as she unzipped her bag and withdrew her Glock 19. Having seen the empty AK-47, she really didn't want to have to resort to it, but as the voices drew closer, clearly formulating a plan that involved surrounding her, she had to remind herself that these men would attempt to hold her ransom to a government that would do little to nothing to get her back.

As she tried to determine which side would be best to cover, a sudden, sharp blast rang out like a single peal of thunder inside her own head, so startlingly loud that her heart skipped a beat.

A stun grenade, she realized. She couldn't help but wonder how desperate Zero and Reidigger's situation was but hoped it was now improving. She had yet to improve her own, but maybe this was the chance. If the blast distracted the pirates half as much as it did her, she had a few seconds to spare.

Maria pushed off from the pallet of ammo boxes and broke into a flat-out sprint toward the fence.

They're not going to shoot me, she said in her head as she pumped her legs over the concrete as fast as they would go. She hurtled the remains of a collapsed wire crate and spotted a jagged hole in the chain-link fence ahead. Behind her the voices were angry but distant. As she ducked to scoot through the gap in the fence she dared to glance back and saw three of them, all armed, chasing her at a rapid clip.

The leg of her jeans snagged on a sharp spoke of wire in the fence's hole. She pulled it hard to free herself, tearing not only denim but skin as a sharp pain seared in her shin.

But she'd had much worse and still might before the day was over. Once through, she broke into a sprint again, heading straight across open ground toward a residential area about a hundred fifty yards away.

To call it a "residential area" was being polite. She entered a veritable shantytown, comprised of a handful of concrete, flat-topped buildings that were either crumbling or had been bombed out, most of them missing entire walls and roofs, some of those patched with corrugated sheet metal or even just fabric and others simply open to the elements. In between and around the buildings were makeshift tents, not unlike Hannibal's parachute tent in the Addis Merkato, and an occasional stack of the boxcar-like containers that she and her teammates had nearly been forced into, here piled two or even three high haphazardly.

Maria holstered her Glock. There weren't many people around, at least not outside, but those who were eyed her suspiciously. She couldn't have been more of an outsider if she'd had green hair and glowed in the dark. She didn't speak the language and doubted many of these native residents spoke much, if any, English. There was no pleading with anyone for shelter or warning them to remain indoors in case shooting started.

This is their life, she realized horridly. *Extreme poverty and a stone's throw from a pirate port.* Even as she thought it she spotted a young girl, wearing an oversized T-shirt cinched at the waist like a makeshift dress and playing with a rag doll. For some reason, despite lacking any similarities at all, the girl reminded her of Mischa, still held in a cell on a sublevel of Langley.

But her thoughts were interrupted by an explosion, even louder and more pronounced than the flash-bang had been. She spun, wide-eyed, to see a fireball topped with black smoke roll up into the sky barely more than a couple of football fields' distance from her position, but there was too much in the way for her to see the source.

Not that she needed to. Obviously the boys had blown something up. She could only hope it wasn't themselves.

The citizens of the shantytown screamed, shouted, and scurried off the narrow intersecting streets at the deep tremble of the explosion, which a moment later was followed by a second, and then a third smaller blast. A chain reaction on the port. She paused then, in a narrow alley of the shantytown, torn between running for cover and returning to the bombed port to find Zero and Alan.

Stick to protocol, she told herself. *Get safe, and then make contact.*

But the sudden evacuation of bodies on the streets made Maria an even more visible target than she already was, which was evidenced by a short gout of automatic gunfire and a stone façade exploding a few feet from her head.

Two Somalis stood down the narrow alley from her, no more than twenty yards—an easy shot. They hadn't been trying to kill her, just scare her. But they could have hit someone else; in fact, Maria quickly glanced behind her where she had seen the young girl playing with the dingy doll. Thankfully she was gone, probably having scurried inside when the explosion occurred.

The pirates barked angrily at her, now and then tossing out a command in English: "Stop!" "Stay!"

Like hell.

They had the drop on her, guns aimed if they felt like filling the alley with bullets, so she didn't even try to raise the Glock. Instead she took three big, quick steps backward, as not to give the impression that she was fleeing, and then sidestepped around a corner.

The Somalis shouted again as they rushed forward.

A car with broken windows sat on its rims beneath the second-story window of the closest concrete building—not a window, per se, but rather a square opening cut into the side of the building and loosely covered with a sheet for a curtain. Maria bounded onto the car's hood, and then its roof, which was so badly rusted she feared for a moment that it would give way beneath her weight, but it held enough for her to leap upward and grab the sill of the opening with both hands.

With a tremendous grunt she hefted herself up and tumbled into the window headfirst, rolling on a shoulder and coming up on one knee with her Glock snapped up in both fists. Then she immediately lowered it.

The two small children in the room stared back at her in terror.

Outside the window, the pirates who had pursued her were shouting to each other, no doubt wondering where she could have gone. She put a finger to her lips to indicate silence from the children, two boys, no older than eight or nine. Then she smiled, hoping to come off as non-threatening.

The younger of the two took a deep breath, and shrieked at the top of his lungs.

Dammit! Maria was on her feet in a heartbeat, shoving through a thin door into another room of whatever sort of living space this was, bursting out into a corridor, feet pounding against loose floorboards that squealed beneath her in protest, as if they too were calling out to the pirates. The corridor ended in stairs leading downward, and daylight through a doorway. But as soon as her foot touched the top stair, a shadow fell into the doorway and a Somali holding a machine pistol glared up at her.

"You!" he bellowed. "You stop!" He pointed the gun at her.

Pop-pop!

It took two seconds, if even that. The instant she saw the barrel tracking upward toward her, she raised her pistol and squeezed off two shots in quick succession. The first hit center mass, just below the heart. The second, just under the left eye, piercing the zygomatic bone.

For a moment the Somali stayed upright, the machine pistol continuing its upward trajectory. But the barrel trembled and faltered, and the man collapsed at the foot of the stairs.

Maria felt a pang of… not remorse, but something close to it. She had to remind herself that even if this man hadn't wanted to shoot to kill, it was only because he wanted to hold her hostage in the hopes of a ransom that would never come.

She vaulted down the stairs, holstering her Glock and snapping up the machine pistol as she stepped over the man's body. She cleared the exit and, seeing no one, slipped out into the narrow dusty street.

A fusillade of bullets tore at the air and she dropped instinctively, unsure of where they'd come from or how close they'd come to hitting her. She saw a flash of movement at her two o'clock—a dark doorway, the hint of a limb as someone hid behind it. She scrambled to her feet, aiming with the machine pistol. As soon as the man positioned himself for another burst, she fired.

He screamed as bullets tore at his arm and torso. The pirate fell through the doorway, his rifle dropping to the dirt. Maria kicked the gun away and kept moving. He would bleed out in seconds.

Two down, she thought. But hadn't there been a third pursuer?

"Do not turn around!" a deep accented voice shouted from behind her.

There *had* been a third—and he had the drop on her, full stop. She had little doubt a rifle was aimed at her back so she did as he said and stayed motionless, staring ahead.

"Drop the gun." Though his accent was pronounced, this man's English was good. She imagined he was likely a translator for the pirates' raids on western vessels.

She tossed the machine pistol to the ground. "Did Hannibal tell you who I am?" she asked him without looking back.

"American government." The man's response was a confident one.

Of course the smuggler hadn't said they were CIA. The Somalis might have known they would never get a ransom that way.

"That's right," she agreed. "My father is the Director of National Intelligence." That part wasn't a lie at all; it just wasn't the whole truth. "The only man he answers to is the president. Harming me would be putting yourself and your people in considerable danger. I'm going to turn around now. Okay?"

The pirate did not reply, so Maria glanced back at him. He was young, mid-twenties at best, holding an AK-47 with no stock at an angle that was just awkward enough to suggest he had very little experience using it. Not that a weapon like that required much.

Slowly she turned around until she was facing him.

"You will come with me now," he demanded.

"Okay. I will. But... your safety lever is up."

The man frowned at her. "What?"

"The safety lever? On the right side of the gun. Above the trigger. It won't fire."

Of course he looked.

Maria drew the Glock in one smooth motion and fired a single shot. The pirate yelped as his body jerked to the right, the bullet penetrating his thigh. He fell in the dirt, but didn't let go of the rifle. Before Maria could cover the distance between them, he aimed the AK at her face as he snarled at her in pain.

She hadn't been lying. The safety lever really was in the upper position.

The man yelped again as she kicked the gun out of his hand.

"Put pressure on that," she told him, gesturing to his leg. "Both hands. Good. Tell your friends that if any of them keep coming after me, they won't be as fortunate as you."

She left him there, hurrying through the shantytown and out the opposite side, where a road stretched toward the tall buildings of downtown Mogadishu. On the outskirts she came across a dirt bike leaning against a small boxy home. The bike was layered in dirt and looked like it had been made of spare parts, but it was better than nothing. It took her only seconds to wire it, and by the time a man came screaming out of the house after her, the whining engine was already drowning out his voice.

She tore away down the road, looking for any place to lie low in this hostile city long enough to rendezvous with Reidigger and Zero. She hoped they were okay, because this entire excursion had already been a monumental dead end. The weapon was still out there, and they were no closer to finding it.

CHAPTER EIGHTEEN

Sheikh Salman appreciated this place. There was a natural beauty to it that was largely unseen in his corner of the world. He stood on the white sand beach with his gaze on the horizon, listening to the surf as it gently rolled in, ebbing and flowing, the perfect metaphor for the cyclical nature in which most things worked.

He found it as amusing as he did strange that he had to resist the urge to kick off his shoes and stand barefoot in the surf, feel the cool water, let the white foam bubble over his old ankles. But a man of his station could hardly be seen doing so, especially not in the company of a half dozen elite members of the Royal Saudi Land Forces.

Masirah Island was, these days, largely a fishing and tourism hub. Located less than ten miles from the eastern coast of Oman, the island—*Jazīrat Maṣīrah*, in the sheikh's native tongue of Arabic—was once an industrious place known for traditional shipbuilding. Later the island was used as a military storage facility, first by the British and later by the United States, though nowadays the most interesting denizens of the island were the loggerhead turtles that used it as a nesting ground.

It was admittedly somewhat dangerous to rendezvous here, with the regular patrols of US Navy vessels in the Arabian Sea and the Gulf of Oman. But the same reason made it ideal; their purpose here would appear innocent enough, and the island itself was of such little note to anyone other than the citizens of its few small towns that it fell far beneath the radar of any naval power.

King Basheer had wanted to personally accompany Salman on this excursion. The former crown prince and recently crowned king was still headstrong and preferred to do things firsthand; he would need to learn how to delegate. Fortunately for him, Salman would be there to offer him tutelage. Instead, Salman had been accompanied by six Saudi commandos, dressed in ordinary garb as not to attract the wrong type of attention, their sidearms concealed and other weapons hidden in bags. Five of them would be exchanged in the trade; one would accompany the sheikh back to Saudi Arabia.

"It is time." The bearded commando that would become Salman's attaché upon his return, a solemn man with a trimmed black beard named Ali, held a thick pair of long-range binoculars to his eyes. "They have arrived."

The sheikh merely nodded and followed Ali to the skiff that waited for them on the beach. Two commandos sat in the low-slung bow, then two more on either side of Salman at its center, and finally two in the stern, including Ali, who shoved the skiff off the beach, started the engine, and piloted them two miles off the coast of Masirah Island into the Arabian Sea.

Salman's sight was not what it was in his youth; he loathed eyeglasses and could not bring himself to even attempt contact lenses, so he was certain the commandos spotted the boats long before he did. But at long last he saw them, first a couple of nebulous shapes but rapidly coming into sharper relief.

One was a noticeably shabby boat, its hull chipped, the paint faded, its railings and fittings on the edge of rusting. It was an open vessel, lacking any sort of cabin; even though the weather here in Oman was a pleasant eighty degrees, he had to imagine that where the Somalis had come from had seen them through some truly frightful weather.

The second vessel, however, was the prize. It was quite a sight to behold, sleek and beautiful, its reflective hull somehow appearing to be a silvery gossamer and the deep blue of the sea at the same time. It was a modern miracle, a work of art; not merely for the aesthetic, Salman knew, but equally so for the treasure it held in its bosom.

A white man stood on the bow of the South Korean ship, square-jawed and sandy-haired. The German had garnered quite a reputation in the last few years, masterful at the art of killing but always true to his word. And true he had been. Salman had been hesitant to hire him, especially considering the insanely steep price at which he came, but the outcome, obvious before even his poor eyes, was positive.

Ali cut the engine and the Saudis' skiff slowed, lolling in the water not ten yards from the Somali boat. The sleek Korean vessel bobbed in the water just to the east of them.

"Well done," Salman told the Somalis in English. The seven men on the ragged boat looked surly, and rightfully so. "You have traveled far and endured much, all while evading capture. That is commendable."

He was, of course, simply placating them. They had only managed to avoid capture by staying in close enough proximity to the technologically advanced ship, benefiting from its radar invisibility and signal-scrambling defenses.

Even so, they deserved to hear a few kind words before their deaths.

"The money," one of the Somalis demanded. He held a pistol in one hand, loosely but with a finger on the trigger.

"Of course. My colleague, Krauss, has your payment. He has had it the entire time." Salman gestured to the German. Each and every Somali face turned toward the man on the bow of the third ship—and in the instant their heads were turned, the Saudi commandos opened fire.

In less than six seconds, the pirate crew was dead, their boat rapidly taking on water. In that same span, Krauss smoothly drew a pistol and fired only two shots, one each through the heads of the two Somalis who had helped him pilot the vessel this far.

Salman had not lied, not technically; for what he was paying Krauss, he could not also pay the Somalis. The German had their payment, already transferred and distributed between several Swiss accounts he held. He had insisted on an upfront payment—likely in an effort to avoid this particular type of scenario from people he deemed potentially untrustworthy.

Krauss pushed the second body over the side and into the Arabian Sea before passively turning back to Salman. "Sheikh. This is, as its creators dubbed it, *Glimmer.*"

"How banal." The sheikh could not help but grin. "The weapon is operational?"

"It is."

"And you know how to operate it?"

"I do."

The German was a man of few words, and soft ones when he was so inclined, so Salman raised an eyebrow expectantly as an urge to elaborate.

"Posing as security," Krauss continued at last, "gave me full access to their research facilities under the guise of sweeps and checks. No one questioned my presence or scrutiny."

"Ali." The sheikh nodded to the commando at the stern, who carefully piloted the skiff closer to the newly minted vessel—*Glimmer,* as it supposedly was. As planned, five of the Saudis climbed aboard to join Krauss, only Ali remaining with Salman.

"My men are briefed on the next step. They will tell you where you need to go and what your objective is. En route, I expect you to teach them as much as possible about piloting the ship and using the weapon."

Krauss merely nodded once.

"Sheikh," said Ali urgently. He handed the binoculars to Salman and pointed to the horizon. "We are not alone."

Salman held the heavy binocs to his eyes and squinted. Three shapes, far away, hazy. And quite large, if they were visible at this distance. It seemed the Somalis had not gone completely under the radar as he had hoped.

Yet this was to be expected, and Salman had not been without a plan for this kind of contingency.

"Krauss." The sheikh handed the binoculars back to Ali. "I will take my leave shortly. But first... grant me a demonstration."

Seaman Evan Crane was excited as he stood on the broad deck of the USS *Pierce*, a destroyer-class battleship currently churning its way toward the eastern coast of Oman at its top speed of thirty-two knots, or approximately thirty-seven miles per hour. He looked through the telescope again, crouching slightly since the bulky gray scope was attached to a steel swivel riveted directly to the ship's deck.

"Negative," he informed command. "No visual yet, sir. Over."

For the past four months—maybe more than that now, he'd lost track—the USS *Pierce* had done little but regular patrols in the Indian Ocean, sometimes north to the Arabian Sea. They were not looking for anything in particular, and to Crane it even seemed as if the exercise was for little more purpose than putting the might of the US Navy on display.

But now was different. Now they were chasing *pirates*. Actual, honest-to-goodness Somali pirates.

Three ships did seem a bit like overkill to him—all of which were armed with Harpoon missiles, anti-submarine rockets, anti-aircraft weaponry, essentially enough firepower on any single one of them to take out a small city, all of it powered by the Aegis Combat System. The *Pierce* was the largest of the three ships at one hundred fifty-five meters long, but not by much; their two companion ships, the USS *Coolidge* and USS *Cleveland*, were just shy of one hundred fifty meters bow to stern, trailing at a short distance of only a few hundred meters to the north and south of the *Pierce* as it headed east through the Indian Ocean.

Just yesterday, the three US destroyers had been deployed to chase down pirates. All of them, all the manpower and firepower, to find and pursue one Somali pirate ship. It seemed strange, but he wasn't in a position to question it and wouldn't even if he was. He couldn't wait to tell his buddies back home about this—and he had no doubts that between then and now, the one pirate ship would become a fleet, and their slow chug across an ocean would become a thrilling chase in his retelling.

On a ship this large, crewed by just over six hundred souls, it wasn't uncommon for not everyone to be clued into what they were doing when (or if) they had a specific goal in sight. And the speed at which they were suddenly deployed yesterday made it all the more difficult, having had little time to brief the entire crew properly.

Crane knew only two things: that they were chasing pirates, and that those pirates had stolen a boat from the Pacific Ocean. Other details were foggy and based largely on hearsay around the ship; Crane had heard tell from other sailors that the pirates had taken the ship's crew hostage and were trying to ransom them back to their government. An ensign in the mess hall claimed their bounty was a military ship stolen from South Korea. And the buzz around the flight deck was the rather bold assertion that the pilfered ship held a North Korean weapon aboard it.

Whatever the case might be, they were chasing pirates, and twenty-three-year-old Seaman Evan Crane thought that was very cool.

His job on this mission was simple enough—painfully so. He stood on deck, waiting for orders from command when line of sight was needed and confirmed visual. That was it. Still, it was much better than bumming around the base at Diego Garcia, the tiny island just south of the equator in the Indian Ocean. Time grew painfully boring when he was on rotation there; the nearest civilization to the island was the Maldives, or Sri Lanka, nearly a thousand miles to the northeast.

Even crouching in front of a telescope intermittently while being barked at through a radio was preferable to the excruciating monotony of Camp Justice. Besides, when they finally caught up, Evan Crane would be the first to actually lay eyes on the pirates, albeit through the lens of a scope.

"Seaman." The radio crackled with the unnecessarily stern voice of his CO on the bridge. "Confirm visual? Over."

Evan Crane gritted his teeth. They'd tracked the pirate ship this far on sheer luck, a visual confirmation from a drone flyover that the USS *Coolidge* had piloted too far out to sea. The drone's connection had been lost and it crashed into the ocean—but not before catching a glimpse of the boat they were after, a tiny thing with only seven or eight men aboard. From there they had managed to get a radar ping on it, or so his CO had claimed, but they must have lost it because they hadn't updated the position of four miles out, north by northwest.

So Crane rubbed his eyes and checked again. He scanned carefully, aware that a boat that small and at that distance could easily be construed as the crest of a wave or a gull flying low over the water.

Was that something? He caught just a glimpse of a shape that could have been a boat, but it was hazy with the miles between them and the floaters in his own eyes. He rubbed his palm against them, seeing colors dance behind his eyelids, and looked again.

He scanned left and right carefully, a single degree at a time, seeking confirmation on the shape he had thought he'd saw.

A flash of blue engulfed his vision, bright as a flashbulb going off in his eye. Bright enough to hurt.

"Aah!" He leapt back and cried out, his hand flying to his eyes. But in the same instant he cried out—no, in the instant *before* that—a jarring explosion rumbled over the deck, up through his body, shaking him to the core.

Crane staggered, one hand over both eyes, feeling heat from somewhere, disoriented, certain he'd been blinded. Panic wrung its claws in his abdomen, churning his insides. At last he dared to look out of his left eye, keeping his hand clamped over the injured right.

He fell to his knees at what he saw.

Where the USS *Coolidge* had been only moments ago was a fireball, a still-spreading conflagration of exploded missiles, torpedoes, and warheads. The blast looked as if it was moving in slow motion, rolling upward. If there was anything left of the ship itself it was invisible under fire and thick smoke and swirling water.

That's impossible.

The *Coolidge* was simply gone, in an instant. That blue flash had annihilated it. Nothing was that fast. They had the most sophisticated combat system in the world; no missile or torpedo could just slip past it and cause that sort of damage.

Only one thing was certain: the probability of anyone surviving was zero.

Only then was Crane aware of the ringing in his ears, backed by the vague sound of panicked shouts, screams of alarm, of terror. Boots pounded on the deck as Crane sat there on his knees.

Then—the *Cleveland* exploded.

The shock of it shoved Evan Crane to his side, the boom of it throwing his equilibrium and blurring the vision in his single good eye.

Impossible, he thought again. How much time had gone by between blasts? He wasn't sure. Ten seconds? Fifteen maybe?

A harrowing thought gripped him and, for the first time since he was twelve years old, Evan Crane found himself in the grip of anxious hyperventilation. There was one boat remaining, and quite likely less than fifteen seconds to the same fate.

He climbed to his knees. "Our Father," he wheezed, "who art in Heaven, hallowed be ... thy name. Thy kingdom—"

CHAPTER NINETEEN

"**W**hat do you mean gone?!" President Rutledge stood up with such force that the chair behind him rolled back into the wall.

The Secretary of Defense closed his eyes solemnly, or perhaps remorsefully, but did not offer a further answer.

"The incident occurred seven minutes ago," Tabby Halpern offered quietly. Across from her, the R&D weapons specialist, Dr. Michael Rodrigo, averted his gaze from meeting anyone's eyes.

It was the usual suspects in the Situation Room, sans DNI Barren but with the preferable presence of VP Joanna Barkley, seated to Rutledge's right at the rectangular table. And despite how preferable that presence might be, it didn't deter from the fact that it was four o'clock in the morning Eastern Standard Time, and the president hadn't yet slept a wink having to deal with this absolute mess.

Rutledge seethed. *The incident occurred seven minutes ago. The incident?* Three American warships destroyed—no, *obliterated*—in the span of forty-five seconds, and it was being referred to as "the incident." Though perhaps that was at least minimally better than General Kressley's pained assessment of the situation, which was to say they were simply "gone."

"How many?" Rutledge paced the short width of the room for lack of anything more he could do. "How many men?"

Kressley cleared his throat. "Approximately eighteen hundred—"

"No, how many *exactly*?" the president demanded.

The general referred to a sheet in front of him. "One thousand, eight hundred and twenty-three. Sir."

"Jesus." One thousand eight hundred and twenty-three Americans. Soldiers, officers, crew, pilots, engineers. Husbands, wives, brothers, daughters, parents.

This is a nightmare.

"Oman has already denied any knowledge or responsibility," Tabby told the room. "Which we knew they would and have little choice but to believe them—"

"Was this the railgun?" Rutledge addressed the young doctor in the room, but couldn't for the life of him remember his name, and in his anger resorted to snapping his fingers quickly in the man's general direction. "You, was this the weapon?"

"Rodrigo, sir."

"Right. Dr. Rodrigo, was this that?"

"I..." The doctor gulped. "I believe so, sir. The Aegis Combat System would have seen anything else coming."

"Which means," said the Secretary of Defense, "that whoever has it knows how to use it."

Joanna Barkley spoke up. "So we have to consider the fact that it may no longer be in Somali hands. They could have already had a buyer in place before they stole it..."

"Or could have been hired by someone specifically *to* steal it," Tabby agreed.

"We can't discount the Somalis yet," said General Kressley. "They are the known aggressor here. Once we start eliminating them as a possibility, we open it up to literally anyone—"

A Secret Service agent slipped into the room, so discreetly that Rutledge didn't notice him until he was handing Tabby Halpern a folder, and he left again just as quickly and quietly.

Her eyes scanned the content in seconds. "Sir, the USS *Pierce* had a radar blip on a ship they suspected was the Somali vessel. The area in which the blip went dark was just searched; a Somali boat was found sunk a few miles off the coast of Masirah Island. Nine bodies have been recovered, all believed at the moment to be the Somali crew of the ship that stole the railgun."

That clinched it. This situation, this "incident," had just gone from nightmare to unfettered catastrophe. The Somalis were a scapegoat all along; whoever had the railgun could be anyone in the world.

But they can't be anywhere.

"Then it was there, right?" Rutledge asked quickly. "The railgun must have been there. How far could they have gotten in seven minutes? We have people there right now, and resources, right? Get them searching. Get them on it, whatever they have to do—"

"Sir," said the Secretary of Defense. "I assure you, they are doing exactly that in every capacity they are able."

"Then find it!" Rutledge slammed a fist down on the table. Rodrigo and Tabby both jumped slightly. Barkley didn't bat an eyelash.

"Mr. President," she said, her gaze flat but not passive. "Jon. Calm down, please."

"I'm sorry," he breathed. He couldn't lose his composure, not now. The Ayatollah of Iran was arriving in Washington in the morning, which Rutledge was still thinking of as "tomorrow" despite it being quite early the same day, expecting a historic meeting that was scheduled for that afternoon. His attaché was traveling ahead of him, due to arrive at JFK Airport and head directly to the United Nations Building to review the treaty.

Rutledge had been dealing with this mess for hours and was facing the very real possibility that he might not be able to greet the Ayatollah in person on arrival in DC, which alone would be a very bad look. He couldn't risk another.

"I'm sorry for the outburst." He wheeled his chair back to the table, sat down, and straightened his tie. "I want the Fifth Fleet on this, as many resources as they can spare. Whatever it takes to find it. This thing got from the Pacific to the Arabian Sea in less than three days; in one more day it could reach any city in..."

He trailed off. He hadn't even considered the possibility, but now that the railgun was in Middle Eastern waters it made all the sense in the world.

"Europe," Barkley said quietly. "Any city in Europe."

"Or Jerusalem," Kressley added, "if we're considering anti-Israel aggressors."

"And at its maximum range of approximately two hundred miles," said Dr. Rodrigo, "it wouldn't even have to get close."

"It's time to alert the UN," said Tabby. "I know you don't want to, but you know it's the right move."

"It was the right move yesterday," Rutledge murmured. As soon as they did that, the media would have the full story. But that was a paltry and selfish complaint in the face of lives lost and cities destroyed. If this weapon could take out three battleships with no effort, it could lay waste to any static target less than a couple hundred miles from the coast—which was where ninety percent of most populations dwelled.

"Do it." He nodded to Tabby. "Have a statement drafted."

"Yes, Mr. President." She rose and rushed from the room.

Rutledge leaned back in his seat and rubbed his face. Through his fingers, his gaze fell upon the one man in the room who had not spoken yet—and at the moment it appeared that he had little desire to speak at all.

"Give Director Shaw and me the room please."

The others dutifully stood from their chairs and filed out, closing the Situation Room's double doors behind them.

"Where are Zero and his team?" Rutledge asked, skipping any pleasantries. "What are they doing about this?"

JACK MARS

"I'm afraid I can't say, sir." Shaw folded his hands upon the table.

"You understand I am the president—"

"I don't know, sir," Shaw admitted. "Zero and his team were dispatched as you ordered. They were given explicit instructions by Deputy Director Walsh based on a carefully curated report of the situation, and they chose to ignore those orders."

"So they've gone dark?" Rutledge asked, though only marginally familiar with the term from films and television. "You have no idea where they are or what they're up to?"

"We know that the jet they took landed in Addis Ababa, in Ethiopia. They left the pilot at Bole International Airport and he fled to the embassy there. His report claims that Zero coerced him to fly them to Ethiopia under ... forceful means."

"Forceful?"

"At gunpoint, sir."

Rutledge frowned. That did not sound like the Agent Zero he knew ... but the man's tactics were not what anyone might call "refined."

"From there, we lost them," Shaw continued. "Any means we had to track them were left behind. However ... there was an incident in Mogadishu very recently. I was briefed in the past hour about an explosion at a small port and several Somalis shot. It was a known pirate port. The source of the explosion and firefight, however, is not known."

The president nodded slowly. If Shaw was to be believed—and Rutledge was not about to say that he was with any certainty—it was too much of a coincidence for Somali pirates to be attacked by an unknown force when a covert CIA team was out there searching for leads.

"Mr. President," said Shaw. "You must understand how this might play out. We now know that the Somalis are not our targets. Agent Zero, however, is not aware of that, and whether he was behind this recent attack or not, he will continue his hunt for the pirates with no knowledge that they are being fished out of the Arabian Sea. We have no way to contact him. And we must avoid unnecessary incidents at any cost."

"What are you suggesting, Director Shaw?"

"It's not a suggestion. It is protocol, sir. The CIA—and by extension, the United States government—must disavow Agent Zero and his team." Shaw sighed as if it genuinely pained him to say it. "That is, if he is even still alive. We have no way to know that the events on the port in Mogadishu didn't claim his life."

Rutledge didn't like it. He didn't like Shaw's obsequiously bureaucratic approach; he didn't like his obviously feigned dismay at denying any responsibility or support for Zero. But ultimately, he was right. If Zero had been looking for the stolen railgun and had gotten into some sort of trouble in the pirate port, he didn't exactly handle it with panache. And the US could not afford the liability that might come with another incident.

"Do what you must," Rutledge muttered.

"Thank you, Mr. President." Shaw rose quickly and swept out of the room—no doubt to set about his task with speed, efficacy, and possibly some measure of satisfaction. Zero and his teammates were about to be cut off from the United States, at a presidential authorization, or something close to it.

If they're even still alive. He could only hope they were.

Chapter Twenty

"Well, this is cozy," Alan muttered.

"Sure is." Zero chuckled, his voice echoing down the long culvert and back despite being barely more than a whisper. The concrete pipe was about five feet in diameter and an indeterminate length, receding into absolute darkness after about twenty-five yards or so. Zero and Alan sat facing each other with their backs against the curved wall behind them at the edge between darkness and vague silhouettes.

After stealing Hannibal's orange Jeep, they peeled out of the pirate port and drove a few miles down the Mogadishu coastline, making erratic turns and doubling back a couple of times just in case anyone was following or watching. Eventually they ditched the Jeep on the side of a road and hoofed it for about half a mile, into a stretch of barren wilderness where they found a long-dried stream bed and the culvert.

"Since we're waiting..." Alan dug into his black backpack and pulled out two miniature bottles of whiskey, just a few ounces each, and passed one to Zero. "Nicked 'em off the Gulfstream."

"Thanks." He could always count on Alan to keep the mood casual, even when he knew Zero was worried. And he was worried—they had already attempted to call Maria on the satellite phone to no avail. There was no point in trying again; if she was in danger or trying to be sneaky, a ringing phone would not help her. Protocol dictated they find a spot to lie low and stay put until they got a call back from her and established a rendezvous point.

If *we get a call back from her.*

He pushed the thought out of his head and unscrewed the cap. "Cheers." The liquor was syrupy on his tongue and burned at the back of his throat in the best possible way.

"So. You want to talk about it?"

Zero winced. He was afraid that Alan was eventually going to ask about the incident back at the port.

"Not really."

"Hm," Alan grunted. He took a second swig from the tiny bottle, comically small in his thick hand. "Even so, I think we should. I don't ask for much. I'm asking for this."

Dammit. He knew this would come sooner or later. The man who had done so much for him and asked nothing in return was calling in the favor at last—and all he wanted was the one truth that Zero didn't want to give.

It was nothing but fair to tell him. His simple failed recollection of how a Zippo worked could have killed them both.

Zero finished his own tiny bottle and tossed the dead soldier into the darkness, where it clattered twice and rolled as he wondered where to start and just how much he'd have to say.

"Not everything came back," he began. "I thought it did, when my memories returned. But then again, I wouldn't have any way of knowing if something didn't, right?"

He chuckled a little. Alan did not.

Zero cleared his throat. "New things pop up from time to time. Not often. Some stimulus, or even necessity will bring it on." He decided to gloss over the still-unconfirmed memories that had resurfaced of his time as a CIA assassin and skip ahead to the important part. "And, on the flip side of the coin... other stuff gets lost sometimes."

"What kind of stuff?" Alan asked.

"Well, like how to work a Zippo." It was much more than that; the lighter had been entirely foreign in his hand, just a rectangular silver box that held absolutely no meaning to him at the time. "I don't even know when I lost it. I could have forgotten it months ago, and never would have known it because I never had a need to—"

"But you needed to," Alan interjected, not harshly but firmly. "There aren't many times that a lighter is going to mean life or death, but here it could have. When you needed it, it wasn't there. Has that happened any other times?"

Zero didn't respond at first. Back in November, he'd forgotten how to load a Glock—but that happened in Bixby's lab, not in a firefight when he needed it most. Still, the fact that it had happened then during an innocuous moment meant it very well could happen again in a confrontational one.

"No," he said at last. "Other times it's been pretty innocent stuff. I, uh..." There was a loose pebble near his hand and he picked it up, desperate for anything that didn't require looking Alan in the eye. "I forgot Kate's name."

Reidigger blew out a breath. "Sorry," he murmured. If anyone knew how devastating it would be to Zero's mental and emotional function to forget the mother of his children, it was Alan. "What about Guyer? Did you talk to him?"

"I did. He ran some tests, but he doesn't know why this is happening or if it'll keep happening." That part was actually a lie; the Swiss neurosurgeon had in fact told him that it would keep happening, and likely increase in severity until Zero's own brain deteriorated to the point that it killed him.

But there was no way in hell that Zero was going to admit that to his best friend in a dirty culvert in Mogadishu in the middle of an op. It was the right audience, but not the time or the place.

"Are you compromised?" Alan asked point-blank.

Zero looked up sharply to find his friend scrutinizing his face, studying him for any sign that he was being untruthful, while at the same time asking if his impairment might put him or the team in a vulnerable or dangerous position.

Of course I am.

"Of course I'm not." He stared right back at Reidigger, hoping he wasn't giving anything away. "You know me. If I thought for a moment that I couldn't do this, I wouldn't be out here."

Alan nodded slowly. "Good. Because it's not just your life on the line, you know."

Zero's nostrils flared. He didn't need to be reminded that he had teammates, or manipulated to give an emotional reaction, and he was about to say so when the satellite phone chimed.

He snapped it up quickly. "Zero."

"It's me."

He breathed a sigh of relief. "Maria, thank god. You okay?"

"I'm fine. Sorry I missed your call; I was on a very noisy dirt bike. You guys good?"

"We are. Where are you? We'll come to you."

"I can't stay here," Maria told him. "Just stopped to make the call. Can you get to Hannibal's plane?"

Zero thought for a moment; they'd headed in the relative direction of the plane with the Jeep, so they couldn't be more than a mile or so from the airstrip. "Yeah. But why the plane? We can't leave now. We haven't even found the right port, let alone the weapon—"

"I'll explain when you get there." Maria ended the call.

"You ready to hoof it?" he asked Alan.

Reidigger climbed to his feet with a grunt, crouching beneath the sloping ceiling of the culvert. "After you."

"Wait." Zero put a hand on the bigger man's forearm. "Are you going to say anything to Maria?"

Alan hesitated for a moment, and then shook his head. "But you should."

✣ ✣ ✣

Less than twenty minutes later they arrived back at Hannibal's Cessna 206 without incident, other than a few wary glances from windows and passing vehicles. Zero was as surprised that they weren't met with resistance as he was that the plane was still there; he could only surmise that the smuggler had not made it out of the pirate port alive.

Maria knelt beside the plane, checking the contents of her black bag, a shoddy dirt bike on its side nearby. She stood quickly when she saw them and gave them each a brief hug.

"Glad to see you're safe," she said. "Especially after you blew up the port."

Reidigger shrugged. "Had to be done."

"I talked to Penny. You want the bad news, or the worse news?"

Zero sighed. There was never good news. Well, that wasn't entirely true; they were all alive at least. "Bad news first."

"We're disavowed."

Of course we are. It wasn't the first time. But Zero was well aware it could mean trouble down the road, if they got back stateside in one piece. After Penny's warning about Shaw's intentions, he had no doubt that the CIA director was building a case against them.

"So no support," Alan said. "That's pretty much status quo for us. What's the worse?"

Maria stared at the asphalt. "The railgun was used, off the coast of Oman. Three destroyer-class ships, blown to pieces in less than a minute."

Zero's lungs deflated with the news. Not one, but *three* American warships destroyed in under a minute? It sounded impossible. And the lives lost...

"So the Somalis were never planning on coming here," he reasoned aloud. They were more than a thousand miles off base.

"That's the other thing," Maria said sourly. "The Somali boat that was seen in the China Sea? It's at the bottom of the Arabian Sea now, along with nine dead Somali pirates."

The hits kept on coming. The Somalis were a clever diversion by the real aggressors; have someone else steal the weapon, let them be seen, and while every resource was looking for them, kill the pirates and take the railgun.

"No leads?" Alan asked.

"Not one," Maria replied. "Of course the president has everything under the sun trying to track it, but so far they're failing. We're talking about a very small, very fast boat designed not to be noticed."

"What are our options?" Zero asked, though he already knew that there was only one.

"Well, we could give up, go home, and try to sort this mess out with Shaw," Maria said plainly. "Or we can take Hannibal's plane, get the hell out of Somalia, and try to find an upgrade on this hunk of junk while we figure out our next move."

The choice was obvious. None of them were about to give up, especially not now that the weapon had been used and a substantial amount of lives had been lost.

"You got any resources around here?" Zero asked Reidigger.

He shook his head. "Not in this corner of the world. Trust me, Hannibal would have been the last choice if he wasn't the only choice."

"We'll need to think of something, and fast." Zero's mind was chugging at full speed. "Whoever has the railgun plans to use it again, and soon. They wouldn't have shown their hand like that otherwise." He had seen the specs on the South Korean vessel; it could have outrun the destroyers easily and slipped away undetected, but instead the aggressors had opted to use it.

"The Chinese?" Alan suggested. "Bet they're still sore about the ultrasonic weapon."

Zero shook his head. "I doubt it. The Chinese are walking on eggshells right now; if they were going to try something, it would be a lot more covert." Trying to guess who might be behind it was fruitless. And discerning a potential target would be nearly impossible without knowing who first.

Although, he thought, *there is a process of elimination here.* He created a map in his head, examining the route. The pirates had likely stuck closer to the coast, through the Gulf of Thailand and the Bay of Bengal rather than over open water. It was the only way they would have reached the Arabian Sea so quickly. And striking in Oman, so close to the stomping grounds of the Navy's Fifth Fleet, would put the US on alert that the next target might be Middle Eastern.

"I see those gears are turning," Reidigger grunted. "What are you thinking?"

"They could get to the Mediterranean," Zero told them. "Via the Gulf of Aden."

"That would make a whole lot of European cities potential targets," Maria noted.

"Exactly," Zero agreed. "And Jerusalem, Syria, Lebanon..."

"But they could get to the US through the Strait of Gibraltar," Alan added.

"True," Zero said, "but that would require they cross the entire Atlantic. It would take days, if that small of a ship could even make the journey without needing to refuel. Besides, now that they've used the weapon, they know the heat is going to be on more than ever."

It didn't exactly narrow things down. The next target could be a European capital, or densely populated coastal regions, or even a nuclear reactor, like the Chinese had targeted back in November. But it was, at least, a starting point.

"That still doesn't solve our problem of needing a plane that's not threatening to fall apart at the seams," said Maria.

"True." But Alan's mention of Gibraltar got another gear turning in Zero's head. "I know where we can go."

CHAPTER TWENTY ONE

"Your hesitance to tell me where it is," said King Basheer, "is concerning, Salman."

The sheikh smiled graciously. The two of them were alone, in one of the king's private chambers in the palace just south of Riyadh. "It is... in transit, Highness."

Basheer narrowed his eyes. The young king did not like being kept in the dark—but he would learn soon enough that certain matters were best left out of his hands and in those more capable of performing dark deeds. It would be unbecoming of royalty for Basheer to be involved directly in the plot. Not to mention, Salman considered, the king would want more control if he knew precisely what was occurring.

It had been exceedingly easy for the sheikh to slip away from the Arabian Sea. He had taken some delight in watching the railgun in action, the fireball in the distance indicating that it had not only hit its target but worked spectacularly. After the first shot, Salman and Ali had sped back to Masirah Island, abandoning their small skiff at a fishing dock and taking a commercial ferry back to mainland Oman. From there, a private plane was waiting to take them on the swift flight to Saudi Arabia. All said, Sheikh Salman was back in Riyadh less than ninety minutes after the first battleship was destroyed.

"In transit to where?" Basheer demanded. "What is the target?"

"My king," Salman said with a deep bow of his head. "Such details are beneath your station—"

"Or are they being intentionally kept from me?" Basheer said sharply. "You have been given much, Salman, much more than any tribal sheikh before you. But you have *not* been given authority to act on my behalf."

"Of course not, Excellency." Salman would never admit to it, but he had already acted on Basheer's behalf under many circumstances; the deals that the king had established when he was still the crown prince, those that the American vice president had dubbed "unsavory factions," were more than simple arms deals. They were alliances, in anticipation of King Ghazi's death and Basheer's rise to the throne. Salman himself had made promises that he was not sure he could keep—at least not at the time. But with the weapon, the plasma railgun, they would establish themselves as a power and unify Islam under their banner.

But only if they could prove capable of seeing their plan through and destroying their enemy.

"I act not on your behalf, but in your name—and that of Allah, praise be upon Him." Salman's attempts to placate the young king did not seem to be working terribly well; Basheer folded his arms and glared, seemingly trying to come off as authoritative but looking to the sheikh more like a petulant child.

"The weapon is en route over the Atlantic," Salman said at last.

King Basheer frowned. "Traveling over the Atlantic? That will take far too long! We will miss our opportunity!"

Salman felt the corners of his mouth pulling into an involuntary grin. "I did not say, my king, that it was in the water."

Zero was certain that the Cessna was going to quake apart at the seams as they rumbled over Moroccan airspace. Reidigger's announcement over the headset didn't help any.

"We're running on fumes," he told them as the plane gave a shudder. "Looks like this landing is going to be a glide-in."

"You're enjoying yourself, aren't you?" Zero practically shouted over the din of the engine.

"What can I say?" Reidigger pushed the yoke gently, easing the plane lower in altitude. "There's a special place in my heart for old hunks of junk."

Finally, mercifully, the Cessna's tires bounced down on a short, bumpy airstrip in the Moroccan desert, just outside an American forward operating base—or so it appeared to anyone who would care to look twice.

Designation H-6 was a CIA black site where the worst of the worst were sent to be shoved into holes and forgotten by the world. Hell-Six, as it was called by those who ran it, was home to high-risk acquisitions that were too valuable to kill but too dangerous to be allowed anywhere else.

The site was in the rough shape of a square, surrounded by an uneven chain-link fence topped with barbed wire and plastered with signs in several languages that threatened all sorts of bodily harm to trespassers. Inside the fence were rows of semi-permanent canvas tents of varying sizes, interrupted here and there by squat, domed steel structures. Zero had been in one of those domes before; he knew that inside was nothing but dirt and a steel grate in the ground, beneath which was a hole, and inside which was a prisoner.

They disembarked from the Cessna to find a half dozen Special Forces soldiers pointing weapons at them, each one very much the stereotype of what anyone might expect: beards, sunglasses, bandanas tied over their heads, tattoos up their exposed forearms.

"Quite the greeting." Reidigger muttered as he stepped off the plane with his hands empty and overhead.

But one of the soldiers lowered his gun, letting it hang from his shoulder by the strap. "At ease, fellas." Sergeant Jack Flagg stepped forward, wearing Oakleys and an olive-drab scarf around his neck. He extended a black-gloved hand. "Agent Zero, Agent Johansson. Always a pleasure when you drop out of the sky unannounced in a heap of garbage."

Zero shook Flagg's hand. "Sergeant. Wish I could say it was nice to see you, but it's never under great circumstances."

Flagg grinned at that. The sergeant was a Green Beret who was hired to take on management of H-6 when he was up for retirement and realized it didn't suit him. A lifelong military man, Flagg handpicked his staff from fellow Special Forces retirees and operated completely off the grid; despite the place being a CIA black site, the agency didn't actually intervene with operations. The brutal truth of it was they didn't know what went on there and didn't want any culpability, so long as things ran smoothly.

All of that meant that Flagg was in the dark and would have no idea that Zero and his team had been disavowed. Similarly, Shaw would never guess that Zero would go to such a place, let alone that he had friends there.

"You all look like you could use a hot meal and a shower," Flagg joked as he led them through the gates and into the encampment of H-6. "Sorry to say we have neither."

"How about a plane?" Zero asked.

Flagg threw a glance over his shoulder at the beat-up Cessna. "Why, you starting a collection?"

"That one's yours," Zero quipped back. "Consider it a gift."

"Ran out of fuel, huh?"

"Yeah. And it won't get us where we need to be fast enough."

Flagg halted outside one of the wide canvas tents. "As you can see, we're a little short on airplanes at the moment." He gestured beyond the fence to the general nothingness of the desert. "But there are places we can call when we need air support, and they don't generally ask questions. Of course, they might start if we're asking them to drop off a plane and have their pilot find another way home."

"Which is what we'd be asking them to do," Zero said.

"Think you can make it work?" Maria prodded.

Flagg tugged off his black baseball cap and smoothed his matted hair. "I think I could come up with something." He jutted his chin toward the tent in front of him. "There's a cistern in there. Everything's purified, so you can wash up, have a drink. I'll make the call."

"Thanks," Zero said. "And Sergeant? Not to complicate things, but we're in a time crunch."

"ASAFP, got it." Flagg trotted off. That was the benefit of having friends in low places like Hell-Six. They were happy to help and didn't ask questions.

Zero lifted the flap of the canvas tent for Maria and let her go in first. "You coming, Alan?"

Reidigger hesitated. "I'm good for now. Just gonna take a moment to myself."

Zero nodded. He didn't want to push the issue, especially given the information he'd shared not too long ago about his own problems. So instead he followed Maria into the tent. A large steel tank, at least two hundred gallons, sat in the center with a black pump affixed to the side, emptying into a thick plastic basin sitting on four legs. The wastewater drained into a small barrel-shaped tank beneath the basin, and through a filtration system and back into the cistern.

Hanging over the basin from two thin ropes was a dirty mirror, probably for shaving—though it didn't seem like any of the men at H-6 bothered with that. Zero glanced in it. Flagg was right; he did look a mess. It was no small wonder that the sergeant even recognized him. His face had streaks of dark soot from the explosion on the dock in Mogadishu. His forehead near his left temple was caked in dried blood. His eyes were bloodshot, the bags beneath them looking deeper than they had a day ago.

"Go ahead," Maria offered, gesturing to the basin.

"Thanks." He dug both hands into the water. It was cool and instantly refreshing. He made use of the gritty hand soap, splashed water liberally on his face, and took a drink from his cupped hands.

As he did, he felt Maria's arms slide around his midsection, and then her head came to rest on his back, between the shoulder blades, as she liked to do.

"I think you should stay here."

Zero turned suddenly, causing Maria to release him and take a quick step back.

"What? Why?" he demanded.

"Because Shaw is obviously gunning for you. I don't think he's all that interested in me or Alan, but you—if you keep this up, if you stay with us, you're just going to be giving him more fuel for the fire."

Zero shook his head. This didn't make any sense; on any other day Maria couldn't care less what Shaw thought or tried to do. In fact, it was her idea in the first place to ignore the orders that came in an envelope from Walsh.

"You'd just be painting a bigger target on your back," she persisted. "If you're here, you have a confirmable alibi. Flagg will vouch for you."

Zero scoffed as he realized what was happening here. "Alan told you what happened." It was the only explanation for Maria's sudden change of heart. She tried her best not to give it away, but he could tell from the pained look in her eye that he was right.

But how? When? He was with them the whole time. Unless—of course. Alan had promised not to *say* anything to Maria. But he didn't have to, because he could text her just as easily with the satellite phone while they were flying to Morocco.

He couldn't help but feel a little betrayed.

"You told me you were fine," she said. "You're not."

"I am," he insisted. "It's under control—"

"What if it gets you killed?"

"What if me not being there gets *you* killed?" he countered.

Maria scoffed. "Is that what you're afraid of? That things will go south because Agent Zero isn't around?"

"No! That's not it. I..." How could he put it into words? How could he tell her that he was struggling to reconcile their professional relationship with their personal one without it sounding like some kind of machismo? He didn't think her incapable, nor Alan, neither by a long shot. It was just that...

It was just that she was right.

"Yes," he admitted. "Yes, I'm afraid that something might happen to you and I'm not there. Not because I don't think you can handle yourself. Not because I don't think you're a great agent. I just... I love you too much to let you go. It's all in my head. I know that. But I'm not staying behind."

Maria nodded slowly. "You're right. It is all in your head. You've loved and lost before."

Fresh guilt stabbed at him like a torn scab. Even after all this time he still felt the sting of Kate's death. He wasn't there for her. He couldn't save her from the lethal dose of TTX administered by Agent John Watson, a man whom Zero had called a friend.

"But that doesn't mean you'll lose me too," she insisted. "And it certainly isn't worth putting yourself in unnecessary risk over."

"I'm not just going to—"

"Don't be selfish," she interrupted. "Did you ever consider that I feel the same way about you? I don't want something to happen to you out there that I can't do anything about. If you're here, I know you're safe. If you're out there, even if it's with me, something could still happen. You could lose something important." She took a step forward and grabbed his hand in both of hers. "Don't you see? You had a great love of your life. You know what it feels like. I don't. This is a first for me."

"Don't," he said quietly. She wasn't being fair to herself. "Don't compare yourself to Kate. That's not healthy for anyone. I know I've been more fortunate than most. They say lightning doesn't strike twice, but it did for me. I've been..."

Wait a second.

"Fortunate..."

"Kent? You okay?"

Lightning. That's it.

"Son of a bitch," he murmured. "Get Penny on the phone, right now."

Maria didn't hesitate. She whipped out her sat phone and put it on speaker as she made the call.

"León," Penny answered quietly on the second ring.

"It's Zero. Maria's here with me."

"I can't really speak now," Penny told them, "unless it's an emergency. Shaw is watching the lab pretty closely..."

"Penny, this is urgent," Zero told her. "Listen, do you know the ILDN?"

"The International Lightning Detection Network, based in New Mexico. Sure, I know it. They have hundreds of sensing stations around the world that send signals to satellites so they can determine the location of a lightning strike within seconds... son of a bitch."

"That's what I said," Zero agreed.

"I don't follow," Maria admitted.

"The plasma railgun emits a powerful electromagnetic burst." Penny was speaking excitedly now. "More powerful than an average lightning strike, but not all that dissimilar of an energy signature. If the railgun's emission was powerful enough to register on the ILDN's network when it fired on the Navy ships, then their meteorological equipment could pick up on it."

"And we may have a way of tracking the weapon," Zero concluded.

"But wouldn't that require them to use it again?" Maria asked.

"Well... yes," he admitted. "But even if it's only once, we could pinpoint a precise location within seconds."

"And we, or someone, would have to be there," Maria added.

"Also yes," Zero conceded, growing frustrated with the holes she was punching in his plan. "Look, I've got nothing better. Do you?"

"Not really."

"Penny, do you think you can get ILDN on the phone? See if they picked up on the railgun's signature in Oman and convince them to keep tabs on it?"

"Sure," the doctor said. "And if they deny me, I'll just hack their system. That's the easy part. The difficulty will be doing so while staying off of Shaw's radar."

Zero shook his head. "To hell with Shaw. The worst he'll discover is where we're headed. The only thing that matters is finding the railgun."

"On it." Penny ended the call.

"Think this will work?" Maria asked.

"Not sure." First they had to get a plane. Then they had to get a hit. Which meant they actually needed the railgun to be fired again—and then to somehow stop it before it could lock onto its next target.

Chapter Twenty Two

Reidigger meandered through the camp at H-6, intentionally giving Zero and Maria some space. He felt terrible about telling her what had happened back at the pirate port, but he knew at the same time that Zero wasn't going to. His friend had always been the first to rush into a fight, to lead the charge, to take the leap, but when it came to facing his own problems, his internal demons, he often seemed to find a way to put on blinders.

He spotted a group of four soldiers sitting in lawn chairs under a canvas tarp, dealing cards on a shabby folding table. They were playing blackjack, it looked like, betting with miniature candy bars and cigarettes.

This site wasn't just a prison for those that needed to be forgotten. This was the kind of place that people went when they wanted to forget about the world around them.

He wondered if he could ever settle in a place like this. Forget everyone else and all their problems. Just sit in the shade in the desert and play some cards.

As bad as he felt about telling Maria the truth, there was a bigger looming concern weighing on his mind—more so even than Zero's admission that he was losing memories.

New things pop up from time to time.

That's what Zero had told him, and that's what had Alan worried the most. Back when Zero's memories had returned and he'd finally recognized the burly mechanic Mitch as his supposedly dead friend, Alan had had a minor moment of panic that Zero had in fact remembered everything.

But no. Somehow one small detail had eluded Zero, even to this day; a detail of which Alan was painfully aware but hadn't divulged to save his friend from the unnecessary pain that had inspired him to have the memory suppressor installed in his skull in the first place.

Zero knew, or had known, that the CIA put the hit out on Katherine Lawson.

He knew, back then, that the lethal dose of TTX that took her life had been administered by a CIA dark agent, a glorified assassin, just like Zero had been when he'd started his career.

He did not know that the hitman was Oliver Brown, the man who went by the alias Agent John Watson, but neither did Alan at the time.

Zero knew, that night on the Hohenzollern Bridge when he faked his own death, that there was no other way out than to let Alan Reidigger kill him. If he didn't, he wouldn't stop. Zero would have torn the CIA apart in search of his wife's murderer, and very likely would have died in the process, leaving his girls orphaned.

It was only through Alan's discovery of the memory suppressor, stealing it from R&D, seeking out Dr. Guyer, and convincing Zero it was a better path than death that he was still alive. That either of them were still alive, if he was being honest, because Alan would have followed Zero to hell.

He didn't want to think that his motivations were out of cowardice or self-preservation, but they sure felt that way sometimes. It was a huge part of the reason that Alan had such ire for the agency, the bureaucracy of it all, the callousness of diluting someone's life down to a rubber stamp on a classified file.

Regardless, Zero hadn't recovered that particular memory. It was as if his brain had filled in the blanks, had taken the pieces and created a patchwork memory, one that led him to believe a version of the story that was mostly the truth but falling just short enough to be a horrible lie.

The fact that Reidigger knew it and had said nothing was an enormous betrayal of their friendship, and he felt it daily. That was why he would do whatever Zero needed of him, whatever was asked of him, and ask for nothing in return.

But new things pop up from time to time.

"Hey, man, you want to join us?"

Reidigger snapped out of it to see one of the soldiers at the card table waving him over. His cheeks reddened as he realized that while deep in thought, it must have looked like he was staring idly at them.

"Uh… no. No thanks. I'm good." He waved to the soldiers and turned to head back toward Zero and Maria, but found Sergeant Flagg striding toward him.

"You're the pilot, right?" Flagg asked.

"Uh… yeah. Mitch."

"Mitch." Flagg grinned as he shook Alan's hand. "Is that Agent Mitch?"

"Just Mitch."

"Okay, Just Mitch. Some buddies of mine at an outpost in Algeria happen to have a decommissioned EA-6B they can lend. You know it?"

Alan nodded. "A Northrop Grumman Prowler. Four-seat cabin. Max speed of six hundred and fifty miles an hour. That should do." The Prowler was a twin-engine aircraft built for electronic warfare, jamming radar systems and gathering radio intelligence. But all they needed was for it to be flight-worthy.

"You know your stuff," Flagg said, impressed. "Can you fly it?"

Alan shrugged a shoulder. "Probably. What's the ETA?"

"About forty minutes."

"All right, thanks." Over Flagg's shoulder, Reidigger saw Zero and Maria striding quickly in their direction. It was time, he supposed, to own up to squealing to Maria. "Excuse me, Sergeant."

Alan stepped past Flagg and met his teammates halfway, expecting to be hit by a diatribe of betrayal and hurt feelings.

"We may have a lead," Zero said excitedly.

"Huh?"

"We may have a way to *get* a lead," Maria corrected.

"The railgun's discharge registered on a lightning detection network," Zero told him quickly. "Penny's working on trying to use it to track the energy signature the next time the weapon is used."

Alan frowned. "But that means it needs to be used again to pinpoint a location."

"That's what I said," Maria muttered.

"I know it sucks, but it's all we've got," Zero said firmly.

"I think we should tell someone," said Maria. "I know we're disavowed, but we still have a responsibility."

"Tell who?" Alan asked. "The CIA?"

"No way." Zero shook his head. "They'll get the military involved and throw everything they have at it. Boats, planes, missiles, and too many personnel. This thing already destroyed three of the most advanced ships the US Navy has to offer. It could sink an aircraft carrier and shoot planes out of the sky. If we want to avoid loss of life, we need to keep this small and tight."

"And we *need* to keep someone that's not us in the loop," Maria insisted. "Because this thing has to fire at least once. What if it fires twice before we can get to it? Or three times? There has to be a contingency."

"Maria's right," Alan conceded. But so was Zero; it couldn't be the agency.

"Rutledge." Zero rubbed his chin and the thin stubble that had sprouted there. "We tell Rutledge. Have Penny deliver him a message securely, and only to him. I'm sure she can pull it off. Tell him we're alive, well, and have the means to find this thing. But none of this will work if there are too many hands on deck, and we don't need to give the railgun any more targets like they did in Oman."

Reidigger nodded. "If you think that's the right play, and that he'll listen, then let's do it. Flagg's got a plane for us inbound. As soon as it's hear, we'll take off and head north, toward the Mediterranean and the most likely targets as far as we can discern." It wasn't much, but it was a plan.

"So I guess you're not staying behind then," Maria noted.

"Not a chance," Zero replied. And then to Alan, under his breath, he muttered, "Tattletale."

CHAPTER TWENTY THREE

President Rutledge felt like a zombie, shuffling down the hall of the West Wing toward the White House master suite, the aptly named President's Bedroom, capital P and capital B for all the pomp it was worth. It had always been funny to him how many people believed that the president slept in the Lincoln Bedroom, a guest suite on the second floor, made all the more amusing by the fact that not even Lincoln had slept in the Lincoln Bedroom.

He chuckled to himself and then thought, *I'm going delirious with exhaustion.*

As if the sleepless nights in the wake of the Ayatollah's impending visit weren't enough, it was now six in the morning EST and he still hadn't caught a moment's rest. The sun would be rising in another hour, and in three more, after the Ayatollah's stopover at the UN, Rutledge would be expected to be greeting Iran's leader fresh-faced and bushy-tailed—though by the looks of things it was going to be more like blotchy-faced and bedheaded.

It was Tabby who had finally ushered him out of the Situation Room and off to catch a couple hours' sleep. No one was any closer to finding the railgun. Fifty trillion dollars this country had out on the water and they couldn't find one tiny boat. Despite being the President of the United States, alleged by many to be the most powerful man in the developed world, he felt utterly impotent. Even if someone found it, a ship or a drone or a plane or even Zero, his presence would be entirely unnecessary to do what needed to be done. He'd issued all the orders he could issue. Short of going out there himself to look for the damned thing, it was now little more than a fraught waiting game, one that he could only pray would end in finding the boat and the railgun and not another target being destroyed.

Bed was the only place he was needed at the moment. Or so he told himself.

He glanced over his shoulder at the pair of Secret Service agents trailing about ten paces behind him and casually waved them off. "G'night, Terrence. Phil."

"Good night, sir." They took the hint and positioned themselves further down the corridor, though not out of sight. Rutledge had trouble sleeping knowing that anyone was right outside his door, regardless of their purpose.

Once inside the bedroom, he tugged off his tie and kicked off his shoes. After peeling off his socks he decided that was as far as he was getting and collapsed onto the bed in his shirt and trousers. The First Lady was out of town, and for a moment he even forgot where Deidre had jetted off to this time, a fundraiser for one of the eight hundred or so charities she supported. He admired her work ethic. It was certainly better than his.

"Dammit," he muttered, his face pressed into a downy pillow. He'd forgotten to turn the lamp off, but the thought of getting up again was downright horrible.

Screw it. It's dark if I close my eyes.

But before he could, the light flickered off on its own.

"What the hell?" Rutledge sat bolt upright and looked out the window. The room was eerily dark—not because just his lamp had gone out. The electricity in the entire White House had gone out, throwing the grounds of the estate into shadow.

Urgent voices shouted outside his room, growing distant. Rutledge froze. Was this an attack? Where were they going?

Rutledge shimmied to the edge of the bed to stand.

"Please stay seated, Mr. President."

The hairs on the back of his neck stood to attention. The voice was soft, female, and if he didn't know any better, accented in proper British. It was strange how non-confrontational it sounded while still instilling abject fear in him that someone had managed to slip into the President's Bedroom.

Suddenly the lights came back on, his lamp and through the window, and Rutledge found himself blinking at a young woman. He'd never met her before, or at least didn't believe he had. Her hair was a curly chestnut around her shoulders, framing her brown face. She wore jeans and a red Hard Rock Café T-shirt, looking not only completely casual but utterly out of place.

"Who are you?" he managed, baffled by this random stranger appearing in his room.

"Please keep your voice down," she said. "My name is Dr. Penelope León. I'm with the CIA. I'm visiting you on behalf of Agent Zero, with whom I am still in contact."

"Zero! He's alive?"

"Very much so. Now please tell your people that you're fine."

An instant later there was a brisk knock at the door. "Mr. President?"

Rutledge hesitated, determining whether to hear her out or call for help. But if she was here and had spoken to Zero, perhaps she had news. "I'm fine, Terrence. What's going on out there?"

"Just a power outage, sir. Appears all of DC went out for about eight seconds. We're back up now."

"Thank you, Terrence." Rutledge waited until the footfalls retreated from the closed door. "All of DC?"

The young woman, this Dr. León, shrugged one shoulder. "I have been accused in the past of having a flair for the dramatic."

"I'll say. A phone call would have sufficed."

"No, sir, it wouldn't. I was asked to personally and securely deliver a message to you, so that's what I'm doing."

The president frowned. "Okay. What's the message?"

"Agent Zero and his team believe they have identified a way to track the railgun."

Rutledge leapt up from the bed, his heart surging in unison. "That's incredible! How?"

"I'm not going to tell you that."

"What? Why not?"

"Because we believe it will risk more lives than it might save," Dr. León said simply.

"I don't understand."

"The method of tracking requires that the railgun is fired at least once more…"

"That's preposterous!" Rutledge couldn't help his outburst. "How is that saving lives?"

"Because we believe that if you know how to locate it, you'll throw everything you have in its path." She explained it slowly, as if to a child, only adding to Rutledge's frustration at being kept in the dark. "The weapon has already demonstrated immense destructive potential. We don't need to give it more targets."

Rutledge's chest swelled as he opted to pull rank. "I am the President of the United States, and I have more right to know than anyone—"

"I'm aware," the young woman told him, seeming bored with the trajectory of the conversation. "That doesn't mean I'm going to tell you anything."

His cheeks reddened, his irritation at this alleged doctor who was allegedly with the CIA growing rapidly. With one shout he could have this room filled with Secret Service, have her arrested, detained, forced to tell them…

"Do you trust him?"

Rutledge blinked. "What?"

"Agent Zero. Do you trust him? Do you believe that he can stop the perpetrators and the railgun, if given the opportunity to track it, even if that means that it must be used again?"

"I…" Rutledge forced himself to calm. "Yes. I suppose I do."

"Then let him try." Dr. Penelope León lifted her right hand and opened it, showing a small black remote control or fob of some sort. "And Mr. President? I hope we can keep this between us."

She pressed a button on the fob, and the lights instantly went out again. He saw a shadow flutter through the room. A few seconds later, the lamp turned on again, and again he heard harried shouts from outside the bedroom.

"Sir?" Terrence called through the door.

"Another outage, Terrence?" Rutledge tried to sound convincing. "Try to find out what's going on, would you?"

"Yes sir, I will."

What a strange young woman, he thought as he sat again on the edge of the bed. It made perfect sense, in a strange way, that she'd be an ally of Zero's.

But what she had asked of him was monumentally troubling—to stand by and do nothing even if the railgun's location was discovered. Could he do that? It would be a flagrant neglect of his office, regardless if was Americans endangered or not.

He made a resolution to himself. If Zero found the weapon first, Rutledge would not intervene. But if someone else did, he would have to act, regardless of what it might mean for Zero or anyone else.

142

Chapter Twenty Four

Sara awoke as the sun was rising, the sky outside her window a flat gray and threatening the possibility of snow. She heard rustling from beyond her bedroom and sat bolt upright suddenly, listening, before the veil of sleep lifted and she remembered the night before. Camilla, her former roommate from Florida, had shown up unannounced, fleeing an abusive ex-boyfriend.

She tossed the blanket off of her, pulled her hair into a haphazard ponytail, and padded out barefoot to the kitchen where she found Camilla digging a fist into a cereal box.

"Hey! Good morning," Camilla said brightly. She dug out a handful of fruity cereal and scooped it into her mouth. "Sleep good?"

"Sure. You?" Sara made her way to the coffee machine. None had been made yet, so she grabbed a filter and the can of grounds.

"Yeah. Definitely. Couch was nice." Sara had slept in Maya's bed and offered her friend her own, but Camilla had opted for the living room couch instead, claiming that the ambient noise of the TV helped her fall asleep.

Sara turned on the brew cycle and leaned against the counter, struggling to come around. She'd never been much of a morning person; not like Maya, who could wake before the sun and run seven miles before breakfast. But something was off this morning. Her brain was just still too foggy to put it together.

"So what do you *do* around here?" Camilla asked. "You got like a job or something?"

"No, no job. I'm studying for my GED. And I take some art classes at the community center."

"Art classes? What, like pottery or something?" Camilla snorted. "Forget all that stuff today. You know I'm flush. Let's go do something fun!"

Sara looked at her, really looked at Camilla for the first time that morning. Her eyes were bloodshot. She was in the same clothes from the night prior. A quick glance over at the sofa showed a blanket tossed over it, but no divots in the cushions, no signs that the pillow had been used.

"You're high."

Camilla blinked at her. "What? Girl, I told you I was clean—"

"Yeah, you said that. But you're high right now." Sara felt the anger coming then, rising like heat from her chest into her neck and up to her cheeks. "I checked your bag. Where'd you stash it?"

"I swear, I'm not high!" Camilla protested.

"You didn't sleep at all!" Sara accused. "You took the couch so that you could do it after I fell asleep!"

Camilla was shaking her head now, over and over, like she was stuck on some kind of loop. "No, I'm not, I'm not..."

"What are you on? Uppers? Coke?" Sara marched over to Camilla's bag, lying on the living room floor, and snatched it up. "Where are you hiding it?" She tore the bag open and looked again, but found nothing odd—other than the thick roll of cash she'd seen the night before.

"Wait!" Camilla cried.

A-ha. Sara took the rubber band off the roll of dough and let the cash unfurl. It was a clever hiding place, stowing the drugs inside the money roll.

"Sara, don't! It's gone!"

She looked up sharply. "What do you mean, gone?"

"I mean... yes. I had some." Camilla stared at the carpet. "I did everything I had last night. You're right. I didn't sleep." Her red-rimmed eyes grew moist with the threat of tears. "I need help."

"You *need* to leave," Sara said lowly. "I asked you *one* thing and you couldn't do it. You couldn't be honest..."

She trailed off as she glanced down at the stack of money in her hand. "What the hell...?" The edges of the bills were curled in on one another, fanning themselves naturally after being rolled so tightly. The top few bills were fives and tens, but every bill beneath them was a hundred. Dozens of them, maybe even a hundred hundred-dollar bills.

These were not just tips from bartending amounting to a few hundred bucks. This was close to ten grand easily.

"Camilla? What is this?"

"It's nothing," she said quickly. "Please, just give it to me? The drugs are gone. Just give me the money, Sara."

"First maybe you tell me why you're running away from this abusive ex of yours again."

"Sara, give me the goddamn money!" Camilla shrieked.

Then she shrieked again, this time out of fear, as a brisk knock sounded at the door.

"Here." Sara shoved the money into Camilla's hands. "Take it and leave." She brushed past the older girl to see who was knocking.

"Wait, wait!" Camilla's face had gone ashen. "Please, check to see who it is first."

Sara was about to roll her eyes—she always checked the peephole first—but something about the fear in her friend's voice gave her pause. She padded to the front door and put her eye to the tiny lens.

On the other side of the door was a young white guy, mid-twenties at best. He wore a white tank top with a heavy leather jacket over it, the loose collar displaying a dark tribal tattoo swirling up his collarbone and reaching his neck. His hair was short, nearly shaved, and his eyes were deep set and ringed in shadow, as if he hadn't slept in days.

A knot of panic formed in Sara's stomach. She didn't have to ask to know who this was.

When she turned away from the door, Camilla had her back against the wall of the small foyer. Sara's expression must have betrayed her instantly.

"Don't open it," she whispered.

"How did he know to come here?!"

"I don't—"

The man on the other side banged on the door with a fist. "Hello!" he shouted, more of a demand than a question.

Sara rushed into the kitchen and snatched up Camilla's cell phone, lying on the countertop. She opened the GPS app and checked the settings.

"Son of a bitch," she hissed. "Your location sharing is turned on!"

"Oh my god." Camilla looked terrified. "He must have done it when I wasn't looking ... that's how he always knew where to find me ..."

"And you didn't think that was strange?!" Sara asked furiously.

"I didn't even know that was a thing!"

"Open up!" The man slapped angrily at the door with a palm. "Whoever you are, I know she's in there! This doesn't have to get ugly! I just want my money!"

Oh shit. The money that Camilla had, the thousands in the roll of cash. "You stole from him."

Camilla didn't answer, but her gaze darted left and right nervously.

"You have to give it back," Sara said firmly. "If you do, maybe he'll leave."

The older girl shook her head, her unwashed hair swinging in her face. "I-I can't. I spent … a lot of it."

"You stole more than ten grand from him?!" *And then you came here?* Sara wanted to add, but she held her tongue. Instead she rushed back to the door.

"I'm gonna give you to the count of three," the dealer threatened, "and then I'm kickin' it in."

I'd like to see you try. Fortunately her dad had the foresight, after several break-ins, to convince the landlord to allow him to install a heavy-duty security door. Even the frame was reinforced with steel. Aside from the lock on the knob, there were also a sliding chain lock and two deadbolts, one an ordinary twist lock and the other a heavier bar that slid into the door frame.

Sara slid it over now, as quietly as she could. But it settled into place with a heavy *chunk.*

"Yeah? You think you can lock me out?" the guy shouted from the other side. Sara checked the peephole just in time to see him winding up a kick.

The impact rattled the door in its frame and caused Camilla to let out a small scream. He tried a second time, and then a third before realizing the door wasn't budging.

Sara tried to think. *Christ, I haven't even had coffee yet.* The guy couldn't get in through the door; of that she was certain. But he'd also clearly driven through the night in pursuit of Camilla, from Florida all the way here to Bethesda, so he wasn't likely to just give up and go home. He knew she was here even if they turned the location sharing off.

And the door was not the only possible way into the apartment, if someone was crafty and persistent enough.

Think. What would Maya do?

That wasn't helpful; her older sister would probably open the door and kick the guy's ass. Sara was in no position to take on a guy who had at least eight inches of height and fifty pounds on her frame, not to mention the strong possibility that his midnight run north was likely fueled by drugs.

"What's his name?" she asked.

Camilla stared at her like a deer in headlights. "Huh?"

"His name. What's his name?"

"Rex. It's Rex."

"Rex?" Sara scoffed. "For god's sake, Camilla … never mind. Just don't say a word." She positioned herself just outside the door and carefully glanced through the peephole again. Then she cleared her throat and said loudly, "Rex?"

The guy was gearing up for another kick, but his foot slowly lowered back down. "So she is in there."

"Yes." There was no point in trying to hide it. He'd never believe that Camilla's phone was there while she wasn't. "But she's not coming out, and you're not getting in. If you don't leave, right now, I'm calling the police."

"Sara..." Camilla said in a small voice behind her.

Through the peephole, the guy called Rex grinned maliciously. "Sure. Go ahead, call 'em. But maybe ask Camilla first. See if she thinks that's a good idea."

Sara frowned at that. "What the hell does he mean?"

Her friend shook her head again. "You can't call the cops. You can't. I have a record."

"What did you do?"

"I helped him move some stuff. A cop stopped me for speeding and he found it on me."

Sara's head was starting to ache. "Let me guess. There's a warrant out for you in the state of Florida. You needed to skip town to avoid jail, so you stole from Rex and took off."

"That's..." Camilla gulped. "That's pretty much how it shook out. And Rex has never been busted. His record is clean. If you call the cops they might get him for trying to break in, but I'll get sent back, it'll be worse. I can't go to jail, Sara."

"I can't *believe* you brought all this on me!" Sara screeched. "What is wrong with you?" She had half a mind to unlock the door and throw her friend to the wolf.

"Please." Camilla suddenly looked like a lot less like the hotheaded bartender she had known and much more like a frightened child. "Help me."

Sara's nostrils flared. Without another word, she stormed to the closet and yanked the door open. In the pocket of her dad's old tweed coat was the silver revolver.

Camilla's eyes widened in shock at the sight of it, and then even wider when Sara expertly opened the cylinder to check it was loaded.

"Rex," she said through the door in a voice that she hoped sounded confident. "Maybe I won't call the cops. But you can bet your ass I'll do anything I have to do to keep you away from her and out of here. I'm armed. It's two against one. Do you like those odds?"

Through the peephole, Rex sneered. "Aw, two frightened little girls shackin' up together. Thinkin' you're tough. But let me ask you something, little girl." He moved closer to the peephole, so that through the fisheye curvature of the lens Sara saw only a leering mouthful of yellowed teeth.

"You think I came alone?"

He vanished suddenly from the peephole's view.

Sara sucked in a breath as she rushed through the apartment, to the sliding glass door that led to their small balcony. She checked it carefully but saw no one, so she swiftly closed the blinds. "Close those curtains," she hissed at Camilla, but her friend was frozen it seemed, her back to the wall and both palms flat against it as if she could become a part of it if she tried hard enough.

"He's going to kill me," she said meekly. "He's done it before, I know he has."

"No, he's not going to kill you." The revolver already felt too heavy in her hand. It had been far too long since she'd even shot a gun. She set it down on the counter and grabbed up her cell phone.

"No! Please, no cops!"

"I'm not calling the cops," Sara insisted. She was calling for help. There was only one person she knew who could even the odds against someone dangerous like Rex. But that was only if he could get there before the dealer found a way inside.

CHAPTER TWENTY FIVE

Stefan Krauss remembered every kill.

He catalogued them in his mind like a bloody library. His memory was not exactly what experts called eidetic, but it was quite excellent, and whenever he wanted he could conjure up the memory of a past engagement as easily as pressing play on a video, rich with detail, precise in actualization.

He did so now, with the odor of diesel fuel stuck in his nostrils, the taste of it acrid in his throat. He still stood on the bow of the small, sleek ship called *Glimmer*, but the ship was no longer in the water; it was thousands of feet above it.

To distract himself from the rumbling engines, impossibly loud in his ears, and the overpowering scent of fuel, and even the chatter of the Saudis as they shouted in their foreign tongue to be heard, he replayed a memory in his head. His first kill.

His name had not always been Stefan Krauss, but he had not gone by his birth name in many years, would never answer to it again. The real Stefan Krauss was a German footballer who had played for the Dortmund club for only one season. He'd been an instant star, his movements so fluid that it appeared his body made the decisions instinctively for him. But a month after the season ended, the athlete Stefan Krauss was killed in an automobile accident outside Dusseldorf.

He was fourteen when he adopted the name, for the simple reasons that he thought it sounded pleasant to the ear, easy to remember, and the actual Stefan Krauss was no longer using it.

Fourteen. That was his age when he killed for the first time. There had been fights before that, schoolyard scraps that ended with bloody knuckles and busted lips. Wrestling matches in the dirt, ruddy faces and name-calling.

He'd had a sister before he was Stefan Krauss. Two years his junior. Spirited and amusing and curious. He'd had a mother, too young to have a fourteen-year-old, who worked two jobs to feed them. He'd had a stepfather, in lieu of the one who abandoned them years prior.

And at age fourteen, he had learned what his stepfather had been doing to his sister.

There was a word for people like him, or at least one that they would use to describe him. In English, that word was "sociopath." Amusingly enough, despite the German propensity to have far more interesting versions of English terms, the same word in his native tongue was simply "*Soziopath.*"

But he did not believe that he was one of them. Not in the true sense. He had a conscience. He had feelings. He knew that because on the day that he learned the unspeakably untoward things that his stepfather was doing to his sister, he came home from school enraged and killed the man.

His stepfather had been between jobs, yet again, drinking a Schöfferhofer while seated in his ratty recliner. The boy had barged into the house, fists balled, and accused him of what he knew his stepfather had done. The older man had stared for a long moment, finishing his beer, standing slowly. Then he lunged with the bottle and smashed it over the boy's head.

That was a pain he would never forget. His vision had been doubled; blood ran into his eyes. But he'd held his own. It was a spectacularly bloody fight—the bloodiest of his life, before he had learned patience and efficiency. It ended with the boy atop the man, pounding his stepfather with both fists, realizing that he could not do the damage he wished to inflict. He'd grabbed the nearest object—a hand weight. A small dumbbell that his mother used for calisthenics. A mere five pounds.

It took only five pounds, over several blows, to crush a skull.

He'd slain the monster. He'd done what he believed was right. But when he looked up again, covered in the blood of an abuser, breathing hard, adrenaline coursing through his veins in those moments before everything would begin to hurt ... *she* was there.

His sister. The victim. And in that moment, *he* was the monster. She screamed and ran from the house. Only then did he fully realize what he had done. So he left. He became Stefan Krauss that day.

That was twenty-two years ago. He'd been Stefan Krauss for longer than he'd been that boy. And now he stood upon the bow of a stolen ship carrying a plasma railgun, the ship in turn being carried in the belly of an Antonov An-124, a strategic airlift quadjet capable of loading and unloading cargo without landing. This particular plane was decommissioned twelve years earlier; the last known use was Qatar. Sheikh Salman had purchased it a few years prior in a seemingly clairvoyant move of foresight that he might one day have use for something like it.

Or so the sheikh claimed. In the last two months the plane had been outfitted with specifications that Krauss had been transmitting out of South Korea while posing as security for the railgun's technical crew. After firing on the Navy ships in Oman, the Antonov had swept out of the sky and low over the water, opening its cargo hatch and slowing its airspeed until *Glimmer* was able to safely slide into the rotund plane's belly. Wide rollers facilitated their transfer, and enormous rubber bumpers caught them before they crashed into the cargo hold's wall.

All in all, it had been relatively smooth.

Over the din of the engine, the PA system crackled and a voice made an announcement in Arabic. Krauss frowned; he did not know the language.

"It is time," one of the Saudi commandos told him in English. Though the warning was unnecessary; he could feel that they were slowing and dropping in altitude.

"Brace," he told the Saudi. Then he gestured to the other commandos. "Tell them." Stefan Krauss lowered himself to his knees and wrapped a bow line several times around his forearm. The landing would be a bumpy one, he knew; the rope was just in case he was flung overboard.

The rear cargo hatch of the Antonov rumbled downward then, instantly bringing a frenzy of whipping, frigid wind over the boat. Krauss zipped up his jacket. February in this part of the world was anything but pleasant.

Then a buzzer sounded, even louder than the engine, so loud he winced. Before he could exhale, the boat rocketed backward. Suddenly he felt his stomach drop out with the telltale sensation of falling; he was able to register a single thought (*I wonder how far the fall is*) before the boat crashed into the water, stern first, and then bow dropping.

Stefan Krauss grunted as his body pitched forward. He caught himself on his forearms and slid into the railing at the bow. Somewhat painful, but at least the rope had been unnecessary. The Atlantic in February could kill a man.

Glimmer rocked a few times and settled, the waves they had created growing smaller with each ebb. Krauss stood then, the Antonov droning in his ears as it took to the sky again, climbing in altitude.

"Good?" he asked the Saudi commandos at the stern, flashing a thumbs-up.

"All good," one of them said in English, though at least two of them looked queasy. Krauss couldn't help but wonder why Salman had sent five when he only needed two others to effectively pilot the boat and fire the weapon. Perhaps they were going to kill him when their goal was accomplished. Though that made little sense either, since Krauss had already been paid. For now, he was still the only one who could use the railgun, and he moved to the console to exhibit that now.

The heavy doors at the center of the boat whirred as they opened upright. The head of the railgun rose slowly, almost casually. He appreciated this weapon immensely; it had no interest in showing off. It was in no hurry to demonstrate its power. It had purpose, and performed it efficiently and quickly. The railgun, in many ways, reminded him of himself.

"What are you doing?!" shouted one of the two Saudi commandos he had heard speak English thus far.

Krauss keyed in the line-of-sight targeting (there were no coordinates needed, and their target was not a static one) and locked onto the plane before answering. "There can be no trail. No one to answer questions."

"Those are our people!"

Krauss frowned at the commando. "I was told you and your men knew the plan. But now I wonder how much Sheikh Salman did not tell you?"

The man's jaw flexed; he wanted to say more, but he refrained.

The railgun pivoted upward, aiming skyward, and then the apparatus swung around one hundred and eighty degrees. Krauss flicked up a small red plastic shield, and then the switch to fire. He directed his attention to the long barrel of the railgun, enjoying the way that it made minute adjustments, tracking its target even during the eight seconds it took to power up.

And then, in the most beautiful blue flash, the Antonov exploded in the air.

Krauss smiled as he started the engines and powered down the weapon. *Glimmer* did an about-face, and then he opened the throttle toward their destination. It was cold, but he didn't mind it. They were only about six hundred miles from the coast. They could reach the eastern shore of the United States in four hours.

CHAPTER TWENTY SIX

The EA-6B Prowler on loan from Sergeant Flagg's "friends" in Algeria roared into the air from H-6 in Morocco and headed north by northwest toward the Strait of Gibraltar. Alan took the yoke, he and Maria seated side by side in the front-most of two cockpits. Zero sat behind them in a secondary cockpit, strapped in with a headset over his ears so they could communicate.

It had been a while since Zero felt this claustrophobic, boxed in by a domed windshield overhead and his black pack between his feet. But that was the least of his concerns. They needed a hit on the railgun, and soon. Otherwise they were flying aimless.

"We'll head to the Strait and go east," Alan's voice crackled through the headset. "If you're right and the boat headed up the Gulf of Aden to the Mediterranean, we should be close enough to find it by visual."

"Close enough to do what?" Zero couldn't help but ask. The decommissioned Prowler had no missiles, no armaments.

"This plane was built for electronic warfare," Alan explained, "with an AN/ALQ-99 system. That's fancy-talk for advanced signal jammers. If we can locate the boat, we might be able to at least keep the railgun from being able to lock onto a target. The pods are still there, affixed under each wing. They should still be operational..."

"Should?" Maria asked.

"Do we ever work on certainty?" Alan retorted.

"Fair point. And if that fails?"

"Then we get coordinates and call in a strike to anyone that will listen," Zero said. It was a long shot, but it was the only one they had—short of crashing the plane right into the damn boat, which was not an option any of them would discount.

The screen of the sat phone in his lap lit up with an incoming call, the ring tone muted by the Prowler's twin engines. Zero patched the call through the headset so Alan and Maria could hear. "Penny? Give us good news."

"Wish I had some," the young doctor's voice was low and urgent. "ILDN got a hit on the railgun's signature, just now—"

"Where?" Zero interrupted, realizing sheepishly that she was about to tell them.

"In the Atlantic. About six hundred miles off the east coast of the United States."

"What?!" Zero's heart skipped a beat even as Reidigger instantly changed their heading. That was impossible; even a ship as advanced as the one the South Koreans had built couldn't get that far that quickly.

Unless...

"What was the target?" Maria asked.

"Unclear," said Penny. "Something exploded over the Atlantic. Satellites are trying to determine what it was. A ship, maybe, or a—"

"Plane," Zero interjected again. That was how the boat got to the Atlantic as fast as it did. "They moved it by plane, and then blew it up."

Just like the South Korean crew had entirely been eliminated, and the Somali pirates who stole it, now the crew of whatever cargo plane had transported the boat were dead too. This was a suicide mission for all involved—which meant that whoever was on that boat with the railgun was not only willing to die for their cause, but knew damn well that they would.

"Feds are investigating the explosion currently," Penny said quickly, "but you know that the railgun is going to be at the forefront of everyone's mind. They're going to know what we know pretty soon, and then it's going to be havoc."

"She's right," Maria agreed. "If anything within two hundred miles of the coast can be a target, the choice would be massive chaotic evacuations or heavy loss of life."

But, Zero realized, *not anything could be the target.*

"The railgun doesn't fire like a missile," he pointed out. "It fires like a gun, requiring a direct and unobstructed path. Which means that something like the White House or the Pentagon can't be a viable target to strike from the sea."

"But the United Nations building in New York could be," Reidigger pointed out. "It's right on the water."

"Unless their goal is simply heavy casualties," said Penny, "in which case any major metropolitan hub on the coast would be fish in a barrel."

Think! Zero shouted internally. The perpetrators had gone through a hell of a lot of trouble to get this far, and the railgun had traveled halfway across the planet. To do all that just for heavy casualties didn't make sense, especially considering the pinpoint accuracy of the weapon. No, their target had to be specific. It had to be calculated. So far it had been used on three warships and an airplane—but no static targets.

"Moving targets," he murmured aloud.

"Zero, repeat that?" Reidigger said.

That was it. The railgun was adept at hitting moving targets. Perhaps the only reason they fired on the cargo plane at all was to let their location be known. The threat of its proximity to the US coast would be cause for evacuation—movement.

They won't have to hit the White House. Because that's not where Rutledge will be.

"Alan, can we make it before the ship reaches shore?" Zero asked suddenly.

"Before it reaches shore? Yes. Before it gets into range of the coast? I ... don't know."

"Let's try like hell. I think I know what their target is. Penny—I need you to do whatever you can to keep the president from getting on Air Force One."

CHAPTER TWENTY SEVEN

It was almost nine in the morning by the time Maya reached the city limits of Columbus, Ohio, in search of the agent formerly known as Seth Connors. She had decided against getting a motel room and tried to drive straight through the night, but around three in the morning her eyelids grew heavy and she feared she'd fall asleep at the wheel, so she pulled into a rest stop and caught a couple hours' sleep in the parking lot, setting an alarm on her phone that she almost ignored. But she forced herself awake again, purchased three sixteen-ounce energy drinks (which had a disconcerting warning on the side to not consume more than two in a twenty-four-hour period) and pressed on.

The morning traffic of the city was surprisingly not heavy, and her GPS told her she should reach the address that Dr. Bliss had given her—501 Willow Street—in ten minutes. The Skylark had performed better than admirably, making the eight-hour drive almost pleasant.

She clicked on the radio for some background noise, hoping for some music but instead getting a rapid female voice reporting on some new development out there in the world.

"Breaking news from the United Nations' Security Council, an investigation is being launched into a weapons project developed by South Korea in secrecy. Anonymous reports claim that the weapon was stolen three days ago, though the perpetrators and the nature of the weapon are currently unknown..."

A short blast of a honking horn startled Maya. She checked the rearview; a black car had swung into traffic on an illegal left turn right behind her, cutting off a honking truck.

Ordinarily she might have chalked it up to rude drivers. Except she recognized the car. It was a late-model Lincoln with a boxy grille and wide headlights. She'd noticed it earlier, as the sun was rising and she was still on the highway. That same model car had been within a few paces of her for a good fifty miles.

Maybe even that same car.

Did Bliss sell me out? she wondered. *Or am I being paranoid?*

There was only one way to find out. At the next intersection, as the light was turning from yellow to red, Maya hit the gas and did a quick left turn without signaling. She elicited a few honks herself but ignored them and kept an eye on the rearview.

The Lincoln didn't follow. She breathed a sigh of relief, and even allowed herself a chuckle at her own expense and paranoia.

I guess that's what happens when you spend too much time around Dad, she thought wryly as she made a right turn to go around the block and double back on her route. But as she made the second right, a car turned from the opposite direction, only a few feet away, practically on her bumper.

The black Lincoln.

"Okay," Maya told them in the rearview. "Never been in a car chase before, so this should be fun." She slammed the accelerator.

The Skylark lurched forward, forcing her further into her seat. She came up fast, too fast on the car in front of her and swerved quickly into the oncoming lane. A blue sedan screeched to a halt as Maya narrowly zipped around it, putting a car between her and her pursuers.

Her heart leapt into her throat as she ran a red light, missing a T-bone collision with an SUV by no more than an arm's width. But the Lincoln was not far behind her, using the path of stopped cars in her wake to keep pace.

You can't outrun them in the city. She slowed the Skylark and fell into the flow of city traffic, doing about thirty and coming up on the next traffic light. The Lincoln stayed right on her tail, close enough that she couldn't see its headlights. Nor could she see through the dark-tinted windshield enough to discern who might be driving.

Time to try something fancy. At the green light she suddenly jerked the wheel to the right, into a sudden turn. The Lincoln predictably kept right up with her—but instead of braking into the turn, Maya hit the gas and spun the wheel further.

The sports car responded perfectly, the back wheels fishtailing out as the Buick did an about-face almost in place. She hit the accelerator again, passing the Lincoln in the opposite direction and, even though they couldn't see through her windows either, gave them the finger.

"Ha!" she shouted victoriously. Behind her, the Lincoln was struggling to do a K-turn on the tight city street, cars blaring their horns as it cut off traffic. She made a quick right, zoomed two blocks and then a left, turning randomly and hoping to lose them.

You're in one of the most conspicuous cars you could possibly be in, she thought. She had to get the Skylark off the street. There was a good chance, she reasoned, that her pursuers knew the car but not her.

Two blocks later she saw it, a large white sign with vertical letters in red spelling PARK. She turned quickly into the parking garage, drove up the ramp, and threw the car in park, grabbing her cell and the purse that still held the Glock inside. She left her rucksack in the trunk and shoved the keys and a credit card to a bewildered attendant.

"I need this parked somewhere that's not visible from the street or the entrance. Please."

The young attendant blinked. "Um...sure. Okay. Just give me a sec to print you a ticket..."

"No time." Maya glanced over her shoulder. If the Lincoln passed by the garage they could easily see her and the car there. "I won't be long; you'll remember me. Is there a back exit to this place?"

"Are you in some kind of trouble?" the young man asked, as if seeing a possibility for a chivalrous act. "Because I can call someone if you need."

"I'm good, thanks. Back exit?"

"Uh, yeah. Through that door and down the stairs."

"Thank you." Maya hurried through a white-painted steel door, took the concrete stairs two at a time, and jogged down a short corridor to a security door that opened onto the street at the rear of the three-level garage. She checked her GPS; her short car chase had led her closer to the address, but not by much. She still had a twenty-five-minute hike to get there.

She pushed through the door and out onto the street.

They don't know your face, she told herself, despite having nothing much to base that on. She walked as quickly as she could while still looking casual, keeping her eyes cast downward at the sidewalk while clutching her phone in her hand and trying to keep passing cars in her periphery, like her dad had shown her. It was hard resisting the urge to look up, to check behind her every few seconds to make sure no cars were slowly tailing her.

It was a fraught walk, but after about twenty minutes she entered a less-than-attractive neighborhood, crumbling brick facades tagged in graffiti and bars over windows. A few minutes later she reached her destination—and frowned as if it had personally offended her.

The address that Bliss had given her was a Chinese food restaurant. And given the early hour, it wasn't even open yet to question anyone.

There must be something. She refused to believe the doctor had lied to her and sent her all this way for nothing. Either he'd been a terrific actor or he'd shown true remorse over what he'd done.

She took a few steps back and looked up—the building had a second story. Possibly some sort of apartment, she reasoned. It too had bars over the windows, like many of the buildings in this part of the city, but they were dark, obscured by curtains behind them. And if Maya wasn't mistaken she thought she could make out something else covering the panes behind the bars, something yellowed with age. Newspaper, taped over the glass.

She hurried around to the side of the building and then to the rear, finding a set of gray wooden steps leading up to a door. Each step creaked under her feet, broadcasting her arrival to anyone who might be inside no matter how much she tried to shift her weight.

The door was white, the paint chipping badly, with a small window to the left of it with the same bars, curtains, and newspaper over it as the ones she had seen from the street.

Suddenly this entire ordeal felt very strange. She was in a city she didn't know at an address she couldn't confirm to find a man she wasn't certain still existed and had definitely been pursued by *someone*.

But she was here, and she didn't know what else to do—so she knocked.

There was no answer. She put her ear to the door but heard nothing. No fluttering of the newspaper at the window to see who was out there.

"Hello?" She knocked a second time, louder. Still nothing.

Maya scoffed. She didn't come all this way, didn't take Alan's car and drive through the night and get into a car chase just to be stymied by a closed door.

She identified two locks, both deadbolts, one a standard residential and the second a heavier commercial grade lock. From her purse she fished two tools, one an L-shaped pick with a flat head and the second a thin pick with a jagged, almost key-like tip, called a long rake pick. She inserted the head of the L-shaped pick in the bottom of the commercial lock's tumbler and carefully maneuvered the long rake in, making subtle adjustments as she worked the first pin.

A gentle touch and patience were virtues in lock-picking; force and speed had no place here, though expedience came with a practiced hand. Often she found that once the first pin fell, the others came easier.

When she felt the final pin in the tumbler fall into place, she took out the long rake and slowly twisted the L-shaped pick counterclockwise. The deadbolt slid into the door. Then she repeated the process for the standard lock. Both were open in less than two minutes.

"Okay," she bolstered herself aloud. "If someone was in there, they would have made themselves known by now." No one sat idly by while watching their locks forced open.

She dropped the pins back into her purse and her hand brushed the Glock. Her first instinct was to draw it, but she decided against it and reached for the doorknob.

The chipped white door opened about six inches and stopped suddenly, straining a chain lock from the inside.

"Oh, come on!" Maya muttered in exasperation. Her arm wasn't small enough to snake inside and try to undo the chain.

Am I really going to do this? Technically she'd already committed breaking and entering. She might as well go the whole nine.

Maya raised her right foot and planted a powerful kick just above the knob. The chain broke off from the molding and the door flew open, hitting a chair. She froze, waiting and listening a moment, but heard nothing.

The first thing she noticed stepping over the threshold was the smell. There was a musty odor with an undertone of mildew, not overwhelming but reminiscent of a place that didn't get a lot of air flow, like a neglected shed. She was standing in an outdated but relatively tidy kitchen. There were a couple of dishes in the sink and two empty beer bottles on the counter. The refrigerator was white and conventional; a small round table on the other side had only a single chair.

She took a few cautious steps and entered a living room. With the newspaper over the windows and the curtains drawn it looked like perpetual dusk, but she could see a sole recliner, a boxy television set in the corner with a DVD player on top of it. A handful of war movies scattered on the floor.

Behind her was a small bathroom; she would clear that last. Facing her was the dark doorway of what she assumed was a bedroom. She took a step toward it—and then froze as a figure moved in the darkness toward her.

She would have leapt back, or perhaps even rushed toward him in attack, but the sight of the silver gun pointed between her eyes seized her limbs. This wasn't the first time she'd had a gun pointed at her, but that didn't stop fear's icy pick from stabbing into her heart.

"Who are you?" the man behind the gun asked softly.

Maya forced herself to look away from the gun to him. She didn't know what he had looked like before, but it didn't seem that time had been kind to him. His hair was shaggy and long, hanging over his ears, and it looked as if he hadn't shaved in a week. His eyes were dull, uninterested even, and he held extra weight in his chin and neck.

"Who are you?" he asked again.

Her tongue felt like cotton in her mouth. "M-my name is Maya. Maya Lawson. Are you..." She almost said "Seth Connors" before she caught herself, remembering what Bliss had told her. He didn't know that name anymore. "Are you John Graham?"

"They told me you would come," he murmured.

Maya frowned. "Who told you?"

"The men on the phone."

"What men on the phone, John?" Maya pressed. "Please. I'm not here to hurt you. I'm here to help you."

"They ... they call me. They make sure I have what I need." Seth Connors's gaze drifted away for a moment, his eyes nearly glazing over. For a moment she even had an opening to disarm him. But she stood her ground. "They make sure I don't leave. Or else, people will find me." His attention snapped back to her. "People like you. They said, 'They'll come for you, and you have to fight them.'"

"No, no, John. I'm not going to fight you." Maya's heartbeat doubled. He was clearly confused, he had a gun in her face, and had been convinced that she was an enemy. "I promise I won't. I just need to know some things. These men that call, are they with the CIA?"

"CIA," Connors said, slowly and pensively, as if he was reaching out for the word. "That's ... that's something I used to know."

Maya blinked. Bliss said the chip in his head had wiped his memories. How did he know what he used to know?

"What else, John? What else did you used to know?" Maya's gaze wavered between the barrel of the gun and his face, which was quickly contorting with uncertainty.

"The men on the phone, they said there was an accident. It was bad. My head ... no. My brain was injured. I forgot who I was. But I knew things, back then, things that were danger-ous to know." Connors spoke softly, methodically, in a way that suggested to Maya that he was regurgitating information he had been told over and over. "That's why I'm here. I have to stay here. It's not safe anywhere else."

Maya had a choice. She could keep him talking, despite the gun pointed at her face, and hope it wasn't used. Or she could try to disarm him and in the process prove that the "men on the phone" were right. There was no way to do it that wouldn't seem like an attack.

"I know some things," Maya told him. "I know the name 'Seth.' Is that something you know too? Seth?"

Connors blinked at her. "I ... yes. I know that name. Sometimes, in my head, I hear people, calling it out."

"That used to be your name. It was Seth Connors. Not John Graham. You were Seth Connors."

He shook his head adamantly. "No. I would remember that."

Maya decided, against her better judgment, to press further. "You had a daughter. A little girl."

"I didn't..."

"You volunteered for an experiment to have your memory erased, Seth—"

"Don't call me that!" he snapped.

"Okay. Okay. Please, let's calm down," Maya urged. "Just... think for a moment. Do the things I'm saying make sense to you?"

Again he glanced away and down, at the carpet, though the gun stayed aimed. "I've seen a girl." His voice was almost a whisper. "Sometimes. When I sleep. She said 'daddy.' But that wasn't... it wasn't me."

Maya's mind was churning. She wasn't entirely sure what was happening, but it seemed that some things were starting to poke through the memory-suppressing chip. She wondered if it had a shelf life and was failing. Or if it was malfunctioning somehow. Bliss had said it was a prototype; maybe they hadn't considered longevity in the design.

That's why they've kept him alive. To see how long it would last.

But what did her dad want with this man? Was it some injustice he'd unearthed that he felt an obligation to make right? Or was it more...

Suddenly Maya thought back to her mother's death. The weeks afterward when he was gone and she and Sara had stayed with their Aunt Linda. Then he was back. He felt different then. For two years, things had been fine. And then he went back to the CIA. He changed...

No, she told herself. *There's no way.*

Seth Connors was staring at her oddly, his head cocked at an angle like a quizzical dog. "Who are you?"

The guy's brain was scrambled, his short-term memory clearly fried. Maya would have to figure the rest out later; for now there was still a gun aimed at her. "Listen to me, please. You are Seth Connors. You are a former field agent with the CIA. You volunteered for an experiment after the death of your daughter and had your memories suppressed."

"No," he said plainly. "You're lying. You're with *them*."

"There is no 'them,' Seth—"

"Don't call me that!" he shouted, raising his voice for the first time.

"You're being kept here as a test!"

"No!" Connors shouted again, squeezing his eyes shut and shaking his head vigorously. "No! No!" His hand trembled, his finger on the trigger.

Maya saw no other choice. Talking wasn't working; she had to act. While his eyes were squeezed shut, she sprang forward, using her right hand to push the gun out of her face. With her left she grabbed his elbow, and she twisted her body ninety degrees while going down to one knee.

Connors's body came with her, thrown off balance, tumbling over her hip and crashing to the floor with a loud gasp. She reached for the gun to twist it from his grip, but didn't expect him to react with such speed.

Before she could reach the pistol his other fist slammed into her solar plexus, doubling her over, forcing the air from her lungs and causing an instant wave of nausea. Connors scrambled to his hands and knees, trying to get to his feet. Maya responded with a kick to his stomach, and then a second one to the hand that held the gun. Her shoe crunched against his fingers and he howled as the pistol skittered across the carpet.

Connors gritted his teeth and leapt at her in a tackle. He had both size and weight on her relatively small frame—so Maya let him take her to the ground. She planted a foot on his hip and used the inertia to throw him backward, off of her, into a heap of limbs in the doorway between the kitchen and living room.

Breathing hard, she grabbed the pistol from the floor. But she refused to point it at him. Disarming him was the goal, not letting him believe she wanted to hurt or kill him. He stared at her wide-eyed as she popped the magazine from the gun.

Then she snickered. She couldn't help herself. The gun wasn't loaded. However he'd acquired it, Connors seemed to have forgotten ammunition.

This man wasn't hostile. He was confused. Memories of his former life were starting to resurface and his brain couldn't reconcile what he had been told with what he was recalling. In that moment, seeing him cowering on the floor and holding his injured hand, she felt horribly sorry for him and everything he'd lost.

"I don't want to hurt you," she said. "I promise. But...I think I want you to come with me." She held out a hand to help him up. "Will you come with me, Seth?"

He eyed her warily for a moment—and then he reached for her hand.

"Step away, please."

Maya looked up sharply to see two men standing in the still-open doorway of the apartment. Both wore black suits and long overcoats. Their features were remarkably forgettable, and in that moment she knew who they were before they even flashed their CIA credentials.

"I'm Agent Riggs, this is Agent Fraser, CIA. Miss Lawson, I'm going to ask you to come with me."

"Why?" she demanded.

The agent smiled at her wolfishly. "Where to begin? Grand theft auto, breaking and entering, assault with a deadly weapon, terroristic threats, the unlicensed handgun you're carrying without a permit...oh, and the classified documents of national intelligence that you stole."

"I didn't steal those, I—" She was about to argue that she'd been given those, but not only was that not entirely true, but she also didn't want to implicate Alan or his hacker friend into her mess.

She offered her wrists. "Fine. Take me in." She glanced down at Seth Connors. "What about him?"

"Don't worry," said Agent Riggs. "He's coming too."

CHAPTER TWENTY EIGHT

"Camilla, get away from the window!" Sara said harshly. Her friend had been nervously glancing through the blinds ever since the drug dealer, Rex, had threatened to try to get them.

Sara stood in the kitchen, her hand closed around the revolver and her cell phone on the countertop. The keypad was open and the numbers 9-1-1 were punched in so that all she had to do was press the call button if need be.

She didn't want to do that unless it became absolutely necessary. Not only was she not particularly fond of police, but if they came and found Rex with nothing on him and no record, there wouldn't be any reason to arrest him. Camilla, on the other hand, would be taken in for her outstanding warrant and failure to appear in court.

Besides, she'd already called for help. She just needed him to get here.

In the meantime, she stood in the kitchen with a clear line of sight on the front door, which was nearly impenetrable unless Rex happened to have a SWAT-level battering ram, and the rear patio, a sliding glass door that led to a small balcony. It would take quite an effort to climb up there, but it certainly wasn't impossible. They were the only entrances in or out for Rex and whatever thugs he had brought along for the ride.

"It's going to be okay," Sara said aloud, as much for her own benefit as Camilla's. "My friend is coming."

Camilla seemed uncertain. "Just promise you won't call the cops?"

"I ..." She wanted to promise, but it simply wasn't fair to ask her to sacrifice her own safety for Camilla's sake. "I won't."

Sara looked down at the silver revolver in her hand. It was an elegant thing, contoured and shiny. It was almost hard to believe that such a thing was capable of killing.

But am I? She was holding the gun for comfort, for confidence. But when it came down to it, would she use it? Would she be able to?

Just for good measure, she grabbed a paring knife from the butcher's block and stuck it in the back pocket of her jeans.

A rattling sound caught her attention. It sounded like it was coming from the bedroom.

Shit. The fire escape!

"Stay there!" she hissed to Camilla as she dashed toward her and Maya's shared bedroom. She couldn't believe she'd been so stupid, forgetting the iron stairs that led straight up to the wide window facing east.

Sara threw open the curtains and pointed the revolver. Through the glass, a chubby man in a Gators cap jumped back in shock. He'd been trying to jimmy it open, but at the sight of the gun he put his hands up quickly.

Glass shattered elsewhere in the apartment. Camilla shrieked. The chubby man outside sneered, and Sara realized he was just a distraction.

She dashed back to the kitchen. The sliding glass door was broken; one of the metal chairs her dad kept on the balcony was on the floor inside. Chilly February air rushed in, along with the drug dealer, Rex. Camilla looked frozen in horror as he reached out and grabbed a handful of her hair. She shrieked as he shook her.

"Where is it?" he demanded. "Where's the money?"

"Hey!" Sara leveled the revolver at him. "Let her go, asshole."

Rex's gaze slowly turned toward her. He frowned. "Christ. What are you, fourteen?" He let out a sharp, braying laugh. "This is who you go to for protection, Cammy? Is that thing even loaded?"

Sara cocked back the hammer with a thumb. "You're about to find out." Her heart jackhammered in her chest. She couldn't shoot someone who was unarmed. Even if he was a criminal who would hurt her if he had the chance.

Rex glanced between her and Camilla, as if trying to decide whether or not to test his luck. Suddenly glass shattered again, this time from the bedroom.

The chubby guy on the fire escape was making a move.

Sara's head whipped around instinctively in that direction, and Rex used the opportunity to shove Camilla roughly at her. The older girl collided and they both fell to the floor. The revolver slipped from her grip. Sara tried to pull herself after it under Camilla's flailing weight when a black boot came down hard on her outreached hand.

She screamed as pain shot up her arm.

Rex leaned over and plucked up the revolver. The chubby guy in the Gators cap had climbed through the window and stood over them, leering, as Camilla rolled off her and Sara sat up, cradling her hand. She couldn't move two of her fingers; something in her hand was broken.

"Well," said Rex, "you tried. Now, Cammy, you are going to give me my money back. And for every thousand missing, my buddy Brody here is going to cut off one of your fingers."

Fear shot through Sara as Camilla's breath came in ragged bursts.

Rex scoffed. "Quit sniveling and get my—"

A fist pounded on the front door. "Police!" a deep male voice boomed. "Open up!"

Rex shot a glare at Sara. "You didn't."

"You promised!" Camilla wailed, seeming to forget the very recent threat of grievous bodily harm.

Sara shook her head. She hadn't called the cops. But maybe a neighbor heard the windows shatter. Or someone on the street saw the strange man climbing to their balcony. Still, that would have been an incredibly fast response time.

Unless it's not the police at all.

"All right, listen up," Rex said quickly. "I'm going to have to answer the door. You're going to tell them we're all fine in here. We were messing around, things got out of hand, a window got broken. You say *one* wrong word, and I'll shoot this cop. Then Brody will shoot the little blonde one. Got it?"

The chubby guy, Brody, lifted the hem of his white jersey to show the black pistol he had stuffed in his pants.

The pounding fist was at the door again. "Police! Open the door!"

"Yeah, I'm coming," Rex called as he tucked the revolver into his jacket. Sara's mind raced. If it really was a cop, they were putting another life at risk. If it wasn't, then whoever was at the door had no idea what was waiting for him on the other side.

Rex opened both deadbolts, took the chain off, and pulled the door open. "What?" he said brusquely.

"Hi there." A familiar voice. He'd disguised it when he shouted through the door, but now Todd Strickland pushed past Rex and into the foyer. "I heard there was a problem here."

"Yo, what are you doing?" Rex demanded. "Cops can't just walk into people's homes!"

"Oh, I'm not a cop. I'm a friend of the family." Todd barely paid Rex any attention as he headed into the kitchen. "I just know that door is damn near impossible to break down." Todd was thirty, with close-cropped dark hair and boyish features that clashed with his physique. He was the kind of guy that Sara might have found attractive if he was on TV, but knowing him in person only made him kind of irritating.

She did notice, with a mild amount of alarm, that his left arm was currently wrapped in a beige cast and hanging from a sling over his shoulder.

Todd glanced over at the chubby guy, Brody, who folded his thick arms to look menacing. "You okay?" he asked Sara.

She nodded, still cradling her hand.

"Let me see." She winced as Todd took the hand gently. It was already swollen and turning purple. "Ooh. Definitely broken. Which one did it?"

She gestured to Rex behind him.

"That's enough of this shit..." Rex reached for the revolver in his jacket.

Strickland's left foot shot out behind him in an instant, catching Rex low in the abdomen in a mule kick. The drug dealer gasped as his eyes bugged and he fell to one knee. Without missing a beat, Strickland spun in place, planted his left leg, and in the same motion drove his right knee into Rex's face.

Blood erupted from both nostrils, flinging in an arc across the floor as his head snapped backward and his body fell flat to the tiled floor.

Brody reached for the gun at his waist. "Motherfu—"

Sara saw her chance. She yanked the paring knife out of her back pocket with her good hand, crouched low, and drove it into the larger man's thigh.

Brody howled in pain as the leg gave out and he crashed to the floor. Sara quickly pulled the pistol from his pants.

Todd nodded, impressed. But behind him, Rex was staggering to his feet, struggling to level the shaking revolver in his hand.

There was no time to shout a warning or even to think twice. Sara raised the black pistol and squeezed the trigger.

The shot was deafening in the small apartment. Camilla shrieked. Todd ducked instinctively. The shot winged Rex in the shoulder and spun him as he fell face-down to the floor again.

Sara breathed a sigh of relief. She hadn't even been aiming properly and could have taken off half his head.

"Phew!" Todd chuckled as he grabbed the revolver from the floor. "Close one. Thanks. That guy didn't want to go down easy."

"What took you so long?!" Sara practically shouted as every emotion from the last five minutes suddenly rushed through her.

"Sorry, I had to drive with one hand! I got here as fast as I could."

"And what was with the fake-cop routine?" Sara demanded.

"I had to assess the situation, didn't I?" Strickland said defensively. "I didn't know how many there were, if they were inside, if they had a gun to your head..."

"God, you are *such* a boy scout."

Strickland grinned and squeezed her shoulder. "Really though, besides the hand, are you okay?"

"Yeah." Sara looked around as Rex moaned from his place in the foyer and Brody took hissing breaths between his teeth, both thick hands clamped over his bleeding leg. "I'm okay."

"Listen, we're going to have to call the cops," Todd told them. "Someone will have heard that shot and likely report it. And you need medical attention for that hand..."

"Sara?" Camilla said meekly. She'd almost forgotten her friend was still there.

"Oh. Right." Sara sighed. "Todd, this is my friend Camilla, from Florida."

Strickland narrowed his eyes. "Yeah. I remember." While Sara had been living in Jacksonville, Strickland had been keeping close tabs on her for her dad. He was well aware of the sordid types she tended to hang around with back then.

"The thing is," Sara explained, "she's got an outstanding warrant in Florida. If the cops run her name, they'll see she skipped a hearing and she'll go to jail."

Todd sighed deeply, accompanied by a small moan of exasperation. "All right. Let me make a couple calls, see what I can do."

"Really?" Camilla asked brightly. "Wait, are you in the CIA too?"

"She knows about that?" Strickland asked in surprise.

But Sara wasn't thinking about any of that. She was thinking that if Todd was able to use his pull to expunge Camilla's record, she would be able to go home—where she would fall back into the same routines and bad habits that had gotten her here in the first place.

"On one condition." Sara turned to Camilla. "If he can get you off the hook, you go to rehab."

"Rehab?" Camilla parroted weakly.

"Yes. I know a place, down by the coast. They're good people. I went there... for a little bit." Strickland snickered behind her, but she ignored him. "It's rehab or jail. You pick."

Camilla seemed to ponder it for longer than she should have, considering her options. At last she asked, "Will you visit me?"

"Yes. Of course I will."

She nodded. "Okay then. I'll go."

"Will somebody call an ambulance already?!" Brody howled from the kitchen floor. "I got a fuckin' knife in my leg!"

Todd looked him over. "First time, huh? Don't pull it out or it'll bleed a lot worse." He shook his head. "Never a dull moment in the Lawson house."

CHAPTER TWENTY NINE

The Prowler hurtled over the Atlantic at six hundred and fifty-four miles an hour, Reidigger pushing it to its limit to reach the South Korean ship and the railgun. In the smaller cockpit behind Maria, Zero was a ball of nervous energy. He could hardly move with the buckles over his chest and the domed canopy over his head, so he had to settle for a knee bouncing in anticipation of catching up to the boat before it reached the range of the United States.

He glanced down at the sat phone's screen for the five hundredth time. Penny had patched him into the ILDN's map, which showed a blue blip where the railgun was last fired.

They'd passed that mark thirty minutes ago.

Any minute, he thought. *Any minute we'll be on top of it.* But would they see it from up here? They wouldn't see it on radar. They wouldn't get a signal. The only way to find it would be an actual visual, to spot its wake on the water—or if it fired again.

What if we already passed it and didn't even notice? he worried.

"Hey, just so everyone is aware," Reidigger said through the headset. "We don't have enough fuel to make it to the coast."

"What?" Maria said loudly. "And you're just bringing this up *now?*"

"I didn't want anyone to worry ..."

"What are our options?" she asked.

"Well," Alan said, "we can find the ship and try to somehow get from in here onto there. Or we can crash into the ocean and die."

"Sounds about right," Maria grumbled.

"No one's dying," Zero said firmly. They were going to find the boat. He craned his neck left and right, trying to get a visual on the water and struggling.

Penny's voice crackled in his headset. "Team?"

"Penny! You have good news?"

"Agent Zero," she said quickly, "from now on, let us assume that unless I begin a call with 'I have good news,' it will not, in fact, be good news. The FAA has ascertained the identity of the aircraft that was shot down. It was an Antonov cargo transport with a flight plan registered to Bermuda. They had some trouble discovering it because its transponder had been turned off. And, of course, it didn't get to its destination..."

"Because it dropped off the boat and got blown up," Alan finished for her. "At least that explains why the boat was dropped so far from the coast. To avoid suspicion if the plane deviated from its flight path."

"What was the plane's origin?" Maria asked.

"That's the surprising part," Penny admitted. "The Antonov was flown out of Iran."

Zero wanted to say that he could hardly believe it, but he'd dealt with Iranian extremists before. When it came to zealots, particularly ones that were religiously motivated, there were few things they weren't willing to do. And if the Antonov came out of Iran, it could have easily dropped south a short ways to pick up the railgun before sweeping east toward the US.

"Hang on," Maria said sharply. "Isn't the Ayatollah of Iran due to visit the US today?"

"That's right," Penny agreed. "Do you think it's related?"

"I think it's too coincidental not to be," Zero admitted. Iran's leader had historically expressed high disdain for America, its leaders, and its people. Could he be involved in this attack? To be on the soil of the foreign nation you hated at the time of a calculated attack was a bold move, one that didn't actually make much sense to him...

Unless it's to provide an alibi. The Ayatollah's presence in the US during an incident would be a terrific excuse for not being behind the plot.

"What's the word on Rutledge?" he asked.

"The news just gets worse from there," Penny told them. "The government has surmised the same thing that we already have—that the Antonov was destroyed by the railgun and it is closer to the US than anyone is comfortable with. We're in emergency protocol, Agents. I can't get through to the president or even close to him. He's going to be moved, and quite possibly on Air Force One."

Dammit. If the perpetrators had any knowledge of the protocol, then they might have known this ahead of time too. It made the presidential plane all the more likely a target. "What about Shaw? Did you try getting through to him?"

"Of course I did. But I can't keep helping you if he knows that I'm helping you, so I had to tell him under the pretense of an assumption. He won't listen."

"Well, if the president gets blown up, that's negligence on Shaw's part," Alan mused.

"Not the time, Alan!" Zero snapped. "Penny, what else?"

"Key locations and personnel within the range of the railgun from DC up to New York are being evacuated," she said. "That includes the United Nations, Liberty Island, any stadiums that would be accessible by line of sight, like in Baltimore, obviously most of DC, Annapolis … oh, and there is one other thing."

"Jesus, what else?" Zero groaned.

"A squadron of bombers has been dispatched to attempt to find and destroy the railgun before it gets into range."

He shook his head in disbelief. "I thought Rutledge agreed he would let us take our shot."

"He did, but again, Agent, emergency protocol. General Kressley ordered the strike, and he doesn't need executive authorization under the circumstances."

Railgun fodder, he thought bitterly. *That's all you've given them.*

"We must be close," he said, more to himself than anyone else. "We have to be. If that thing fires again, we need the ILDN coordinates right away. You got that, Penny? Patch it directly through to my—"

"Zero." Reidigger murmured through the headset. There was no alarm in his utterly flat tone, which made it all the more alarming. "Zero, look."

He leaned forward and squinted through the cockpit's viewing pane. "What am I looking f—"

A bright blue flash ignited on the water, some distance from them, so bright that it made even the daylight seem dimmer. In the same instant, an orange fireball blossomed in the sky. From Zero's perspective, the explosion was barely the size of a dime.

"My god," Maria murmured. "The railgun…"

"And the bombers," he finished.

"What's happening?" Penny demanded. "I just got a hit on ILDN…"

"It's firing on them," Zero said quietly. "It's going to pick off that whole squadron like flies."

"Alan, how far is it?" Maria asked.

"Um … we're at about nine thousand feet, so our max visual would be … about a hundred sixty miles? Give or take due to air pollution and light refraction. So the bombers must be closer than that, and the railgun between us. So it's got maybe a hundred miles on us currently."

Zero did some quick calculations of his own. "At max speed we should be on it in ten to twelve minutes. Can we make it?"

"We can make it," Alan confirmed.

Another flash lit upon the ocean, and another fireball burst like an orange bubble in the atmosphere.

Despite his horror, Zero forced himself to count. *One, one thousand, two, one thousand, three, one thousand...*

"And then what?" Maria asked.

"Wait," Zero said harshly. *Six, one thousand, seven, one thousand, eight, one thousand...*

Another blue flash. Another fireball in the sky.

Eight seconds between shots. The railgun required eight seconds to reload and charge.

"Alan, get us lower as we approach," Zero told him as he unzipped the black backpack between his feet.

"We need a plan. What are we going to do when we get on it?" Maria asked again.

"For starters, I'm activating the signal jammers," Alan said gruffly. "With any luck, that'll keep them from locking onto us as we approach like they did with the bombers."

"Okay," Maria said impatiently, "that's a start. But *then* what?"

Zero pulled out the pieces of the Beretta PMX, the submachine gun Penny had supplied them. He couldn't answer her question because he wasn't yet sure. Whatever it was, it was bound to be incredibly foolish, inherently dangerous, and with only the slightest possibility of actually working.

There was only one thing he could say for now. "Then we stop it."

CHAPTER THIRTY

The black SUV screeched to a halt on the tarmac of Andrews Air Force Base, home of the two Boeing VC-25As dubbed Air Force One. It had surprised even Rutledge to learn that there were actually two planes that carried the call sign; almost the entirety of the public only knew of one plane that ferried the president and his entourage, but the Air Force had commissioned two of them since 1990, to have a backup, which were collectively known as the "presidential fleet," though it seemed odd that a fleet would consist of only two planes.

A Secret Service agent pulled open the door and ushered Rutledge out. They had parked mere feet from the stairs of Air Force One to minimize the amount of time that the president would be exposed. Several other cars began pulling up, carrying cabinet members and chiefs of staff who would be joining him.

It had all happened so fast. One moment he was preparing to receive the Ayatollah of Iran, making sure his hair was combed and wondering if there was anything the on-staff stylist could do about the bags under his eyes. The next instant the room was filled with activity and chattering voices: he needed to be moved. A plane was shot down over the Atlantic. The railgun was moving into range of the US coast. They had no visual on it, electronic or actual. Several key locations, including Congress and the United Nations, were being evacuated and transported inland.

Suddenly he was outside, and then in a car, and then at Andrews AFB in suburban Washington, DC, near Morningside, Maryland, and now being ushered—which was a kinder term than the unnecessarily pushy agent deserved—up the stairs and into the plane.

"What about my wife?" Deidre was across the country, at a charity event in Redondo Beach. "Has she been informed? She's supposed to fly back today ..."

"Sir, the First Lady is informed and will be joining you at an undisclosed location inland, far from the weapon's range," the agent told him.

"And the VP? Where's Joanna?"

"Marine One is en route to Vice President Barkley's location. Please, sir, we need to get you on the plane."

But still he lingered, until a familiar face jogged to him despite wearing heels, concern etched on her face.

"Mr. President, come with me." Tabby Halpern offered her arm and Rutledge took it, as if he was an old man that needed help up the stairs. The truth was the sleeplessness, the exhaustion, the worry, and the dizzying speed at which all of this had happened was confounding him.

Tabby boarded the plane alongside him and directed him to a cream-colored leather seat opposite her, an oak desk between them affixed to the floor. "You okay, Jon? You need some water?"

"I need a stiff drink," Rutledge muttered.

"We're going to find it," Tabby said confidently. "Before it does any damage."

The president glanced out the window as the cars pulled away and personnel hurried aboard the jet. "Zero will find it."

Tabby frowned. "Zero...?"

"POTUS is aboard Angel One," a Secret Service agent said into an earpiece radio. "Wheels-up in three minutes." The agent leaned over. "Phone call for you, Mr. President."

Rutledge nodded, though he felt a tinge of anxiety over whatever matter would require his attention in a moment like this. He plucked a white phone from its place on the wall. "This is President Rutledge speaking."

"Sir. It's Kressley." The general spoke gruffly, as if he was already on the defensive for whatever it was he was about to explain. "I have confirmation that the railgun is approaching the eastern coast."

"How?" Rutledge asked carefully. "How do you have confirmation? A visual?"

"Not exactly, sir." The Secretary of Defense cleared his throat. "I authorized the deployment of four B-2 Spirits to find and eliminate the target."

"And... did they?" the president asked dully.

"They're gone, sir."

Gone. The same term the general had used when the railgun had destroyed three destroyer-class naval ships. Just... gone. As if they had merely blinked out of existence.

Rutledge rubbed his forehead. He didn't know much about planes, but he did know that the B-2 was the most expensive one on their budget sheets—and the most technologically advanced. "But did they *see* it?" he pressed. "So far no one has actually *seen* this boat, Kressley."

"Negative, sir. But we were able to triangulate an approximated area and a predictive model of its heading. I am requesting your authorization, Mr. President, to launch a missile strike into the approximated area."

Rutledge blinked. He wasn't sure he'd heard that precisely right. "General, you want to carpet bomb a section of the Atlantic Ocean a couple hundred miles from the American coast in the hopes of hitting it? Is that about the gist?"

"Not exactly 'carpet bomb,' sir. It would be a carefully calculated long-range missile strike. But... I suppose the spirit of the request is still there. Our guidance systems won't be able to get a lock on the target, so we'll be shooting blind."

"How do we know there aren't people out there in this 'approximated area'?" Rutledge demanded. "There could be boats out there, commercial ships, cruise ships..."

"Frankly sir, we don't know that," Kressley said candidly. "And we don't have time to confirm or get them out of the area. The time to act is *now*. We are left with zero other options."

Zero. It was clear now that he wasn't coming. The thought didn't anger him or even disappoint him as much as it made him realize his own shortcomings. He'd put too much faith in one man, assigned him an insurmountable task that, for all Rutledge knew, might have cost Agent Zero his life.

Kressley was right, and though the decision pained him greatly knowing that they might be dropping missiles on unsuspecting seafarers, the potential loss of life if the railgun reached range would be significantly higher.

"Do it," President Rutledge said as Air Force One taxied down the runway. "And may God have mercy on us."

CHAPTER THIRTY ONE

"**C**oming up on an approximate location!" Alan called through the headset. "Descending to two thousand feet. Keep your eyes peeled!"

Zero felt as if he was about to burst with energy, confined in the cramped cockpit, craning left and right to try to get a visual as the Prowler dipped in altitude. "I don't see anything!"

"The hull is coated in a reflective material," Maria reminded him. "From this height you won't see anything. Look for a wake; this boat could be traveling at a hundred twenty miles an hour, maybe even more. They might be invisible to radar, but they can't help but create a trail."

Zero held the Italian-made compact machine gun across his lap, assembled, locked, and loaded. What he was going to do with it, he wasn't yet sure. It was just somehow more comforting. *Better to have it and not need it, right?*

"Visual!" Maria all but screamed into the headset. "There, two o'clock!"

Zero practically pressed his face against the cockpit dome, wishing his field of vision wasn't so restrained. The right wing dipped as Alan dropped in altitude again, and Zero saw it—a long, thin white wake with an oddly vague shape heading it.

His pulse quickened. Finally laying eyes on the thing after all this time felt like he'd just spotted Bigfoot or the Loch Ness monster. It was real. It was there. And as the plane dipped precipitously again, Zero's stomach lurching with the sudden drop, he could make out the shapes of men on the deck—and a long, dark shape rising from the blue of the ocean itself.

The railgun was out of its hold, and without the reflective coating on the weapon itself it appeared almost as if it was skating along the water on its own.

The Prowler zoomed past the boat in an instant, their speed greatly higher than the ship's. "The weapon is out!" Zero warned.

"That must be why they slowed," Alan grunted. "They can't be doing more than sixty or seventy; there's no way in hell we can match their speed. But with the signal jammers, they shouldn't be able to get a direct lock onto us."

The bombers had come at them head-on and in formation, Zero realized, making them easier targets and not requiring a direct visual to fire. Now, with the Prowler, the railgun had a direct visual but no way to directly lock other than manually—assuming the likely outdated signal jammers were operational.

"Just to be safe," Zero said, "you need to keep us moving." Even as he said it he put his face to the glass to see the railgun's long barrel rising up toward them. "They're aiming, Alan!"

"I see 'em. Hang onto something."

Alan shoved the yoke forward and the Prowler nosedived, sending Zero's heart into his throat, and then leveled again, the inertia feeling as if it had rearranged his insides. He banked hard to the left, swinging into an arc that would have looked to be a turn with a predictable end.

But as they came out of the arc he pulled up.

The blue flash of the railgun illuminated the cockpit. For a second, Zero imagined that it was the light he might see when fate finally took him. Or perhaps it had, and this was it. But then he felt his stomach lurch again and he knew he was still with the living.

The railgun's shot missed. As long as Alan kept up the erratic flying and the signal jamming pods stayed active, the railgun was like trying to shoot a fly with a BB gun.

But we can't do this forever. The boat was still moving steadily closer to the coast, and they had no weapons. No, that wasn't entirely true. The plane had no weapons. He had a Beretta PMX on his lap, a Glock 19 at his hip, a Ruger in an ankle holster.

"Three... four... five... six..." Alan's voice was in his headset as Zero snapped back to reality. He was counting the seconds before the railgun would be able to fire again.

"Eight!" Alan banked hard to the right as another deadly blue flash, like lightning directly in their faces, lit the Prowler's cockpit.

"Jesus, that was close!" Maria gasped as Alan resumed his count.

You know what you have to do.

He just didn't know if he could actually do it.

Zero tore open the backpack and pulled out two items. One was the square black parcel with shoulder straps and the letters XI-B stenciled on it in white. The second was a round magnetic tracker.

"Eight!" Reidigger cried as he rolled the Prowler. For an instant Zero was weightless; Maria's shriek caught in her throat over the headset.

But there was no blue flash that time. *They're trying to be unpredictable.*

Alan came out of the roll and dropped the Prowler another fifty feet or so. They were flying no more than seven or eight hundred feet over the water, presenting a bigger target to the railgun operator.

He banked hard again as the railgun fired. The Prowler actually shook with the proximity of the blast.

"Can't keep this up forever!" Reidigger shouted. "Open to any ideas!"

"Maria," Zero said. "I love you."

"I love you too," she practically gasped from the cockpit in front of him. He couldn't reach for her or hold her hand. Couldn't hug her. They didn't say goodbyes; that was a rule they'd made long ago. But one last kiss, just in case, would have been nice.

He unbuckled his harness, slipped the XI-B pack over his shoulders, and refastened himself into the seat. "If we live through this, let's get married."

"Yeah," she said breathlessly. "Okay. But we have to keep it small..."

The plane banked again, flying sideways for a fraught second or two, and then leveled out and pulled up, climbing again into the sky.

"Of course," he agreed. "Just you, me, the girls. Alan. Todd. Your dad?"

"Maybe we don't tell him about it."

"Yeah. Maybe we don't." He smiled as he tightened the strap on the Beretta diagonally over his chest so he wouldn't lose it. "As soon as the tracker is on, give Penny the coordinates for a missile strike. Then have them blow that thing out of the goddamn water."

"What?" Maria said, panicked. "Kent, wait, what are you—"

Zero tore off the headset, reached for the red lever near his right foot, and yanked it hard.

Two things happened in the span of a heartbeat. First, the dome of the cockpit exploded away and went flying off into the Atlantic Ocean. Second, a powerful burst detonated beneath him, ejecting the seat—and him—about one hundred and fifty feet into the air.

Zero's lungs deflated with the sheer and sudden force of ejection. He felt his spine compress as every muscle in his body went to jelly. Cold wind tore at him as the edges of his vision darkened, threatening to lose consciousness with the sudden and excruciating g-force.

The Prowler was gone from beneath him, jetting ahead, wings wagging as it tried to evade any potential railgun blasts.

The seat fell away, leaving only the frame and the parachute behind, and then he was falling too. For one terrifying moment, he realized he had absolutely no control over this process, and that this was, in all likelihood, a very bad idea.

A shadow fell over him as the white parachute unfurled. He winced against the sudden drop in descent, the straps straining against his chest and shoulders.

Zero sucked in a gasping breath. He hadn't expected that to be as painful or jarring on his system as it had been.

Come on. Get it together.

He scanned the ocean below as he descended and spotted the white wake of the boat to his northeast. The Prowler had gotten ahead of it when he ejected, but it was coming up fast and he would only have one chance to get on it.

One very slim chance.

The railgun's barrel lifted like a bird looking skyward, tracking the Prowler as it dipped and arced in the sky. He could only imagine what Maria and Alan might be thinking right now—hopefully worrying about themselves and not him.

The Prowler banked hard as if going into a roll. The railgun barrel tracked it, moving slightly left with the action.

Just get clear, Alan. There's nothing more you can do here.

The plane leveled suddenly, feigning the roll—but whoever was behind the railgun saw it coming.

The railgun fired. Without the cockpit and the plane's engine to contend with, Zero heard the blast—not so much a blast as a resonant *thoom*—and the ship lit up blue for a fraction of a second.

The Prowler flashed orange as its right wing was torn from its body.

"No!" he heard himself scream.

The jet spun wildly as it fell from the sky. Zero could do nothing but watch and drift closer to the ocean as the Prowler whipped around and around. As if slow motion, he watched it hit the sea at an angle, skipping across the surface of the water twice like a stone on a river. Finally it stopped, tipping upward on an angle, bobbing twice.

Then it began to sink.

His breath came ragged in his own ears. He no longer felt the cold, or the biting wind, or the pain in his spine from the hasty ejection.

Alan. Maria.

It didn't feel real. He felt detached, as if floating instead of falling slowly.

Part of him wanted to give up. To fall into the icy ocean and let it take him too.

He forced himself to tear his gaze away from the sinking Prowler. The ship had nearly reached him. He was still about four hundred feet in the air, give or take. He wouldn't reach it in time. Not with the parachute; he needed to be another hundred feet or so northward to even have a shot at landing on it.

Figures on the small boat pointed at him. People. The perpetrators. They were the target. Not the railgun or the ship that carried it. The ones who had stolen it, the ones who had fired it, the ones who had killed every soul aboard three battleships and shot the Prowler out of the sky.

A deep rage bubbled up inside of him, the likes of which he hadn't felt since he discovered his wife's assassin.

A fusillade of automatic gunfire tore at the air. The figures weren't pointing at him; they were armed, shooting at him. No, not at him. At his parachute.

The white canopy over his head shredded. At the same time, Zero clawed at the straps still connecting him to it.

He managed to free himself as the parachute folded, and he plummeted to the ocean.

CHAPTER THIRTY TWO

Zero felt weightless as he fell through the air, as if the ocean was rising up to meet him. He reached for his right shoulder, fingers finding the ripcord there, and he pulled it. The XI-B pack on his back burst open, the lightweight aluminum frame springing to size and supporting a blue sailcloth the same azure color as the sky above. Once again he was thrust into shadow as the personal glider expanded outward on either side of him.

The glider caught on the wind, yanking hard on Zero's already-sore shoulders. His descent slowed, but his angle was too sharp; the glider directed him downward, ever closer to the water. He gritted his teeth and twisted his body, angling his shoulders back and straightening his legs beneath him to increase drag.

Pull up, dammit!

The glider leveled as his right foot skipped across the ocean's surface. He sucked in a breath as he sailed mere feet over the Atlantic, wishing he'd had even ten minutes of practice with the glider before deciding to eject himself out of an airplane with no other safety net than trying to land on a rather small boat.

The South Korean ship was mere yards away. Zero angled himself toward it as three men on the bow aimed guns at him.

His left hand groped for the Beretta PMX as he struggled to keep his body angled slightly upward, to keep himself from crashing into the frigid ocean at forty miles an hour.

He wasn't sure if the fire selector was on full-auto or not as he raised the compact submachine gun, easily one-handing the five-pound weapon, and fired. A dozen nine-millimeter rounds exploded from the barrel in a second. The three men hit the deck; he wasn't sure if they leapt for cover or he'd hit any of them.

But the force of the blast put him slightly off-kilter. The glider angled too far to the right.

I'm not going to make it.

The only chance he had was to radically overcompensate.

A bellow erupted from his throat as he twisted his body to the left. At the same time, the South Korean boat veered, trying to steer away from him. The glider's frame groaned with the sudden action, threatening to fold.

Zero soared over the port side of the fifty-foot boat. It was under him now, but he was moving too fast to land. He was going to glide right over it.

He pulled his legs in, his knees to his chest, his arms hugging them and head tucked, curling himself into a ball. The glider dragged, angling sharply downward.

Shots rang out behind him as he hit the deck. He rolled once, bouncing, the glider still catching the wind—and he tumbled off the starboard side.

A hand shot out and grabbed onto the railing before the glider pulled him right off the side of the boat. He shouted with the pain, his shoulder threatening to dislocate even as his other hand fumbled with the clasp of the straps holding him in place.

The glider slipped away from his shoulders and drifted off on the air like a paper airplane.

Zero clung there for a moment, just a few seconds, panting and hanging by one hand and expecting that any moment one of the Middle Eastern men he had seen on the ship was going to aim a gun over the side and fire it into his face.

He heard shouts then in a language he understood: Arabic.

"Where did he go?"

"He fell over the side! He must have!"

"Idiot, there was no splash!"

Now's your chance. Zero clenched his teeth. He took up the Beretta in one hand, the other clinging to the railing, and with his foot against the reflective hull of the boat, he forced himself upward with a shout and unloaded the rest of the PMX's magazine in a spraying burst over the deck.

One man cried out and fell as bullets penetrated his midsection. Another dove behind the weapon for cover even as several rounds struck the railgun, sending up sparks.

Where's the third? Zero quickly hauled himself over the railing, letting the spent Beretta fall to the deck—he hadn't brought a spare magazine—and drawing the Glock 19 at his hip. The railgun rose from the center of the ship, standing about nine feet tall, the barrel of it comprised of two parallel rails close to twenty feet in length.

It would have been a sight to behold had Zero not been preoccupied.

A three-round burst rang out as he spun to the right. Pain seared in his abdomen even as he leapt in front of the railgun's barrel for cover.

"Stop shooting, you fool!" someone screeched in Arabic. "You will hit the weapon!"

"I hit him!" the shooter shouted back. "I got him!"

The shooter was right. Zero winced as he pressed a hand against the place where two bullets had struck his midsection.

There was no blood. They hadn't penetrated. The long-sought question of whether or not the jacket Penny had supplied was infused with a graphene mesh had been answered. His ribs would be bruised to hell, but at least his insides were still intact.

But they don't know that.

"Confirm it!" a voice shouted. "Then throw the body over!"

The boat's engines were surprisingly quiet; Zero could hear the careful footfalls of boots coming his way. He crouched low, to one knee, and when the man whipped around to the front of the railgun, his rifle raised to his shoulder, Zero fired twice into his chest. He sprang to his feet and kicked out, sending the commando staggering backward. The man toppled over the railing, his scream cut short when he hit the Atlantic.

Two down.

"Hassan!" a voice called out. And then in English: "Bastard!"

The frigid wind whipped around him as he held his position on the bow. He wondered for a moment if he could disable the railgun by shooting at it in key places—but he had no idea where those places would be or if it would even work.

Besides, I might need the ammunition.

He dared to peer around the railgun, down the length of the ship even as it raced closer to the coastline. He saw no one except the man he'd shot with the Beretta, lying face-down and motionless. It gave him an idea.

Zero sprawled on the deck with a view beneath the weapon's long parallel rails. A moment later a pair of black boots came into view, slowly heading toward the bow. Zero aimed and fired, just once, the bullet passing beneath the railgun and striking an ankle. The man screamed and fell.

As soon as Zero saw his head, he fired a second time, and then scrambled to his feet. That made three down. How many had he seen from the air? At least five, maybe six—and he knew where to find the others.

He stole quickly down the length of the ship to the stern. Behind the raised railgun were two steps down, a thick windshield rising up, and behind it, an impressively complex control panel.

Three men stood at the controls. Two of them were Middle Eastern, much like the three he had just killed, but the third was fair-skinned, with sandy, slicked hair, a black tac vest over his jacket. European, most likely. He stared at Zero through the windshield even as his hand hovered over a lever.

There was something cold in his stare, almost lifeless. It reminded him all too much of the psychopathic assassin Rais, Zero's former nemesis that he had finally killed on the walls of Dubrovnik.

It takes three to pilot the boat, he realized. These men could not fend Zero off or the boat would stop. Most likely was that only two were piloting, and one was operating the railgun—and Zero had little doubt that the man behind the weapon was the sandy-haired mercenary with the cold stare.

The image of the Prowler spinning into the water ran through him again, and his fury warmed him.

He raised the Glock and fired it, once, twice, four times, seven.

The windshield stopped the bullets. They did not ricochet, but stuck in the glass as if it were made of ballistics gel.

The European shook his head, and then showed Zero the pistol he held in his other hand, the one not hovering over the controls. If Zero tried to get around the side for a clean shot, he'd be in a straight shootout with the European and would have to hope he was faster. If he stood here, he was at an impasse.

He had to try. He gripped the Glock tightly, knowing he had only a few rounds left, and took the first step. The European cocked his pistol casually.

But then the man frowned. Zero did too; there was a sound, even above the ship's engines. A roar in the distance.

A plane?

The European looked skyward.

Zero dared to as well, but saw nothing.

"Incoming!" one of the men behind the windshield shouted.

A rocket-propelled streak fell out of the sky, something long and white and trailing orange that collided with the surface of the ocean not two hundred feet from the ship.

The Tomahawk missile exploded, its sensitivity set to detonate on any impact. An orange fireball plumed on the water as black smoke rolled into the sky. The boat raced onward, leaving the blast behind quickly—when another missile struck at their ten o'clock, closer this time.

The ship lurched with the sudden wave. Zero fell to the deck. The Glock slipped from his grip but he opted to grab a rope instead of the gun; the optimal choice, it seemed, since the boat was rocked again by another too-close impact and rocked sharply the other way. Zero bounced, clinging to the rope.

The Glock skittered over the side and into the ocean.

A missile strike. The US had only a vague idea of where the ship was; they were firing blindly, carpet-bombing the ocean in the hopes of hitting it and nearly had. Missiles struck further out, up to a mile away, exploding on the water in front of them and behind them.

It was only then that Zero realized the boat had slowed. They were still moving forward, but coasting along, their speed falling rapidly.

He yanked the small, silver Ruger LC9 from his ankle holster and got to his feet, keeping his knees bent and his stance wide to accommodate the still-rocking motion of the ship.

Behind the windshield, the three men who had been at the controls were sprawled. The European's eyes were closed and his forehead was bleeding; it looked as if his head had bounced off the console when the missile struck. One of the Iranians was staggering to his feet, putting out a hand to help the other up.

No. This boat would go no further.

Zero rounded the windshield and fired once into the standing commando.

For Alan.

The man on the deck put out both hands. "Wait," he said in Arabic.

Zero fired once, through his forehead.

For Maria.

And then there was one. The European. As much as Zero wanted to shoot the man outright, he couldn't help but wonder who he was and why he was working with the Iranians...

Zero paused. He'd been thinking of them as Iranians because of the supposition he'd made earlier. But they were speaking Arabic. The chief language of Iran was Farsi; only about two percent of the population spoke Arabic, and it was highly unlikely that an entire crew of Iranian commandos would be speaking a relatively rare language for their part of the world.

"Not Iranians," he murmured. He knelt beside one of the dead men to look for some identification or insignia, but found none.

"No. Not Iranians."

Zero whirled around with the Ruger—but not fast enough. The European caught his arm, twisting it into a lock and pinching a nerve in the hand. The gun fell from his grip. A knee slammed him in the abdomen, doubling him. Then an elbow swept upward, catching his chin.

Stars exploded in Zero's vision as his head rocked back and his body followed. He hit the deck but barely felt it, as if he'd sunk into the ocean instead.

The man was fast, too fast, and Zero was hurting and slow.

"You are brave," the man said as he stooped and picked up the LC9. His accent was definitely German by the sound of it. "I will give you that. All you've done to get here was quite admirable. But I am afraid you have failed." Another Tomahawk exploded over the water, a quarter mile from them, and he winced slightly.

Zero staggered to his hands and knees, struggling to clear his double vision. "I've killed your people. This boat... it's not going anywhere."

"Maybe not," said the German. "But you see, *mein* friend, we are already in range."

"Of what?" Zero demanded. He tried to stand, but the German kicked him squarely in the chest with the flat of his boot and he sprawled again, the air knocked from his lungs.

The German chuckled. "Of what? Of America. Of your coast. You believe there is only one target? You believe we would steal such a magnificent weapon for a single goal?"

He flicked up a plastic shield covering a wide red button.

No...

Before Zero could react, the German's hand mashed down on it and the railgun whirred to life.

CHAPTER THIRTY THREE

Officer Warren Mills had been on the NYPD's Emergency Response Team for eight years. In that time, he had been a part of an evacuation response at the United Nations Secretariat Building, on the waterfront at 405 East 42nd Street, on three occasions.

"Let's move in an orderly fashion, please!" his deep voice boomed as he ushered employees and visitors alike out of the UN building and back behind a row of sawhorses set fifty yards across the courtyard. "Keep moving, quickly now, thank you!"

The first occasion had been his first year with ERT, a bomb threat that had turned out to be fruitless. The second time was just a couple of years ago, when terrorists managed to get submersible drones carrying heavy payloads into the East River.

The third time, of course, was today.

"Hey, you!" Mills barked at a young man in black eyeglasses who was scurrying back toward the entrance of the building. "Hey!"

"I'm sorry," the young man called back nervously, even as he bumped roughly against a woman exiting the building hastily. "I just need to retrieve my laptop—"

"This is an evacuation! Back behind the sawhorses!" Mills commanded.

But the young man ignored him and disappeared into the building.

"Son of a..." Mills muttered. He considered going in after the guy and physically dragging him out, but there were still plenty of people to get out of there. "You believe that? Like they don't have a care in the world."

"Hey, you gotta admit," said Chalmers, his partner, "ninety-nine times out of a hundred, these threats don't pan out."

"Yeah," said Mills lowly. "And that one other time could be 9/11. We don't mess around with stuff like this, you got that?" Chalmers was young, only twenty-four, a rookie who had gotten a spot on ERT through some sort of nepotistic means, an uncle high up in the hierarchy or something.

"Right. 'Course not," Chalmers muttered.

Mills sighed, hoping that whatever this threat was wasn't going to eat his whole day. Tomorrow was Valentine's Day and he (in a totally boneheaded move) had signed up for rapid intervention renewal. To make up for it, he'd booked a table for tonight at Yvette's favorite date-night restaurant, a midtown sushi joint that looked like it was straight out of Tokyo.

Sushi wasn't so bad, he thought. He liked his steak rare, so why not his fish too?

"Mills." The radio clipped to his shoulder squawked. "How's the eastern entrance?"

"Coming along," he replied. "Key personnel are out; we got some stragglers though. Just had a guy run back in for personal belongings. Unreal, you know?"

"I want you on sweep team," his lieutenant told him. "Bring Chalmers along, he needs to see how it's done."

"Ten-four." Mills rolled his eyes. Sweep team meant going floor to floor, room to room after the evacuation to ensure everyone was out. If the threat was a bomb, they had to put on bulky EOD suits to do it.

Is this a bomb threat? he wondered. They hadn't told him.

"Mills," his radio squawked again, this time with the voice of Earnhardt, one of the officers covering the western-facing exits. "You got eyes on the Iranian attaché?"

Mills sucked in a breath. "Sorry, what?"

"Three members of the Ayatollah's attaché are unaccounted for," Earnhardt told him. "We may need to send some people in."

He knew that the leader of Iran had been scheduled to arrive at the UN that morning—his buddy Ray had been part of the NYPD motorcade that had escorted the Iranian diplomats from JFK earlier that morning, ahead of the foreign leader's personal plane. But to hear that they were unaccounted for meant that someone on the inside had dropped the ball big time and left them behind.

"Shit," he muttered. Into the radio he said, "All right, we're on it. Send a couple more guys our way." To his partner he said, "Yo, Chalmers, looks like we're going to have to—"

Mills winced instinctively. It was purely reflexive, his body's natural reaction to the sudden blue flash in the sky, not only because his brain couldn't comprehend what he was seeing, but equally because it happened quickly, in an instant, so fast he wouldn't have been sure he had seen anything at all if in the same instant, the UN building hadn't exploded.

The impact struck the eastern sea-facing side of the building, a massive and sudden explosion at the structure's center mass that took out several floors in one blast. Windows exploded outward, raining glass and chunks of concrete down as people ran, screaming, covering their heads.

"Bomb!" Chalmers hollered. He sounded far away; Mills hadn't even realized that his own legs were moving, propelling him forward, grabbing the arm of a woman who had fallen, bleeding from her forehead. He pulled her to her feet and they ran as the building burned and rained fiery debris.

There are still people inside.

Steel groaned high overhead as floors above the impact site collapsed and the upper third of the building threatened to topple.

"Get clear!" Mills bellowed, waving his arms at people gathered behind the sawhorses. "Move back, go!"

"It was a bomb!" Chalmers was still shouting, this time into his radio. "We need ... we need emergency ... everything! Just send everything!"

That was no bomb. Mills couldn't be sure what it was. But he had seen *some*thing, that blue flash that streaked across the sky in the instant before the explosion. It wasn't a bomb, and it wasn't a missile. He had no idea what it was, and that was what scared him the most.

The young man in the thick black eyeglasses entered the building on the eastern side; there had only been two officers there guarding the entrance, and while their attention was elsewhere he dashed for the door.

"Hey, you!" An NYPD officer with a square jaw and angry eyes shouted at him. "Hey!"

"I'm sorry," Leonard Stark called back, even as a woman bumped against his shoulder roughly as she rushed out of the building in heels. "I just need to retrieve my laptop ..."

It was a lame excuse, he knew, but he couldn't stop to explain to the officer how important it was.

"This is an evacuation!" the cop had shouted back, but Leonard didn't hear the rest of it because he was already ducking inside, darting left and right to navigate the thin trickle of still-evacuating UN employees.

Leonard was just an intern—that was a phrase his mother used when she was passive-aggressively chastising the career choices that had led him down this path at age twenty-six, "just an intern"—but by virtue of years of contract editing and extensive knowledge of legalese, he had made it onto the small team doing the final review on the peace treaty between the US and Iran.

If this truly was a legitimate bomb threat, the physical treaty was in danger. Removing it without authorization, even in a crisis, could be considered a federal crime, but he had a digital copy on the secured laptop in the ambassador's office.

This was not at all about heroics. This was not about ensuring peace (though he very much hoped it would be construed as such later). No, this was about his career not ending here, about elevating himself above "just an intern" to a well-paid aide to the US ambassador to Iran.

The eastern entrance of the UN building opened on the lobby to the visitors' center, which he practically sprinted across as he sidestepped oncoming foot traffic and vaulted up the stairs. The ambassador's office was on the third floor and Leonard, despite his wiry frame, was in pretty good shape.

He reached the third floor in less than forty-five seconds, ran down the hall, then left, into the office, there was the laptop, he grabbed it, turning back—

There was suddenly an immense pressure in his head, accompanied by a thunderous sound, the combination of which seemed to disrupt all of his senses at once in an instant. He was vaguely aware of being off the ground. The lights overhead blinked out.

The bomb. The thought came to him dimly, like something far away that was just out of his reach. *There really was a bomb.*

And then he struck the carpeted floor, having been thrown clear through the office doorway and into the corridor. The impact was painful enough to jar him back to his senses. His shoulder burned with pain and his legs felt like jelly.

The building was trembling beneath him. Wherever the bomb had gone off, he was not exactly at ground zero but couldn't have been far. Was it above him? At ground level?

Metal groaned. Somewhere nearby, something collapsed, bringing with it a new cacophony of unknown debris cascading down.

Above me. The bomb went off above me. So his only choice was to go down, and quickly, before more of the building came tumbling down around him. Somehow Leonard managed to get his feet under him and moving, one leg at a time, moving fast but certainly not sure-footed.

He heard a groan and stopped dead in his tracks.

"Hello?" he called out. "Is someone there?"

"Here." The voice came weakly, a male voice, accented slightly even on just the lone syllable.

Leonard followed the sound. "Say something, please!"

"In ... here."

He rounded the corner where he'd made the left and skidded to a harrowing stop. What used to be a conference room was now a disaster of rubble, broken pieces of furniture, entire chunks of floor and walls.

The ceiling of the conference room had collapsed. Leonard glanced upward, through the gaping hole, and saw that the floor above had been a victim of the one above it, and through that—he could see sky, sunlight filtering through the thick dust. There was heat, too; fire above him.

He frowned, for a moment forgetting why he was standing there. *That doesn't look like the work of a bomb.* It looked like the building had been hit by something, struck from the exterior…

"Here," said the voice again, straining.

Leonard snapped back to it, coughing on the excessive dust as he carefully climbed over broken tables and overturned chairs, jagged exposed beams that had fallen at odd angles.

The first man he found was not the one who had been calling out. Leonard leapt back in horror as he realized the man was dead, his wide-eyed face a mask of his final moment of utter shock.

He tore his gaze from the body and picked his way to the other side of the former conference room. The man who had been calling to him lifted an arm slightly. It was the only limb exposed; the other three, and most of his body, were pinned beneath a large section of the floor that had fallen in from above. His face was visible, a cut below one eye bleeding copiously and his face streaked with brown dust.

"Are you hurt?" Leonard asked quickly. "I mean, can you move?"

The man squeezed his eyes shut and rattled off something rapidly in another language.

"I'm sorry, I only speak English…" Leonard told him.

"I… think I can move." The man definitely had an accent, Middle Eastern by the sound of it. "But I am not strong enough to lift this."

"Okay. I… I might not be either," Leonard admitted. He only now realized that he was still carrying the laptop, and set it down so he could help.

Overhead, metal groaned in warning. They had to move quickly.

"Together, on three. Ready? One… two… three!" Leonard hefted with all his might. The section of floor moved slightly, just a couple of inches—enough for the man to move his limbs, to get some leverage under it. He pushed with both legs, his face contorting as they both strained.

After a several-second struggle, the floor slid away and off of him. Leonard sucked in a breath; he could see that the man was bleeding from several places and could only hope that adrenaline would get him out.

"Come on, we have to get out of here." The frame of the building groaned again, louder this time. Leonard helped the man to his feet and put one arm over his own shoulders, grabbing up the laptop in his other hand.

The man grimaced in pain as they staggered out of the conference room and back to the dust-filled corridor. His leg buckled, yanking on Leonard's neck.

"You can do this," he told himself as much as the man. "Come on now, we have to go." His throat felt dry, the dust threatening to clog his throat, but still he opted to try to distract them both from the pain and precariousness as they made their escape. "Where are you from?"

"I am ... I am from Iran," he said breathlessly.

That's right. He'd nearly forgotten that the Ayatollah's attaché had arrived separately, before the leader, who was due for a visit to the UN that very morning ...

"Oh my god," Leonard exclaimed suddenly. "The Ayatollah ... he wasn't ... was he?"

The man shook his head. "No. He was—he was rerouted. Direct to Washington."

Thank god for that.

"And the others?" Leonard recalled the ambassador saying that there were four in the Iranian group.

But the man simply shook his head.

They didn't make it.

They reached the bottom of the second-floor stairs when the building groaned once more, followed by the thunderous and terrifying sound of a floor above them collapsing.

"We have to move!" A surge of energy shot through Leonard as he half-dragged the man along with him. The man winced in agony, but this wasn't the time to be tender or careful.

He dared to glance behind him, upward, just in time to see the top of the stairs swallowed in darkness and dust as the floor collapsed.

He heard a cry of surprise and panic that might have come from his own throat as they nearly fell down the stairs to the first floor. The visitors' center lobby opened up before them, empty and looking untouched compared to the carnage they'd just experienced, but he knew it was only moments away from devastation itself ...

"Hurry up, let's go!" A voice. A man—a police officer. The square-jawed cop that had shouted at him for entering the building was running across the floor, supporting the injured man on the other side. "Move it!"

Then they were running to the glass doors, to fresh air, to sunshine. There were two other officers there, grabbing onto them, practically carrying them to safety as the ceiling of the visitors' center behind them collapsed.

CHAPTER THIRTY FOUR

Zero could only stare in horror. Just a moment ago, the blue spark of plasma danced down the length of the railgun's electrodes and vanished across the water at seven times the speed of sound toward its target.

"That," the German said, "was the United Nations building."

Zero took no solace in being right about the target. He had to stop this man. He climbed to his knees, but the German waved the Ruger in his direction.

"Do not, please," he asked gently. "I would be disappointed to have to kill you."

There was a sound, a chime; the German reached into a pocket for a satellite phone and glanced at it. "Ah," he said simply.

Tomahawk missiles rained down over the Atlantic at varying distances, getting closer. It seemed the missile strikes had swept out from their area and were coming back for a second salvo. The German seemed to realize it as well and turned back to the console, punching numbers into a keypad. Coordinates, if Zero had to guess.

Another target?

"You have a choice," he told Zero as he input the numbers. "I cannot pilot the boat on my own. It requires two. We are one hundred and sixty miles from the coast. We can stay here and both die when a missile strikes the boat. Or we can work together and try to make it to the coast. Come what may beyond that—perhaps one will kill the other then."

That explains why he hasn't killed me yet.

Maria was gone. Alan was gone. His daughters were grown enough to take care of themselves. Shaw wanted him fired, if not imprisoned.

He couldn't help but laugh dismally—not at his situation, but at the lunacy of this man believing that Zero cared whether he lived through this ordeal or not.

"What is funny?" the German asked, cocking his head slightly even as the rain of destruction continued to draw nearer.

"We're both going to die out here."

"Hmm," the man said. "Seems you have a German sense of humor." He reached for the plastic shield again, the one concealing the round red button that activated the railgun.

Zero let out a primal shout as he surged forward.

The German was quick—quick enough to get a shot off with the Ruger. It hit Zero right over his heart.

It hurt. God, did it hurt. But the German didn't know about the graphene, and Zero did not slow down. He tackled the German to the deck, swinging rapidly, a flurry of punches at the smug face. Some glanced off, his knuckles scraping the rough floor of the boat. Others split his lips and blackened his eyes.

The German got both hands on Zero's lapels and, with a ferocious grunt, hefted him over onto his side. Something hard and blunt jammed into his ribs—the LC9.

But the man was already scrambling back to the control panel. He reached up.

Zero raised the pistol and fired.

The German slammed a hand down on the red button.

A missile exploded not a hundred feet from them and the boat rocked.

"Oh." The German slumped, a bullet in his back, as Zero scrambled to the control panel.

Eight seconds. He had eight seconds to do something.

He mashed buttons, flicked switches, hitting everything on the control panel, anything that might stop the railgun from firing.

Six... five...

A missile struck closer, tipping the boat precariously. Zero grabbed onto the edge of the bulletproof windshield to keep himself from bowling over.

Four... three...

He spotted a control stick, just a thin gray stick that looked utterly innocuous, practically hidden among the red buttons and green lights and LED displays of the console. He grabbed it and pulled it back.

One...

The railgun's barrel shifted upward as it lit up blue and fired a plasma projectile at Mach 7. The tilt was just a few degrees. Barely an angle.

But at a hundred and sixty miles away, that tiny angle could have made all the difference. He would have no way to know if he had saved anyone or anything.

Behind him, the German laughed weakly. "Do you think that was enough?"

"I don't know." He turned to the man, who sat with his legs splayed before him, blood running down his back and forming a pool around him. "Who are you?"

The man winced as he adjusted his weight. "My name is Krauss. Stefan Krauss. Remember it. We may meet again—in this life or the next."

Zero scoffed. These sociopaths always seemed to be part-time philosophers.

"And you?" Krauss asked him.

"Agent Zero."

Stefan Krauss's eyes widened as an eerie, bloody grin lit upon his face. "Really," was all he said.

He checked the console. The numbers that Krauss had entered into the keypad were 1-2-2-8-0-1. They weren't coordinates, but he had no idea what they could mean.

Not that it mattered. The boat wasn't going anywhere. Zero had no way to communicate with anyone on the shore. The South Korean vessel did not appear to have any sort of radio, which made sense; the boat was built for absolute stealth, and a radio frequency could be tracked. He wished he'd had the foresight to bring the satellite phone when he'd ejected from the Prowler.

His heart ached with the loss of Maria and Alan. But he'd be joining them soon enough. Another Tomahawk detonated, but it was further than the others and west by about two hundred fifty feet.

What if one doesn't hit? he thought. The railgun was too powerful a weapon to fall into anyone's hands—even the United States'.

You could take matters into your own hands. He reached for the thin gray control stick and pushed it forward. The railgun's barrel responded in kind, pivoting downward, further, until it was pointed at the bow of its own ship.

Krauss let out a pained laugh. "Well. That is certainly a design flaw."

"One I'm glad for," Zero said dryly. "Goodbye, Krauss."

He pressed the red button.

For a moment, he thought about jumping before the railgun fired. What would be more preferable, he wondered: a fiery death or a frozen one?

He sat at the console and waited, staring out over the sea on the starboard side. The ocean was calm, tranquil over here, the opposite direction in which missiles were falling.

The railgun lit up blue, and the bow exploded.

It happened so quickly that Zero's brain felt as if it short-circuited. He heard the blast, but before he saw anything he felt heat, and then impact—the ballistic-resistant windshield came off in one piece, blasting outward and taking him with it.

Next he was off the boat, in the air, tumbling end over end. He hit the water and it was as if every nerve ending in his body screamed. He broke the surface, gasping a lungful of air, but he couldn't stay above water. His muscles seized; his limbs would not respond. His hands grasped blindly, hoping that the windshield had landed nearby, but if it had he couldn't find it.

He sank again.

This is it.

He tried to move his arms, to just tread water, but it was so shockingly cold and everything hurt, as if a thousand pins were in his skin.

An icy hand latched onto his wrist and tugged at him, and he was certain it was Death.

CHAPTER THIRTY FIVE

Death, it seemed, looked a lot like Alan Reidigger.

Zero gasped and sputtered as Alan pulled him into the yellow inflatable life raft, first by the arm and then by the back of his pants, hauling him easily out of the water.

"Okay, you're okay," he said over and over.

"Here, put this on." Maria was there, wrapping him in a silver crinkly sheet that looked like aluminum foil. A Mylar emergency blanket.

He trembled terribly, teeth chattering, lips refusing to move properly to address the questions that he needed to ask.

"Don't try to talk." Maria positioned herself against him, sharing her body heat. "We're okay." The front of her shirt was bloody and her jacket torn down one arm. Alan had a purple bruised eye that was nearly swollen shut and a gaping cut across the back of one hand that would certainly require stitches.

They were alive. Their cockpit had still been sealed shut when he ejected. They'd survived the crash and, somehow, miraculously, had managed to escape as the plane sank.

It was a story Zero very much wanted to hear, but it would have to wait until after the threat of hypothermia had passed.

"Penny." Alan had a sat phone to his ear. "We got him. The railgun is destroyed. Do you have our position? Good. And would you ask them to stop shooting missiles at us?"

He lowered the phone. "A chopper is on the way. We're not dying out here today." He clapped a hand on Zero's shoulder. "You did good, pal."

Zero stared out at the South Korean ship, its devastated bow already sunk, the glimmering stern rising as the sea swallowed it. The back half of the railgun was still visible, its barrel facing downward in the water. He wondered if Stefan Krauss was still in there or if he too was flung with the force of the explosion. It didn't matter; the German was undoubtedly dead.

He shook his head. "N-not ... not over."

Maria frowned. "What's not over?"

Talking was difficult. But they still had to determine what it was that Krauss was trying to destroy, and why—and if he had been successful.

The CH-46 Sea Knight roared over the Atlantic toward the Virginia coast, carrying three soggy and battered CIA agents, one pilot, and two medics. After being hastily airlifted by harness from the life raft to the cabin of the tandem-rotor transport helicopter, Zero stripped out of his wet clothes and into a spare gray pilot jumpsuit they had onboard. He sat with a warm, dry compress around his neck, his breathing returning to something like normal, as the medics tended to Alan and Maria as best they could.

Everything hurt. His skin was red and felt raw. His spine and shoulders ached. His ribs, he'd noticed while changing, were badly bruised after being shot at multiple times. The superficial cut on his forehead had opened again—or perhaps it was a new one, he wasn't sure—so he'd used his wet T-shirt to clean as much of the dried blood away as he could.

But they weren't finished.

"The railgun operator said he targeted the UN building," he said loudly into a headset. "What's its status?"

Both of the medics avoided his gaze, focusing on their tasks.

"Destroyed, sir," the pilot told him. "It was hit."

Zero shook his head. *I could have stopped that.* "How many casualties?"

"Unknown at the moment," the pilot said. "I heard tell that most were evacuated. But there were still people in the building."

Zero frowned. It didn't make sense. The United States was already aware that the railgun was en route before Krauss was even in range. Key personnel would have been evacuated. So why strike at the UN building? Was it symbolic? A show of force?

"There was a code punched into the railgun's targeting system," he told the chopper. "A six-digit code. It was one-two-two-eight-zero-one. It doesn't sound like coordinates. Something else. Does that ring any bells in any heads?"

"An abbreviated date?" Maria spitballed. "Something he wanted you to see and figure out?"

"Could be a security code, maybe," Alan suggested, wincing as the medic stitched his hand. "Did the railgun require an access code?"

Zero shook his head. They weren't bad ideas, but neither made much sense.

"Sounds like it might be a transponder frequency," the helicopter's pilot mentioned.

Zero twisted in his seat. "It does?"

"Sure. Every plane registered with the FAA has a transponder to send and receive radio signals, and every transponder has a unique frequency code for them to identify it."

That's it, he thought, recalling that Penny told him the downed Antonov had been difficult to determine because it had turned off its transponder.

Krauss had been aiming for a moving target by using its transponder frequency. He didn't even know the railgun could do that, but it made sense; how else would it find its target a distance that didn't have direct visual?

"Alan, your sat phone." Zero took it and made the call as he adjusted the headset off one ear. "Penny, I need you to contact the FAA and find the plane with this transponder code." He recited it to her, and then quickly added, "I need to know where it came from, where it went, where it is now, and who was on it."

"It would probably be faster for me to just back-door their database ..." she said.

"Then do that."

"Stay on the line."

Zero twisted again to address the pilot, his back aching in protest. "What's our ETA to the coast?"

"About twenty minutes, but I can probably cut that down by a few."

"Then do that," he said again.

A moving target... a plane. Was I right? What if the target really was Air Force One all this time? What if the railgun blast that he had adjusted by just a few degrees had been intended for President Rutledge?

But no, he realized; that didn't add up. Emergency protocol had already been in place before the UN building was destroyed. If the president was the target, Krauss wouldn't have wasted time on the static attack before his moving quarry.

"Zero," Penny León's voice came through the phone at his ear. "I found your code. It's not a plane; it's a helicopter. It took off from JFK with a proposed destination of Blair House but never made it there. Instead it landed at Joint Base Andrews near Washington."

"And who was on it?"

"It's not in their system, which means classified."

Classified—that meant someone important whose identity they didn't want known was on the helicopter. He knew of Blair House, the presidential guest house that comprised four buildings across the street from the White House in Washington, DC. It was named for an advisor to Andrew Jackson and was sometimes jokingly referred to as "the most exclusive hotel in the world" on account of being closed to the public and reserved only for guests of honor of the United States government...

"The Ayatollah," Zero realized. "The target was the Ayatollah of Iran." He had erroneously believed that Iran was behind this. But even Krauss had confirmed that it was not Iranians who were responsible.

Because their leader was the target.

Maria chewed her lip as she worked it out for herself. "He was due to arrive this morning for the meeting with Rutledge—but he was supposed to visit the UN first..."

"But when the railgun threat was imminent, they must have sent him straight to DC," Alan reasoned.

"His attaché was already at the UN," said Penny. "Along with the treaty."

Destroying the UN building was a calculated measure on Krauss's part, Zero deduced. Even if the Ayatollah wasn't there, the Iranians' diplomats and the treaty itself were.

And then, he recalled, *Krauss got a message to his sat phone. Someone told him where the Ayatollah really was—or at least the transponder code of the helicopter he was in.*

The shot that Zero had misdirected was intended to strike the aircraft carrying Iran's leader. "Take us to Andrews AFB!" he instructed the pilot.

"Roger that."

"Penny, find out where they took him," Zero said urgently into the phone. "Likely a bunker at Andrews, or a safe house nearby..."

"That could be difficult," Penny admitted.

"But you can do it," he insisted. "And do *not* alert anyone, do you understand?"

"Got it. Will call you back." Penny ended the call.

"Zero," Alan frowned, "the railgun is gone. The crew is dead."

He nodded. "I know. But Krauss couldn't have just assumed that the helicopter carrying the Ayatollah was in the air. That would have been too big a risk to take. And I saw him receive a message—someone had to have given him the transponder code of the aircraft."

Maria's eyes widened. "Someone that's with him... maybe part of his own detail?"

That was what Zero feared most. Whoever the mole was, they were willing to die for this cause, willing to be blasted out of the sky along with the leader of Iran.

And if they were still there with him, as soon as the news came that the railgun had been destroyed, they might be inspired to try and finish the task they'd set out for.

CHAPTER THIRTY SIX

Zero was out the helicopter's side door before the Sea Knight was fully wheels-down at Andrews Air Force Base, less than a twenty-minute drive from the White House. The pain in his back sent a shockwave up his spine as he landed on the flat tarmac. The February wind bit through the gray flight suit and his feet felt frozen in his still-damp boots, but he did his best to ignore it.

Come on, Penny. He needed a location. *They* needed a location, since Maria and Reidigger were at his side, despite his protests of going alone. They were both injured worse than he was—or so he'd tried to claim. Neither quite bought that either.

"Where?" Alan asked breathlessly, winded from scrambling out of the chopper and jogging a far enough distance to hear each other over its rotors.

Zero didn't know. All around him, personnel of the base hurried in this direction or that, shouting orders to one another, fueling jets and getting planes into the air. It seemed that the news of the railgun's destruction hadn't yet reached them—or else was not public knowledge just yet, considering the powers-that-be would demand evidence of it.

Thankfully no one questioned their presence there, in part to the jumpsuit that made him look like he belonged and partially due to the Marine helicopter that had just deposited them there.

"Here," said Alan, discreetly slipping him a Glock 19. "It'll do you more good than it will me." He gestured to his wounded hand. He wouldn't be able to hold and fire a pistol without popping the stitches.

Zero slipped it into the baggy pocket of the jumpsuit as he looked around desperately. He couldn't very well just ask someone. *Excuse me, is there a secret bunker around here in which you hide foreign leaders?*

Thankfully, the satellite phone rang. "Penny! What have you got?"

"I have nothing, Agent," she admitted somberly. "I'm sorry. But there is simply no record to find of the Ayatollah's current whereabouts. It's not something anyone would note anywhere, and anyone who could tell us is obviously unavailable. His trail went cold where you're standing."

Dammit. They had no other options; they had to report it and hope that the spy didn't have a chance to act. It was a huge risk, and not one he was eager to take...

He spotted a familiar sight on the next runway over. For a moment it confused him; what was Air Force One doing here at Andrews if Rutledge and his cabinet had been evacuated?

Then he remembered—there were two Boeing VC-25As dubbed Air Force One, and when not in service they called the runway at Andrews AFB home.

Curiously, though, there was an airstair alongside the massive jet, a white-framed set of red steps leading to the closed clamshell door.

"Zero?" Maria was at his shoulder, staring in the same direction. She saw it too. "You don't think...?"

He shook his head slowly. It made sense, in a way; a foreign leader with plenty of known enemies needs to be spirited away during an attack that suggests foreign dignitaries might be targeted by way of the UN building's destruction. Where would they hide him? In the bunker of an Air Force Base was a possibility.

But inside the unused Air Force One? No one would guess that. He'd heard tell that the body of the plane could sustain a nuclear blast; even on the ground, it was as secure as any safe house and still within the confines of a military base.

Which would make getting inside it almost impossible.

"Can't exactly just knock on the door," Alan muttered, as if reading his mind.

"What about the cargo hold? Can we access it from the exterior?"

"If this was a regular Boeing?" Alan said. "Probably. But this is the president's plane, Zero. They've thought of that."

"Fair enough." He had to think of something, and fast. "Follow me." He jogged toward the blue and gray plane, hoping he didn't simply get shot on approach, and put the sat phone to his ear. "Penny? Would you be able to patch me through to Air Force One? Not the one carrying Rutledge—the one on the ground at Andrews."

"I believe I could," the young doctor said. "Give me a moment..."

"What are you thinking of doing?" Maria asked as she trotted alongside him. He held up a finger for her to hang on—mostly because he wasn't quite sure what he was going to do yet, only that he needed the people inside to open that door.

"Okay," said Penny, "patching you in three, two, one..." There was a crackle, and then silence, and then a man's voice came through the phone, low and more than a little heated.

"This is Agent Kenney with the United States Secret Service. Who is this?"

"My name is Agent..." He almost said Zero, but stopped himself. Anyone who hadn't heard of him would think that was crazy. "Agent Alan Reidigger, Central Intelligence Agency. There is a bomb on the plane. I repeat, we have reason to believe there is a bomb on the plane."

The words simply tumbled out of his mouth before he had a chance to really think it through. Zero had no way to confirm that this man was really Secret Service or that he wasn't the traitor. But in the two seconds of silence that followed he became fully aware that he had just committed a felony—calling in a fake bomb threat—which was probably made much worse considering the location.

Act now, apologize later.

To Agent Kenney's credit, despite the brief silence that followed Zero's proclamation, he did not ask further questions. It sounded as if the phone was dropped, and then he heard the agent's booming voice: "We're evacuating the plane! Let's go, right now! Get the Ayatollah off the plane!"

I was right. And, in an oddly circuitous way, Air Force One was still the target—just not the one he'd thought it would be.

By the time the shouting began through the phone, Zero had reached the airstairs. He sprang up them quickly, ignoring the pain in his limbs, as Alan huffed behind him and Maria shouted a warning.

"Wait! Are we really going to do this? We're essentially hijacking Air Force One."

But he didn't have time to answer. The blue clamshell door of the plane opened, and the black-suited agent on the other side—presumably Agent Kenney—froze in bewilderment as he came face-to-face with Zero.

Luckily Alan took point. He reached past Zero, grabbed the agent's wrist, and twisted his body as he pulled. Agent Kenney yelped as he was yanked through the door, over Reidigger's shoulder, and tumbled down the staircase, landing unconscious at the bottom.

"Sorry," Reidigger grunted.

Zero pulled out the Glock and swung into the president's plane. "Freeze!" he shouted at another Secret Service agent. "CIA! Don't move!"

Behind the agent were four Middle Eastern men who he surmised were the Ayatollah's private security detail, and then the man himself. The Ayatollah was tall, six-two without the black turban wrapped around his cranium, and a shrewd gaze surrounded by creased, aged skin. His beard was entirely white, though his eyebrows were oddly still dark.

Two of the Iranian security detail reached for the guns at their hips when Maria and Alan rounded on them as well, entering the plane.

"Stop!" Maria commanded in Farsi. "Do not move!"

"There's a traitor among you," Zero said directly to the Ayatollah. "Someone here wants you dead."

Iran's leader did not have to speak loudly for his basso voice to be heard easily. "I would assume," he said in flawless English, "that the ones pointing weapons are the ones who wish me dead."

"No, sir, we're trying to keep that from happening." Zero looked from one Iranian to the next. *Which one?* He had no idea. "Someone on this plane gave crucial information about your location. The helicopter that you flew on. Who was it? Who made a call?"

"My men are loyal," the Ayatollah said, perfectly patient and seemingly unafraid. "And none made calls."

None... Zero shifted his attention to the other Secret Service agent. The agent had his hands up at ear level, his eyes narrowed, his square jaw set firmly.

And just the tiniest bead of perspiration on his forehead.

"You." Zero pointed the Glock at him. "The railgun is gone. It's at the bottom of the Atlantic. The crew is dead. Krauss is dead."

"I don't know what you're talking about," the man insisted.

"I think you do." Zero could see the anxiousness etched in his face. "You were waiting to hear that news, weren't you? When the helicopter never exploded. You boarded at Blair House and commanded the pilot to return to Andrews, but nothing happened. So you were sitting here, waiting to be told that Krauss had failed so you could assassinate the Ayatollah yourself—"

The agent's lip curled in a snarl. One hand whipped down, reaching for his gun. Zero pulled the trigger on the Glock.

Nothing happened. The trigger lock was on.

Biometrics. Zero had forgotten that Alan's Glock would be useless to him. The gun was keyed to Reidigger's thumbprint, not his.

The agent pulled his pistol in one smooth action, even as the Iranians went for theirs. One of them leapt in front of the Ayatollah, forcing their leader to get down.

A single shot rang out.

The agent's head snapped back as blood plastered the wall of Air Force One.

Maria holstered her gun. Her shot had been perfect.

"Thanks," Zero breathed.

"Anytime."

Sirens sounded outside, screaming closer. At the bottom of the airplane steps, Agent Kenney groaned as he came around.

They had a *lot* of explaining to do.

Chapter Thirty Seven

Sheikh Salman literally quaked with rage as he watched the footage of the US Navy pulling the remains of the railgun from the ocean floor.

His men had failed him. Krauss had failed him. Even the Islamophobic agent he had recruited had failed. The man was suffering from PTSD and had even made an attempt on his own life before Salman had discovered him, thanks to a sleeper cell in Virginia who had infiltrated the veterans' support group. The Secret Service agent had come at a steep price, an eight-figure sum for his family, and Salman was quite content to kill him in the process.

The agent could have had a hundred chances to murder the Ayatollah, but had been ordered to do so only if the railgun failed. The plan that Salman had been concocting for two years was to show strength, ingenuity, and power—power that was supposed to unite the separated fundamentalist factions under a single banner, *their* banner.

Thus, he had failed as well. King Basheer would be furious. Currently the young king was away from Riyadh, attending the wedding of a cousin on the other side of the country, but he would return tomorrow and there would be punishment for Salman. Of that there was no doubt. Perhaps he would be cast from the palace. The very thought made him queasy.

He stormed to his private quarters, an outbuilding opposite the courtyard. It was a magnificent space, one he had come to think of as his own, more than a thousand square meters total that held a king-sized bed, a lounge, his own wading pool, and even a small topiary and garden.

Salman pushed open the double doors and closed them again behind him. Dusk was settling over the palace, throwing the chamber into shadow. He reached for the nearest lamp, switched it on, and leapt back in fright.

An African-American man sat on the edge of the four-poster canopied bed. He was dressed quite ordinarily for a westerner, in denim jeans and a dark jacket, which somehow made the black pistol in his lap all the more alarming. The barrel of it was long, thin, designed to suppress the sound of its shots.

Salman struggled to force his heart to slow as he stood tall in the face of this intruder. "Who are you?" he demanded in Arabic.

"Hello, Sheikh Salman." The man spoke English; he was American, or so his accent dictated. "My name is Oliver. I'm here to kill you."

The sheikh sneered. Who did this man think he was? Despite the presence of his weapon, he wouldn't dare to kill a king's advisor in the middle of a royal palace. The notion was lunacy.

"You see," the man called Oliver continued, "complex problems can sometimes be solved with fairly simple solutions. I find those solutions. I fix the problems. Usually those problems can be solved by removing a particular variable."

Sheikh Salman took a cautious step to the right. In the bureau against the wall, not ten meters from him, there was a pistol. If he could get to it…

"Please don't," the man said. "The gun's not in there. I've already swept the room."

"Just who do you think—"

Oliver stood suddenly. The simple act was threatening enough to silence Salman and he shrank back two quick steps.

"As I was saying. I find solutions. Our current problem is that we don't want to go to war with your country. We'd prefer to avoid a bigger international incident than we already have. The US enjoys the benefits that have come of our relationship, and frankly, it would create a whole mess of new problems. We know that Saudi Arabia was responsible for the railgun's theft and use. We know that King Basheer was at least mildly aware of the attempt on the Ayatollah's life. But we also know that the plan itself was of your design, Sheikh Salman."

"You know nothing," the sheikh hissed, "and you can prove less."

"Yes." Oliver smiled at that. "You're right. Burden of proof *is* a burden. Which, again, is where I come in. Men like me don't have to prove anything."

"You are speaking in circles," Salman spat. "I don't believe you're here to kill me. You're here to threaten me, like a common American thug. Your country would never sanction a crass assassination like this—"

"Make no mistake, Sheikh. I am here to kill you."

He said it so coldly, so candidly that a chill ran up Salman's spine. He thought about shouting, screaming for help, but that would only inspire this Oliver to use the gun faster.

"Ordinarily," the man continued, "that part would be done by now. You probably wouldn't have even noticed me before you were dead. As I said, I don't have to prove anything; for example, I don't have to prove that you have been whispering in Basheer's ear for much of his life. I don't have to prove that you are clearly the variable that requires removing in order to solve the problem. There's really only one reason you're still breathing."

Salman gulped. His head was shaking back and forth and he didn't know how long he'd been doing it. "You ... you can't. You wouldn't dare. Killing me would make a martyr! Those I have aligned to our cause would rally against you and your country. It would be war regardless! You would only be helping my plan, not hindering it! And not just here, but across the entire Middle East!" He was ranting now, sweating, his palms damp and clammy.

"No," said Oliver. "Your death will be written off as a suicide for the failed terrorist attack. I think we both know that Basheer will deny any knowledge of the plot and pin the attempt entirely on you and your radical followers. They, in turn, will either be captured or abandon your cause. Without your influence, Basheer will play nice with us, or he'll face a potential conflict that he is woefully unqualified to handle. Your name, Sheikh, will die in ignominy. Just like you are about to."

"No!" Salman cried. Even the threat of death paled in comparison to being relegated to a traitor and forgotten. "You cannot! I ... I have information!"

"I know you do. That brings me to the reason we're talking. Who is Stefan Krauss?"

Salman blinked in surprise. That certainly wasn't the type of information he'd expected to be asked. Krauss was a nobody, a killer for hire who, in hindsight, had been far overpaid. "What does that matter? He is dead now."

"Maybe," said Oliver with a small shrug. "Maybe not. His body has not yet been recovered, even though we found all five of your people. We know that Stefan Krauss is not his real name. Intelligence suggests he's been involved in up to a dozen high-profile assassinations in the last five years. He was able to infiltrate the South Korean research team flawlessly. I think he led you to believe he was a simple mercenary, maybe an assassin. But the little that we've gathered suggests he's former intelligence, perhaps a spy, and is still able to access sensitive information. That kind of man is very dangerous. He's been a ghost, and whether or not he is now in the literal sense is something I would very much like to know. How did you find him?"

"Amnesty," Salman gasped. "I will tell you for amnesty."

"I already told you, I'm here to kill you."

"Please ..."

"Last chance," Oliver warned quietly. "Krauss?"

"I ... I didn't find him. He found me," the sheikh admitted. "One of the factions we made an arms deal with, they had contracted him. Somehow he knew what I was doing, trying to unite them, and had assumed I was creating a plan ..."

Oliver frowned. "Did Krauss tell you about the railgun?"

"Yes." The sheikh was practically whimpering now. "Amnesty, please."

But Oliver was not paying him any attention. He looked pensive. "Interesting. So Krauss knew not only about your arms deal, but also about the railgun well before it was completed. That means he already had a way to get into the research team posing as security." He looked up. "Sheikh Salman, I believe he played you for a fool."

Salman did not understand, and at this point did not care. Krauss was certainly dead. There was no way he could have survived. But the sheikh still had a chance.

"I have money," the sheikh protested. "Whatever they are paying you, I will double it. Triple it! Whatever you want! You can go wherever you want. You don't ever have to go back."

Oliver smiled sadly at that. "That's the thing, Sheikh. I already can't ever go back. And they don't pay me for this. Call it ... atonement."

He raised the pistol.

Sheikh Salman squeezed his eyes shut. There was nowhere to run.

He did not even hear the sound of the shot before the bullet entered his skull.

CHAPTER THIRTY EIGHT

Zero, Maria, and Alan sat side by side on one end of a conference table with nine empty seats around it. The surface of the table was equally empty other than a triangular black speakerphone in the center. It was after eight o'clock at night and Zero was exhausted, aching, and really just wanted to get home to his girls and his own bed.

After the debacle on Air Force One, which had occurred several hours ago now, they had been detained, questioned relentlessly, and eventually released—no thanks to Director Shaw or Deputy Director Walsh, but because Dr. Penelope León had arrived. Despite all three being disavowed, Penny had created backups of their CIA records and credentials and was able to prove their identity.

Their wounds were cleaned and treated; they were fed and brought clothes to change into. Then they were whisked to Langley by two expressionless agents who said almost nothing before depositing them into the conference room and locking the door behind them. The pair of agents then went through a debrief—an amusing exercise to Zero, not only because their account was probably bordering on unbelievable but especially since the presence of the two agents was practically unnecessary, as the whole exchange was recorded.

The two agents had left twenty minutes earlier, and now the three of them simply sat there, waiting for the next part, which none of them had been told but they all knew was coming.

"Certainly taking their time," Reidigger muttered.

As if on cue, the door swung open and two men entered briskly: Director Shaw, his expression as solemn as it ever was, and the shorter accountant-like lackey Walsh. They did not address or even look at them as they took seats at the head of the conference table.

"As far as I'm concerned," Shaw said finally, "you should all be in jail."

"Hello to you too, sir," Maria said snidely.

"And you're welcome," Alan added.

At last Shaw looked up at them, and the disdain in his gaze was palpable. "You're all fired." He shook his head in disgust and opened his mouth to speak again when the door to the conference room opened once more.

Penelope León entered, dressed in corduroy and a purple V-neck and sporting bangles around both wrists.

"Dr. León," Walsh said sharply, "this is a confidential meeting—"

"I helped them." Penny took a seat beside Zero in solidarity. "I was communicating with them during their entire operation. I supplied them with weapons and gear. I copied their records from the CIA database in order to prove their identities to the authorities. Whatever falls on them for their insubordination should be equally visited upon me."

Shaw frowned so deeply Zero feared his face would get stuck that way. Walsh was simply stunned.

Penny sat with her hands in her lap and, Zero noticed, a small black box in her fist. Some sort of remote, it looked like. Her thumb pressed a button, but nothing happened. At least not that he could discern.

"Well then," said Shaw. "I'll repeat myself for Dr. León's sake. As far as I'm concerned, you should all be in jail. You're certainly all fired. For now you will be placed under strict house arrest until the events of the last two days can be fully investigated and charges can be filed. There *will* be hearings. You *will* be charged with crimes. In the meantime, you *will* be watched carefully. If any of you attempt to leave the country, you will be jailed immediately and without due process. Do you understand?"

Reidigger yawned.

"I have to admit, that doesn't really work for me," Penny said casually.

Shaw finally reacted with some character, by virtue of his eyes going so wide they looked like they might fall out of his head. "I don't think any of you understand the severity of what you've done. You deliberately disobeyed orders, you committed scores of crimes, you took the law into your own hands, you held a foreign leader at gunpoint, and you think after all of this you can simply *waltz* back in here and tell me no?!" He was shouting by the end of his rant, his face growing red. "I have half a mind to toss you all in the holding cells right now and throw away the—"

"Excuse me," said a male voice. It sounded tinny, as if coming through a speaker—because it was. It was coming from the triangular speakerphone in the center of the table. "I think I've heard enough."

Zero knew that voice. It was President Jonathan Rutledge.

Shaw knew it too, and his red face suddenly paled. "...Mr. President?"

"Regretfully I can't be at this meeting in person," Rutledge said. "Obviously there has been a lot to attend to, including my delayed meeting with the Ayatollah. For what it's worth, team, he sends his regards and appreciation."

The remote, Zero realized. Penny had planned this. She crashed the meeting and patched the president through on the sly. He almost laughed aloud.

"And the Saudi king, sir?" Maria asked.

"King Basheer has predictably declared the incident an act of insurgency by a radical group within his borders," Rutledge told them, "led by a tribal sheikh who was found dead by self-inflicted gunshot wound today."

"Mr. President," Shaw said quickly, "let me just say that what I meant just now may have been misconstrued out of context—"

"I heard what you said, Shaw. I understand your position, and you should understand mine. You can try to bring charges against these people. But if you don't think I'll use executive power to pardon the people that risked life and limb to stop that weapon, you're very mistaken."

Alan folded his arms smugly. Zero allowed himself a smirk; maybe Reidigger wouldn't be so quick to naysay operations now that he too had a powerful friend in the White House.

"Furthermore," the president continued, "Dr. León shared with my office the briefing package that you supplied these agents with at the onset, after my explicit order to involve Zero and his team. I think we both know it was a disgrace intended to discredit them."

"Sir, that was absolutely not my intent—"

"I'm still talking, Shaw. For all of their indiscretions, your own were clearly negligence. However, finding a new CIA director would be a hassle and there's enough to be dealt with right now. Believe it or not, besides your clearly troubled relationship with this team, I think you're doing a decent job on the whole.

"So here's what we're going to do," Rutledge continued. "In the coming weeks, after the dust settles on this mess, we're going to establish a new division, outside the realm of Special Activities Division and SOG. This team will operate under the umbrella of the CIA, but will work autonomously and answer directly to either the DNI or me."

Zero saw Maria stiffen in her seat. Mouthing off to Shaw was one thing; answering to her father, DNI David Barren, would be another matter entirely.

We'll burn that bridge when we come to it, he thought wryly.

"Is that amenable to you, Shaw?" the president asked.

"Um... yes. Yes, sir. It is."

Despite the consternation that Maria would undoubtedly have, it was plenty amenable to Zero as well. Not having to deal with rookie deputy directors or answer to Shaw anymore would solve a lot of problems. It would be the same crew in a new division. They'd bring Strickland, of course.

And Zero had not forgotten his promise to the pilot and aspiring agent Chip Foxworth. Maybe he'd make a good recruit.

"Until that time, I believe these three agents have earned some time to recuperate from this ordeal," Rutledge added. "Go home to your families. The United States thanks you."

"Thank you, sir," Zero said on behalf of all three of them. Some time off would be very welcome.

"Was there anything else, Dr. León?"

"No, Mr. President, I believe that covered just about everything."

"All right then. Thank you for your service, and good night, all." There was a click, and President Rutledge hung up.

The conference room was silent for a long moment. Walsh looked to Shaw. Shaw looked as if he very much wanted to say something, but couldn't make up his mind.

It was Maria who finally spoke. "There's one more thing, Director Shaw."

"I ... yes, Agent Johansson?"

"The girl that's being held, Mischa. I want her released into my care."

Zero's head whipped around so fast he was pretty sure he pulled a muscle.

"You're holding her unlawfully. You can't prove that she's done anything wrong," Maria continued, her tone rising an octave. "I don't think that the president, or anyone else, would be too pleased to discover that the CIA has been keeping a twelve-year-old girl in the basement."

"Pardon me?" Penny gasped.

"Dr. León," Shaw said very nervously, "the call did end, right? Doctor?"

My god. Zero could hardly believe what he was hearing. That girl was still being held down there? He had assumed long ago that she'd been transferred to a minimum-security facility somewhere. Guilt stabbed at him for not having followed up—but it seemed Maria had.

And Maria wants to ... do what, exactly? Adopt her?

That was definitely a long conversation they were going to have in the very near future. But he agreed that getting her out of there was the primary concern.

"I will see what I can do," said Shaw carefully.

"I wasn't asking," Maria told him firmly. "You'll make this happen by the end of the week."

Shaw stared for a moment and then nodded once, tightly, as if it was against his will. Walsh looked like he wanted to be anywhere else at the moment.

"Great, glad that's all settled." Reidigger rose to his feet with a groan. "If we're finished here, I'm in pretty dire need of a shower." He glanced pointedly at the directors. "Unless there was anything else?"

"Um, no. You ... you're dismissed," Shaw said meekly. The director had clearly marched in here thinking he was about to score a victory against the agents he saw as insubordinate, and the tables had flipped so suddenly that he was at a loss for words and, likely, coherent thought too.

Zero got up as the four of them filed to the door. He too couldn't wait to get home, to find out what his girls had been up to the last couple of days.

"Oh, I'm sorry, one moment," said Penny. She turned to Shaw. "Would you also release Agent Zero's daughter from custody?"

Zero got whiplash for a second time in the span of two minutes. "Sorry, *what?*"

Chapter Thirty Nine

"Okay." Zero slid into the passenger seat of his SUV with a wince, letting his eldest drive him home so he could focus more on the pain his body was in—and exactly why she had been in a holding cell at CIA headquarters. "You're going to tell me everything, starting with why my car is out here near Alan's garage."

"Sure, I guess I owe you some answers." Maya started the car. "But first, how are you? You look like hell."

"Uh-uh, no deflecting. Out with it, young lady." He tried to sound stern, but she only chuckled at him.

Upon hearing that Maya was being held by the CIA, his first instinct had been to hit Shaw in the jaw. He restrained himself (mostly by virtue of Alan putting his bulk between Zero and the director) and instead demanded he be brought to her. Every horrible thought ran through his head on the way to the sublevel—that Shaw had done this as revenge against him, that his daughter was being humiliated, possibly even tortured—but when he arrived at the glass-walled holding cell and spotted her, she grinned sheepishly and flashed him a thumbs-up.

Then, after being released, she told him that his car wasn't in the Langley parking lot and Reidigger needed to give them a lift back to the garage.

"Still waiting..." he said singsong in the passenger seat of his SUV.

Maya sighed, keeping her eyes on the road ahead. "I found the guy."

Zero frowned at her. "Who? What guy?"

"The man you told me about. The one you were looking for. He's alive. His name is Seth Connors, but he was going by the name John Graham and being kept in a safe house."

A knot of panic formed in Zero's stomach and the only thing keeping it from turning to nausea was his utter bewilderment that Maya had actually followed through and found the man—inside of two days. A hundred questions formed in his head and jammed up at his mouth. "You—what? How? Why?"

"How? Let's see ... by heading off Alan's hacker guy, threatening a neurosurgeon, driving through the night, and having a gun pointed in my face by a man who has clearly lost his mind." She lowered her voice. "Why? Because, Dad ... you needed help and I knew you wouldn't ask for it."

"I needed help? Is that right?" He scrutinized her. "Since when are you so charitable?"

Maya rolled her eyes, though her shoulders slumped a bit and her features softened in a rare display of vulnerability. "Fine. Also, maybe, it was just a little bit because I felt I ... needed to. To do something like that. To prove to myself that I could."

Zero rubbed his forehead. "Maya, you don't have to go running off on an insane mission like that to prove anything. You know that you can do anything you set your mind to—"

"You have to say that. You're my dad. I needed to *know* it."

There was that pang of guilt again, this time over a trait he'd clearly passed down unwillingly. "I get that."

She glanced over at him sharply. "Do you?"

"Eyes on the road. And yes. More than you know." If he was being honest with himself, which was generally as rare as Maya's moments of vulnerability, the primary reason he'd even pursued the railgun halfway around the world and back again was to prove that he could. It certainly wasn't to prove anything to Shaw or anyone else.

"So," he asked carefully. "What did you discover?"

"I ... I think I need to think about that for a little while."

He frowned. Maya did not know about the memory suppressor. She did not know that for two years he had been completely and blissfully unaware of his involvement in the CIA. She did not know that his memories had, for the most part, returned, and she certainly, absolutely did not know about the deterioration that was occurring in his skull.

He very much wanted to keep it that way if he could, no matter how much she deserved to know the truth.

"I think," she continued, "that sometime very soon, you and I and maybe even Sara too are going to have a long and difficult conversation."

A lump formed in his throat, not because of what she was suggesting but because of how right she was. It was a long overdue conversation, one that they deserved.

"But before we have that conversation, I think I have to consider what exactly I want to say, and what I want to ask," she told him candidly.

Despite all of his fears, he was immensely proud of her. He wasn't particularly pleased with the danger she'd put herself in, or how blasé she was about it, but he was proud that he'd raised such an intelligent, capable, headstrong, and occasionally vexing young woman.

"Would you tell me just one thing?" he asked. "How was he? Connors."

"Confused," Maya admitted. "He'd lost his identity and had no choice but to believe the lies he'd been told. But ... some things were coming back. Poking through. I think he's starting to remember again, even if only a little."

"And the safe house. Is he still there?"

Maya shook her head. "They brought him in too. I don't know where he is."

So he's at Langley. Zero mentally marked that as an item on his to-do list in the near future: speak with Seth Connors personally somehow. He was sure his new friend Dr. León could help facilitate a meeting.

They drove in silence for a couple of minutes before Zero's cell phone rang, startling him.

"It's Alan." He frowned. Then he answered and put it on speaker. "Hello?"

"Zero," Reidigger said gruffly. "Would you mind asking your daughter if she's seen the 1972 Buick Skylark that was parked in my garage?"

"Oh, crap." Maya's eyes widened. "Right. Um ... so that is in a parking garage. In Columbus. Ohio. I don't have a ticket for it. But it's there. Sorry."

By the time they reached home, the second-floor apartment in Bethesda, Maryland, Zero was so exhausted his feet were literally dragging up the steps. But before he could put his key in the door, Maya stopped him gently by the elbow.

"Listen," she said quietly. "Sara's been by herself the last couple days, for the first time in a long time. I'm not sure how she handled that, so maybe we don't lay all our stuff at her feet?"

Zero smiled. "Course not. We'll keep it light."

Maya nodded as he opened the door.

The first thing he noticed was that it was freezing inside, as if every window had been opened despite being the middle of February.

"Oh," he heard Maya exclaim softly. "Okay ..."

He closed the door behind him and followed her gaze down the foyer and into the kitchen, blinking at what he saw.

Todd Strickland was there, his left arm in a sling as he tried to duct-tape long pieces of cardboard over their back patio door, which by the looks of it had been completely shattered.

Sara knelt nearby, struggling to sweep glass into a dustpan on account of her right hand being wrapped in a thick splint.

She looked up in surprise and stood quickly. "Hey! Hi. So...I know this looks bad. But before I say anything, I promise I'm okay." Sara glanced down at the splint on her hand. "Uh, mostly okay."

EPILOGUE

Maya sat up in bed, every muscle feeling relaxed after a very excellent and much-needed night's sleep. She checked her phone; it was nine thirty in the morning. It had been a long time since she'd slept in that late.

She rolled out of bed and padded down the hall barefoot to the bathroom of Maria's bungalow-style house, the one that she used to share with her dad and now was again. Last night, after seeing the broken patio door and window and hearing Sara and Strickland's tale of forced entry at the hands of two drug dealers, her dad had called up Maria and asked if they could crash at her place, which she had graciously agreed to.

Sara had taken the couch, giving Maya the twin bed in the spare room. But when Maya reached the bathroom she was surprised to see her sister already up, brushing her teeth.

She leaned against the door frame. "Huh. Nine thirty is kind of early for you, isn't it?"

Sara spit before replying. "Huh. Nine thirty is kind of late for you, isn't it?" She pulled her blonde hair back into a ponytail. "I'm heading down to the community center this morning."

"You have an art class?" Maya asked.

"Something like that," Sara said cryptically as she relinquished the bathroom.

Five minutes later Maya had her sweats on, sneakers laced, earbuds around her neck and sweat band on her forehead as she prepared to go for a run. She thought about skipping a day, but then decided to just do five quick miles so she didn't feel lazy. After all, she'd slept in—

Her phone buzzed from the nightstand. Maya frowned; the number displayed was a familiar one. It was the office of Brigadier General Joanne Hunt.

The call she'd been delaying for more than a month now was making itself to her.

She hesitated for the slightest moment before answering. "Good morning, Dean Hunt."

"Ms. Lawson," said the authoritative voice crisply. "I had expected to hear from you by now."

"Yes, ma'am. I'm sorry. I ... I've been busy." She winced at the lame excuse.

"I'm well aware, Ms. Lawson."

Uh-oh.

"Just as you are well aware that I am very good acquaintances with the Director of National Intelligence," the dean continued.

Oh no.

Maya was indeed well aware that Joanne Hunt and DNI David Barren had a professional relationship; she'd been in a meeting with the both of them before.

"So it should come as no surprise," said Dean Hunt, "that I am equally aware that a number of rather impressive charges were recently levied against your record. Considering that you are still enrolled in West Point despite your leave of absence, those charges were remitted to my office."

Maya's heart sank. The decision she'd been putting off had been made for her—she was being expelled. "Ma'am, I can explain—"

"I'm sure you can," the dean interjected. "However, what I am more interested in is why those charges suddenly vanished from your record this morning."

Maya blinked.

"Vanished as if they never existed," said Hunt, "though I am certain as the earth is round that I saw them with my own eyes. Care to explain that?"

"I, um ..." Ordinarily Maya was very good at coming up with excuses, but she couldn't bring herself to lie to Hunt—especially considering that the dean might have been aware of what had happened and wanted to see what she'd say. "I'm afraid it's classified, ma'am."

"Hm. I'm sure it is." She could hear the smirk in the dean's voice before the authority returned in full force. "You will be returning to the academy in March."

It wasn't a question; it was an order.

"Uh, yes. Yes, ma'am. I'd like that. If you'll have me back."

"I refuse to let a talent like yours fall by the wayside. You will make up for the time you've missed before the summer. And when you arrive, my office will be your first stop. I want to personally lay eyes on you and make sure you're present. Is that clear, cadet?"

"Very clear, ma'am. Thank you."

"Enjoy the rest of your time off, Ms. Lawson." Dean Hunt hung up, leaving Maya bewildered at the one-eighty the conversation had taken.

But her future was clear. She was going back to school.

❧ ❧ ❧

The community center still smelled like cedar chips, but this time it had an undertone of lavender and linseed oil on account of the floors recently being mopped. Sara made her way down the hall, forcing herself forward with each step.

You've come this far. Can't turn back now.

She reached the door with the sheet of white paper scotch-taped to it, the sign that read:

Common Bonds
Sharing Trauma, Sharing Hope

The door was ajar just a few inches and she peered inside. It was nearly ten a.m. and several somber-faced women were present, preparing for the meeting that was about to start, stirring instant coffee and arranging their chairs in a semicircle as they chatted quietly amongst themselves.

I can't do this.

She turned back and nearly ran headlong into a brunette woman.

"Oh! Excuse me," the woman chuckled. It was the pleasant-faced soccer mom, Maddie, carrying a box of donuts. "Hi, Sara. It's nice to see you again. Please, come inside."

"Um... okay." She couldn't flee now. She followed her into the room.

"Good morning, everyone!" Maddie announced brightly. "We have someone new joining us today. This is Sara."

"Hi, Sara," the group of seven women said in unison.

"I think Sara is just going to sit and listen today." Maddie gave her a reassuring smile. "I hope we can make her feel welcome."

Sara's throat felt dry as she grabbed a folded metal chair from a rack and joined the semicircle. Beside her, a woman in her thirties who had certainly seen better days gave her a shy smile and a nod.

"Hi," Sara murmured.

Maddie took a seat and put her purse at her feet. "Let's get started. Does anyone want to begin?" She looked around the circle. "Gail. I'm sensing you have something you'd like to talk about."

Sara looked over at the woman named Gail. Her hair was going gray and she had a noticeable bruise beneath her left eye.

The woman nodded. "I do. Um..." She trailed off, tears forming in her eyes before she could even begin.

"Take as much time as you need," Maddie assured her.

Camilla was in rehab now, and had promised to stay there as long as Sara visited her twice a week. The drug dealer Rex was in jail, along with his friend Brody. Despite her injured hand, Sara should have felt victorious.

But as Gail slowly began her story, a tale of an abusive ex paying her an unexpected drunken visit late last night, Sara did not feel triumphant. She did not feel fulfilled.

She felt infuriated.

Common bonds and sharing hope might be cathartic, but it was not enough.

She remembered vividly the feel of the revolver in her now-broken hand, and an idea began to form in her head.

Zero scrolled on his tablet, looking for the perfect recipe for that evening but coming up short. *Maybe we'll just go out,* he thought. He hadn't exactly had time to plan anything.

Maria swept into the living room, affixing the stud of an earring as she looked for her shoes. "Hey," she said quickly, "I'm heading out for a little bit. Just a couple of hours, I promise."

He raised an eyebrow. "Is it paperwork?"

She paused with one foot in a sneaker. "I'm going to visit Mischa. Which I've been doing for the last few months. And I'm going to light a fire under Shaw about releasing her. And I know we should have talked about that first, and I'm sorry, but—"

He held up a hand to stop her. "Hey. The only thing we need to talk about is the logistics. It's the right decision. I'm not going to argue that."

She smiled and scoffed at herself. "It's going to be hard. I don't think I've really thought it through at all."

Zero set the tablet down and stood, crossing the room and wrapping her in a hug. "In my experience, some of the very best decisions come from not thinking too hard about it. Follow your instincts and roll with the punches." He shrugged. "Besides, I've got some experience raising screwed-up girls..."

"I heard that," Maya called from the kitchen.

Maria laughed shortly, but her smile faded. "Stay."

He frowned. "Where would I go?"

"No, I mean stay here. Move back in. Don't go back to the apartment. The girls too. We have the space, and—maybe we can finish the basement, make it a living area or another bedroom..."

"Okay," he agreed. "You don't need to sell me on it." He squeezed her again. "Happy Valentine's Day."

"Oh shit," she groaned. "I'm so sorry, I totally forgot."

"Don't worry. We'll all go out for a nice dinner together tonight."

"You'll never get a reservation!" Maria insisted.

"Just call up your pal the president," Maya called out. "He could probably pull some strings—"

"Quit eavesdropping," Zero called back.

"It's a small house!"

"Go visit Mischa," he told Maria. "By the time you're back I'll have a plan for tonight."

"Sounds great." She kissed him, slipped on her other sneaker, and whisked out the door. "Hey, Sara," she said in passing as Zero's younger daughter came in.

"Where were you?" he asked.

Sara shrugged. "Paperwork."

"Uh-uh, you're not stealing my line!" he protested.

She headed to the kitchen and Zero followed, finding Maya snacking on a can of mixed nuts that Sara dug a fist into.

There was one more thing, and now seemed like as good a time as any.

"While I have you both here," he started, "there's something I need to ask you."

The girls exchanged a wary glance.

"While I was away," he told them, "there was a point when I...well, I was pretty sure I was going to die, to be honest, and in the moment I sort of...I sort of proposed to Maria."

Sara shook her head. "Oh, man."

Maya snorted. "Just what every woman wants. The empty gesture of an imminent-death proposal."

"That's not—it wasn't empty!" This wasn't going very well. "What I'm trying to say is that I meant it then and I mean it now. I want to do it right. But before I do that, I want to make sure that it's okay with you. Both of you."

"So you're asking our permission to ask Maria to marry you?" Maya clarified.

Sara wrinkled her nose. "Are you sure she'll say yes? You come with a lot of baggage."

"Yes, and probably yes," he answered in turn.

Maya smiled. "Dad, you don't need our permission to be happy."

"But since you're asking," Sara said pensively, "I'll have to give it some thought..."

Smartasses, he thought with a grin. *I've raised a couple of smartasses.*

"Bigger problem," Maya said around a mouthful of cashews and almonds, "is what you're going to do about getting a table for four on Valentine's Day."

"That's true. Will you help me?"

They both pulled out their phones and got to work, swapping notes as they did. Zero just watched for a little while, marveling at how they'd grown and how far they'd all come.

He had realized, after yet another brush with death, he had too much to lose. His brain was still going to continue its slow deterioration. There was no avoiding that, at least not for the time being. But he could still make the most of whatever time he had left. There would be a new living arrangement. A new wedding. A new addition to their odd little family. A new division, with possibly a new team member.

He could put the past behind him. There was a lot to look forward to.

Now Available for Pre-Order!

CHASING ZERO
(An Agent Zero Spy Thriller—Book #9)

"You will not sleep until you are finished with AGENT ZERO. A superb job creating a set of characters who are fully developed and very much enjoyable. The description of the action scenes transport us into a reality that is almost like sitting in a movie theater with surround sound and 3D (it would make an incredible Hollywood movie). I can hardly wait for the sequel."

—Roberto Mattos, Books and Movie Reviews

CHASING ZERO is book #9 in the #1 bestselling AGENT ZERO series, which begins with AGENT ZERO (Book #1), a free download with nearly 300 five-star reviews.

The Palestinians decide they want to make peace with Israel—and they want the U.S. President to broker the historic treaty on their territory. Agent Zero advises the

President against the dangerous trip, but he insists on going. After a series of dramatic and shocking twists, the most dangerous 48 hours of Zero's life ensue, forcing him into an impossible mission: save the President at all costs.

CHASING ZERO (Book #9) is an un-putdownable espionage thriller that will keep you turning pages late into the night.

"Thriller writing at its best."
—Midwest Book Review (re *Any Means Necessary*)

"One of the best thrillers I have read this year."
—Books and Movie Reviews (*re Any Means Necessary*)

Also available is Jack Mars' #1 bestselling LUKE STONE THRILLER series (7 books), which begins with Any Means Necessary (Book #1), a free download with over 800 five star reviews!

CHASING ZERO
(An Agent Zero Spy Thriller—Book #9)

Made in the USA
Las Vegas, NV
21 February 2022

44322197R00146